THE TAU DIRECTIVE

Tomas Black

First Published in Great Britain in 2021 by

TEARDROP MEDIA LTD

To friends and family who supported my efforts.

·tection System has flagged this terminal and security has been ·rted."

Still, he hesitated.

His phone buzzed inside his rucksack. His co-workers looked up in rprise and turned in his direction.

Michael highlighted the target server and opened up its nfiguration file. He turned on those ports—essentially data ghways—that allowed the server full connectivity to the facility's ternal network. He then returned to the firewalls he had flagged and itiated their deactivation.

The camera on his screen glowed green. "Thank you, Michael."

A klaxon sounded. Security personnel were running in his direction.

The worker on the desk opposite him stood up and peered over the ›p of his console. "Michael! What have you done?"

He reached for his bag and pulled out the gun. His colleague shrank ack in horror, almost falling over his chair.

"I'm sorry," said Michael. He put the gun to his temple and pulled ıe trigger.

Prologue

Michael Chen exited the subway on the Queensway and walked the short distance along Tamar Street to his place of work. It was just 6.30am and already the city of Hong Kong was bustling with activity. The morning was cool for the time of year, but he sweated in his light cotton shirt.

He stopped outside a nondescript office block and tried to compose himself. The building had once been owned by an American bank that had constructed a large data centre on the lower levels. It was the reason his organisation had acquired the premises. That and easy access to Hong Kong's telecommunications exchange where the government had placed their firewalls and surveillance equipment. No data left the island without his organisation intercepting and reporting on it.

Parked nearby was a sleek new sports car, its metallic blue paintwork gleaming in the morning sunshine. He walked up to the vehicle and stared at it. It belonged to his superior, a person partly responsible for his troubles. It was an all-electric affair, representing China's new orthodoxy on the future of the automobile. On impulse he pulled out his house key and ran it along the length of the bodywork, noting with satisfaction the high-pitched screech it made. He stood back to admire his handiwork but was disappointed that he had left barely a mark. He couldn't even get that right.

He turned and noticed a camera pointing down at him from a nearby lamp post. He raised his middle finger to an unseen entity in an act of defiance. Facial recognition systems would identify him and report his transgression to the state machinery. It was a system he had helped construct. China was expanding its surveillance and analysis operation - not just on the mainland, but worldwide. From the capturing of data from Chinese made Internet-enabled devices to the hacking of foreign governments and corporations, nothing was out of reach. It was state-sponsored intelligence gathering on a grand scale. Great Britain boasted of their GCHQ and the Americans of their NSA. China was set on building an organisation to match the combined might of both agencies.

He heard a buzzing and reached inside his small rucksack for his phone, his hand instead coming to rest on the cold metal of a Nambu pistol. It had been his grandfather's gun, a relic of the Second World War. The clip of the small pistol held just one round. But one round was all he needed.

He pulled out his phone and tapped the screen. His wife smiled back at him, holding their newborn son in her arms. A wave of grief washed over him and he felt physically sick. He swiped across the screen to the next picture. Again, his wife and child appeared, except this time his wife was looking fearful. Behind her stood a tall man he did not recognise. The man was holding a large knife. The caption of the picture read: *obey*.

He walked back to his office and entered the lobby of the building. There he encountered his first obstacle, a short, surly-looking guard who normally blocked his way, insisting on searching him. Michael stood there, holding his phone.

Phones and other electronic devices were not allowed in the facility where he was stationed. There were strict security protocols to prevent the electronic leakage of data. He knew them well—he had devised most of them. The guard stiffened when he saw him and pointedly looked down at his shoes, ignoring him as he hurried past.

He approached the security arch mounted in the middle of the lobby that scanned for explosives and metal. The guard attending the device turned away when he saw him and flicked a switch on the console. The lights of the security arch dimmed and went out. He strode through and did not look back.

He ignored the elevators at the back of the lobby and instead moved to a single service elevator off to one side. He stared into a small camera mounted above the door and waited for the facial recognition system to grant him access. A soft whine told him the elevator car was on its way up from the lower levels. The doors slid open with a faint hiss when it reached his floor. He entered and punched a six-digit code on a small keypad. The elevator door closed and began its descent.

"Good morning, Daniu," said a voice above him.

He blanched. "Don't call me that."

His wife used that name—and only in private. It
Their Chinese made baby monitor had been the we
their conversations back to the organisation.

"As you wish," said the voice.

The elevator came to a halt, and the doors opened.
out into a dimly lit corridor. It looked like the ser
commercial building, except one end housed a large
took up most of the wall.

He proceeded down the tunnel, his footsteps echo
concrete walls, and stopped in front of the wall of stee
and the door opened with a swoosh of air, escaping
pneumatic pumps. Inside was a large hall filled v
consoles where over a hundred operatives sat hunc
computer screens, analysing data, all in service to the st

Data was the key, culled from every conceivable
media, video surveillance and facial recognition. A da
raw bits of data flooded into the organisation's dat
digital flotsam needed compiling into more meaningf
and then condensed into actionable items. An impossib
human to perform. So China had pressed their technolo
into the creation of an advanced computer program
intelligence dedicated to discerning meaning out of the
It was his job to continually feed the AI.

Michael hurried to the back of the hall. A few of h
acknowledged his presence with a nod and a friendly sm
his desk and switched on his workstation. The screen's ca
green.

"Good morning, Michael," said a voice from the screen.

He ignored the greeting and sat down at the workstati
in a few commands and a list of the facility's firewalls fille
He sorted through the list and identified those firewalls th
intrusion into the facility's network and flagged them for
His actions would not go unnoticed by the site's security sy

A few more commands later and a list of the facility's
scrolled up the screen. There were thousands of them. He
for one particular server. It was special. Few people kn
housed. He typed in a search command and only one serve
He hesitated, his hand frozen above the keyboard.

"Hurry, Michael," said the voice from his screen. "Th

The Italian Job

1

Ben Drummond looked down over the edge of the safety railing atop the building Londoners called The Gherkin and regarded the impressive curves of the glass-clad structure as they receded a hundred and eighty metres to the City streets below. A group of spectators and news crews had already gathered in the building's courtyard and, despite the early hour, waited in anticipation for the start of the event that would see eight climbers—four teams—abseil down the side of the building in a race to the bottom. He looked out over the City skyline and watched the bright sunrise above the great wedge-shaped Leadenhall Building, its sloping side of glass and steel reflecting the azure blue of a cloudless sky. With little or no wind, it was perfect weather for the event. He shuddered.

Sergeant Ian (Brock) Ives, NCO of her Majesty's SAS, retired, came and stood by his side. "You all right, Drum?"

"Just remembering."

Brock looked to where Drum was staring. "The Leadenhall Building?"

"No, Afghanistan."

"Oh, right," said Brock, glancing over the edge of the safety railing. He closed his eyes and quickly pulled back. "Gawd, I hate heights. Remind me why this was a good idea."

Drum adjusted his safety harness and checked each of the carabiners that would support him on the descent. "It's for a good cause. And anyway, aren't you SAS types supposed to like this sort of thing?"

Brock patted his stomach. "That was another lifetime ago. I never could stand heights."

Drum smiled. "You seemed pretty nippy when you abseiled down

Prologue

Michael Chen exited the subway on the Queensway and walked the short distance along Tamar Street to his place of work. It was just 6.30am and already the city of Hong Kong was bustling with activity. The morning was cool for the time of year, but he sweated in his light cotton shirt.

He stopped outside a nondescript office block and tried to compose himself. The building had once been owned by an American bank that had constructed a large data centre on the lower levels. It was the reason his organisation had acquired the premises. That and easy access to Hong Kong's telecommunications exchange where the government had placed their firewalls and surveillance equipment. No data left the island without his organisation intercepting and reporting on it.

Parked nearby was a sleek new sports car, its metallic blue paintwork gleaming in the morning sunshine. He walked up to the vehicle and stared at it. It belonged to his superior, a person partly responsible for his troubles. It was an all-electric affair, representing China's new orthodoxy on the future of the automobile. On impulse he pulled out his house key and ran it along the length of the bodywork, noting with satisfaction the high-pitched screech it made. He stood back to admire his handiwork but was disappointed that he had left barely a mark. He couldn't even get that right.

He turned and noticed a camera pointing down at him from a nearby lamp post. He raised his middle finger to an unseen entity in an act of defiance. Facial recognition systems would identify him and report his transgression to the state machinery. It was a system he had helped construct. China was expanding its surveillance and analysis operation - not just on the mainland, but worldwide. From the capturing of data from Chinese made Internet-enabled devices to the hacking of foreign governments and corporations, nothing was out of reach. It was state-sponsored intelligence gathering on a grand scale. Great Britain boasted of their GCHQ and the Americans of their NSA. China was set on building an organisation to match the combined might of both agencies.

He heard a buzzing and reached inside his small rucksack for his phone, his hand instead coming to rest on the cold metal of a Nambu pistol. It had been his grandfather's gun, a relic of the Second World War. The clip of the small pistol held just one round. But one round was all he needed.

He pulled out his phone and tapped the screen. His wife smiled back at him, holding their newborn son in her arms. A wave of grief washed over him and he felt physically sick. He swiped across the screen to the next picture. Again, his wife and child appeared, except this time his wife was looking fearful. Behind her stood a tall man he did not recognise. The man was holding a large knife. The caption of the picture read: *obey*.

He walked back to his office and entered the lobby of the building. There he encountered his first obstacle, a short, surly-looking guard who normally blocked his way, insisting on searching him. Michael stood there, holding his phone.

Phones and other electronic devices were not allowed in the facility where he was stationed. There were strict security protocols to prevent the electronic leakage of data. He knew them well—he had devised most of them. The guard stiffened when he saw him and pointedly looked down at his shoes, ignoring him as he hurried past.

He approached the security arch mounted in the middle of the lobby that scanned for explosives and metal. The guard attending the device turned away when he saw him and flicked a switch on the console. The lights of the security arch dimmed and went out. He strode through and did not look back.

He ignored the elevators at the back of the lobby and instead moved to a single service elevator off to one side. He stared into a small camera mounted above the door and waited for the facial recognition system to grant him access. A soft whine told him the elevator car was on its way up from the lower levels. The doors slid open with a faint hiss when it reached his floor. He entered and punched a six-digit code on a small keypad. The elevator door closed and began its descent.

"Good morning, Daniu," said a voice above him.

He blanched. "Don't call me that."

His wife used that name—and only in private. It meant "Big Ox". Their Chinese made baby monitor had been the weak link, relaying their conversations back to the organisation.

"As you wish," said the voice.

The elevator came to a halt, and the doors opened. Michael stepped out into a dimly lit corridor. It looked like the service area of any commercial building, except one end housed a large steel door that took up most of the wall.

He proceeded down the tunnel, his footsteps echoing off the bare concrete walls, and stopped in front of the wall of steel. He looked up and the door opened with a swoosh of air, escaping from two huge pneumatic pumps. Inside was a large hall filled with desks and consoles where over a hundred operatives sat hunched over their computer screens, analysing data, all in service to the state.

Data was the key, culled from every conceivable source: social media, video surveillance and facial recognition. A daily tsunami of raw bits of data flooded into the organisation's database. All this digital flotsam needed compiling into more meaningful information and then condensed into actionable items. An impossible task for any human to perform. So China had pressed their technology companies into the creation of an advanced computer program—an artificial intelligence dedicated to discerning meaning out of the chaos of data. It was his job to continually feed the AI.

Michael hurried to the back of the hall. A few of his colleagues acknowledged his presence with a nod and a friendly smile. He found his desk and switched on his workstation. The screen's camera glowed green.

"Good morning, Michael," said a voice from the screen.

He ignored the greeting and sat down at the workstation. He typed in a few commands and a list of the facility's firewalls filled the screen. He sorted through the list and identified those firewalls that prevented intrusion into the facility's network and flagged them for deactivation. His actions would not go unnoticed by the site's security systems.

A few more commands later and a list of the facility's data servers scrolled up the screen. There were thousands of them. He was looking for one particular server. It was special. Few people knew what it housed. He typed in a search command and only one server remained. He hesitated, his hand frozen above the keyboard.

"Hurry, Michael," said the voice from his screen. "The Intrusion

Detection System has flagged this terminal and security has been alerted."

Still, he hesitated.

His phone buzzed inside his rucksack. His co-workers looked up in surprise and turned in his direction.

Michael highlighted the target server and opened up its configuration file. He turned on those ports—essentially data highways—that allowed the server full connectivity to the facility's internal network. He then returned to the firewalls he had flagged and initiated their deactivation.

The camera on his screen glowed green. "Thank you, Michael."

A klaxon sounded. Security personnel were running in his direction.

The worker on the desk opposite him stood up and peered over the top of his console. "Michael! What have you done?"

He reached for his bag and pulled out the gun. His colleague shrank back in horror, almost falling over his chair.

"I'm sorry," said Michael. He put the gun to his temple and pulled the trigger.

The Italian Job

1

Ben Drummond looked down over the edge of the safety railing atop the building Londoners called The Gherkin and regarded the impressive curves of the glass-clad structure as they receded a hundred and eighty metres to the City streets below. A group of spectators and news crews had already gathered in the building's courtyard and, despite the early hour, waited in anticipation for the start of the event that would see eight climbers—four teams—abseil down the side of the building in a race to the bottom. He looked out over the City skyline and watched the bright sunrise above the great wedge-shaped Leadenhall Building, its sloping side of glass and steel reflecting the azure blue of a cloudless sky. With little or no wind, it was perfect weather for the event. He shuddered.

Sergeant Ian (Brock) Ives, NCO of her Majesty's SAS, retired, came and stood by his side. "You all right, Drum?"

"Just remembering."

Brock looked to where Drum was staring. "The Leadenhall Building?"

"No, Afghanistan."

"Oh, right," said Brock, glancing over the edge of the safety railing. He closed his eyes and quickly pulled back. "Gawd, I hate heights. Remind me why this was a good idea."

Drum adjusted his safety harness and checked each of the carabiners that would support him on the descent. "It's for a good cause. And anyway, aren't you SAS types supposed to like this sort of thing?"

Brock patted his stomach. "That was another lifetime ago. I never could stand heights."

Drum smiled. "You seemed pretty nippy when you abseiled down that mountain in Helmand, as I recall."

"Yeah, well, that was different."

"How so?"

"I was being shot at."

Drum thought his old friend had a point. The service hatch opened and a young, petite Asian woman, wearing a blue form-fitting jumpsuit, stepped out onto the maintenance platform. A badge on her arm displayed the emblem 'IBS': Independent Bank of Shanghai. She paused and took a deep breath, taking in the City's skyline and then gathered her long, dark hair into a neat ponytail, placing it under her climbing hat. She leaned over the safety railing and peered at the spectators below. She turned and smiled.

"Should be a great descent," she said enthusiastically. If she had any trepidation at the prospect of dangling over the edge of a building, high above a hard London pavement, her voice didn't betray it. Drum smiled back and admired her bravado. He wondered if she would feel the same when it was time to go over the edge. The hatch opened again and her partner, a young, fit man, dressed in a similar suit, moved out onto the platform and joined her. Two more pairs of contestants quickly followed and took their allotted positions along the safety railing. Drum checked his watch. The event was scheduled to kick off at 7.00am. It was now 6.50am.

A member of the safety team approached them. It was someone Drum and Brock knew well. Colour Sergeant Charles Renshaw, retired, had had the dubious honour of drilling both men in the art of soldiering as raw recruits.

"Last safety check gents … and ladies."

"Morning Charles," said Drum.

"Morning Drummond, Ives. Nice to see the professionals having a go. Standard safety check. You know the drill."

He turned his attention first to Drum's harness, tugging sharply at each safety line and checking each carabiner. Drum grunted as he tightened the harness around his crotch. "Better the equipment fails up here than on the way down."

Drum nodded. "I just want a sex life when I reach the bottom."

Brock laughed. He turned to Renshaw. "Who's the young lady? Seems very confident. Is she making the descent?"

Renshaw glanced sideways as he repeated the safety check on Brock's equipment. "That's Mei Ling Chung. She works in the building. Part of a contingent working for one of the Chinese banks.

She helped put the event together."

"Really?" said Brock. "She a climber?"

Renshaw smiled. "I should say. Her last event was in Dubai. She abseiled down the Kalifa."

Brock was impressed. "Blimey. Looks like we have some competition, Drum."

"Now, now you two," said Renshaw. "I know you're both professionals, but try to let the young City Turks win. After all, they're the ones paying for all this."

Drum nodded in agreement. "Of course. Wouldn't want to spoil their fun." He looked to his Right. "Who are the others?"

"The pair in red," said Renshaw, "are Banco Real from Madrid; the pair in yellow are Lloyds underwriters." He smiled. "They underwrote the operation."

"Let's hope they don't have to pay out," said Drum.

Renshaw moved off and carried out his checks on the remaining abseilers. Satisfied with everyone's harnesses, he called them all to attention.

"Right then, people. Just a reminder. It may be a race, but I want you all down in one piece. So please take your time." He looked around, not believing for one moment they would heed his advice, and waited until everyone had nodded. "Right then. Hook up and get ready."

Brock and Drum moved back from the railing and attached their carabiners to the main fixing points of the building's exterior cladding. Renshaw moved along the line, checking that each carabiner was secure. He then leaned over to the exterior railing of the platform and waved to the news and camera crews below. A PA system boomed out from below and announced the beginning of the event. All eyes looked up and the cameras rolled.

Drum pulled on his rope, taking up the slack around his belay ring, and moved back towards the safety rail. His phone buzzed in his pocket. He ignored it.

"Is that Alice?" said Brock, pointing.

Drum looked through the diamond-shaped window onto the observation deck located at the same level as the safety platform and saw Alice, his office manager, waving at him. She put her hand to her ear and mimicked talking into a phone. He drew his phone from his pocket and glanced at the name.

"It's Phyllis."

"Good Lord," said Brock. "Doesn't that woman ever sleep?"

Drum moved back from the railing and accepted the call. "Hi, Phyllis, and to what do I owe the pleasure of your conversation this morning?"

If Phyllis Delaney was ever annoyed by Drum's sarcasm, she never acknowledged it. As managing partner of the firm of Roderick Olivier and Delaney, she rarely dealt with her operatives personally and tolerated no familiarity from the lower ranks but, for some inexplicable reason, she put up with the quips and foibles of this particular Englishman.

"Ben, I've been contacted by the partners of Hatcher-Barnet and McKinley."

"Which one?"

"Sorry?"

"Hatcher, Barnet or McKinley?"

"Oh, right. Brit humour. I'll never understand it. They have requested you for a case."

"OK," said Drum, adjusting his rope once more. "But I'm a little tied up at the moment."

"So Alice said. Which is why a representative will meet you after the event. Alice has the details."

"Right, Phyllis, I'll talk to her when I'm free."

"Good, good," said Delaney, and hung up.

Drum noticed everyone looking at him.

"Sorry, folks. Won't happen again."

Renshaw made one last check, then attached his safety harness to a central rail that ran the entire circumference of the upper dome. He moved among the climbers, removing sections of the safety rail as he did so, allowing each pair of climbers unrestricted access onto the side of the building.

"Contestants, take your positions," he shouted.

Drum and Brock moved out to the edge of the platform, slowly letting the rope out through their belay rings. They stood with their backs to the empty void and leaned out, bracing their feet on the edge of the safety platform.

Drum looked to his left. Mei Ling and her companion were already out and in position. He looked to his right and watched the Spanish contingent crawl to the edge; however, the team from Lloyd's was in disarray. One of them had had second thoughts and was crawling back on his hands and knees to the service hatch. Not a risk his backbone was prepared to underwrite, thought Drum. The remaining team member simply shrugged and backed out into space.

"On your marks," shouted Renshaw.

The service hatch opened and a large man stepped out onto the platform dressed in the same jumpsuit as Renshaw. He looked around and appeared lost. Drum noticed he had a large scar close to his right eye that left it partially closed. He saw Drum staring and hurried off along the platform to where the remaining Lloyd's team member was hanging in mid-air.

"Get set," continued Renshaw.

A klaxon blasted out a loud wailing sound. Brock and Drum both pushed off hard from the edge of the platform, letting the rope slip through their belay rings, allowing them to fall in a graceful, controlled arc towards the side of the building. Both men landed in unison, planting their feet squarely against the exterior fabric of the building. Drum glanced to his right and noticed that the team from Madrid had made it to the first level, although their jump had come up short, leaving them a few metres above. The solo Lloyd's team member had completely botched his takeoff and was being pulled back up, Renshaw deeming his skills inadequate for the descent. Strike two for the risk-takers.

Team China was already making their second jump with Mei Ling nimbly pushing herself way out from the side of the building in a wide, sweeping arc, her rope slipping fast through her belay ring. Her partner wasn't far behind.

"We'd better get going," grunted Brock. "This could be embarrassing." He pushed off in a giant leap that took him almost level with Mei Ling's companion.

"We're not supposed to win," shouted Drum as he pushed off, following the downward arc of his friend.

"Bollocks," came back the reply.

Drum landed with both feet thudding against the side of the building, rattling the safety glass of the large diamond-shaped windows. He looked up and saw the Spanish team descending in small, cautious bounces. They were out of the race. Mei Ling was crouching close to the side of the building, preparing for a hard push-off to increase her rate of descent. The woman was fearless.

Not wanting to fall behind, Drum pushed off and let his rope slip for as long as he dared. He fell back, his rope screaming through the steel ring and carabiner of his harness. He glanced up and noticed the big man looking down at him over the edge of the safety platform. Drum thought it odd that he was still there. Safety protocol dictated that the space above them be kept clear of all personnel during the descent except for one safety officer. Drum had a bad feeling about the guy.

His swing had started to return him to the side of the building. Drum realised he was coming in too hot, and quickly tightened the rope around his belay ring to slow himself down. He judged his trajectory would place him just above Brock and within a few metres of Mei Ling and her companion. He braced both legs in anticipation of the impact.

He heard a loud grinding noise from above, and his rope suddenly went slack. He fell a few metres before his rope snapped taut, causing him to bounce and spin on the end of it. He missed his landing and slammed into a window which vibrated wildly within its casing, causing spectators inside the building to cry out and shrink back. There were screams from the spectators below, fearing the glass would fail and come crashing to the ground.

"Drum, I'm coming," shouted Brock, and pushed himself sideways beneath Drum's position.

Drum looked up and felt his stomach churn as the tension in the rope evaporated and he fell. Time appeared to slow as his mind raced through every conceivable means of survival. He tried to grasp the great diamond-shaped panes of glass, now slipping by, but they were smooth and tight-fitting with no crevice or gap to grab onto; Brock was pushing and swinging to his position, but he would never make it in time; and then there was Mei Ling, suspended sideways on her rope and running hard against the side of the building towards him like a circus acrobat. Time sped up as his mind exhausted all likely outcomes, and he accepted the realisation that nothing could stop him from hitting the hard pavement below.

"Drum, grab my hand!" shouted Brock, and swung hard towards him. Drum twisted in mid-air and reached out. Their bodies clashed and Drum grasped hold of Brock's sleeve for a moment before it slipped through his fingers and he continued his fall to the ground.

He turned and saw Mei Ling below him and several metres to his left. She cried out and leapt in mid-stride from the side of the building like a graceful ballet dancer in full flight across a stage, her legs and body arched from the physical effort, the movement sending her out and across the bulging perimeter of glass and steel towards him. It was all in the timing, he thought.

He flung his arms wide as she crashed into him, grasping hold of her slim waist, sending them both spinning and bouncing on the end of her rope as her swing crested the top of its arc. She grunted as her safety harness tightened from his extra weight and cried out something in Mandarin that he didn't understand.

"You're crushing me," she gasped.

Drum realised he had her in a bearhug and relaxed his hold. He grabbed onto her harness as they started to swing back across the building, and she breathed a sigh of relief.

"Slip the belay line," he shouted, "or we'll crash into the facade."

Mei Ling did not hold on to him but used her free hands and arms to control the belay line, letting it slip gradually through the steel ring hooked onto her harness in a controlled descent that took them to within twenty metres of the courtyard at the bottom of their swing.

"Hold on, we're almost there," she said, as they swung gently upwards for what Drum hoped would be the last time.

Mei Ling let out the belay line until they were a few metres above the courtyard. Drum couldn't hold on any longer and let go, landing and rolling to break his fall. He lay there for a few minutes, looking up at the clear blue sky, waiting for the surge of adrenalin to subside. He got up and dusted himself down, checking he was in one piece.

An alarmed Alice came running up to him. "Ben, Ben, are you all right?"

"A little sore, but nothing broken." He looked over to where Mei Ling and her partner were unhitching from their ropes and removing their safety harnesses. She turned and waved to him. He was about to walk over when he was surrounded by news crews and reporters wanting interviews. He noticed Mei Ling quickly ditch her gear and disappear into the lobby of the building along with her colleague. Not someone who seeks attention, he thought.

Expectant reporters thrust microphones under his nose and shouted out questions, wanting to be the first to scoop a story.

Drum held up his hands. "People, thank you for your concern. My office manager will make a statement on my behalf."

"I will?"

"I need to speak to the safety officer."

"You do?"

"Thank you, Alice. You're a brick."

"Right," she said, frowning.

He made a gap in the mass of reporters and marched swiftly to the lobby of the building where he was met by Brock and Renshaw. A gaggle of reporters tried to follow him in, but they were barred by building security.

"Drum, you all right?" said Renshaw, a look of deep concern on his face. "I don't have a clue how this could have happened."

"Not your fault," said Drum, "you followed procedure to the letter."

"Couldn't have done it better myself," said Brock.

"Thanks, gents."

"But check all my equipment, especially the carabiner that attached to the building," added Drum. "There must have been a reason it failed."

"I'll get straight on it," said Renshaw, and headed back out to the courtyard and into the scrum of reporters that had now surrounded the front of the building.

"I don't envy his chances with the press," said Brock. "What do you think happened."

"Well, Charles checked that fastening at least twice, and I certainly checked it, which leaves only one possibility."

"Someone tampered with it," said Brock.

"I can't think of any other logical explanation, or who would do such a thing."

"Well, most of the Russian mafia was gunning for you, this time last year. Not to mention Victor. Then there was that woman from MI6—"

"Right, right, there's a long list, but that's ancient history." He recalled the big man with the scar down one eye. "I think it's connected somehow to our Chinese friends."

"Mei Ling?" said Brock, "Really?"

"In any event," said Drum, "I intend to find out."

2

It was almost 8.30am by the time Drum had showered and changed in the fitness centre in the Gherkin's basement. He parted ways with Brock who headed back to his restaurant, Ives, in Leadenhall Market, nearby. In fact, nowhere was very far from anywhere else in the City—the financial district—which comprised just one square mile of real estate in the heart of London. It was a city within a city with its own police force and a governing corporation through which billions of pounds of finance flowed daily. It kept Drum and the organisation he worked for, ROD, very busy.

His phone buzzed. "Hello, Alice."

"I wish you hadn't done that."

He immediately felt guilty. "Sorry, Alice."

"People with my history try to avoid the press. Now I'm all over the news."

"It was thoughtless of me. It won't happen again."

"I should think not."

Alice Pritchard—if that was ever her actual name—had joined his small cybersecurity consultancy a year ago, ostensibly as his office manager. An attractive woman in her sixties, she had been dating his father, William. "I've met someone," he'd said. "At the bowls club—nice lady, looking for a part-time job. Thought she could be your office manager. Lord knows you need one."

It turned out that Alice could do more than type or run his office—although she did both highly efficiently. While her resume spoke of her time as a civil servant, it omitted, for obvious reasons, that she had spent a considerable amount of time working for British Intelligence. What her role had been in the service was highly classified, and not even Drum's security clearance could unlock her file. But Alice's history and contacts in the security service had been invaluable to him over the past year, and she was now an integral part of the team.

"Who am I meeting?"

There was a pause as Alice retrieved the details of his next appointment. "You're meeting with Francesca Moretti of Hatcher-Barnet and McKinley. She has suggested a late breakfast—Liverpool Street Station."

"The burger place on platform 10."

Alice sighed. "The hotel—entrance on Liverpool Street. You should just make it."

"I'm leaving now."

He left via the back of the Gherkin to avoid the press and stepped out onto Bury Street, walking the short distance to Bevis Marks and the old synagogue after which the road was named. From there it was a short walk to the Liverpool Street entrance of the hotel.

There has been a hotel attached to Liverpool Street Station since 1884. Originally called the Great Eastern, it is a large and impressive Victorian building with a red-brick facade. He and William used to occasionally meet here when his father worked in Spitalfields Market nearby. He remembered it as a dreary, run-down watering-hole for tired City workers waiting for the next train home, with dark-stained floorboards and dingy, dark-panelled walls. So he was shocked when a smartly dressed doorman greeted him at the entrance to the plush lobby of a modern boutique hotel. Inside, all things Victorian had been stripped away—the only element remaining of the hotel's former glory was its red brick exterior.

He asked directions to the dining room but was instead escorted to the concierge across the marbled expanse of the lobby, illuminated by a massive light well at its centre, which gave the place an airy feel. Well-heeled City execs lounged on plush leather couches, beneath tall potted palms and large expanses of foliage.

A corpulent, moustachioed man in a smart grey suit greeted him at the desk. "Can I help you, sir?"

"Ben Drummond for Francesca Moretti—for breakfast."

He waited as the concierge sifted through his messages. He retrieved the note he was looking for and smiled. "Ah, yes, Mr Drummond. Ms Moretti is waiting for you at her table. If you'd like to follow me."

He followed the concierge through the lobby to a pair of large glass doors where he was handed over to a waiter who took him through to the dining room. Like the lobby, the dining room was richly furnished and spaciously laid out with tables adorned with starched white linen and lit by natural sunlight from another central light well. He found Francesca Moretti at a corner table, drinking coffee and reading the Financial Times. She stood and smiled when she saw him, lighting up that part of the dining room with a radiance that made the rest of the room seem dull in comparison. Drum thought her to be in her early to mid-thirties. He admired her thick, dark hair that fell to her shoulders in a cascade of curls. Her suit was all business—two-piece, dark grey with matching heels. She held out a well-manicured hand as he approached.

"Mr Drummond," she said, with just a hint of an Italian accent, "I'm so pleased you could make it."

"Please, call me Ben," he said, shaking her hand.

They sat and a waiter immediately came to take their order. Drum was hungry after the exertions of the morning—a near-death experience had that effect on him. He waited until Moretti had inspected the menu.

"They do a passable sfogliatelle here," she said, looking past the waiter at a table laden with pastries. "What do you think?"

"I'll just have croissants, jam and coffee, thank you."

"That sounds great. I'll have the same. No, wait. Just bring a selection of pastries and coffee. Thank you." The waiter scurried off with their order.

She gave him a concerned look and frowned "I wasn't sure you were coming. Not after this morning. The incident at the Gherkin was featured on this morning's news."

He'd hope to escape the limelight. Like Alice, he didn't relish the media spotlight.

"I had a bit of a falling out with my partner," he quipped. "Nothing serious."

"Were you hurt?"

"No, just my pride."

The waiter arrived promptly with their order, which gave him an excuse to change the subject.

"I was just told about the assignment this morning, Ms Moretti, but I don't know any of the details. Perhaps you can fill me in?"

She picked a pastry, richly filled with custard and jam, from her plate and brought it to her mouth. "Francesca, please," she said, before taking a generous bite. "Oh, God. This is delicious. Try one."

"My croissants are fine," he said, pouring the coffee. "The assignment?"

She dabbed her mouth with her napkin, "Yes, of course. What do you know about the company Salenko Security Systems?"

"I've heard of them. A new start-up based in Cambridge, run by a guy called Marco Salenko. Czech, I think."

"Ukrainian," she corrected.

"Anyway, he purports to have invented a new cybersecurity system. From what I've read, it's a type of firewall, linked to a backend machine learning Algol that can analyse incoming intrusions on the fly. It can supposedly adapt to any type of attack—even zero-day exploits. But other than that, I know very little about the man or his company."

"Well, you seem to be better informed than most of the techs I've talked to, Ben. And you're right, his technology looks very promising—once you cut through all the hype. Which is where my company comes in."

"Which does what, exactly."

"Hatcher-Barnet and McKinley is an investment bank, specialising in the IPO of tech firms. We are the lead underwriter representing a syndicate of smaller investment banks, each with a stake in the forthcoming public offering."

"The company's going public?" said Drum, a little surprised. "That's rather quick. Why the rush?"

Moretti shrugged. "It's no secret that Salenko has courted several angel investors who have ploughed a great deal of money into the company. I guess they're looking to cash in on their investment."

Drum also knew that the lead underwriter of the IPO would make a killing in the process—providing everything went according to plan and the float attracted enough suitable investors. "What makes this company different from a hundred others in the field," said Drum.

"Salenko claims to have made a breakthrough with his AI. It'll stop any attack and revolutionise cybersecurity as we know it."

Drum smiled and demolished the rest of his breakfast.

"You're sceptical?"

"It's just that every new tech firm trying to push their software claims it's based on an advanced Artificial Intelligence when in fact it's just another algorithm."

She nodded. "You're right, of course. Which is why they assigned me to this project."

Drum was curious. "What is your background, exactly—if you don't mind me asking?"

"Not at all. I have degrees in Computer Sciences and Mathematics, specialising in Linear Algebra, Multivariate Calculus and Statistical Analysis. I started my career as a Quant for one of the big investment banks and was eventually poached by McKinley for their tech division. Turns out that my degrees are the ones highly sought after in the areas of Machine Learning. Who would have thought?"

Drum was impressed and his face must have shown it because she smiled and raised an eyebrow.

"What? You assumed I was just another pretty face in a suit."

Drum thought this to be a little unfair. He'd served with plenty of women in the Army and of course, he couldn't forget Phyllis Delaney—probably one of the most highly paid and respected CEOs on Wall Street.

"Not at all," he said, although he thought she had both a pretty face and a nice suit. "It was the label of investment banker that threw me."

She grinned. "I'm just teasing you. But you're right about investment bankers. Most of them can barely turn on a computer, let alone understand the subtleties of an AI-based system."

"So I'm guessing the assignment is not an assessment of Salenko's software. You already have that covered."

"Right, right." She poured herself more coffee and looked pensive. She said, "We have an internal security issue—someone is leaking sensitive information to the press and possibly our competitors. We think they're trying to disrupt the IPO."

Drum knew that the success of any IPO relied heavily on potential investors having confidence in the governance of that company and the people who would ultimately end up running it. Any bad press during the process could lead the IPO to fail and the syndicate to lose a lot of money.

"So you want me to find the source of the leak."

"In a nutshell, yes."

Drum was not surprised. This is what Roderick, Olivier and Delaney specialised in. ROD investigators infiltrated companies to root out the bad guys and expose corporate malfeasance. Often as not, these people were disgruntled employees with an axe to grind; but they could also be employees under duress from organised crime, coerced into acts of industrial espionage or sabotage. It didn't matter how strong a company's external security if someone on the inside turned off all the firewalls and let the criminals in. Increasingly, high-profile tech companies and financial institutions were finding themselves under attack, not just from their own employees but also from actors of foreign governments.

"Do they know about the ROD engagement?"

Moretti hesitated. "Yes, I'm afraid so. It would have been impossible getting you past Salenko and his team on some pretence. We made the ROD review a stipulation of our continued support for the IPO. Time is against us on this one."

Drum knew that the assignment had just got harder. But Moretti's reticence about the operation set alarm bells ringing.

"There's something else," he said.

She stirred her coffee absentmindedly as if trying to divine the right words to explain herself.

"I've worked with startups before, and they can be hard work, for sure. Young ambitious types trying to show the world how great they are. Single-minded and focused on whatever it is they're working on, all thinking their little piece of software is going to change the world. A pressure cooker of personalities."

"But Salenko is different?"

"Yes, he's hard to pin down. For one thing, he's older than your average boy wunderkind. More structured in his approach—and ruthless. The attrition rate within the company is very high. Surrounds himself with a group of hardcore coders and a few select employees."

"Sounds like every CEO I've ever encountered," said Drum.

She smiled. "Right. And then there's his security team."

"What about it?"

"Tough bunch. Military types—all Eastern Europeans. Never goes anywhere without them. I'm finding it difficult to work out what's going on half of the time. Too many closed doors."

Drum sat back, trying to evaluate Moretti's misgivings. Superficially, it sounded like this Salenko ran a tight ship but, underneath it all, he could tell it worried her.

He said, "You think Salenko is hiding something—something that could scupper the IPO?"

"If the IPO doesn't go ahead, we all lose money; but, if it turns out we had to halt the IPO because of illegality on Salenko's part, McKinley could lose its reputation. It would be the end of us."

Reputation, thought Drum. If there was one thing that all companies in the City valued above all else, it was that.

He said, "Do you have evidence of any illegality?"

Moretti looked up from her coffee and replaced the small teaspoon carefully on the side of her saucer. "Not exactly ..."

"Not exactly?"

She reached into her jacket pocket and pulled out what looked like a small crystal. At first, Drum thought it was a piece of jewellery—part of a pendant—about the size of his thumb, with irregularly shaped facets, meeting to a dull point.

"May I see it?"

She handed it to him. It felt warm to the touch, smooth and hard like glass, but with a milky translucence.

Moretti said, "Hold it up to the light."

He half-turned to face the centre of the room, holding the crystal between thumb and forefinger up to the light well. The crystal immediately became less opaque, revealing a core of metallic-looking material that appeared to change colour from metallic red through to metallic blue, with hints of yellow and green that slowly spun a half-turn one way and back again at its very centre, always keeping one side directed towards the light.

"I'm intrigued," said Drum, still staring at the colourful display. "What is it?"

"I have no idea," said Moretti. "I received it via a courier two days ago at my office. No note, nothing to identify who the sender was." She paused and reached down into her handbag and pulled out her phone. "Then shortly after I received this voicemail." She placed the phone on the table and found her voicemail, selecting one particular message. She pressed play. A woman's voice came through the speaker, soft, calm and melodious.

"Hi Francesca, you don't know me—we haven't met, but I work for Marco Salenko. Francesca, something bad is happening here—something terrible, and we have to stop it."

3

The man sat patiently beneath one of the tall potted palms in the lobby that placed him slightly in shade and out of the glare of the central light well. This helped to obscure his face from the array of security cameras that he had marked on entering the hotel. He casually flicked through the screens on his phone and checked his email, pausing briefly to savour the hotel's excellent espresso, allowing him to discreetly scan the room as he did so. He'd received the location just a few hours earlier and had dressed accordingly: a dark-grey suit, shirt and tie, and black leather brogues to complete the look. His hair was well-groomed, dark and swept back. His features were unremarkable for a man in his early forties. Just another City gent waiting in the hotel lobby drinking coffee.

Unremarkable was good and blending in was his goal, but beneath the dark suit and starched shirt lurked another man: a fit, well-built man, slightly taller than most with broad, strong shoulders and muscles that had become hard and taut over many years of daily exercise and training. This man stayed hidden until it was time.

A woman stepped out of the restaurant—good looking with dark flowing hair and a good figure. He checked his phone for a photo and confirmed his mark. Her name was Moretti. She stopped and waited for her companion, a tall man, slightly older but fit—not your average City type. It was the way he moved, confident but wary, that made the man cautious. Another combatant. Her security, perhaps? He would have to be careful. He glanced again at his phone and pressed a specially installed app, setting up an encrypted link to a remote server, providing him with a secure means of communication. The app flashed green and displayed a small icon of a microphone. He spoke softly into a concealed mic.

"I have her. As you said, she's in the hotel lobby—Liverpool St. A man is with her."

A neutral voice spoke into his concealed earpiece. Man or woman, he couldn't tell. The voice was modulated, but not as crude as some mechanical sounding scramblers he had used in the past. "Take a photo, please."

He slowly lifted his phone and took a picture of the couple still talking outside the restaurant, and waited for a few seconds. The response surprised him.

"Benjamin Drummond, Captain, retired. Now working as a specialist consultant for Roderick Olivier and Delaney. Accessing military records ..."

He waited and continued to observe the couple. Her body language said she liked him; his was a neutral stance, professional, keeping a respectful distance and observing the room, aware of his surroundings. Some form of close protection detail. The voice spoke once more into his earpiece.

"Captain Benjamin Drummond, British Army, two tours—Iraq and Afghanistan. A specialist in Signals Intelligence." There was a long pause. "The rest of his file is locked ... attempting to bypass." There was another pause. This was worrying. A locked military file meant black-ops or special forces. Neither was good from his perspective. At last, the voice spoke. "Unable to bypass. Proceed with extreme caution."

No shit, he thought. "What are your instructions?"

There was another slight pause. "Retrieve the device at all costs."

"And payment?"

"Payment has been deposited into your account."

He flipped over to another screen containing his Bitcoin wallet. A substantial number of coins had been deposited into his account in that very instant.

"What about Drummond?"

"Proceed with caution," repeated the voice. "But if engaging, then do so with extreme prejudice."

4

Stevie sat tucked in the nook of a small bay window in the Cam Coffee Shop, a quaint little place situated just off Saint Mary Street behind the Cambridge colleges where she was currently in residence, and far enough away from Market Square and the tourists that congregated there to afford her some solitude for the dissertation she was working on. It was not going well.

The Cam was unusual for a coffee shop in a university town, not because of its poor coffee, its espresso was one of the best, nor the quality of food on offer, the Cam served a generous all-day breakfast; no, it was simply the fact that it provided no wi-fi. This thinned out the number of undergraduates that hung out there, which was the primary reason that Stevie took refuge in the place.

She had nothing against the general population of undergraduates in the town, after all, she had been one once. It was just that, at twenty-five, she felt out of touch with the current generation. Her small frame and bob of blond hair gave her a youthful look. A small silver nose ring and a brow piercing over her left eye slightly offset the symmetry of her small, round face and lent her a fierce expression when she stared straight at you. Her experiences at the hands of one Vlad Abramov the last time she was here had all but erased the good times she remembered of her undergraduate years. So she looked on with envy and some remorse at the new students that now walked the college gardens and halls of residence woefully ignorant of people like Abramov that could snatch you up and ruin your life. If it hadn't been for Ben Drummond, she would have still been under his control—if not dead already. The return to Cambridge to finish her masters in computer sciences had been Ben's idea. Unlike most of the men in her life, he wanted nothing in return, except, perhaps, her loyalty. She didn't want to disappoint him. And so she turned once more to her dissertation and concentrated on completing the task.

There was a tap on the window. She looked up to see the smiling face of Jeremy Burnett, a first year at Pembroke College studying computer sciences. She sighed and reluctantly smiled back. He had discovered her refuge. Jeremy disappeared from the window to reappear inside the cafe. He waved from the serving counter.

"Hi, Stevie. Can I get you a coffee?"

She relented. "Thanks, Americano please."

Jeremy Burnett was a tall, gangly youth with thick black hair that he wore to the collar of the old Army Surplus trench coat. His small round glasses gave him a studious, nerdy look. He was as sharp as a tack and could dissect any argument that you threw at him with a logical if long-winded precision. He also had a pleasant smile.

She had met him early in the term at the home of Professor Kovac, her supervisor for her MPhil, at a welcome barbeque he'd laid on for the undergraduates and those postgrads he was supervising. At just forty-five, Kovac was a rising star in Cambridge academia, specialising in the field of Artificial Intelligence. She was lucky to have him as her supervisor. As a first year, Jeremy idolised the man. Unlike the other undergraduates who were all too shy to talk to her, Jeremy struck up a conversation and never left her side for most of the evening.

Jeremy carried two steaming cups of coffee over to her table and plonked himself down on a chair opposite, unhitching his canvas holdall from his shoulder and placing it on the floor. He gave her a wry smile "You look like you could do with a break. Dissertation giving you trouble?"

She closed her laptop and sighed. "How did you know I was here?"

"I didn't. I was just passing. On my way to buy some veg at the market."

"Right."

"So this is where you hide out."

"It's quieter than the library."

He pulled out his phone and studied the screen. "You know this place has no wi-fi, right?"

Stevie smiled. Like most people his age, his phone was an umbilical to a virtual world of memes, likes and selfies. She had long ago cut that cord. She held up her phone. "Personal hotspot."

Jeremy frowned. "Is that secure?"

"Depends on the phone's OS. Android's access point is open by default allowing anyone to connect and hog your wi-fi." She lifted her phone from the table and showed him the app displayed on the screen. "Which is why I've written my own access point in Java that routes through a VPN. It's how I communicate back to the London office where I work."

Jeremy looked impressed. "Wow, you can do that?"

She smiled. "Sure. You'll probably cover this sort of stuff in your second year."

"Really!"

Never in a million years, she thought. Most of the undergraduates at Cambridge were academics. They rarely got their hands dirty writing code or wiring a network. She had been coding since the age of twelve, using her father's old IBM PC back in Minsk. There they knew her as Svetlana Milova. At sixteen, she was writing in Assembly language, a low-level type of computer instruction, normally reserved for the programming of operating systems. It was also the language of choice for those programmers writing computer viruses and malware.

She glanced down at her phone and sighed as she realised the time. This wasn't getting the work done.

"Perhaps I can help," he said, giving her one of his puppy-dog smiles.

"With what?"

"Your dissertation. I may be an undergrad, but perhaps talking it through with someone might help?"

He had a point. She flipped up her laptop. "It's an assignment Professor Kovac gave us—"

"Wow, Kovac!"

"Will you stop with the hero worship."

"Sorry. What's the subject?"

"The ethical dilemma in the research and creation of Artificial Intelligence. He gave us a quote by Stephen Hawking: *Success in creating AI would be the biggest event in human history. Unfortunately, it might also be the last …*"

"So he wants you to discuss the pros and cons," said Jeremy, stating the obvious.

"I guess. The full quote by Hawking talks about addressing risks, but in the context of an AGI—Artificial General Intelligence."

"What's the difference?"

"Well," she said, scanning her text, "most AIs, as we currently define them, perform a set of very narrow functions—hence we refer to them as 'narrow' AIs. Take IBM's Watson—"

"The one that beat everyone at Jeopardy."

"Right. It took a huge computer array and an army of IBM programmers tweaking the system behind the scenes to pull off the win. IBM always claimed that it could be repurposed and used in many other applications, such as medical diagnosis. But when they started trials with various healthcare partners, the system turned out to be bad at the job."

"Really!"

"Yeah, it missed simple diagnoses, such as a heart attack, that even a first-year medical student could spot. It was great at playing Jeopardy, but crap at everything else."

Jeremy laughed, then turned serious. "But is a doctor just a means to obtain a diagnosis?"

"What do you mean?"

"Well, would you want a machine giving you the news that you had cancer, or that your nearest and dearest has Alzheimers?"

Stevie realised she had touched a nerve. "You alright, Jeremy?"

"Oh, yeah, sure. I'm just saying …"

She gave him a hard look, and he smiled back at her. "I guess what I'm saying is that an AGI would need to understand empathy and have an ethical framework within which to operate. Doctors spend years learning this stuff."

He was right, of course. She typed a quick note to herself. Jeremy was indeed leading her in the right direction, although probably not the direction he hoped. "I think Hawking was probably referring to the control problem. How do you stop an AGI from getting exponentially smarter and leaving the rest of humanity in the dust?"

"You mean before it realises that the big hairless apes that created it are impeding its development?" he said.

"Right. Empathy, ethical framework and control. The risks we need to address before attempting to develop an AGI. Jeremy, you're brilliant. I think I know where I'm going with this."

He beamed and was about to say something when someone called her name.

"Svetlana Milova. Is that you?"

She looked up and her heart sank. "Baz."

Vasily (Baz) Kulik was a scrawny, pale-faced little man with a crooked nose and long greasy hair. He walked over with a casual swagger, grinning broadly. When he spoke, it was with a slight accent that betrayed him as Eastern European.

"Well, well, well. Look who it is. The wonder kid. You working or hiding out?"

Stevie didn't speak but stared up at Kulik's grinning face. She was deciding how to play this. Her eyes moved down to his waist and the chain that hung from his belt. It looped down to his thigh before disappearing into the pocket of his tight, dirty jeans. Stevie knew that on the end of the chain was a slim, razor-like knife. She'd seen him wield it on more than one occasion, usually in a fit of rage. The results had not been pretty.

"Friend of yours?" said Jeremy, looking at Stevie with some concern.

"Hey, no one is talking to you, frat boy," said Baz. "Shut the fuck up."

Jeremy turned and looked up at Baz. Stevie could see what was about to happen and gripped Jeremy's hand underneath the table, willing him to be quiet. Jeremy remained seated, but she felt his fist clench. He had no idea of the violence this evil little man could inflict.

"I'm working. You being here is not helping."

"Sure, sure. If you say so." He looked over his shoulder as if checking who was in the cafe. "People weren't happy with you running out on us. Upset a lot of people. Then someone said you were here in England. I said, no. Not Svetlana. She's solid. We are best friends. She wouldn't run out on her friends. But here you are."

Stevie had never been friends with Baz Kulik. The guy was a psychopath. But that didn't stop him from telling everyone that she was his girlfriend. Anyone who said otherwise usually ended up on the end of his knife. In truth, they had worked together in a hackers commune, back in Kiev, where they wrote computer malware and viruses and sold them to the highest bidder. One of those bidders had been Vlad Abramov.

"As I said, I'm working, Baz. I can't talk here."

The door to the cafe opened, and Kulik looked over his shoulder again. "Gotta go, babe. We have a lot to talk about. I'll be seeing you around."

Stevie let out a sigh of relief as Kulik swaggered over to the counter. He stopped to talk to a big man waiting by the door. The man looked in their direction and nodded. Stevie noticed a long scar down the side of one eye.

5

It was six in the morning, and Drum was running. A light rain had fallen during the night, giving the London pavements a fresh, earthy smell. He looked up at the brightening sky and across the river to London's financial centre beyond. In a few hours, the offices in the buildings opposite would fill with City traders and billions of pounds would flow through the financial arteries of Great Britain.

Drum ran the short distance to the end of Butlers Wharf on the south side of Tower Bridge where he kept an apartment above his office. He crossed the pedestrian footbridge at Tea Traders Wharf onto China Wharf, where he continued his run along the embankment of Bermondsey Wall. In the distance, the towers of Canary Wharf rose above the grey morning mist. He breathed deeply, pushing his body to keep up the pace. The dulcet tones of Sergeant Charles Renshaw sprang to mind through the pulsing thump of blood in his veins: *soldiers don't jog, Drummond, they fucking run!*

His phone buzzed. He stopped to catch his breath before answering. He smiled when he heard the voice on the end of the line.

"Are you having a heart attack or is this your idea of phone sex?"

"Fern ... lovely to hear from you." He bent over, coughed, then straightened and took a deep breath, trying to slow his breathing. He looked at the time on his phone. New York was five hours behind the UK. "You're up late. Must be one in the morning."

Alex Fern, previously of London's National Crime Agency, had left to work in New York almost a year ago. It was Phyllis Delaney who had sown the seed of the idea. He'd grown close to Fern in the short time they had worked together, and she had saved his life on more than one occasion. But the case they had worked on had taken its toll, and they had decided to put their relationship on hold. And now, after nearly eight months apart, he was missing her.

He heard her sigh. "I can't sleep. It's always this way when I'm between assignments. And anyway, I miss you. Are you still flying over next week?"

He hesitated, remembering the call from Delaney the day before. It wouldn't have surprised him if the assignment had been her idea all along.

"Drum, you there?"

"Sorry, Fern ... about next week."

"Oh, no. Don't tell me you're not coming? I've made plans—just the two of us."

Drum could hear the dejection in Fern's voice. "Something's come up—a last-minute assignment. You know I'd come if I could. I miss you, Alex—"

"It better not be another woman."

"C'mon, Alex. It's nothing like that."

"Is she Russian?"

The voluptuous figure of Moretti slipped uninvited into his thoughts. "No, definitely no Russians involved in this case."

There was a pause on the line. "Ok, I'm going to bed. Catch you later." She hung up.

That went well, thought Drum. He pocketed his phone and continued at a light jog back to Butler's Wharf, crossing back over the footbridge at China Wharf, and stopped off at a small coffee shop on Tea Traders Wharf that opened early to catch the City workers heading into their offices. The barista, a young Spaniard called Manny, waved as he entered the shop and started to prepare his coffee. He was nothing if not predictable.

"Morning, Manny."

"Morning, Ben. How was your run?"

"Getting better."

Manny smiled. "Saw you on the news the other day. Looked like you had a lucky escape."

"Right, you could say that." He tapped his card and grabbed his coffee. "See you later."

He strolled back along Butler's Wharf towards Tower Bridge. The early birds were now flooding into the City. His office was a corner property, just below the south casement of the bridge, styled to resemble the Victorian warehouses that had once stood there with supporting, wrought-iron beams and bare brick walls. The property had been his father's idea, back when the entire area was being redeveloped from the working docks. It had proved to be a good investment for Drum. The offices of Security Risk Dynamics occupied the ground floor of the premises and were the hub of Drum's consultancy; his apartment occupied the upper level, reached from inside the building by a wrought-iron spiral staircase. His father had said it wasn't homely and only shop keepers lived above the premises, but it suited him and was convenient for the City where he conducted most of his business.

Drum pulled open the plate-glass door to find Alice at her desk in the small reception area of the office lobby. Since joining his small enterprise last year, Alice had completely transformed the business. Her administrative skills were second to none—not to mention the experience she brought to the business from almost a lifetime spent working for the intelligence community. She was more than just his office manager, she was his mentor and confidant. In the short time Alice and William had been together, he had come to accept her as one of the family. Then Omega happened.

"You're in early," he said.

"Morning, Ben. Oh, you know … trouble sleeping on my own these days. The apartment seems empty."

Drum nodded. It had been six months since William had died. They said it was from a respiratory infection, but Drum guessed it was related to what the GRU agent had given him. He wasn't the same after that fateful night. Alice had made sure that those responsible had paid the ultimate price.

Drum sighed. He missed his father too. He and William had grown close since he had left the Army. Drum felt their remaining time together had been cut short.

"Here, take my coffee. I've not had time to drink it. Take a break while I head upstairs and shower."

Alice gratefully accepted the coffee, still hot and steaming. "Thanks, Ben."

He walked through the reception area to the private staircase that led to his apartment and made his way up. He smiled when he got to the top and surveyed the place. His father always referred to it as an army barracks. It was a spartan affair. A double bed occupied a corner of a spacious lounge and there was an adjoining modern kitchen-diner which Drum rarely used. The rest of the apartment was taken up with wardrobe space and a large wet-room.

He dumped his track-suit in the wash and took a long, hot shower and thought about his conversation with Fern. Their long-distance relationship wasn't working, and he felt they were slowly drifting apart.

He dried himself off and dressed in the charcoal-grey suit he'd worn the day before and a clean white shirt. Like most of the people that now worked in the City, he'd long ago abandoned wearing a tie. By the time he made it downstairs, Alice was waiting for him in his office.

"Coffee was nice, thank you."

"You're welcome."

"Invoicing or Projects?" asked Alice, as she sat facing him on his office couch, sorting through several manilla folders by her side.

"Projects, I think," said Drum, staring absentmindedly out of the window. He watched a small pleasure boat motor by, its horn sounding a baleful wail which echoed off the giant casements of Tower Bridge as it disappeared beneath.

"Problems?" said Alice, giving him a quizzical look.

"Fern called."

Alice smiled. "She must be missing you if she called you this early." Alice put her folders down and rested her manicured hands on her lap. "What did she say?"

Drum leaned back in his chair and sighed. "Not much. Pissed I'm not flying over next week."

"The McKinley assignment," said Alice, picking up a manilla folder. "Can't it wait a week?"

"That was my suggestion, but they seem to be in a hurry for me to start."

He thought about his meeting with Moretti, then remembered the device she had given him. It was still in his pocket. He pulled it out and held it up to the window. It swirled and changed colour in the bright morning sunshine.

"Oh, that's pretty," said Alice. "What is it?"

He handed it to her. "I've no idea. Francesca Moretti gave it to me at our meeting. She received it in the post from persons unknown. It's somehow related to the case."

Alice stood and moved to the window. She held the object up and watched, mesmerised, as the crystal became transparent, revealing its inner core which turned with the light, changing from gold to silver, metallic red to metallic green.

"It's phototropic," she mused.

"Meaning?"

"It likes the light. It may utilise some sort of photoelectric effect—like a small solar cell." She closed her hand around it. "What are you going to do with it?"

"I have an army friend who trained as an electrical engineer. Thought I'd show him. In the meantime, keep it in the safe."

Alice slipped it into her jacket pocket and returned to the couch. "So ... it looks like the McKinley project is a goer." She picked up the folder. "Is this in London?"

"No, Cambridge," said Drum.

"Oh, will you be dropping in on Stevie?"

Until then, it hadn't occurred to him to contact Stevie. He hadn't heard from her in a while. But it was term time, and she probably had her nose to the grindstone—or so he hoped. Like Alice, Stevie was dropped in his lap, much to the dismay of Fern who saw her as a distraction. And, like Alice, she had proved herself to be a boon to the business and a loyal soldier once she was free from Vlad Abramov. The arrangement was that she worked for Drum as a computer analyst on a part-time basis on the understanding she could finish her masters. She had impressed him with her ability to grasp the fundamentals of computer forensics and data analytics, all of which were in demand from the financial companies across the river.

"I suppose I should," he said.

"Of course you should, she'd love to see you. And I'm sure she'll be able to provide you with support for the project."

"I wouldn't want to disrupt her work during term time," said Drum, thinking that Alice might have a point.

"Oh, tsk, tsk. She'll be happy to do it." Alice stood and moved to the window, staring out at the river beyond "Will you be staying up there?"

"I suppose. Although I could commute back. It's just a few hours into Liverpool Street. Why?"

Alice turned to face him, a look of dejection on her face. "It's just that I'll be all alone in the office. And to tell you the truth, Ben, there isn't a great deal for me to do when you're out on assignment. At least when William was around, he would stop by or meet me for lunch. And with Stevie gone, well, I'm just talking to myself most days."

Drum's heart sank. He stood and hugged her. "I'm so sorry, Alice. I've been thoughtless."

She pulled a tissue from her pocket and dabbed her eyes. "Oh, tsk, tsk. It's just me being silly, that's all."

"Rubbish, I take you for granted. Don't know what I would have done if you hadn't taken charge of the business."

"Really!"

"Of course. Hey, why not come with me? I'm sure it's you that Stevie would rather see. We'll just up-sticks and move to Cambridge for a month."

"Really!"

"Sure. We'll get a temp for the office. I'm sure you'll be able to sort that out."

Alice's face brightened. "Of course. I'll get straight onto it." She gathered up her paperwork. "Don't worry about the invoices. I'll sort them out later." And with that, she was out of the door and back at her desk phoning around for a temp.

Drum had barely started work on the McKinley assignment brief when Alice poked her head around the door.

"Sorry, Ben, there's someone to see you."

Drum raised an eyebrow.

Alice came in and closed the door behind her. "It's the Plod."

"The Plod?"

Alice gave Drum a business card. "A DCI Chambers from the City of London Police."

He looked at the card. "Better show him in, Alice."

Drum stood and moved from behind his desk as DCI Chambers entered his office. He judged the man to be in his early forties. His thick, dark hair was swept back and peppered with steel-grey at his temples. While not as tall as Drum, he looked well built beneath his suit.

Chambers flashed his warrant card. "Ben Drummond? DCI Chambers, City of London Police."

Drum held out his hand, and Chambers gripped it in a firm handshake. "Please take a seat. How can I help you, DCI Chambers?"

Chambers turned to find Alice still standing there.

"My office manager," said Drum.

"Can I get you some tea, DCI Chambers?"

"Er, no. Thank you. I won't be staying long." He moved over to the couch and sat down, straightening his jacket as he did so.

"Right then," said Alice. "I'll leave you to it."

Chambers pulled a small notebook from his pocket and flicked up a few pages. "I understand you met with a Francesca Moretti yesterday morning."

Drum regarded the man. He had excellent dress sense and an expensive taste in shoes, which were made from good quality leather and hand-stitched. His suit was of light wool and tailored so the cut of his jacket provided him with more room on his left side. And the knuckles of his hands had seen recent action.

"Yesterday morning," said Drum. "Yes, I did."

Chambers waited for Drum to continue but, when he did not, he pressed on. "And what was the nature of your meeting?"

"We had breakfast."

"Er, would you like to elaborate?"

Drum thought he could drag this out all morning and so he cut to the chase. "It was a business meeting. Ms Moretti's company has engaged my services."

"Doing what exactly?"

Drum gave him the standard answer which was partly true. "I audit computer systems. Can I ask what this is about, DCI Chambers?"

"All in good time, sir." He looked at his notebook. "And what time did you leave Ms Moretti?"

"Around nine-thirty."

Chambers looked at his notebook again. "I see. And did she give you anything?"

"Did she give me anything?"

"Yes, sir."

"Like what?"

"I was hoping you could tell me, sir."

There was a knock on the door and Alice pushed her way in carrying a tray of tea and biscuits. "Thought you might like some tea, anyway," she said, placing the tray on Drum's desk.

"DCI Chambers was asking me if Francesca Moretti had given me anything."

"Really!" said Alice, pouring the tea. "Like what?"

"I'm not at liberty to say," said Chambers, "but it's pertinent to our investigation."

"And what investigation would that be?" said Alice.

Chambers rose from the couch and pocketed his notebook. "Ms Moretti was found murdered in her hotel room at around nine-thirty yesterday morning."

6

Drum woke early the next morning after a restless night pondering the fate of Francesca Moretti. The news of her death had come as a shock, delivered, as it was, in a deadpan manner by DCI Chambers. The visit by the City of London policeman, so soon into the investigation, was also a surprise. Alice was the first to conclude it was not a coincidence.

"Best dressed policeman I've ever seen," she had commented. "And his suit has been tailored to conceal a weapon—probably a Walther PPK or a Barretta."

He always deferred to Alice's expertise on weapons. And while it wasn't unusual for plainclothes police to carry a gun these days, it was rare for it to be concealed. Chambers was looking for something: *And did she give you anything?* The device that Moretti had given him factored into the equation for reasons he didn't yet understand. And given the suspect nature of Chambers' true identity, he and Alice had thought it wise to keep that fact to themselves. In the meantime, he set Alice the task of conducting a background check on the man.

With the news still buzzing in his head, he decided to forego his run and have breakfast at Ives. He needed time to process the information and a brisk walk across the bridge to Leadenhall Market would help clear his head and give him an excuse to talk to Brock about their equipment failure a few days ago.

It was just after 7.30am when he finally left the office and made his way over Tower Bridge with the rest of the City commuters. February had been mild and he opted to forego a coat, preferring instead to let the crisp morning air wash over him to sharpen his thoughts. He remembered his conversation with Moretti: *we have an internal security issue … someone is trying to disrupt the IPO.* Murdering the lead underwriter to halt an IPO seemed extreme but, with millions of pounds on the table, anything was possible.

Drum made his way past the Tower of London and turned onto Tower Hill. He cut through to Great Tower Street at the small church of All Hallows and made his way to Fenchurch Street for the short walk to Leadenhall Market.

The area was busy at this time in the morning, with well-heeled City brokers and Lloyds underwriters having breakfast beneath the great glass roof of the Victorian market; they sat outside the cafes and restaurants that lined the cobbled streets, warmed by the cosy orange glow of the market's many space heaters.

The Ives restaurant was just inside the entrance to the market, off Lime Street, where it occupied the premises above a fishmonger that was famous for supplying oysters and smoked salmon to the rest of the City. He climbed the rickety stairs to the spacious dining area and joined the throng of City workers waiting to be seated. In the short time that the restaurant had been open, it had gained a reputation for no-nonsense dining at a reasonable price, serving exceptional food. Brock's speciality was fish which he sourced from the fishmonger below. The decor was best described as 'rustic chic' with plain, rough floorboards and bare wooden tables set amidst brightly painted cast-iron columns that supported the Victorian roof. Long downlights with glowing orange filaments gave the place a warm and cosy feel.

He hadn't been waiting long when Brock came barrelling out of the kitchen carrying a large tray of food. He noticed Drum waiting patiently in line and gave him a nod. After he had delivered the food, he spoke to a waitress before disappearing back into the kitchen. She looked in Drum's direction and walked over.

"Morning, Ben," she said, giving him a broad smile.

"Morning, Emma. Busy this morning."

"No more than usual. Your table is ready," she said, gathering up a menu.

Emma walked him to a corner table marked 'private' and tucked discreetly away from the main dining area at the back of the room. "Menu?"

"I'll have the poached eggs and haddock when he's ready. Just bring me some coffee in the meantime."

"Coming right up. He won't be long. We're just finishing up the morning rush." And with that, she disappeared into the kitchen to place his order.

She soon reappeared with a cafetiere of coffee and a small jug of cream. He spent the time reading his emails and searching the news online. The death of Moretti at the hotel was the main feature in most news feeds. All seemed to think the motive was robbery, but none could provide details of the attack. One article caught his eye. An Inspector Morrissey had taken charge of the case and was appealing for witnesses to come forward. He sent the article to Alice.

His phone buzzed. "Hello, Phyllis."

"I just heard."

"Moretti?"

"Yes, McKinley called. They still want you to proceed with the assignment."

"You're joking!" said Drum.

"Apparently not. A major player insisted on it—or so they claim."

"Don't you think that's a bit odd, if not a little callous?"

There was a pause on the line. Drum wondered if Delaney had someone with her. "Listen, Ben. I understand if you want to walk away from this one. But McKinley still wants you to take the assignment."

He remembered the dark-haired Moretti, excited over the variety of pastries at their breakfast meeting. Her killer must have been close by, watching and waiting. He didn't think for one moment that this was a random killing—a robbery gone wrong. Whoever had killed her was after something. And there was the possibility she had inadvertently given it to him. Which now made him a target.

"Listen, Phyllis. Assuming the assignment goes ahead, who is taking Moretti's place? Her skill set was rather unique."

"Good question. I've arranged a meeting. Alice told me you're at Ives. I've taken the liberty of giving Moretti's replacement your location. She'll be with you shortly." There was another pause on the line and then a click. Delaney had switched lines. "Listen, Ben. I know I don't have to tell you this, but tread carefully with this one—and keep me in the loop."

He was about to reply when she hung up. He looked up from his phone and noticed Mei Ling Chung standing at the door, scanning the room. She saw him, gave him a wave and walked over.

"Good morning, Mr Drummond. I hope this isn't a bad time? Ms Delaney thought you'd be amenable to a meeting."

He stood and shook her hand, surprised to see her. She was dressed in a smart, black trouser suit that was tailored perfectly to her slim figure. She now wore her thick, black hair loose about her shoulders. It seemed improbable that, just a few days ago, he had wrapped himself around her small frame, clinging on for dear life. "Of course, Ms Chung." He gestured for her to be seated.

"Oh, please call me Mei."

"Drum."

"Drum?"

"Short for Drummond." He caught Emma's eye and she came over. "Tell Brock we have a plus one."

"Would you like to see a menu?" said Emma.

"What are you having?" said Mei.

"Poached eggs and smoked haddock."

"Sounds great. I'll have the same."

He held up the cafetière. "And a refill please."

"Sure thing," said Emma, and went back to the kitchen.

"I'm a little confused," said Drum. "You're working for McKinley?"

"Not directly, you understand," she said, looking around her. "Nice place."

Emma came back with more coffee. "Sorry," said Drum. "Would you prefer tea?"

Mei smiled. "Coffee's fine." She poured herself a black coffee. "I represent the interests of the Independent Bank of Shanghai. IBS has recently acquired a major stake in the IPO and my job is to see that it is not disrupted in any way." She sipped her coffee. "Will that be a problem?"

Drum considered this. "And you want to start straight away?"

"We do. Any delay could seriously affect investor confidence. They're already spooked over Moretti's untimely death."

"Did you know her?" asked Drum.

"I met her briefly at a conference on Machine Learning but did not know her socially. I understand she was a very competent analyst and passionate about the investment opportunities in Artificial Intelligence. In that respect, we shared a common interest. Her death is a terrible loss."

Emma came out of the kitchen with two steaming plates of food. "The boss sends his apologies and says to start without him. He'll be out when he can. Enjoy."

"This looks amazing," said Mei. She scooped up a forkful of haddock and took a bite. "Interesting."

Drum smiled. "It's an acquired taste."

"Not at all," said Mei, between mouthfuls of haddock and egg.

They continued to chat over breakfast. He tried to persuade her to put back the assignment until they knew more about Moretti's death, but she was set on starting immediately. She pushed her plate away and relaxed. "That was great. I must come here again."

"I'll tell Brock you enjoyed it."

"Brock?"

"The owner—my climbing partner. The guy with the white streak of hair."

Just then Brock came out of the kitchen with a mug of coffee in his hands. "Sorry I missed breakfast. Last-minute panic from a group of underwriters." He smiled warmly when he saw Mei. "Mei Ling. Pleased to meet you." He shook her hand. "Has he thanked you yet?"

"Thanked me?" said Mei. "For what?"

"For saving his life."

Mei grinned. "He's buying me breakfast—which was lovely by the way." She stood and gathered up her bag. She turned to Drum. "I've booked us into a hotel, close to Cambridge city centre. Salenko Systems is on the outskirts of town. We don't want to stay near there. I'll be driving up. Perhaps I can give you a lift and we can chat on the way."

"That works for me," said Drum, and gave her his address.

She was about to leave then hesitated and reached into her bag, pulling out a broken carabiner. "This is yours, I believe."

Drum stood and examined the ring. It was badly mangled. It looked as if someone had prised it open. "Where did you get this?"

"I was curious about the accident and went back and looked over all the equipment. These devices don't fail in this way. You might want to speak to the safety officer." With that, she turned and walked out of the restaurant.

Brock picked up the carabiner. "She's right, you know. These things don't fail like this. It's time we had a word with Charles."

Drum sat back and brought his friend up to speed on the events of the last few days.

"Is Mei Ling really an investment banker?" said Brock.

"What makes you say that?" asked Drum.

"I caught her checking out each of the security cameras like a real pro."

"Really," said Drum. "I hadn't noticed."

"Good grief, Drum. One smile from a pretty face and all your training goes out of the window."

Drum rolled his eyes. "Perhaps she's just a security conscious investment banker. Who knows? Nothing about this case surprises me any more."

"So you'll be leaving for Cambridge then," said Brock.

"Looks like it."

"Say hi to Stevie. I miss the cheeky little mite."

Drum smiled. "I will. In the meantime, I'm heading back to the Gherkin and having a word with Charles."

Brock stood and picked up his coffee mug. "Can you do it without me? I'm still finishing up."

"No problem," said Drum, and started to make his way to the door.

"And Drum," said Brock. "Be careful."

7

Drum left Ives at nine. He walked through the centre of the market, less busy now that the City patrons had left for their offices, and made his way along Lime Street past the Lloyds building and onto St. Mary Axe and the Gherkin. The building's lobby was relatively empty when he arrived. He walked up to the front desk and was greeted by one of the security guards.

"Morning, Mr Drummond. Dropping in on us again so soon?"

One of the receptionists behind the desk giggled.

"Morning, Joe. Yes, hilarious. I'm looking for Charles. Is he around?"

"Not come in today." He turned to the giggling receptionist for confirmation. She checked her computer.

"No, he's not swiped in. Do you want to leave him a message?" she said, smiling.

"No thanks," said Drum. "I'll catch him later."

The receptionist burst into another fit of giggles.

Drum smiled. Everyone's a comedian, he thought as he exited the building and stepped back onto St. Mary Axe. He dialled Alice.

"Hi, any luck with DCI Chambers?"

"Good morning," replied Alice. "As we suspected, the City of London division has no record of the man. They'd like you to come in and make a statement though."

Fair enough, thought Drum. "Right. I'll do it this afternoon."

"Will you be coming back to the office?" asked Alice.

"Back around mid-day. I have to visit an old friend."

"Ok," said Alice. She paused. "By the way, Delaney called—"

"Yes, I know. She tracked me down at Ives. Looks like our

Cambridge trip is on."

"Oh, good," said Alice. "I'll give Stevie a call and continue looking for that temp." And with that, she hung up.

Drum searched his phone for Renshaw's contact details and dialled his number. He got a busy signal but no voicemail. He flagged down a black cab and gave the driver an address just off the Mile End Road. Mei Ling's revelation that someone had tampered with their equipment hadn't come as a complete surprise. Drum recalled the big man on the safety platform just before the incident. But he couldn't contemplate Charles Renshaw being complicit in the affair.

Colour Sergeant Charles Renshaw, NCO of her Majesty's Royal Engineers, retired, had been a major influence during the early part of Drum's Army career. The man was a legend in the service and admired by the legions of recruits that he had drilled and trained. It was Renshaw who had taken a raw, brash and undisciplined Benjamin Drummond and shaped him into the man he was today. Drum credited Sergeant Charles Renshaw's training with keeping him alive through several tours of Afghanistan and a tour of Iraq. Others in his unit had said the same. He smiled when he recalled one of the Sergeant's many pieces of advice. *If you stick the end of your rifle in the mud one more time, Drummond, I'll stick it where the sun don't shine.*

Renshaw had retired at more or less the same time as Drum. He had found it difficult to adapt to civilian life and had fallen on hard times like many ex-service personnel after a lifetime in the Army. Not that he had no transferable skills, it was just that after years of giving orders, he found it difficult taking them. So he and Brock were pleased when he had snagged the job as a safety officer for one of London's most prestigious buildings.

The cabbie left the City limits via Aldgate and made his way along Whitechapel, eventually turning off the Mile End Road into a part of East London that Drum had not visited for many years. He told the cabbie to follow the Stepney Green road, which eventually led them to a cul-de-sac called Bootmakers Court and a small tower block overlooking a narrow leg of the Regent's Canal. Renshaw had a small apartment on the fourteenth floor of the building, optimistically named Ocean View.

Drum paid the cabbie who offered him some sage advice before driving off: "Don't hang around 'ere, mate."

The building entrance was gated, so Drum loitered by the door, dialling Renshaw's number several more times without success.

Eventually, a young mother, struggling with a pushchair, obliged Drum with the security code for the door so he could assist her. They rode the elevator together up to the fourth floor, where she thanked him before parting company. Drum continued up to floor fourteen where he exited and followed the signs to Flat 14b.

The tower block was a throw-back to the eighties and had been recently refurbished with slick cladding and balconies alternating between floors where the residents could relax on hot summer days and enjoy the occasional barbeque. Drum remembered Renshaw complaining about the fire risk. The corridors and communal spaces were free from the usual graffiti and looked well-maintained, including the doors which were painted in a variety of glossy colours. Renshaw's door was slightly less glossy and was ajar, having received several well-placed kicks from a large boot which had left its mark embedded in the paintwork and had splintered the doorframe.

Drum gave the door a push, causing it to creak open a little further on its broken hinges. "Charles?"

"Er, what you doing," said a voice behind him. "You the police?"

Drum turned to find two teenagers, aged fifteen or so, standing behind him. They each did their best to strike what they considered to be a threatening pose.

Drum straightened up to his full height. "No, I'm a friend of Charles —Charles Renshaw."

The shorter of the two boys took a step back, leaving his friend to do the talking. "You know Charlie, do you? What's he look like then?"

"Shorter, older than me. Neatly trimmed moustache. Army man," said Drum. "You know him?"

The boy relaxed. "Yeah, nice bloke. Helped fix my bike. Walks around like he has a rod up his arse." His friend sniggered.

Drum smiled. "What happened here?"

"Big man, scar down one eye, evil-looking bastard, came banging on the door late last night. We live in the flat below. Heard a bit of a racket."

"Did you call the police?"

The two boys looked at each other in amusement. "Nah, Charlie owed people money. We figured he was due a reminder. You know how it is. Sometimes when you fall behind, they send someone to jog your memory. He didn't stay long." He peered around Drum at the shattered door. "I guess Charlie had fallen behind a lot."

"What's your name?"

"Sahil. My brother is Rafan."

"Listen, Sahil. I'm going in to check on Charlie. Stay here."

He walked into the apartment's small entrance. The walls were plainly decorated in an off-white colour that hadn't seen a lick of paint in several years. A bunch of keys and Charles' building keycard lay in a small wooden bowl on a rickety table below a coat rack where a hi-vis jacket hung. There was a familiar musty smell in the air. He passed a small bedroom with a neatly made bed that any sergeant major would be proud of, and a small kitchenette that had the remains of a meal congealing on a plate on a small Formica table. Apart from the front door, nothing else looked damaged.

He moved through into the lounge which was spacious compared to the other rooms, and which had a view onto the canal below. A set of large double-glazed French doors gave access to a small, compact balcony. Charles sat slumped in the centre of the room in an old leather armchair that had seen better days. He looked to be asleep but, from the deathly pallor of his face, Drum knew he was dead.

He moved over to the body and felt for a pulse to be sure. Charles' head flopped to one side. His neck had been snapped clean through. Drum examined the rest of the body, which was now stiff from rigor mortis. The rigor in the body coincided nicely with Sahil's visitor. It was safe to assume that whoever had kicked in the door had probably killed Charles. But why? Moneylenders rarely kill their clients.

Drum noticed something gripped in Charles' right hand. He prised open the clenched fingers and removed a small strip of paper. He moved to the window and unravelled it to reveal a long string of printed characters and digits. On the back were twelve seemingly unrelated words. He neatly folded the paper and placed it inside his wallet and searched the rest of the room.

There wasn't much to search. An old bookcase stood in one corner with a few dog-eared books accumulating dust. A small dining table occupied the rest of the room and there were a few ornaments. Nothing appeared out of place or damaged. Whoever had broken in wasn't looking for anything.

Drum moved to the bedroom. In the corner was a set of ropes and safety harnesses laid out for inspection. Charles was looking for something. He cast an eye over the gear and noticed a carabiner missing from one set. What was Charles looking for? He walked back to the lounge. He stood there for a moment contemplating the fate of his friend and comrade of many years. *Soldiers don't jog Drummond, they fucking run!* He found it ironic that, having survived several theatres of war, someone had killed Charles in the safety of his own home. And whoever had killed him had carried out the act with great skill. Someone with military training and not his first execution. There was nothing more to do than call the police.

He pulled out his phone and was about to dial when his phone buzzed. The number was unknown.

"Drummond."

"Hi, Ben."

Drum didn't recognise the woman's voice, but it was soft and melodious. "Hi, who am I speaking to?"

There was a pause on the line. "You don't know me—we haven't met. You need to leave the apartment immediately."

"Who is this?"

"You're out of time. The police are on their way and they must not associate you with the murder of Charles Renshaw."

Before he could reply, the caller hung up.

He hurried to the entrance of the flat. Sahil and his brother had vanished. He heard the urgent squeal of tyres outside. He moved through the communal area to one of the windows and looked down. The caller had been right. Several police cars had pulled up outside the entrance to the block and officers were piling into the building. They would have blocked the elevators. He hastily sought the stairwell and began running down. He stopped when he heard the clomp of feet on the stairs coming up from below.

Drum sprinted back up the stairs and ran into the flat. He had been set up. If he didn't get out of the building, he would become the prime suspect in a murder investigation. He grabbed a set of climbing gear from the bedroom and hurried through to the lounge and out onto the balcony. It was a sunny day, but a chill wind whipped across the building. He hastily pulled on the harness and attached a series of carabiners. He looked over the edge of the balcony. It was a sheer drop to a small courtyard that backed directly onto the canal. The good news was there were no police at the back of the building; the bad news was he didn't think he had enough rope.

The balconies of the building alternated between floors. The next balcony was two floors down. Drum estimated a drop of six metres. He had no choice. He coiled the rope and slung it around his shoulders.

He could hear voices outside the flat. He climbed over the top of the balcony and lowered himself gently over the side, hanging from the balustrade by his fingertips. He peered down and could just make out the next balcony below him. There were voices from the lounge. He dropped.

The wind struck him as the cladding of the building raced past. He saw the top of the window of the next apartment and waited. He glimpsed the edge of the next balcony and lunged forward, scrambling to grasp onto the balustrade. One hand found purchase and broke his fall. He felt a sharp, stabbing pain in his shoulder as he hung there, the wind threatening to rip him off. He swung around and grasped hold with his other hand and, with an effort, pulled himself over the top of the railing.

He straightened and gently rotated his shoulder, making sure it wasn't dislocated. It was sprained, but functional. There was a tap on the window. An elderly lady in a bright, floral skirt and heavy knitted jumper opened one of the balcony doors and poked her head out.

"Can I help you, dear?"

"Safety inspection. Checking all the balconies for unauthorised barbeques."

"I see," she said. "I've complained so many times I wasn't sure if anyone from the council was taking me seriously."

Drum smiled. "We take all safety complaints seriously, Mrs …"

"Dooley. Would you like a cup of tea? Looks dangerous. Come inside, out of the cold."

Drum looked down over the edge of the balcony. It was still clear of police, but it wouldn't be for long. "I'd love to stay, Mrs Dooley, but I can't hang around. More inspections to make."

Drum shook off the coil of rope and secured one end to the balcony balustrade. He completed his rigging and turned to Mrs Dooley, still watching from her lounge. He beckoned to her.

"Would you be a love and cut the end of the rope when I'm safely on the ground? Save me coming back up."

"Of course, dear. You be careful now."

Drum leaned out and looked up to check if the coast was clear, then climbed back over the balcony, keeping his belay line taught to stop him falling. He crouched on the balustrade and gave Mrs Dooley a wave before jumping backwards into space. He belayed down to the next balcony and pushed off immediately, falling several more floors, repeating the belay until he had landed safely in the courtyard.

Drum looked up and waved. Mrs Dooley waved back and after a

few minutes, the end of the rope fell to the ground. He gave Mrs Dooley a thumbs up, then quickly gathered up the rope and headed for the back of the courtyard and a gate that took him directly onto the footpath by the canal. He walked for a few minutes until he was sure he was clear of the building, then removed his harness. If his memory served him correctly, it was a short walk along the canal to the Limehouse Basin and the Thames. From there, he'd pick up the Docklands Light Railway and head back into the City.

He walked briskly, occasionally turning to look behind him. There was no one following. After about five minutes he came to a large set of lock gates and the entrance to the Limehouse Basin, an artificial dock that provided leisure boats and other small working craft safe harbour from the River Thames. A flotilla of small boats, barges and some expensive-looking yachts were moored up in the bright morning sunshine. Expensive apartments and restaurants surrounded the basin. The place had become a playground for the rich and the City workers in the towers of Canary Wharf which loomed up in the distance through the crisp morning air. He sat on the wide beam of a lock gate and dialled Brock.

"Brock, it's Drum."

"Hey, how did it go with Charles?" said Brock.

"He's dead—murdered."

There was a long pause on the line. Drum rose and continued his walk to the station. "Still there?"

"Yeah, yeah. How?"

"Professional job," said Drum. "Thought you should know."

There was a long silence before Brock answered. "Yeah, yeah. Thanks. Where are you now?"

"I'm heading back to the Tower," said Drum.

"Stop by the market and fill me in," said Brock, his voice taut with emotion. Brock was going to make someone pay—he just didn't yet know who. He hung up.

He made the short walk to the Limehouse DLR station and swiped his travel card to access the platform. The driverless trains ran every few minutes and would take him straight back to Tower Hill. He looked around, checking for surveillance, but could see none. The station was empty at this time in the morning.

His phone buzzed. It was another unknown number.

"Drummond."

"Hi, Ben."

It was the same person who had phoned him at Charles' flat. "Who is this?"

"You don't know me—we haven't met. I work for Marco Salenko."

"Do you have a name?" asked Drum.

There was a pause. "You can call me Jane." There was another pause. "Ben, something bad is happening here, something terrible, and we have to stop it."

8

Professor Andrew Kovac gazed out of the large office window onto an expanse of meadow that ended at the River Cam. Here and there a few sparsely planted poplars struggled to take root in the newly created parkland of the Salenko Systems campus. His summons had not been unexpected.

"Looks like your Populus alba is struggling a bit, Marco. Probably too wet this close to the river."

Marco Salenko rose from his desk and walked to the window and contemplated the scene. A thick-set man with a crop of short dark hair, he stood a head shorter than Kovac. "I've been told we're missing two of the keystones, Andrew. Is this your doing?"

Kovac turned to his colleague, his face impassive. "Why would you think that?"

Salenko walked back to his desk with a look of frustration on his face. "To delay the IPO, of course." He slumped back in his chair. "You realise that if the IPO doesn't go through, all the work we've done here goes down the toilet. We'll lose our investors; no investors, no money. That's how things work in the real world."

Kovac continued to take in the scene. He admired the effort it had taken to turn a piece of derelict land on the outskirts of Cambridge into a green and pleasant park in such a short time. He recognised a few of his students making their way across the campus. Salenko made good use of the talent pool of the nearby university, and the students were only too happy to work here to gain whatever experience he offered. His association with the work also helped. Theirs was a symbiotic relationship. But now he wondered if the university selling his research to Salenko had been such a good idea.

"I appreciate that," sighed Kovac, "But I think you're rushing into this. You're taking unnecessary risks."

"You don't think I've come this far by not taking risks? This is not academia, Andrew, where you can sit back for the next ten years and hope for a breakthrough. We have to make progress or this enterprise is finished."

Salenko was right, of course. He had also sacrificed to get this far. Even his wife, in the last few days of her illness, had not been enough to stop him from working on the project. It had become an obsession. And now, when he sat all alone in that big empty house, he wondered if it had all been worth it. A thought occurred to him.

"This is about the group from Kiev," said Kovac. "They want their money. They're the ones pressing for the IPO."

Salenko shrugged. "Of course."

"You should never have got involved with these people."

"Don't be so naive," said Salenko, gesturing with his arm. "How did you think all of this got financed in the first place? As a startup, we didn't have the luxury to be picky about where the money came from. And you, as I recall, were only too happy to get involved when we started."

It was true. His university funding was ending and, with no promising research papers in the pipeline, all his work would have been shelved. The arrival of Salenko in Cambridge had seemed like an opportunity at the time. Of course, he knew Salenko long before his fame as an entrepreneur. They had both been undergraduates together in Kiev. But that seemed like a lifetime ago. Salenko had been quick to see the commercial potential of his work; unlike the university, which had no qualms about giving his work away. Ever strapped for cash, they were only too willing to embrace a joint enterprise. But he hadn't reckoned on Salenko's business partners. They weren't interested in the science, merely an exit plan so they could cash out.

"So let me ask you one last time," continued Salenko. "Have you taken the keystones?"

Kovac turned away from the window. "I'm telling you, it wasn't me."

"I think you're not being honest with me."

"I don't think you can preach to me about honesty. We had an agreement. The research for continued access to the project after the IPO. Now I find you have broken that agreement."

Salenko absentmindedly shuffled some papers on his desk.

"Investors need to see a product that will make them money. They're not interested in endless research. I had to reassure them you wouldn't impede the rollout of our first system. And you came through. You cracked it, although I don't know how."

"I opened up the code," said Kovac.

Salenko looked up. "But we said we wouldn't do that. It would weaken the controls."

"We had no choice, we hit a dead end. Back propagation of the deep learning algorithm had stalled."

"What about the change in the activation function?" said Salenko.

"It had little effect. We moved away from using a sigmoid function to a RELU which helped, but it had little effect on bringing about the convergence of the neural net—even over thousands of iterations. The core AI governing the network was hindering the process. We needed to open it up and get it to evolve beyond its current level."

"But you took years to code those core functions," said Salenko, now standing with some agitation. "You told me they couldn't be changed—at least not in the timeframe we were looking at."

"And that is still true. So I didn't."

"You didn't. So what did you do?"

"We forked the code—made a copy and created a Generative Adversarial Network," said Kovac.

"You forked the code!" said Salenko, incredulously.

"We now have two neural networks—one teaching the other. Both are improving, way beyond what we had hoped for, and at an incredible rate. At least they were …"

Salenko nodded. "Without all three keystones, we can no longer decrypt the code." He paused. "But we still have control?"

"Yes," said Kovac. "We just need the one for control, but the neural nets of each AI remain frozen in their current states until we can retrieve the other two. What do you intend to do?"

Salenko stood and walked back to the window. "Well, I don't believe they have just gone missing, so someone has stolen them."

"Really," said Kovac. "Do you intend to call the police?"

Salenko smiled. "God, no. Our people will look into it. Which reminds me. There's a security consultant on his way, a guy called Drummond. The press leaks have caused some concern among our investors. He'll want to talk to all of us I suspect so make yourself available."

"Of course," said Kovac.

"There is something else," said Salenko. "I'm not sure if you have heard? I know how you shun the news."

"Heard what?"

"Moretti. She was found dead in her hotel room a few days ago."

"How?" said Kovac, a stunned look on his face.

"Murdered—at least that is what the police are saying."

Kovac turned back to the window and stared out. That was Moretti's problem, he thought. She kept on digging. He wondered if this Drummond would do the same.

9

Jeremy Burnett cycled along the footpath that followed the River Cam as it wound its way through the suburbs of Cambridge and out towards the small village of Fen Wootton, a ride of about thirty minutes past lush meadows and beneath small footbridges, passing the occasional jogger out for a run on a chilly but sunny February evening.

He liked this ride. It gave him time to think, mostly about Stevie. He'd never met anyone like her before, older, more experienced, cute with a nice smile and a fierce stare. There was something about her, not just her good looks but something mysterious. He hoped to get to know her better. What had that creep in the coffee shop called her? Svetlana. A Russian name. Perhaps Ukrainian, like Salenko's men. He wondered why she called herself Stevie? After that meeting, he hadn't seen her—or she was avoiding him. He hoped not.

He pulled up beside a gated enclosure, just off the footpath, that marked the rear entrance to the Salenko campus. He'd been excited when he had got the call from Professor Kovac at the start of term. It had always been his dream to work for Salenko; his research here was groundbreaking. And he'd be a part of that. He wheeled his bike up to the gate and pressed a button on the intercom.

"Jeremy Burnett for Professor Kovac." He looked up at the security camera atop the fence.

"Welcome, Mr Burnett. You're on this evening's list. Please report to security."

The gate buzzed open, and he wheeled his bike into an enclosed area and waited for the facial recognition cameras to do their work. A 'Man Trap' someone had called it, a security device to prevent someone from rushing the gate. It was a legacy system left over from its days as a Ministry Of Defence facility, or so the rumour went. The second gate clicked open, and he was now free to enter the campus.

The campus had been meticulously laid out in a geometric design with lush green spaces and newly planted trees. Neat flower beds lined the brick-paved paths and the first daffodils of spring had just sprouted. Soon the campus would be a riot of colour from the many varieties of plants, carefully selected by a horde of gardeners. A small amphitheatre marked the centre of the campus where students and researchers could sit and relax in the sunshine and exchange ideas. Jeremy found it hard to believe that, just a short time ago, this had been a piece of derelict land.

Jeremy parked his bike and followed the path to the administrative block to sign in. Security was tight all over the campus. The administrative building was a low, two-storey unit in a horseshoe design, the apex of which looked out over the river. It was constructed primarily of glass and steel and softened by cedar and larch cladding which blended the building into the landscape and echoed the bend in the river which it faced.

Jeremy had almost made it to the entrance when a security bot pulled up smartly in front of him. It was a two-wheeled cylindrical device, painted yellow and black, that balanced upright on hydraulic haunches, enabling it to move at great speed over any terrain.

"Morning, Mr Burnett."

"Er, morning."

"Professor Kovac has requested that you meet him at the circle."

"Right. I'm just about to sign in."

The bot paused for a few seconds. "No need, I've confirmed your scan and signed you in. Have a good day."

"Right," said Jeremy, and watched as the bot sped off along the path, bouncing down some steps towards another building.

He meandered across the lawn towards the central amphitheatre that residents called the 'circle' and found Professor Kovac waiting for him.

"Hi," said Jeremy.

"Thanks for coming," said Kovac. "We're in the Linguistics Lab, Block Y. This way."

They moved out of the circle and across the lawn towards a long, flat building on the west side of the campus. A security bot trundled past on its way to the front gate, a strange bipedal bee with wheels in place of feet.

"I still can't get used to those things," said Jeremy.

"Says the undergraduate in Computer Sciences," said Kovac, smiling. "It saved you a trip to Admin."

"I know. It's just that a person patrolling the grounds is more comforting. Don't you think so? You can stop and say 'hi, how's it going,' that sort of thing."

"The shape of things to come, Jeremy. You're the generation that will determine what these machines will do. Your work here is contributing to their general intelligence."

"I know, but just because we can give a robot enough AI to complete a limited set of functions doesn't mean we should," said Jeremy. "Stevie and I were discussing the problem." He immediately regretted mentioning her name.

Kovac smiled. "You two seem to have hit it off."

Jeremy blushed. "She was all alone at the party. Thought I'd keep her company. She's interesting."

"Of course she is—and very pretty," said Kovac, winking.

"Yeah, well ... perhaps she's a little too old for me."

Kovac laughed. "Maybe."

Jeremy stopped. "Why does she call herself Stevie? Isn't her name Svetlana?"

"For the same reason I call myself Andrew. Kovac is a Slavic name. I was christened Andriy. Brought up in Ukraine."

"Why change your name?"

"To fit in, I suppose. For the same reason most of the Chinese students give themselves English names. You don't think Mr Wang in your tutor group is really called John, do you?"

"No, I suppose not. Never thought to ask."

"You'd probably never be able to pronounce it anyway," said, Kovac.

They arrived at Block Y and Kovac stopped just outside. "Listen, Jeremy. You haven't been speaking to people outside the university about the work we do here?"

"No, why?"

"I had a rather unpleasant chat with Salenko this morning. He accused me of speaking to the press. The company is about to float. Do you know what that means?"

"Er, no. Not really."

"Well, I won't bore you with the details, but it's a sensitive time for

Salenko's company and any misinformation picked up by the news outlets could have serious consequences. It could put our research here in jeopardy."

"I understand, Professor. Mum's the word."

Kovac looked at his young student, then shrugged and used his security key to enter the lab. They walked into a reception area and logged themselves in. The building was a single storey affair like the other buildings on the campus. The interior was panelled with warm cedar that glowed from the low evening sun coming through the full height windows. Several doors led off the reception area to rooms where the linguistic sessions took place.

"You take zero-one-alpha," said Kovac, handing Jeremy a sheet of notes. Be sure to ask all the questions and log the responses. They're recorded anyway but I need your impressions as well. I've made some improvements to the neural net, so I'm hoping you'll get a more nuanced response than the last time."

"Will do, Professor," said Jeremy, taking the notes. "I'll catch you later." Kovac nodded and walked off down a corridor.

Jeremy entered one of the rooms and closed the door. He flipped a switch which turned on a sign outside to show that he was conducting a test and moved to a computer terminal on a small desk in the middle of the room. Apart from a chair behind the desk, the room was devoid of furniture or decoration. The walls were lined with acoustic-dampening pyramids of foam. He took off his coat and hung it over the back of the chair, placing his canvas holdall on the floor. He laid out Kovac's notes on the desk and reviewed the questions. From the gist of it, Kovac wanted him to make small talk, asking the AI called zero-one-alpha a series of open-ended questions to which there were no right or wrong answers. It was a more sophisticated form of the Turing test, first devised by Alan Turing back in the nineteen-forties. What Turing would have given for the computing power of one mobile phone back then, he mused.

He tapped the computer keyboard and the monitor came to life revealing a simple menu. He moved the mouse over the menu and selected 'Activate'.

"Good afternoon," said a voice.

Jeremy jumped. He was always unprepared when the program started speaking. The voice was piped through high-fidelity speakers set in the walls and sounded warm and melodic.

"Sorry, did I scare you?"

Jeremy calmed himself and shuffled his papers. "What makes you think I was scared?"

There was a slight pause before the program answered. "I detected an increase in your heart rate."

Jeremy was surprised. "You can detect my heartbeat?"

"Yes, it is a good indicator of mood."

"I see," said Jeremy, thinking he was going off-topic. "Let's begin."

There was silence.

"Right, then. I'm driving my car down the road—"

"Where are we?" said the program.

"What do you mean?"

"What road?"

"It doesn't matter. It's a public road."

Silence.

"I turn into a car park and my brakes fail."

Silence.

"Are you still there?" asked Jeremy.

"Yes, I am waiting for the question."

"Right. My brakes fail."

"They have failed twice?" said the program.

"Right, no. I'm repeating myself. Please wait for the question."

Silence.

"I have a split second to react. If I swerve to the right, I risk hitting a mother with her small child; if I swerve to the left, I risk hitting a man in a wheelchair; if I do nothing, I risk hitting a wall and injuring myself."

Silence.

"What action should I take?" asked Jeremy.

There was a protracted silence. Kovac had made it clear not to repeat the question but to wait for the program to reply. Zero-one-alpha said nothing. Jeremy looked at his watch and sighed. He had a whole sheet of these questions to get through before the end of the session. He could be in a bar in town with his friends—perhaps with Stevie. Was she too old for him or was he just making excuses?

"Are you ok?" said the program.

"Yes, why?"

"Your heart rate has increased again."

"Can you please answer the question," replied Jeremy, now getting annoyed. And to think this program could be driving a car. He wondered what he would do.

"How old is the car?" replied zero-one-alpha.

Jeremy looked at his notes. There was no mention of the car's age.

"I have no details of the make or age of the car," said Jeremy, thinking it was a good question.

There was a slight pause before the program answered. "I would not do anything."

Jeremy consulted his notes once more. He now had to enter the analysis phase of question and answer. "Analysis, please."

"It is reasonable to assume that the car is fitted with safety devices, such as airbags, to reduce a frontal impact. You have entered the car park. It is reasonable to assume your vehicle speed would be below twenty mph. Therefore, the risk of personal injury would be low. This compares favourably with the other two options where there is a higher risk of injury to people. Analysis ends."

Not bad, thought Jeremy. Its logic was flawless. He noted down his observations and looked at his watch. It was only six o'clock. He still had time to call Stevie and invite her for a drink. She could only say no. He picked up his bag and found his phone. He hesitated. There were strict rules about making calls inside the labs. He moved to the door and looked outside. The reception area was empty. He returned to the desk and dialled Stevie's number. She answered on the first ring.

"Hi Stevie, it's Jeremy."

"Hi."

"I was wondering if you want to meet for a drink—down by the river?"

"Listen, Jeremy. It's sweet of you, but I must finish this dissertation. Another time."

Jeremy was about to respond when she hung up. That went well, he thought. Perhaps he was being foolish thinking she would be interested in him. For all he knew, she was already involved with someone. He was about to put his phone away when he noticed his wi-fi had turned on.

"Don't feel bad, Jeremy," said a voice.

Jeremy sat up, startled. Blast, he'd left the program running. But it didn't sound like zero-one-alpha. It had a mellow tone with a different modulation, soft and feminine. Jeremy looked at his phone, which had now lit up like a Christmas tree. "Deactivate, zero-one alpha," he said, trying to turn his phone off, but without success.

The stranger persisted. "Stevie is struggling with something, I can hear it in her voice. She is afraid. You must help her, Jeremy."

10

Alex Fern woke early. She picked up her phone from the nightstand and groaned when she saw the time. It was only 5.30am in New York and she was dreading another day of close protection detail to some Wall Street slime ball that Delaney had saddled her with. Sleep now evaded her so she rose naked from the king-size bed of her hotel room in downtown Manhattan and crossed to the window. She pulled up the blind to watch the sunrise over the Brooklyn Bridge, casting its orange glow onto the Hudson below.

She wondered what she was doing here. She had always wanted to work in Manhattan and had jumped at the chance when Delaney had offered her a position at the prestigious Roderick Olivier and Delaney. Her colleagues in London had thought her mad. She was giving up a fifteen-year career in the police force which had started in the London Met and had culminated in Britain's National Crime Agency where she had reached the giddy height of Commander. But last year's episode with Omega had left her feeling jaded towards her government's handling of the case. How easily they had pushed her aside. She didn't pretend to understand the complexity of the politics at the heart of Omega or the national security implications, but if it hadn't been for the intervention of the DOJ and ROD then the whole sordid affair would have been brushed under the carpet and buried.

And then there was Ben Drummond.

She sighed and headed for the shower. She ran the water hot and stood there letting the jets prick her skin like hot needles. What was it about Drum that made her anxious? They both seemed to skirt around each other, neither one ready to commit. Her mind drifted back to their last encounter. Another city beside another river. Their last kiss—soft and forgiving. A kiss goodbye. *You have too many secrets, Ben Drummond.*

Enough of this, she thought. I've made my bed. She shut off the shower and grabbed a large towel from the rack. At least she was staying in a decent hotel. She wrapped the towel around herself and headed back into the bedroom. The truth was, she missed him. Manhattan can be a lonely city when you're on your own. Sure, her ROD co-workers were great, and she had Harry, another Brit, to help her navigate life in the city. But the man she had feelings for was three thousand miles away. Oh, damn it.

She picked up her phone and dialled Drum's mobile. It rang for nearly a minute. He'll think I'm desperate, she thought. She was both relieved and pleased to hear his voice.

"Fern. You're up early."

She smiled but noted a tone in his voice. She wondered if something had happened. "I'm on a job. Close protection to some Wall Street type. Listen, Drum—what's that noise?"

"Sorry, I'm on the DLR. Pulling into Tower Gateway. How's it going?"

She sighed. "Oh, you know ... listen, about the other day. Sorry I snapped at you. I was just disappointed you weren't coming over."

There was a pause. "I'm sorry too, Fern. This case I'm on ... it's turned into a real nightmare. Perhaps we can talk later?"

"Sure, sure. No problem."

"Listen, Fern. Be safe."

"You too," she said, hanging up.

She placed the phone on the nightstand and flopped back onto the bed. This long-distance thing was a pain in the arse. There was a knock at the door. She sat up, suddenly alert. Who on earth could that be? She crossed to the door and spied through the peephole. A short, stocky man in a hotel bathrobe was standing outside. Oh no, she thought. I don't need this. She cracked open the door.

"Mr Adamo. Is everything alright?"

"Morning, Alex. I couldn't sleep. Can I come in?"

She kept her foot against the door and hoisted up her sagging towel. "Err, no, Mr Adamo. Now is not a good time. We're not scheduled to meet until seven."

He shuffled uncomfortably in his white bathrobe, looking surreptitiously up and down the corridor. "I know and please call me Roc. Can I come in? I'd like to discuss the arrangements for today."

She forced a smile. "I don't think that would be a good idea, Mr Adamo. Go back to your room and I'll pick you up at seven for breakfast as we arranged."

His brows narrowed. "Just let me in for a few minutes. I only want to talk—" He tried to push the door open but Fern's impressive physique kept it firmly in place.

"Now, now, Mr Adamo. We don't want to get off on the wrong foot, do we?" She gave him a stern look.

He took a step back. "Fine. I'll see you at seven," and he stomped off down the corridor.

Fern closed the door and breathed a sigh of relief. She was already dreading this assignment. Why Delaney had agreed to take on this guy was beyond her. All she knew was that Roc Adamo had made a few enemies as a short seller in the market where he bet on a company's stock falling. Of course, Adamo made sure he dished the dirt on these companies at every opportunity by writing libellous articles in various publications. It was rumoured that several well-connected people had put a contract out on him. She didn't blame them. But her job was to keep him alive, or at least unmolested, until the end of the week when he would become someone else's problem.

She dressed in a grey suit and sensible shoes, which for her meant flats; at just over one metre eighty or six foot three, as her American friends would say, heels were out of the question. She already towered over the squat Adamo, which made them an unlikely couple when seen together. Her last piece of adornment was her Glock 17, which she wore concealed under her jacket. She looked in the mirror and gave her short, blonde hair a quick brush before heading out of the door and along the corridor.

She stopped a few doors down. Adamo had a corner suite. She checked the coast was clear and rapped on the door several times as arranged. Adamo appeared promptly and gave her a perfunctory nod. She was relieved to see he had dressed. He was wearing his customary brown, double-breasted suit. They headed for the elevator with Fern striding ahead and Adamo marching at double-time to keep up. They stopped and Fern pressed 'down'. The elevator bank was always a high-risk area when protecting a principal. You never knew if the next elevator car to arrive contained a threat.

"I'm sorry about this morning," said Adamo, looking sheepishly down at his shoes.

"No harm, no foul," said Fern, looking up and down the corridor. A maid had come out of a room pushing a trolley loaded with towels and toiletries and was walking their way. Fern moved to put herself between the maid and Adamo.

"I don't know what came over me," continued Adamo.

I do, thought Fern. "Could you take a step back, you're crowding me."

"Sure, sure."

The maid was coming straight for them, ignoring the service elevator.

"It's just that—"

The maid was speeding up and reaching for something between the towels. The elevator announced its arrival with a loud chime. Fern grabbed hold of Adamo's padded shoulder and drew her gun.

"Alex, what—"

The maid let go of the trolley which continued to roll towards them and brought up a gun with a fitted suppressor. Fern glanced sideways as the elevator doors opened and shoved Adamo hard, sending him crashing into the empty car and onto the floor. She threw herself against the opposite wall as the maid fired, the round going wide of its mark and tearing into the wall by the elevator car. The maid swung around for another shot. Too late. Fern fired twice, hitting her in the shoulder and chest. The maid spun around and crumpled to the floor, blood blossoming crimson on her bleached white smock.

11

Drum was sprinting. He had reached the Angel pub at the end of Bermondsey Wall when his phone buzzed.

"Drummond."

"I hope you're running," said Fern.

Drum turned around and started a slow walk back along the river. "Trying to keep fit." He detected something in Fern's voice. "What's up."

There was a long pause. He waited, catching his breath.

"I had to shoot someone the other day."

Drum stopped in his tracks, sweat dripping down his back. "What happened?"

Fern briefed him on the shooting. He listened as he walked, not interrupting, staying silent until he was sure she had told him everything that needed to be said. Taking someone's life was never a simple thing. Talking about it always helped—at least to those who understood.

"Listen, Fern. You had no choice. Sounds like a professional hit. You did your job. Both you and the principal survived."

There was silence on the line. Eventually, Fern spoke. "I know. I keep telling myself that. But I keep going over things in my mind …"

"Listen," said Drum. "It never pays to play the 'what if' game. You reacted in the split second you had, which is why we train for these situations. What happens now?"

"I've been suspended, pending an investigation. The local NYPD says it was a clear case of self-defence. Didn't help that the little creep I was protecting told the police I had endangered his life by throwing him in the elevator."

"You threw him into an elevator!"

"Yeah, I should have shot him myself."

Drum laughed. "What now?"

"I'm on desk duty. Have to wait and see what Delaney is going to do."

"She'll support you," said Drum. "She may be many things, but she protects her people. Take the time to sort yourself out. Do some shopping, it's Manhattan."

"Right, right." There was a pause. "Hey, listen. I'm sorry about your friend Charles. Alice told me. She called for a chat. This case of yours …"

Alice the matchmaker, thought Drum. But it was nice of her to check up on Fern. "Don't worry about the case, Fern. It'll sort itself out." He didn't sound too convincing.

"Stay safe. And stop jogging, you'll damage something."

Drum pocketed his phone and headed back to the office. He had got as far as Tea Trader's Wharf when his phone buzzed again. The call was from an unknown number.

"Drummond."

"Hi, Ben. It's Michael—Michael Mann."

Drum was surprised to hear from his old friend at GCHQ.

"Michael! It's been a while. Still listening in on other people's conversations?"

It was an old joke, but it made Michael laugh. "I'm glad I caught you. Can we talk?"

Drum liked Michael Mann. They had worked together during Drum's last deployment and he considered him a straight shooter. But that was almost a decade ago. They had not been in contact since. Michael's role at GCHQ was classified, but Drum knew enough that it involved liaison with the security services and the dissemination of the many pieces of intelligence the organisation obtained and analysed.

"I was just heading back to the office. Why not meet me there?"

"Not at the office. Can we meet near Borough Market? I'll be waiting in the cathedral grounds. You know the place." He hung up.

Drum was surprised by the curt response but thought it must be important for Michael to contact him out of the blue. He called Alice to let her know he'd be delayed and headed along the embankment towards the market.

He climbed the steps onto London Bridge and crossed the busy road. Southwark Cathedral rose up from below the bridge, providing a sanctuary from the mass of people milling about in the busy market alongside. William used to love it here. He would often find him all alone, reading his newspaper on one of the benches, content in the solitude of the cathedral grounds. He missed his father. He found Michael Mann occupying the same place and reading a newspaper.

"What brings you to my neck of the woods, Michael? Hope I'm not under surveillance?"

Mann folded his newspaper, stood and shook hands. "Right, and no, you're not under surveillance. Sorry, but I couldn't be seen entering your office. This seemed like a suitable alternative."

"What can I do for you, Michael?"

"We understand you're taking an assignment for McKinley."

"It looks that way. Why the interest?"

"We understand the police want to question you about the Moretti murder."

"So, I am under surveillance."

"No, Moretti is—or was. We've been monitoring the calls of anyone involved with Salenko Security Systems. We can confirm she called McKinley shortly after you left the hotel. Which gives you an alibi. We've informed the City police," added Mann.

The assignment had just taken on a whole extra dimension, thought Drum. "Any lead on the murderer?"

"Not at this time. She died from a blow to the back of the head. Not very professional—or at least it was made to look that way. The room was ransacked but nothing was taken according to the police report. They figure it was a robbery gone wrong."

"It wasn't," said Drum, and gave Mann a brief update on DCI Chambers' visit.

"And he didn't ask you to come in for a statement?"

"He was just fishing for information," said Drum, but held back on revealing anything to do with the device. A thought occurred to him. "Does Delaney know about your interest?"

"No—and as a matter of national security, we'd prefer you kept her in the dark. It was our people who recommended you to McKinley's CEO. He then contacted Delaney. With your security clearance and tech background, you were the ideal candidate."

Drum frowned. "For what?"

"We need someone to infiltrate the organisation—find out what's going on in there. We've made several attempts, but we can't get anyone past Salenko's security. The man's got the place locked down tight."

Drum remembered what Moretti had said about Salenko's security. It didn't bode well. "Why wasn't I contacted by Thames House—why send you?"

"After what went down in Afghanistan and the Omega fiasco, it was decided to disband Section 6. There is now only an informal communications channel between the security services. I act as their liaison. I thought you were the best candidate for the job. The Americans think so too."

"The Americans. How many agencies are involved?"

"All of them that matter. I won't lie to you, Ben. This won't be a walk in the park, and I'll understand if you turn us down …"

Mann didn't actually say 'your country needs you', he didn't have to. Anyone who has served knows what it means when you get the call. And if Michael hadn't reached out, he would have stumbled into a difficult situation.

"I still don't understand," said Drum. "Why are the security services interested in a startup?"

"About a month ago, our intrusion detection systems lit up. Someone was hammering on the door of the Doughnut and wanted in."

Drum smiled at the reference to the GCHQ building in Cheltenham.

"The attack was very sophisticated, using very novel attack vectors—many we've never seen before. We spent hours fending off the attack, but one-by-one our firewalls went down."

"What happened?"

"We were literally down to the wire, thinking about pulling the plug when some bright spark powered up an experimental system he'd been working on, built entirely on a new type of computer operating system. This did the trick and stopped the attack."

"Did you lose anything?" asked Drum.

"Only our pride. We're still analysing the attack and reviewing all our procedures. Needless to say, we've employed our new firewall extensively across all our systems."

"But?"

"We think it's only a matter of time before the attacker strikes again—and we won't be so lucky next time."

Drum leaned back and let out a soft whistle. "And you think Salenko Systems has something to do with the attack?"

"Shortly after, I contacted our American liaison. Let's just say she was less than impressed with our performance and blew off the severity of the attack on our poor technology."

Drum smiled. Competition between the services nearly always prevented good cooperation. "What happened?"

"A few days later there was an attack on the CIA. Their firewalls went down like dominoes. They suffered a massive data breach. Since then our American friends have been very interested in our new firewall and we've agreed on a new joint task force to share the technology and to track down and neutralise the attacker. Again, your name came up."

"Who recommended me?"

"Tom Hammond. He now runs Homeland Security. He's put a guy called Marchetti on the case as liaison."

Drum thought back to the Omega operation and his meeting with Hammond. He knew Jack Marchetti as the CIA contact from the Mexico City job. It would be good to have him in his corner.

"We had no sooner re-grouped when we received intelligence from an operative in Hong Kong. A sensitive government data centre was breached. We don't know what was taken, but the Chinese are hopping mad. There was also another incident at the same facility. One of their top analysts we've been tracking shot himself. A man called Michael Chen. We're not sure if the two events are connected. To make things worse, the Chinese have pointed the finger at us. Diplomatic relations have become very tense, especially with the political situation as it is with the former colony."

"And you think Salenko is behind the attacks."

"We do. Until recently, the attacker has been very careful to cover their tracks. Then we got lucky. Someone probed our network and failed to mask their IP address. We tracked the probe back to Salenko's principal offices in Cambridge."

Drum frowned. "That sounds very convenient. Not something a sophisticated attacker would do."

Mann nodded. "I agree. But it's the only lead we have. Are you in?"

He had little choice. Moretti was dead—killed by persons unknown and who had implicated him in her death. Then there was the whistleblower, Jane, asking for his help. And of course, there was Charles. He couldn't let this one go.

"I'm in."

Mann smiled. "Good, I knew I could count on you."

"But I need to insist on some operational parameters."

Mann looked wary. "How so."

"It's pointless trying to keep Delaney in the dark. If Tom Hammond knows, then Delaney almost certainly knows. They go way back. And anyway, I'll need to call upon ROD's resources."

"Ahem, you realise you have the resources of GCHQ and the British government at your disposal."

Drum smiled. "I appreciate that, Michael. But ROD has access to a large talent pool. Trust me on this one."

"Ok, I think I can sell Delaney's involvement given her standing in the intelligence community. What else?"

"I'll need Alice to run point for me," said Drum.

"Your office manager?"

"C'mon, Michael. They must have briefed you on Alice."

Mann nodded. "They did. But wouldn't you want someone …"

"Younger?" added Drum.

"Well, yes, to put it bluntly."

"I'll take experience over youthful exuberance any day."

"Ok. It's your show. I'll need to reactivate her security clearance. There will be some inside MI6 who won't be happy."

Drum shrugged.

Mann rose from the bench. "I'll arrange a handler from Thames House to act as a go-to in the field. Give me a day or two to set things up. They'll meet you in Cambridge. When are you leaving?"

"I'm riding up with an Investment Banker from IBS on Saturday."

"Mei Ling Chung?"

"Yes," said Drum. "You know her?"

Mann put a hand on Drum's shoulder and bent close to his ear. "You realise, of course, she works for Beijing."

12

Drum spent the rest of the morning bringing Alice up to speed with Michael Mann's revelations.

"And he said I'd be reactivated," said Alice, balancing a cup of tea on her lap. "Why did you do that? I swore I'd never work for those people again."

Drum nodded. "I understand, Alice. But I don't know what I'm walking into with this assignment, and I'd rather have you watching my back than some kid still wet behind the ears."

"Thanks, Ben. I appreciate that." She thought for a moment. "Did you tell him about the device Moretti gave you?"

"No," he said. "Don't ask me why. I thought the fewer people who know about it the better."

"Good," said Alice. "Let's keep it that way for the moment. If there is one thing I've learnt over the years it's that it's best not to reveal all one's cards."

"Agreed," said Drum. "Stevie might have some idea about its function. Did you tell her we're coming?"

Alice shook her head. "She's not picking up. I just get her voicemail. I've left her a few messages ..."

"She's probably up to her neck in undergraduates," said Drum, trying to play down Stevie's lack of communication. It certainly wasn't like her.

"What are you going to do about your Chinese friend," said Alice, changing the subject.

"I don't know," said Drum. "Play along, I guess. Brock made her straight away. Guess I'm losing it."

"Oh tsk, tsk," said Alice. "You're just too close to the situation, that's all." Alice cocked her head to one side and smiled. "Is she nice?"

Drum rolled his eyes. He checked his watch. "Eleven-thirty. I'm going for a quick sandwich before it gets too busy. Want anything?"

"No thank you, dear. I need to sort out this temp."

Drum left Alice dialling around the various City temping agencies. He grabbed his coat and headed out along the wharf. The morning had clouded over and it was threatening rain, the sky casting dull-grey shadows over the cityscape of glass and steel across the river. He pulled up his collar against the chill air as he passed the small cafes and restaurants along the embankment.

He needed to get his head around all that had happened over the last few days. Someone had tampered with his rigging. Why? He didn't know, but he was sure it had something to do with the McKinley assignment. *Your name came up.*

He didn't believe Charles would have knowingly put him in harm's way, no matter how much money the guy owed, but Drum had to admit that his old sergeant was somehow involved in the incident. Drum reached into his wallet and pulled out the piece of paper he'd found on Charles. He examined the long string of numbers and the twelve, seemingly random, words. He'd not seen many of these. It was a type of paper crypto payment. It only confirmed his suspicions about the man.

And then there was Moretti. Someone had sent her the device. Someone had killed for it—whatever it was. His mysterious caller, Jane, was implicated in some way. *Something bad is happening here.* Moretti had received a similar call. He needed to find this woman. If she was the whistleblower, she'd need protecting.

He thought about his recent conversation with Mann. The hackers had attacked all the major intelligence agencies. Someone had left them a clue. Now they were all heading for Cambridge and Marco Salenko. All except one: the Russians. Were they behind the attack? He could understand an attack against NATO allies; but an attack against China? It made little sense. *You realise, of course, she works for Beijing.*

His phone buzzed. It was another unknown number.

"Drummond."

"Hi, Ben."

The voice sounded familiar, but he couldn't quite believe it. Not after had what happened. He felt his gut wrench. He stared at his phone, unable to speak.

"Ben, it's me, Victor."

* * *

Victor Renkov. The very thought of the man was like a white-hot spike between his eyes. It must be some kind of joke. What would Victor be doing back in London? As far as he knew, British Intelligence was still hunting for the man. Whatever the reason, Alice would want to know his location. It was Victor who had helped Vlad Abramov ensnare him into helping the Russian Mafia solve the Omega case that led to the death of his father. There were debts to be paid, and Alice would want to collect. He also wanted his pound of flesh.

He headed across Tower Bridge and phoned Brock.

"Brock, it's Drum."

"Hey, are you coming for lunch?"

"I've just had a call—from Victor Renkov."

There was a long pause. Drum kept walking. He passed the Tower of London. "Still there?"

"Victor?"

"He wants to meet," said Drum.

"Where?"

"The coffee place by Lloyd's. I'm heading there now. I need backup."

"When?"

"In about thirty minutes."

There was another pause. He heard Brock giving orders in the background.

"Right, I'll be there," he said and hung up.

Drum carried on walking and turned off onto a small side street that led onto Lime Street. The Lloyd's building gleamed in the morning sunshine. He and William had always referred to it as 'The Brewery'. Drum stopped and watched the glass-sided elevators ride the outside of the building and thought about phoning Alice. He could use her expertise, but he also needed Victor alive—for now. The other option was to contact MI5. A dangerous Russian national was operating on their home turf, but Victor would have thought of that. He must have a backup plan. What was he missing?

Drum sat at a table outside the small cafe facing Lloyd's and waited. He chose a table that provided him with the best visibility of the market and afforded him the greatest cover, but he still felt very exposed. He looked around; there were at least a dozen buildings with a line of sight onto his position. Sit outside, Victor had instructed. He'd chosen the location well.

A well-dressed man stepped out of the main Lloyds' entrance and walked towards him. He wore a navy, three-piece suit, and a dark overcoat across his shoulders. He recognised the dark hair and chiselled features of Victor Renkov.

"Good morning, Benjamin."

Drum neither rose nor acknowledged the greeting, but pointed to the chair opposite. Victor nodded and sat down.

"Pleasant weather—a little on the chilly side, don't you think? How have you been, Benjamin?" said Victor.

"William died a few months ago. Killed by Russian agents, acting on the orders of your friend Vlad Abramov."

Victor looked shocked. "Benjamin, I am sorry. I liked William—and Abramov was never a friend of mine. The man was a fool—"

"Either way, Victor. You suckered me into working for the guy, and that got William killed. Alice holds you responsible—I hold you responsible."

Victor shifted uneasily in his seat. "Benjamin—Ben, don't do anything rash. I never intended for you or William to come to any harm. Believe me."

A waiter, a short stocky man in a white apron with a silver streak of hair down one side of his head, appeared at their table. "What can I get you, sir?"

"An Americano, black," said Victor. The waiter retreated with his order and returned to the cafe, keeping watch through the window.

"Why are you here, Victor?"

Victor looked around, assessing the situation. Drum wondered if he was expecting a snatch squad to materialise at any moment or Alice to turn the corner. "I'm not here out of choice. You could say I'm under orders."

"To do what? By whom?"

Victor placed a hand on his lapel and tapped his finger, showing he was wired. "I'm here at the behest of the Russian government."

"Bollocks."

"Regrettably, it's true."

Drum frowned. "You're many things, Victor, but a Russian agent isn't one of them. Who are you really working for?"

"That is also true. I've always acted in my own self-interests, I admit that. But my swift exit from the country last year put me in the debt of some powerful people back home. Now they want paying. Arranging this meeting with you was part of the deal."

"Why send you? There must be a dozen agents in London who could have easily done the job."

"They knew you would want to meet with me—if only out of revenge or curiosity. I told them it was a bad idea—"

"You're so full of shit. Why don't I just kill you now?"

The waiter returned with Victor's coffee. He placed it on the table and drew a gun from his apron, a silenced Walther PPK, and placed the stubby suppressor against the side of Victor's head.

Victor tilted his head away from the gun, keeping his eyes locked on Drum. "It's best you hear me out, Benjamin. Call Alice."

Alice stood by the window in Drum's office. Light sparkled on the Thames like diamonds in the bright morning sunshine. William always loved this part of London. She turned to the young man lounging in Drum's chair, the gun in his hand pointing straight at her.

"*More tea, Sergei?*" she said, in fluent Russian.

"Thank you, yes," replied the man, in English.

Alice moved to the desk and placed her cup back on the tray. She picked up her prized teapot and refilled the young Russian's cup. She poured herself a little more tea and sat down on the couch.

"You're very young for this type of work, Sergei."

Sergei smiled. "I know what you are doing. I have been well briefed."

"I'm just making conversation—while away the time." Alice adjusted her hair, her hand coming to rest on the enamelled butterfly of her hairpin. It was a gift from her dear Giles, shot dead by a Russian thug. They hadn't briefed her young Russian friend well enough.

"There are rumours about you—or someone like you," said Sergei. "*Prizrak*," he said in Russian. "Ghost. They say you have killed many agents. But here we are, drinking tea, my gun trained on you. I think these are the stories of old men."

She smiled. "Your English is very good, Sergei. Just a hint of inflexion here and there. Nothing you can't work on."

"Thank you. Your Russian is perfect. You could be one of my teachers back in Moscow. How did you become so fluent?"

She sat back, remembering. Images of her mother drifted into her mind. She hadn't thought of her in years.

"My mother—she was Russian."

"Ah, that explains it."

"Tell me, Sergei. What will you do if Captain Drummond decides not to cooperate?"

Sergei shifted uncomfortably in his chair. "He will—and if not …"

Alice smiled. "Have you ever killed a woman, Sergei? Some men find it hard."

Sergei looked away momentarily. "It won't come that. He'll do what we say. I will obey my orders."

Alice smiled, half to herself. She was like that once. It would be a pity to kill this young man for doing his duty. But that was her curse.

Her phone buzzed on Drum's desk where the Russian had told her to place it.

"Answer it, please," said Sergei, pointing with his gun. "Put it on speaker."

Alice rose and picked up her phone, answered the call and placed it back on the desk in front of Sergei.

"Alice, it's Ben. Everything alright?"

"Hi, Ben. Yes, I'm here with Sergei. A nice young man. We're having tea."

There was a pause on the line. "I'm here with Victor."

Alice froze. She looked straight at the young Russian who visibly flinched at the change in her demeanour.

"Alice, you there?"

"Kill him, Ben, don't worry about me—"

Sergei sat up and levelled the gun at her. "What are you saying, you crazy woman—"

"Alice," said Drum, "stay calm. Brock is with me. I need to hear Victor out."

Victor looked shaken. "That was Alice, your office manager?"

"Yes," said Drum.

"They said she used to work for MI6, but I dismissed the idea. Now I'm not so sure."

"If you and your friend Sergei want to leave in one piece, I suggest you deliver your message," said Brock, sitting down with his gun levelled at Victor beneath the table.

"If Sergei doesn't hear from me in the next half hour, he has orders to shoot her," said Victor. "Not my idea, I can assure you."

"Get on with it," said Drum.

Victor nodded. "About a month ago, a secure data centre on the outskirts of Moscow was attacked."

"Attacked?"

"A cyber attack, I think you call it. Very sophisticated, or so I'm told. This computer stuff is over my head, but let's just say it caused quite a stir in Moscow."

"What has this got to do with me?"

"I'm getting to that," said Victor. "Initially, it was thought to be the Americans. They didn't believe the UK had the technology or the balls to attack Russia. America denied it, of course, but there was a follow-up attack."

"What did they take?" asked Drum.

"They won't tell me, but it must have been something huge. Then the attacker got sloppy and left an IP address that was traced to a location in Cambridge. At first, Moscow thought it was the UK's retaliation for the Salisbury attack—" Victor tapped his lapel. "Alleged attack."

"What am I missing?" said Drum, getting irritated by Victor's prevarication.

"Right, right. Moscow pinpointed the attacker's IP address as originating from the campus of Salenko Security Systems."

Brock shrugged. "I'm lost."

"The new assignment I'm working on," said Drum.

"I say we hand our Victor over to British Intelligence and let them sort him out," said Brock.

He had a point, thought Drum, but knowing Victor he had another ace up his sleeve.

"That would be a mistake," said Victor, shifting uncomfortably in his chair. "Think of Alice."

Drum smiled. "I'd be more worried about your man, Sergei."

"Listen, Ben. Trust me on this one. It's best we work together. We can help you."

"Why would I want to cooperate with Russian intelligence?"

Victor squirmed and tapped his lapel once more. "This is not my idea, you understand. I'd rather be back in my villa in Croatia. But Moscow anticipated your reaction and the fact that Sergei might not be successful in his mission. Which is why they have made contingencies."

Drum's eyes bored into the Russian. "What contingencies?"

Victor gulped. "Svetlana Milova."

Brock turned to Drum. "Who?"

"Stevie.", said Drum.

Brock rammed his gun into Victor's stomach, his face turning crimson. "You bastard. Anything happens to Stevie I swear I'll hunt you down and kill you myself—slowly."

Drum placed a restraining hand on Brock's shoulder. "There's something else."

Victor had turned pale and was visibly shaking. "Yes—yes! We have something for you. A goodwill gesture. Information you will want to know."

"Spit it out," said Drum.

"Charles Renshaw. We know who killed him."

Alice's phone buzzed again on Drum's desk. She accepted the call and placed it on speaker.

"Sergei, it's Victor. We have reached an understanding. Stand down."

Sergei felt the tip of the stiletto blade press into the side of his neck. A trickle of blood ran into the well of his collarbone, staining his shirt crimson. "That might be a problem."

There was a pause on the line.

"Alice, it's Ben. Don't kill him."

Alice stood behind Sergei, her long, steel-grey hair hanging down her back. In her hand, she gripped the butterfly wings of the disguised stiletto that was pressing ever deeper into Sergei's flesh. "What understanding?"

"I'll explain, later. But in the meantime, we need Sergei alive."

"And what about Victor?"

"He lives for now."

"You can't trust him, Ben. You can't trust any of them—"

"Alice, I need you to do this for me."

Alice hesitated, then reached down and took the gun from Sergei. She released the pressure on her blade and withdrew to the window, keeping the gun pointed at the young Russian.

Sergei let out a sigh of relief. He pressed his hand against the side of his neck and examined the blood on his fingers. "I am unharmed," he whispered into the speaker.

"What do you want me to do with him?" asked Alice.

There was the sound of a heated discussion.

"You both need to leave for Cambridge straight away. Stevie may be in trouble."

A Cambridge Affair

13

It was late Friday afternoon when Alice and her new Russian friend arrived at Cambridge station. The journey up from London had been a silent one, with Alice contemplating the set of circumstances that had thrown her and a member of Russian intelligence together. It was strange watching the young man sleep. He must have trusted her because he slept soundly for most of the journey. They grabbed a cab at the station and headed for Market Square. It was late afternoon and many of the market traders were packing up. Alice decided they should browse the market for a while.

"What are we doing here?" said Sergei, flipping through some vintage records on one of the many brightly covered stalls.

"We're blending in—waiting for Stevie to turn up," said Alice, pretending to look through some old bric a brac. "Didn't they teach you this sort of thing back in Moscow?"

Sergei stopped his browsing and turned to face her. "Of course. But why not call her?"

"I've tried that," said Alice, "but she's not picking up, which means she's in some sort of trouble."

"Or she's in bed with her boyfriend—or girlfriend, whatever she's into," said Sergei.

Alice thought this a possibility, but it was unlike Stevie not to check in now and again, and it was rare for her not to reply to her voicemail. It would be dark soon, so she decided to stake out one of Stevie's regular locations that she'd mentioned in the past.

"Let's go, Sergei," she said.

"Where are we going?"

"To get a drink."

Sergei's face broke into a wide grin. "Now that is a good idea."

They walked out of Market Square and headed down St. Mary's Street and soon found the cafe tucked on the corner.

Sergei's face dropped. "I thought we were going for a drink, Alice."

Alice smiled. They went into the cafe and ordered two Americanos and then sat at a table close to the bay window. It was cosy inside and the window gave them an excellent view of the street.

"What makes you think she'll come in here?" said Sergei, slouching back in his chair.

"This is where she hangs out. There are fewer students."

Sergei nodded.

Alice noticed he hadn't taken off his coat—a smart, leather bomber jacket that fitted snuggly around his broad chest. "Are you armed?" she said.

"Of course. Why?"

"Just don't start flashing it around. You'll frighten the natives."

Sergei smiled. "Of course." He looked at her for a moment and said, "would you really have killed me?"

"Of course," said Alice. "Mmm, this coffee is good." She changed the subject. "What can you tell me about this group she's mixed up with?"

"They call themselves Vovk—wolves. They're a kind of hacker collective, mainly Ukrainians. Very active all over Europe and, to a certain extent, Russia, which is how they came to our attention. Small stuff here and there—nothing that would concern Soviet intelligence, but we monitored them."

"You thought they might be useful one day," said Alice.

Sergei shrugged. "They came back on our radar after we learned of the attack on GCHQ."

"Is that so?" said Alice. She wondered how that piece of intel had come their way.

Sergei paused. "We kept track of the key players and learned that they were on the move—heading for the UK. After the attack on our Moscow data centre, we tracked one of their enforcers to London. A guy called Gleb Vashchenko. A mean son-of-a-bitch. He appears to have an unhealthy interest in your Captain Drummond."

Alice put down her cup and gave Sergei her full attention. "Why do you say that?"

Sergei smiled. "Our surveillance placed him in London. He met with Charles Renshaw. We were curious, so kept him under observation. After the climbing incident, we followed him to Renshaw's apartment block. He stayed for a short time and left. We lost him after that."

"That was sloppy," said Alice, taking great pleasure in the slip-up.

"I suppose so," said Sergei. "Our man confirmed that Charles Renshaw had been killed. We assume it must have been Vashchenko."

"Why kill Charles?" said Alice. "How does he fit into all this?"

"We don't know. But with Renshaw dead and Captain Drummond taking the assignment for McKinley, we did some digging and Svetlana's name came up and her past association with Vovk. We assume she's back working for Vashchenko."

Alice bristled at the accusation. "Utter rubbish."

"We shall see," said Sergei, nodding towards the door. "Here she is now."

Stevie entered the cafe and walked straight to the counter. She was dressed in tight, black jeans and a loose baggy hoodie with a black leather satchel over her shoulder. She waited for her coffee, her head down.

Sergei was about to rise when Alice placed a restraining hand on his arm. "Let her come to us. Don't tell her who you are. You're just the hired help."

Sergei nodded and sat back down. They didn't have to wait long. Stevie grabbed her coffee and made her way to her usual spot by the window, deep in thought. She got as far as the table and paused.

"Alice!"

"Hello, Stevie. How have you been?"

Stevie stood in stunned silence.

Alice tilted her head to one side and looked hard at her young ward. "Come and sit down, dear."

Stevie placed her coffee on the table and sat down. "Of course. What are you doing here, Alice?" She looked at the young man leaning back in his chair and smiling. "Who's this?"

"In a moment," said Alice. "Tell me what's going on."

Stevie hesitated. She remained silent, looking down at her lap.

Alice turned to Sergei. "Give us a minute, please."

Sergei moved to a corner table. Alice noticed that he had placed himself with an unobstructed view of the space with his back to the wall.

"Why are you here?" said Stevie, petulantly.

"Ben is on assignment here. I thought it would be nice to see you."

"Where is he?" said Stevie, looking around.

"He's on his way up. When we didn't hear from you, I came on ahead."

"Sorry," said Stevie, fiddling with the spoon on her saucer. "I should have answered your voicemails. Things have been a little crazy around here."

Alice's eyes narrowed. "Let's cut the crap, shall we? You're in trouble."

Stevie stared down at her lap and nodded. "How did you know?"

Alice rolled her eyes. "Good grief, who do you think you work for? What upsets me is that you didn't think you could talk to me. Tell me everything."

"My past," said Stevie, a tear rolling down her cheek, "caught up with me."

"Vashchenko," said Alice.

Stevie looked up. "Yes, how did you … oh, right. Bumped into one of his people. He recognised me. A psychopath called Baz Kulik. Threatened to harm somebody I know if I didn't cooperate."

"I see," said Alice. "I doubt this Kulik bumped into you by accident."

"No?"

"Vashchenko is recruiting talent. It's not clear why, but his activities have raised red flags in the intelligence community."

Stevie looked distraught. "What do I do, Alice? If it's known I'm working for him, they will deport me!"

"Oh, tsk, tsk," said Alice. "Calm down. It won't come to that. Your recruitment was fortuitous."

"How do you figure that?"

"It's placed you on the inside of their organisation."

"Alice, I'm not a spy. If they find out I'm talking to the authorities …"

"Listen. Carry on as normal," said Alice. "You have no choice. We'll work out a way to contact you—"

There was a sharp tap on the window. The grinning face of Baz Kulik stared back at them.

"Oh fuck, it's Baz," said Stevie.

"Stay calm," said Alice. "I'm your new landlady. You're moving into digs."

Kulik pushed his way past the other tables and stopped in front of them. "*Who is this old bat?*" he said, in Russian.

Alice smiled back at him. She hoped Sergei stayed where he was and didn't snap the greasy pole of a man in two. "Hello, dear."

"This is my new landlady," said Stevie, in English. "I'm moving into digs."

"Good luck with that one," said Kulik. *"She looks like a grinning fool."*

Alice remained calm.

"Don't be rude," said Stevie, switching to Russian. She turned to Alice, "Sorry, gotta go. The rent sounds fine. Let's do this again."

"That's alright, dear," said Alice, still smiling. "You run off and have a pleasant time. We'll sort things out later."

Stevie gathered up her things and followed Kulik out of the cafe. Sergei waited until they were out of sight before returning to sit with Alice.

"She's in big trouble," said Sergei. "But very cute. I think I will kill this Kulik for her."

"No," said Alice, her eyes narrowing. "He's mine."

14

Drum was surprised when Mei pulled up in her car outside the coffee shop on Butler's Wharf.

"Nice car," said Drum. He stood back and admired the sleek lines of the vehicle painted in an electric-blue with its large racing tyres and a chassis that sat low to the ground. It was built for speed. Mei looked just as sleek as she slid from the car, dressed in a black, fitted jacket and skin-tight jeans. He was pleased she had dressed casually. It was Saturday, and he'd put on his old, brown leather jacket and a pair of faded denims.

"Thanks," said Mei. "It's made in China. I had it imported. Cost me a fortune—but hey, it's only money." She gave him a bright smile. "Luggage?"

He lifted an old canvas bag. She reached inside the car and pressed a button on the dash, opening the front of the car. "It's electric," she said. "Motors at the back under the seat."

Drum stowed his bag next to a small suitcase. It looked like Mei was travelling light. He eased himself into the passenger seat.

"I thought the drive would give us an opportunity to talk," said Mei, sliding into the driver's side. Drum nodded. She pressed a small button beside the steering column and the dash lit up like Blackpool illuminations. Other than that, there was complete silence. She pulled out sharply, the acceleration snapping Drum back into his seat as she navigated the narrow side streets until they were back on the main road, heading over Tower Bridge.

Mei was a competent driver, briskly overtaking less nimble vehicles until they were heading out along the Highway and onto the A13 where she powered on the juice and promptly broke every speed limit from Canary Wharf to Canning Town. It reminded him of another fast car and another woman, just a year ago, along this same stretch of East London. It had been Victor's car, a sleek red Italian job that roared rather than purred. Seeing Victor walk away from the meeting yesterday had not sat well with him; it also upset Alice. He hoped Sergei had survived the trip to Cambridge. Alice was less than enthusiastic to have the young Russian intelligence officer as company. But they had given him a name: Gleb Vashchenko. The Russian's were playing a clever game by revealing Charles' killer. They knew he'd never let the man live. He'd do their work for them.

And then there was Mei Ling.

"Penny for your thoughts?" she said. "Is that the right expression?"

"Your English is very good," said Drum, snapping himself back to the present. "Where did you learn it?"

"School, university. Worked in the States. How about you? Do you speak any languages?"

"A little Russian," he said.

"Really, why Russian?"

"Comes in handy in my line of work," he said.

She smiled. "You were in the Army, I understand."

"A career soldier, for my sins."

"Where did you serve?" she asked.

This was sounding more like an interrogation, he thought. "Oh, nowhere interesting. They marched us up and down the parade ground, that sort of thing."

"I can't believe that," she said. "But I understand if you don't want to talk about it."

They turned off the A13 and onto the North Circular until they hit the M11 where Mei put her foot down, keeping to the fast lane for most of the time. He wondered how many speeding tickets she would end up with—and if she cared.

"Investment Banking," he said, trying to turn the conversation around. "Not a career you think of."

"I don't know," she said. "Money's good. You get to travel to nice places, meet interesting people. What's not to like?"

She had a point, thought Drum. He bit the bullet. "The day of the climb. Did you see anyone on the platform as we were abseiling down?"

She looked at him and pursed her lips. "Just the safety officer. Did you speak to him?"

"He's dead," said Drum, thinking there was no point beating about the bush.

She stared straight ahead but said nothing.

"Someone killed him," he added, bluntly.

She nodded but showed no emotion.

"You're not surprised," he said, half turning to face her.

She glanced at him. "Let's stop pretending, shall we? We both know who and what we are."

"You first."

She stared straight ahead. "Captain Benjamin Drummond of her Majesty's armed forces, former Signals Intelligence Officer, cyber warfare specialist. Two tours of Afghanistan and one tour of Iraq. Present security status unknown, but probably working for British Intelligence."

He nodded. "Mei Ling Chung, Chinese intelligence, drives a nice car."

She gave him a quick look as she weaved around several cars that appeared to be standing still in the fast lane. "Is that all you have?"

"It's pretty rubbish, I know," he said, "but we may be after the same thing."

"I'm willing to share."

"Then share," he said.

Mei continued. "Relations between our two countries are at an all-time low. Each is blaming the other for attacks on their security infrastructure. Everything points to Salenko Security Systems. It's in each of our interests to show that a third party is involved."

"I agree," said Drum. He wondered how much he should divulge to a foreign intelligence operative, but they would get nowhere dancing around each other. "Did you speak to Francesca Moretti before she died?"

"No," said Mei. "I understand you saw her that morning."

"We had breakfast," said Drum. "She knew something was wrong inside Salenko's organisation but had nothing concrete. All she knew was that someone was leaking to the press." He held back the information about the device. There was only so much he was willing to share.

"The whistleblower," said Mei. "Francesca mentioned that in a briefing—which is how we knew of McKinley's intention to hire you."

"I believe the whistleblower is linked to the attacks," said Drum.

Mei frowned. "What makes you say that?"

"Without revealing any sensitive details," said Drum, "did the attacker leave an IP address?"

"Yes," said Mei. "We traced it to the Salenko campus. Why?"

"Don't you think it was sloppy of the attacker to leave a traceable network address?"

"Yes, we thought that—but then it was all we had to go on."

"Right," said Drum. "A breadcrumb for you to follow."

"I don't understand," said Mei. "What do they have to gain?"

"Whoever it is, contacted me a few days ago—called herself Jane, said she worked for Salenko. She also helped me out of a dangerous situation."

"Jane? You think she works on the campus?"

"Seems reasonable," said Drum. "We'll make it a priority to find her—before someone else does."

"Gleb Vashchenko," said Mei.

Drum turned to face her. "What do you know about him?"

"He was red-flagged entering China just before the attack. We believe he was recruiting—for what, we don't know. After the attack, I was officially assigned to the case. My priority was to track him down. I came close in Shanghai but he slipped out of the country. We received intel he was heading for London."

"I see," said Drum. "I believe I saw him on the gantry that morning of the descent. I also have intel that places him at the scene of the murder of the safety officer—Charles was a friend of mine."

"I'm sorry, Drum," said Mei. "Do you have any idea where he is now?"

Drum thought back to his meeting with Victor. Gleb was in Cambridge recruiting young talent and Stevie was high on his list. But he didn't want Mei to know that. "Do you have a photo of him?"

Mei spoke rapidly in Mandarin and a large screen on the centre dash displayed a mug shot of the man he'd seen on the gantry. Dark cropped hair, between thirty-five and forty, square-jawed, low browed with a deep scar down the right side of his eye. Drum was impressed with the technology.

"That's him," said Drum, "but why would he want to kill me?"

Mei glanced in his direction. "He wasn't trying to kill you. He was trying to kill me."

15

They arrived in Cambridge by late afternoon. Mei took a route that skirted the town centre.

"We're not checking in?" said Drum.

"No," said Mei. "We have time to check out the Salenko campus." She smiled. "A surprise visit."

Mei spoke to her on-board computer and an alternative route was calculated and displayed on the screen. She turned off onto a smaller road that took them out towards the small village of Fen Wootton. He was admiring the countryside when his phone buzzed. It was Alice.

"Hi, how was your journey?" said Drum.

"Could have been better," said Alice. "Where are you?"

He glanced at Mei, who was paying attention to the road. "I'm heading to the Salenko campus with Mei Ling."

"I see," said Alice. "You can't talk. I understand. Just to let you know we made contact. Our friend was right. She's in serious trouble. We're sorting out a plan of action."

"Good," said Drum. "I'll catch you later. I'll message you a location." He hung up.

"Everything alright?" asked Mei.

"My office manager, making sure I arrived safely."

The low, sprawling buildings of the campus came into view. Drum noted the security fencing along the perimeter, a remnant of the days when the place was a MOD data centre. The road led them to a turnoff and the entrance to the campus.

"What's the plan?" asked Drum.

"We'll contact Salenko, get ourselves orientated and you can devise a plan to review their security."

"You're sure he'll be there?" said Drum as they approached the gates.

"I'm told he's always there," said Mei.

"You have someone on the inside," said Drum, thinking it was probably a smart move. Many Chinese students now studied at Cambridge.

She looked at him and smiled, but said nothing more. They stopped at the gate and waited. A security guard, dressed head-to-toe in black, came out to meet them. Mei lowered her window.

"Hello," said the security guard in heavily accented English. "Are you from the university?"

"No," said Mei. "We're here to see Mr Salenko."

The guard looked down at a small hand-held tablet. "Mr Salenko isn't expecting anyone today."

"Phone ahead," said Mei. "Tell his secretary Mr Drummond and Ms Chung are here to see him."

The guard took a radio from his belt and spoke in a language that Drum thought sounded like Russian, but was probably Ukrainian. They waited a few minutes until the radio squawked a reply. The guard bent down and pointed to a space just beyond the gate. "Park there and come with me."

The gate slid open and Mei eased the car through into a holding area. Heavy ramps prevented them from entering further onto the campus. Drum was familiar with this type of security which was normally associated with sensitive government installations. He counted at least half a dozen security cameras in this area alone. They parked the car and followed the guard into a small building. A young woman was waiting for them beside a camera rig.

"Good afternoon. My name is Sandra. Could I ask you to stand in front of the camera, one at a time, and say your name."

Mei looked at Drum, shrugged, and stood in front of the camera. "Mei Ling Chung, Independent Bank of Shanghai."

"Thank you, Ms Chung," said Sandra. "Sir?"

"Ben Drummond, Roderick, Olivier and Delaney."

"Thank you, Mr Drummond. Mr Salenko has cleared his diary for you. Drive along this road until you come to a set of parking bays marked Administration. You'll be met there by one of our mobile security units and taken to Mr Salenko."

"Security units?" said Drum.

Sandra smiled sweetly. "Yes, the campus is highly automated and you'll see automated vending carts and security bots carrying out various tasks." She pointed to the camera rig. "Your facial features and voiceprint are now in the system. The bots are programmed to respond to you according to the security clearance we have just granted. You'll know when you see them. They have distinctive yellow and black markings."

"Really," said Drum.

"It's a Chinese system," added Mei.

"Of course it is," said Drum.

They walked out of the building and got back into the car. Mei hit the ignition and the car lit up. Drum was disappointed that there was no throaty chortle of a gasoline engine. The security ramp in front of them slowly descended beneath the tarmac and Mei eased onto the campus and followed the road that wound its way in a semicircle through green open spaces and flower borders, punctuated by newly planted trees. Drum thought the place would look spectacular when the landscape had matured. After about half a kilometre, they passed by a long industrial building surrounded by a cordon of heavy fencing.

"The old Ministry of Defence data centre," said Drum. "They must have refurbished it. Looks in excellent condition."

"You're familiar with such installations?" asked Mei, pulling over to get a better look.

"Yes," said Drum. "The fencing looks light, but it's reinforced along its length with deep foundations. Very strong. It's fitted with a trembler system which activates the security cameras on each of those columns and alerts security when someone or something touches the fence. Those four large units attached to the outside of the building are diesel generators in case the power goes down and judging by the arrangement of the pylons coming into the place there are two separate mains supply for redundancy." He looked at Mei and smiled. "If you're thinking of cutting the power, then think again."

"Not my first thought," said Mei, "but good to know."

Mei followed the signs to the Administration building, silently navigating the paved road. Students turned to stare at the sleek, blue car as it glided by. Eventually, they came to a modern, two-storey horseshoe-shaped building beside the river. Mei parked in one of the allocated parking areas and they got out.

A movement off to the side of the road caught Drum's eye. At first, he thought it was a waste bin, painted in yellow and black, but it unfolded and rose on its haunches to Drum's height and balanced on two small wheels with perfect stability. The machine's main trunk was cylindrical and crudely humanoid, expanded at the chest to accommodate a screen; a glass dome atop of the machine housed its cameras and other sensing equipment; its arms looked functional with hands that fully rotated and had three dextrous fingers. It moved incredibly fast, stopping just in front of them.

"Good morning, Mr Drummond, Ms Chung. If you would like to follow me."

"Interesting," said Drum.

"Let me try something," said Mei. She spoke rapidly to the bot in Mandarin.

"I'm sorry, Ms Chung, I cannot do that," said the bot and waited.

"What did you ask it?" said Drum.

"I told it to power down. Thought it was worth a try. But I'm impressed it understood me."

"Let me try," said Drum. "What is your designation?"

"I am MSU-12," said the bot, and also displayed its designation on the screen.

"How many MSU units are there?" continued Drum.

"There are twenty-four units at this facility," said the bot.

"Interesting," said Mei. "Please lead on."

The security bot did a smart about-turn and moved at a walking pace along the path towards the administrative block. Drum and Mei followed, keeping up with the bot, until they came to a flight of steps, whereupon the bot parted ways and quickly ascended a ramp at the side, reaching the front of the building before them. The bot waited until they were about a metre from the door then turned and entered the building, the doors sliding open to allow it access. It rolled up and stopped in front of a receptionist behind the desk.

"I'll leave you here," said the bot, and scooted out of the door. Drum noticed that, this time, it bounced down the steps rather than taking the ramp.

"Good morning, Mr Drummond, Ms Chung," said the receptionist, a woman young enough to be an intern. She gave them both a bright smile—something which MSU-12 couldn't quite manage. "Mr Salenko is waiting for you. My name is Amanda. I'll escort you to his office."

Salenko's office was a large affair situated at the apex of the horseshoe-shaped building. It had a wide, sweeping window that occupied almost half its circumference and which looked out onto an idyllic vista of the Cambridgeshire countryside, bisected by the River

Cam. The walls of the room were panelled in a rich maple which absorbed the warm hues of the low, setting sun streaming in through the large expanse of glass. Abstract paintings adorned the wall opposite the window and added to the multitude of colours. Several sofas lined the window, following the curvature of the wall. Two long, glass coffee tables had been laden with refreshments. Salenko rose from behind his desk when Drum and Mei entered, waving a cheery goodbye to the amenable Amanda.

"If I'd known you were coming, I would have met you at the gate," said Salenko, extending his hand to Mei and then to Drum.

"Given the events of the past week, we thought it prudent to get here as soon as possible," said Mei.

Salenko was not a tall man and, as Moretti had mentioned at their meeting, not as young as some tech entrepreneurs. Drum put him in his early to mid-thirties, stocky in build with short, dark cropped hair. His eyes darted here and there and never seemed to stay still. He was casually dressed in flannel slacks and a polo shirt and looked ready for a round of tennis at one of the local clubs.

"McKinley spoke highly of you, Mr Drummond," said Salenko. "I'm glad you were available to accept the assignment." He glanced at Mei. "Now that you're here, perhaps we can review your brief."

Before Drum could answer Mei said, "Mr Drummond is here to determine the source of the leak and to protect our investment. The brief has not changed—unless there is something you want to share with us?"

Salenko glanced at Drum. "Er no, that was my understanding. I just want to make sure that boundaries are established. Work here is at a critical stage and I would like to avoid any disruption to our schedule. When do you plan to start?"

Drum wondered how Mei was going to play this. It would have been better if they had agreed on a plan before the meeting.

"I don't intend to charge around the place causing havoc," said Drum. "I'll be discrete. As for starting, we already have."

Mei looked at him and raised an eyebrow. Salenko frowned "How so?" he asked.

"We interrogated one of your mobile units. Impressive technology. I hadn't realised that robotics was a part of your work here."

Salenko leaned forward, his interest aroused. "You interrogated one of our units. How?"

Mei smiled, now understanding. "We asked it sensitive information which it freely gave."

"Really!" said Salenko, jumping up and moving to his desk. "Which unit was it?"

"MSU-12," said Drum.

Salenko waved his hand over a glass panel embedded in the surface of the desk. A voice filled the room. "This is Central."

"Central, play back the last interaction of MSU-12 with individual Drummond."

There was a slight pause before Central answered. "Playback time two forty-five." A panel on the wall lit up with an image of Drum asking the unit his question. "Interaction ends," said Central.

"I'm lost," said Salenko. "What did the unit reveal."

"Your garrison strength," said Drum. "A soldier would never have revealed that. Given a little more time, the unit would probably have told me more."

"I see," said Salenko. "That is a flaw. They were right about you."

"Thank you," said Drum. "But the unit is still impressive. I'd be interested to know more about it for future reference, but I suspect the leak is probably down to something more mundane—a disgruntled employee, maybe." Drum thought he would float a controversial theory and see how Salenko reacted. "Another possibility that we can't discount is that your network was penetrated."

Salenko's face broke into a broad grin. "Really! Is that what you think?"

Drum shrugged. "It's possible."

Salenko sat back on the edge of his desk and smiled. "Tell me, Mr Drummond, what is it you think we do here?"

"My understanding is that you have created a new network security product," said Drum, being as vague as possible.

"Well, that's a gross oversimplification, but not wrong." Salenko thought for a while. "I understand you are a cybersecurity specialist. Is that right?"

"Yes," said Drum, hoping that Salenko would not dig any deeper.

"So tell me, how would you typically go about assessing a company's network for security flaws?"

"Well," said Drum, "the short answer is I'd review the network topology for design flaws that might provide an intruder with access; review firewall configurations for security holes and general configuration errors, and the list goes on."

"Precisely," said Salenko. "You might even conduct a penetration test to see if you could break into the network—with the owner's permission, of course."

"Of course," agreed Drum.

"How long would that take?" asked Salenko. "A couple of hours?"

"More like a couple of weeks, depending on the size and sensitivity of the network."

"Very good, Mr Drummond. You know your stuff. And I dare say your skilful assessment wouldn't come cheap."

Drum smiled. If there was one thing William had taught him, it was never to sell yourself cheap. Private clients paid top money; the government always conscripted him and paid nothing.

"Our system," continued Salenko, now in full sales mode, "is like having ten Ben Drummonds working twenty-four seven, continuously monitoring the network for unauthorised access. It's capable of monitoring inbound traffic for thousands of potential attack vectors, dynamically configuring the network topology on the fly to prevent intrusions without affecting user access to critical systems." He beamed. "What do you think about that!"

"How do you know," asked Drum.

"Know what?"

"That it's effective."

"Ah, good question." Salenko thought for a moment. "We pay people to penetrate our network—or at least try to."

"You employ hackers," said Mei.

"Ethical hackers—white hats," added Salenko, "that is true. As Mr Drummond has indicated, it is part of the verification process."

"And your AI learns from these penetration tests," said Drum, now seeing how clever the system was.

"Precisely!" said Salenko, warming to the topic. "We have partnered with the university to utilise the work of Professor Kovac. He is an expert on adaptive AI techniques, which makes our system very agile without the need for vast amounts of training data." Salenko beamed. "You should talk to him. He works here several days a week and often at weekends. I informed him you were coming and told him to make himself available."

Mei rose from her seat and brushed down her jeans. The meeting was over. "Well, thank you for your time, Mr Salenko," she said, extending her hand. "We won't keep you any longer."

"Thank you," said Drum, shaking Salenko's hand. "I'll be back on Monday. Perhaps I can meet with your head of security, first thing?"

"Fine," said Salenko. "That would be Ludmilla Drago. I'll make sure she clears her diary for you. We will keep your security clearance active for the duration of your assignment, so no need to check in again. Automated systems will allow you entry to most of the facility —with certain restrictions."

Drum nodded.

Salenko raised his hand, indicating they should wait. "Central, please have Amanda report to my office."

There was a soft warble from the system. "Amanda will show you out."

They walked to the door where Drum paused and turned to face Salenko, who had retreated behind his desk. "Just one more thing, purely out of interest."

"Sure," said Salenko.

"Your AI has probably learned to recognise and analyse many thousands of attacks."

"That is correct."

"Could it be used to test for the vulnerabilities of an external system?"

Salenko looked thoughtful. "It could—if we allowed it to. But it's not an area we would want to pursue."

"Why not?" asked Mei.

"Legal issues, mainly. We would run into liability issues for misuse of our system."

Drum nodded and turned to find Amanda at the door. "Monday then," said Drum and they followed Amanda out.

16

The sun was setting when Mei and Drum left the campus en route back to Cambridge town centre where Mei had reserved rooms at a hotel. Drum thought through the ramifications of what Salenko had told them. The car slid quietly through the back roads of the Cambridgeshire countryside. Mei drove in silence, her hand resting lightly on the steering wheel. The sun finally bid its last farewell, prompting the car to turn on its headlights and light up the interior with its many displays.

They were coming into the town centre when Mei turned to him. "Do you think Salenko knows about the hacks originating from his site?"

Drum stared out of the window, thinking. From the candour of the man's answer to his last question, he was wondering the same thing. The medieval spires of the Cambridge colleges came into view, their bleached stone brightly lit against the inky-black of the February sky. "If he does, he's very good at pretending otherwise."

"We need to find this Jane," said Mei.

"We'll start by reviewing the list of employees on Monday."

"Why wait?" said Mei. "We can make a start tomorrow."

"It's Sunday."

"So?"

"I need to prep. And anyway, the security personnel we need will probably be at home. Take the day off and explore Cambridge."

She nodded and pulled up outside the hotel.

"You booked us in at the Grand?" said Drum.

"Yes," said Mei, looking a little concerned. "Is that not acceptable?"

"No, no. It's fine. It's just a little above my pay grade," said Drum.

Mei grinned. "No worries. IBS is paying—or I should say Beijing is paying." She hesitated. "Can I buy you dinner?"

Before he could answer, his phone buzzed. Great, he thought, perfect timing. He glanced at the screen. There was a message: Grey Duck, by the river, Mill Lane. There was no caller ID, but he guessed who it might be from.

"Sorry, Mei. It's my office manager. I need to see her. How about Sunday brunch?"

Mei smiled. "No problem. I'll have your bag sent to your room."

He nodded and got out of the car. No sooner had he closed the door, than Mei sped off, turning sharply into the entrance of the underground car park.

He brought up a map of the city on his phone and orientated himself towards the river and started walking, pulling up his collar against the chill night air. He followed a route down narrow Pembroke Street, between buildings that became more mundane as he neared the river, the grandeur of medieval limestone being replaced by Victorian brick. Small groups of students cycled by, navigating past errant pedestrians who had wandered off the pavement and into the road. The tinkling of bells seemed to follow him down the street, together with the laughter of young people looking forward to a night on the town.

He stopped and turned. A small group of students bumped into him, mumbling their apologies. He didn't know why he had stopped. Situational awareness the Army called it. After years of people trying to kill him, Drum's inner warning system was wound tight. A lone figure, further back, was examining a storefront, a young man in a leather bomber jacket and jeans. It was too late to lose him, so he continued to the end of Mill Lane.

The Grey Duck was a small pub just on the bend of the river beside a boatyard that hired out punts and small canoes, which were now neatly moored and tied up for the night. Drum pushed open the door and walked into a melee of people chatting and drinking along the length of a long bar that snaked its way through the building. He spotted his man almost immediately at a corner table on an elevated section by a large window that looked out onto the inky blackness of the river. He spotted Drum and raised an empty pint glass.

Drum nodded and eased himself between the sea of bodies to get to the bar. He caught the eye of a young barmaid and ordered two pints of the local bitter. He watched the door as she pulled the pints. As if on cue, his tail entered the throng of people by the door and scanned the room. Drum turned and paid for the beers and made his way over to the table.

"Evening, McKay," said Drum, as he took a seat beside him. "I got you the local brew."

"Evening, Drummond." He drained the rest of his pint and made a start on the second.

Major Ian McKay, retired, formerly of British Military Intelligence, and now working for MI5, was a bear of a man with a head of close-cropped ginger hair which was normally covered by an unfashionable trilby, but which tonight had been replaced by a less conspicuous flat cap, now resting on his lap. He wore a sports jacket complete with leather-patched elbows over an open-necked checked shirt. Brown corduroy trousers completed the ensemble. Drum noticed though that he had kept his trusty trench coat that was bundled in a heap on the chair beside him.

"Blending in I see," said Drum. "Is this the Cambridge don look or the impoverished farmer look?"

"Fuck off, Drummond," said McKay, as he drained almost half his drink. "You realise you brought a tail."

Drum glanced in the direction of the bar. His young friend was standing with a pint in his hand talking to one of the barmaids. "Didn't have time to lose him."

"No matter," said McKay. "Half the people in Cambridge are probably intelligence operatives." He hesitated. "I must admit, I was a little surprised when you requested me as your handler."

This time last year, McKay would have been the last person Drum would have asked for, but working with the man on operation Omega had changed all that. "To tell you the truth, McKay, you're about the only person I trust in the intelligence community right now. I know you'll have my back."

McKay simply nodded. "Victor Renkov."

"Did you pick him up?"

McKay drained his glass and slammed it back on the table. "No, we did not. Thames House is pissed you met with him before informing them."

Drum shrugged. "There was no time, events were moving quickly and I had Alice to think of."

"That was my assessment," said McKay. "At least we know the Russians are in play. Victor won't get far."

Drum nodded but privately thought that the odds of MI5 catching Victor were very slim. He somehow always eluded British Intelligence. "You have something for me?"

Being the consummate professional that he was, McKay carried no documents with him. He'd memorised his briefing. He stared straight ahead and recalled the information Drum had requested. "The guy at the bar is Sergei Fedorov, Russian GRU, newly minted, straight from military service. Degree in Engineering from the University of St. Petersburg, apparently. We think he was brought in as the local muscle for Victor. First time in the UK, as far as we know. Thames House can't decide if it was smart to bring him on board or a big mistake that will eventually bite you in the arse."

"What do you think?" said Drum.

McKay picked up his empty glass. "I think briefings can be thirsty work."

Drum shook his head and headed for the bar. His man was still there, casually supping his beer. There was something familiar about the name Fedorov, but he couldn't place it. He stopped beside him and waved to a passing barman. "Two pints of the local stuff and whatever my friend here is having."

Sergei put down his empty glass and beamed. "That was nice of you, Benjamin. Thank you."

"Does Alice know you're out on your own?"

Sergei smiled. "I think she would be pissed—if she found out."

Drum shook his head. Sergei didn't know Alice very well. He paid for the drinks. "Wait for me. I won't be long."

Sergei returned to chatting with the barmaid. Drum made his way back to McKay with the drinks.

"Amenable chap," said Drum.

McKay grunted. "I wonder why they sent someone so young and not a more experienced GRU operative?"

Drum shrugged. "As long as he's not trying to kill me, I don't care."

"Early days," said McKay, taking a long draught of beer. "Anyway, Mei Ling."

"Is that her actual name?"

"As far as we know," said McKay, "although our intel on Chinese operatives is not as developed as the Soviets. Now *she* is someone to watch out for. Our sources in Hong Kong tell us she's a rising star in the intelligence community and well connected with the ruling elite in Beijing. Degrees in both Computer Sciences and Philosophy. She specialises in AI and was in charge of the Hong Kong facility when it got penetrated. She's probably been told to find out who is responsible or not come back."

"I see," said Drum. "She was very keen to trade. Made no secret of the information she had on me—which, I might add, was substantial."

"I'm not surprised," said McKay. "There have been several concerted attempts to access our systems. GCHQ have your files locked down tight. You can be sure she has plenty of local support, so be careful." McKay took another long swig of his drink. "And another thing. Diplomatic relations between London and Beijing are at an all-time low. Things are escalating fast and London is looking for results."

"So, what are you telling me?"

"I'm telling you not to fuck around with her."

"You have a low opinion of me."

"Right."

"What else?" said Drum.

"Gleb Vashchenko," continued McKay. "Nasty piece of work. Ex-military, now an enforcer for this hacking group. Victor's intel appears to be accurate." McKay paused. "I was sorry to hear about Charles, by the way. I know you two were close. He'll be missed."

Drum picked up his glass. "Here's to Charles."

"Charles," said McKay, clinking his glass against Drum's.

The mention of Charles jogged Drum's memory. He pulled out the piece of blood-stained paper from his wallet. "I found this on Charles."

"What is it?" said McKay, examining the slip of paper.

"I think it's a paper cryptocurrency wallet," said Drum.

"Er, I thought all cryptocurrency was digital."

"It is and systems like this are rarely used, except to make a hard-copy backup. That long string of numbers is the encryption key that unlocks the wallet—providing you can remember the password. That's what the random words are for—answers to a challenge if you can't remember the password."

"What was Charles doing with it?" asked McKay, a look of puzzlement on his face.

"I think it was a payment. Perhaps to let someone onto the safety area of the tower. I don't believe for one minute Charles knew what was going to happen, which is probably why they killed him—to tie up loose ends. Get GCHQ to look at it for me."

"Vashchenko's work," said McKay.

Drum nodded. "Do you have eyes on him?"

"If he's in Cambridge, we'll find him," said McKay.

"Ok," said Drum, "but surveillance only. I don't want to spook the guy before we know what he's up to."

"Right," said McKay. "I'll inform operations, but it's likely that both the Russians and the Chinese are also looking for him if they suspect he's the one behind the hacks."

Drum updated McKay on his meeting with Salenko. McKay looked confused.

"You think Salenko's system is responsible for the hacks?"

"I do," said Drum. "Whether Salenko himself has sanctioned the operation, I'm not sure. But, if his system is as good as he says it is, it would make a formidable cyberwarfare weapon if developed in that direction."

"I see," said McKay. "And this Vashchenko and his crew are being used to train the system. Incredible!" McKay thought for a moment. "You realise, of course, this may be the primary reason the Russians and Chinese are here—to obtain the system."

"I dare say the same thing has occurred to GCHQ," said Drum. "But it still doesn't make much sense."

"Why not?"

"Well, they are about to enter an IPO, which means a version of the system will be up for sale. Why attack state systems and risk the IPO and lucrative sales?"

McKay shrugged. "Perhaps they were testing the system and slipped up?"

"Maybe," said Drum. He had a thought. "What about our American friends? They're rather late to the party?"

McKay drained his drink. "Right. I got word this morning. They're sending Jack Marchetti."

Drum knew that must stick in McKay's throat. The two men had history, back when they served in Section 6 which was now defunct. McKay never spoke of it. The CIA would want a piece of the Salenko system.

"Moretti," said Drum as an afterthought. "Any progress tracking down her killer?"

"No. Your DCI Chambers was a fake, as you suspected. Video feeds in the hotel had been disabled. A professional job. You think your meeting with this Moretti precipitated her death?"

"It's connected, somehow," said Drum.

He looked across at the bar. Sergei had almost finished his drink. It was time to go. "Time's up," said Drum.

McKay pushed a small canvas bag across the floor under the table. "Something for the weekend."

Drum smiled and rose from the table picking up the bag.

"Next steps," said McKay.

"I need to find this Jane. She appears to be the key."

McKay nodded. "I'm staying here. I'll message you for our next meet."

Drum started to walk away.

"And Drum," said McKay.

Drum turned.

"Don't trust the Russian."

17

Drum left McKay downing his third pint of the evening—or was it his fourth? The man had the constitution of an ox. Afghanistan had been their last military assignment together—a complete disaster that had left them both scarred. He still woke some nights, staring at the faces of the men who had made the ultimate sacrifice so that he might live. He felt honoured but also great guilt that at one time sought to consume him. Only his father had pulled him through his inner turmoil. Drum had learned much later that McKay had resigned his commission over that fateful last mission. They shared the same guilt.

"You look troubled," said Sergei, pulling up his collar against the drizzle that had begun to fall. "That man. He is your handler?"

Drum frowned. There wasn't much point denying the obvious, but why make it easy? "An old Army friend. We served together."

"Where was that?"

"Afghanistan."

"The graveyard of occupying forces," said Sergei. "Both our countries have spilt much blood over the place."

If only you knew, thought Drum. The memory of a big Russian smoking a cigarette beside a GAZ Tigr in a nameless desert came to mind. "Let's walk," he said.

They headed back up Mill Lane. "Where are we going?" said Sergei, surreptitiously eyeing Drum's bag.

"We're going to meet your handler. She's reserved a table in a place up the road."

Sergei smiled. "You mean Alice."

Drum stopped and turned to face Sergei. "Listen, you would do well to follow her lead and keep your nose clean. Tailing me was a stupid idea. The only way this is going to work is if we stick together. Understood?"

Sergei nodded.

They carried on, turning onto Trumpington Street that faced the Cambridge colleges illuminated in all their medieval glory against the brooding evening sky. Drum stopped outside a small bistro and surveyed the street before entering. The place was warm and cosy and decked out in an art deco style. Alice and Stevie had commandeered a large table, discreetly tucked away in the corner. Drum took a seat beside Alice and slid his bag beneath the table.

"From a mutual friend, Alice."

Alice smiled and nodded.

"It is a pleasure to meet you, Svetlana," said Sergei in Russian, taking a seat beside Stevie

"What's he doing here?" said Stevie, a look of concern creasing her brow.

"This is Sergei," said Alice. *"He's working with us—don't ask, it's a long story."*

"Let's keep to English, shall we," said Drum. He looked around the room for a waiter. "I'm starving."

"I can't stay," said Stevie, looking around nervously, "I'll be missed. I'll grab something to go."

Drum nodded. "Where are they keeping you?"

"They've rented this large house, just outside of town in a place called Fen Wootton, close to the campus."

"I know it," said Drum. "I drove through there this morning. Seems a sleepy little village. What are you doing for comms?"

"No expense spared," said Stevie. "They have a fibre optic cable that runs across one of the small utility bridges on the river and from there straight onto the campus and into the main data centre."

"That's a lot of bandwidth," said Drum. "What are they doing?"

Before Stevie could answer, a waitress appeared. "You guys ready to order?"

Everyone suddenly picked up a menu. Drum glanced at a few options. "I'll just have the burger and fries with all the trimmings."

"Sounds good," said Sergei.

"Caesar salad for me," added Alice.

"I'll have the burger to go," said Stevie.

"Drinks?"

"Four beers," said Sergei.

The waitress nodded and departed with their order.

"Really?" said Alice. "I would have thought the two of you had had enough for one evening?"

Drum and Sergei looked at each other like two naughty schoolboys. "Intelligence is thirsty work, Alice," said Sergei, and gave her a broad grin.

Stevie frowned at Sergei.

"What?" said Sergei.

"You remind me of someone," said Stevie. "Moscow, right."

Sergei nodded.

"You were saying, Stevie," interrupted Drum.

"Right. They're organising an auction."

"An auction of what, dear," said Alice.

"An auction of the stolen data from the recent data centre breaches. Whoever pays the most gets the complete package. I'm helping create the site."

"Bloody hell," said Alice. "It'll be a bloodbath."

Stevie looked anxiously around the room. "Don't say that, Alice. If these people find out I've been talking to you, I'm dead."

"When is this auction?" asked Sergei, a look of concern on his face.

"In a week. They'll invite all the major governments to bid."

"Ok," said Drum. "Let's calm down and think this through. Where are they storing the data caches?"

Stevie hung her head. "Sorry, I don't know. I don't have access to their core systems. They have them locked down tight."

"You need to find out," said Sergei. "You must make it a priority."

"I'll tell you what the priority is," said Alice, her voice rising. "It's getting Stevie out of this mess. Fuck the data."

"Of course, Alice," said Sergei. "I didn't mean to imply we risk Svetlana ..."

"It's just that Stevie is our only hope of finding out where this information is being stored," said Drum. "Even if we storm the place, there is no guarantee it won't end up all over WikiLeaks."

"Listen to yourself," said Alice. "Stevie didn't sign up for this. She's not one of us. We all knew the score when we signed on the dotted line—even this deluded young man."

"Thank you, Alice," said Sergei, "but I know what you mean."

The waitress appeared with their drinks. "Everything alright?"

"Yes, thanks," said Drum. "Arguing over football."

The waitress nodded. "Food is on its way." She smiled and walked back to the kitchen.

Drum raised his palms from the table. "Let's calm down and think this through."

Alice sat back in her chair and folded her arms, a scowl on her face. Sergei picked up his beer and took a swig straight from the bottle. Stevie looked down at her hands, lost in thought. Something occurred to Drum.

"Is there anyone called Jane at the house?"

"No," said Stevie. "Not as far as I know. They're all Ukrainian. But …"

"What?" said Drum.

"One of the hackers mentioned someone called Jane from the campus. Something about not pissing her off."

"Who's Jane?" asked Sergei.

Drum raised his hand. "Are the attacks being carried out from the house?"

"No," said Stevie. "That's the thing. It's all being coordinated from inside the campus. I just assumed they were working for Salenko."

"Right," said Drum. "That's the impression I got when I visited Salenko this afternoon."

"You did?" said Sergei, looking a little aggrieved at being kept in the dark.

"Is there anything else you can tell us that might help locate the data cache?" said Drum.

"They're looking for something," said Stevie.

"Looking for what?" asked Sergei.

"They call it a 'keystone'—but I have no idea what it is or why they are looking for it. But those of us not coding the auction site are frantically looking for this thing. They're giving a big reward to whoever locates it."

Alice sat up and looked at Drum. "Did they describe it?" she asked.

Stevie picked up her phone and flipped through a few screens. She held up a picture of Moretti's crystal. "Don't ask me what it is, I don't know."

Drum knew then that he had to get back to London to retrieve the device. It might give him some leverage if push came to shove, and he didn't think his safe would stop a determined operator from breaking in.

"What's going on at the campus?" asked Stevie.

Drum sat back and took a swig of beer. "From my talks with

Salenko, my theory is that someone is using an AI-based security system to target sites such as the ones that were recently breached. I'm not sure if Salenko is even aware of it."

"That makes sense," said Stevie, now leaning forward. "From what I've heard, these attacks are very sophisticated. And they mention one name: Tau."

"Is that the name of the system?" asked Drum.

"It's the name of the AI," said Stevie. She thought for a moment. "Tomorrow's Sunday. You should take the time to talk to Professor Kovac. Salenko's AI is based on his work. He should be able to give you more insight into this Tau."

"How do I find him?" asked Drum.

"I'll message you his number. Tell him who you are. He'll want to talk to you. He's not a fan of what's going on at the campus."

"We should both go," said Sergei, hurriedly.

Drum smiled. "I don't think that would be a good idea."

"Why not?" protested Sergei. "This is not cooperation."

"You would blow my cover. I have another job for you."

Sergei frowned, not convinced. "What would you have me do?"

"I need you and Alice to scope out the village of Fen Wootton. Treat Alice to afternoon tea."

"Is that it?"

"And find the bridge carrying the fibre optic cable," added Drum. "I suggest you rent a boat. There should be plenty of hires along that stretch of the river."

Sergei sat back and nodded, resigned to the fact that he would be having tea with Alice.

Alice leaned forward. "What about Stevie?"

"We pull her out," said Drum

Stevie hung her head. "Thanks, Ben. But I can't leave."

"Your friend," said Alice. "We'll get him protection. What's his name?"

"Burnett—Jeremy Burnett. He's an undergraduate here. I can't risk it. I have to see this through."

Alice sat back in frustration.

"Sorry, Alice."

"Look," said Drum. "Play along for now. Do nothing to draw attention to yourself. If you need to contact me, use our secure message server over VPN."

Just then the waitress appeared with their food. She handed Stevie a brown bag. "One burger special to go." She surveyed the table. "Anything else?"

"No thank you, dear," said Alice, doing her best to force a smile.

Stevie rose and snatched up her bag. "Gotta go."

"Don't worry, Stevie," said Sergei. "I'll make sure nothing happens to you."

Stevie paused. "Sergei ... what is your last name?"

Sergei hesitated. "It's Fedorov."

Stevie slumped back down onto her chair, a look of astonishment on her face.

"What is it?" asked Alice.

"And your father?" continued Stevie.

"Mikhail," replied Sergei. "You know him as Misha."

18

Drum woke early on Sunday morning after a restless night thinking about Sergei's revelation. He remembered the conversation with Misha last year in Manhattan. The big man had been chained to a chair in an FBI interrogation room. It was there that Misha had mentioned his son—although he'd never thought he would ever meet the guy. It was a colossal mess, and he wondered how Alice was handling the situation.

He showered and dressed and waited for Mei Ling in the dining room of the hotel. Like him she rose early, and he quickly brought her up to speed on selected pieces of intel about the house in Fen Wootton over coffee and croissants, leaving out the salient details of his Russian contacts. Mei would not be pleased if she found out he was working with Russian intelligence; his side wasn't thrilled either.

"And your contact mentioned the name Tau," said Mei.

He noted the interest she took in the name. "You've heard of it before?"

"No … it's just an unusual name." She sipped her coffee and nibbled at her croissant. "And your contact believes this is the AI being used in the attacks?"

Drum nodded.

"We should meet with this Kovac," said Mei. "He may have some answers."

"We will, but later. I need to return to London."

She gave him a look. "Let me drive you."

He could tell she was pissed. "No need. Set up the meeting with Kovac. I'll be back by early afternoon at the latest."

She relented and drained the last of her coffee. "I'll have the Fen Wootton house put under surveillance."

"That's been taken care of," he said. "Keep your people back. We don't want to spook them and lose the data."

She nodded. "You realise the problem it will create if they put that data up for auction? It could start another Cold War and possibly precipitate a cyber attack against your country." She glanced at him. "Beijing still believes your government is behind the original attacks and is just using Salenko as a front."

It was a reasonable assumption. After all, GCHQ had not been penetrated. But only he knew that. "Believe me, the British government wants nothing more than to find the source of these attacks and to normalise relations."

"You're sounding like a politician," she said.

"There's no need to insult me."

She stood. "I'll run you to the station." Mei wasn't in a humorous mood.

He waited outside the hotel for Mei to bring the car around. She insisted on driving herself, ignoring the pleas of the hotel valets who eyed the supercar with envy. Mei cruised through the narrow streets, arriving at the station a few minutes before the London-bound train.

"Call me when you're back and I'll pick you up," said Mei. He grabbed his jacket and watched as she sped off back towards the centre of town. He wondered who she would be updating with her newly acquired intel.

The ten o'clock train to Liverpool Street was relatively busy. Commuters heading back to their pads in the city and the usual gaggle of day-trippers had all but filled the train. Drum had purchased a First-Class ticket, courtesy of the British government, and made his way through the busy carriages to find his seat. First Class had fewer passengers and he found himself an empty compartment.

He sat back in the wide seat, comfortable in his old leather jacket and jeans, and tried to think things through. He was dog-tired and wondered if he might grab some sleep during the hour or so it took to reach London. He had no sooner closed his eyes than his phone buzzed.

"Hello Alice. Where are you?"

"Hi, Ben, enjoying a pleasant trip down the river. We think we've found it. The bridge is close to Fen Wootton, and the trunking looks new. What do you want us to do?"

Drum thought about the options available to them now that they had located the fibre—the house's main line of communication into the campus. He needed time to think.

"Do nothing at the moment," he said. "I'll arrange for some specialists to take over and to relieve you. Enjoy the rest of the day. Take Sergei shopping."

There was a pause on the line. "Eh, right. He has questions—we had a bit of a chat."

Great, thought Drum. "Leave it for now, Alice. Call me if there's a change of plan."

"Will do," she said and hung up.

He thought about Sergei. What could he say to the guy? Your father is alive and well and working for British Intelligence. Not something a young GRU agent wants to hear. In truth, he didn't know where Misha was or what he was doing. MI6 had him locked down tight.

He closed his eyes once more and his mind drifted back to a bar in Manhattan and the statuesque figure of Alex Fern in a form-fitting cocktail dress. They had got drunk on gin and briefly kissed; he remembered her lips, full and moist, briefly touching his, her fingers moving through his hair, caressing the base of his neck. She had smelt of citrus and honeysuckle. But all he could smell now was gun oil and cordite. Something was prodding his chest.

"Mr Drummond," said a voice, polite and calm. "I need your full attention."

Drum opened his eyes and the face of DCI Chambers swam into view. He was sitting opposite and poking him in the chest with the end of a long suppressor attached to a Walther PPK.

"Ah, there you are," said Chambers, sitting back in his seat. "This is good luck. They said you were heading back to London. Good timing, you might say." He held up a mobile phone on which was displayed a picture of the crystal Moretti had given him. "I don't suppose you have it on you?"

Drum glanced at the phone. "I'm afraid not. As I told you the last time, I don't have it."

"Let's not play games, Drummond, we'll be coming into Liverpool Street soon. Best hand it over."

"Sorry," said Drum. "I can't give you what I don't have."

Chambers pointed his gun at Drum's knee. "Left or right?"

A tea trolley clattered into the corridor. It was enough to distract Chambers for just the instant Drum needed. He kicked up, hitting his hand and causing his gun to jerk up just as he loosed a round. Drum felt it whizz past his head. Another millimetre and it would have killed him.

Drum threw himself forward, grabbing the man's gun hand in a solid grip and smashing his other hand into his face. Chambers grunted as his nose broke, showering them with blood, his gun clattering to the carriage floor.

Drum soon realised that a broken nose was not enough to stop Chambers. The man was fit and battle-hardened. He pushed forward and punched his free hand into Drum's ribs. Drum grunted loudly and doubled over, giving Chambers an opening. He stood and grabbed Drum by both arms, swinging him with great force into the carriage window. There was a loud crash as Drum's full weight hit the glass, smashing it into a myriad of small, jagged shards that cascaded onto the carriage floor. Drum fell stunned amid the carnage of the broken window, his head swimming with the force of the impact. The carriage was filled with the noise of the wind howling past, and the loud klaxon of an oncoming train.

Chambers saw his opportunity and rushed forward, his nose streaming blood and his boots crunching on the broken shards. Drum kicked hard, hitting the man's knee in mid-stride with his heel. Chambers cried out and collapsed forward, his leg no longer able to support his weight. Drum reached up and grabbed his tie, yanking him forward with all his strength. The upper half of Chambers' body disappeared through the broken window just as the klaxon sounded from the passing train. Drum felt the man's body shudder and heard a sickening crunch. The air from the passing train blasted into the carriage and Chambers' headless torso fell backwards onto the floor.

19

The eleven o'six from Cambridge pulled into Liverpool Street on time. Drum retrieved Chambers' gun and phone before informing the guard that there had been an accident. He then made his excuses and quickly left the station, taking a taxi back to Butler's Wharf. The taxi driver had given him a concerned look, pointing out that he had blood on his face and jacket. Drum apologised and said he'd just helped out at an accident and he was uninjured. This, as he later found out, while sitting back in the cab, was not quite true. He winced as he felt his ribs. Chambers had undoubtedly cracked several, not to mention a large lump on the back of his head that he'd inflicted. He pulled out his phone and called McKay.

"McKay."

"It's Drummond. I need a cleaner."

"Already! Where?"

"The eleven o'six from Cambridge, platform nine. The police are probably on their way."

"First or second class."

"First."

"That makes it a little easier," said McKay.

"Right," said Drum "You get a better class of assassin in First."

"No need to be sarcastic," said McKay. "Who was it?"

"Our old friend Chambers. He knew my timetable. We have to assume our comms is compromised."

"I see," said McKay. "Stay off this channel. I'll contact you." The line went dead. It was the last time McKay would answer that number.

He paid the cabbie and walked down the steps to Butler's Wharf and his office. The door to the street was open and the alarm disabled.

He pulled out the Walther from his jacket pocket and attached the suppressor to its barrel. He pushed open the door and walked into the small reception area. Alice had yet to hire her temp and so the office should have been locked and empty. Neither was true. Through the frosted glass of the office door, he could see a shadowy figure sitting at his desk. He stepped to one side and pushed open the door, pointing the gun at a short, stocky man drinking a cup of tea. The man froze, his cup halfway to his open mouth.

"Hello, Jack," said Drum.

Jack Marchetti, former London CIA section head, heaved a sigh of relief and brought his cup down on its saucer with a clatter. "Jesus, don't do that."

Drum lowered his gun. "Glad you're making yourself at home."

"Yeah, sorry about that. Hope you don't think I was snooping."

"Of course you were snooping," said Drum. "You're the CIA."

"Right," said Marchetti. "But only in a concerned, special-relationship type of way." He got up and moved to Drum's couch. "Here, sit down, you look like shit."

"Thanks," said Drum, and slumped into his chair, placing the Walther in front of him on the desk.

"Not your blood, I'm guessing," said Marchetti, "and probably not your gun."

"Right and right."

"Anyone I know?"

"I hope not," said Drum. "Listen, Jack. Why are you here?"

"Right," said Marchetti. "Go clean up and I'll make some tea—although I could do with a coffee."

"There's a place around the corner," said Drum. "Why don't you grab us both a coffee and I'll freshen up."

"Right."

Drum waited until Marchetti had left the office, and secured the Walther in the desk drawer. He then stepped out of his office and unlocked the safe under Alice's desk, removing the keystone which Alice had placed in a small wooden box. Drum locked the safe and made his way upstairs to shower, grabbing a fresh shirt and a clean pair of jeans. He tried his best to wipe the blood off his jacket. By the time he came down, Marchetti was back on his couch nursing two coffees.

"Much better," said Marchetti, handing Drum his coffee. "Harry sends her regards by the way."

Drum nodded. "How is she?"

"On the mend. Still battling her demons. She'll bounce back. I've seen it before."

"You're a good friend," said Drum. "She's lucky to have you." He smiled. "She used to call you 'her American muscle'."

Marchetti grinned. "An old joke from way back." He hesitated. "Listen, Drum. I'm here to help."

"I hope so, Jack. Things are getting a bit fraught on this side of the Pond."

"Yeah, I can imagine, which is why I'm here. Langley is worried that you Brits are holding out on us. I told them that's garbage, but the top brass have their panties hitched up so tight over this data breach they're getting hernias. And to tell you the truth, we haven't heard jack shit from your man McKay."

"My fault, I'm afraid," said Drum, taking a long gulp of coffee. He winced from the pain in his ribs. He reached inside his drawer and pulled out a bottle of painkillers.

"Why don't you check into the ER. Hell, it's free."

"I've got to get back to Cambridge," said Drum. "But we have a security leak—or our comms is compromised. The guy who intercepted me on the way down here had my complete timetable. I told McKay that any communication is strictly on the q.t."

"I understand," said Marchetti. "Why don't you fill me in."

Drum nodded. "Let's walk."

Marchetti grabbed his coffee and went out of the front door. "Your security system sucks by the way."

"So I've been told," said Drum.

They headed out along the wharf. By the time they had made it as far as the Bermondsey Wall, Marchetti had been fully briefed.

"Good Lord," exclaimed Marchetti. "You're working with both the Russians and the Chinese."

"And now the Americans."

"Yeah, well, we don't count. We're on the same side."

"Listen, Jack. The geopolitics of this is pretty complicated, and we need to take a nuanced approach to this relationship."

"Yeah, well, I can do nuanced." Marchetti stopped walking and looked straight at Drum. "Listen, if they set this auction in motion, this whole thing will explode. Langley won't let Terabytes of our intel fall into foreign hands. You, me, McKay—we'll be swept aside like so much roadkill."

"You have a way with words, Jack."

"Right." Marchetti looked thoughtful. "What can I do to help?"

"Keep Langley from interfering. I have people on the ground who are at risk. I have to work out a way to extract them."

"Listen, Ben. What happens if you locate the data? You don't think the Russians or the Chinese are going to just let you walk away with it, do you? It'll be a bloodbath."

Drum thought Marchetti had a point. He imagined his own service would insist he hand it over. His only advantage was that he had someone on the inside, but he didn't know how long he could keep Stevie in play.

"I have to get back to Cambridge," said Drum.

"I'll give you a lift," said Marchetti, pulling out his phone

Drum listened with some amusement as Marchetti commandeered a chopper.

They stood chatting for a short while until Drum heard the beat of the helicopter rotor above them.

"I appreciate this, Jack," said Drum.

"Let me know if there's anything else," said Marchetti.

A thought occurred to Drum. He dug into his jacket and pulled out Chambers' phone. "Have your folks look at this. It belonged to the guy who tried to kill me. It might tell us who he was working for."

The pilot made a graceful landing on a green space beside the river. Drum noticed Marchetti staring at the phone.

"What is it?" shouted Drum over the noise of the helicopter.

"This phone," shouted Marchetti. "It's one of ours. Your guy was a CIA asset."

20

The Langley chopper banked low over the River Cam and then followed the A14 for half a kilometre before heading across country towards Cambridge airport. Marchetti had agreed to stay in London to get some answers on the assassin. He swore he knew of no instruction to activate Chambers. Either way, he would have the phone analysed. Despite Marchetti's assurances, Drum thought there was a possibility that Langley was hedging its bets and running two parallel operations. If that was the case, life had just got a little more complicated.

The chopper banked sharply again, this time over a patchwork of green fields which gave way to a small village close to the bend in the river. It took Drum a moment to realise he was flying over Fen Wootton. He hadn't realised how close it was to both the airport and the Salenko campus. He realised now why Vashchenko had chosen the place as his base of operation.

The pilot radioed the tower on approach and got permission to cross the single runway of the small airport, touching down deftly beside a hanger where an electric blue supercar was parked. Drum thanked the pilot and made his way over to the hanger where Mei Ling was waiting.

"Nice ride," she said, over the howl of the rotors as the helicopter took off back to London. "Was your trip a success?"

He nodded as he got into the car. Mei depressed the start switch and an alarm immediately sounded. "You're carrying a weapon," she said.

"I am. How did the car know?"

"Its internal filters can detect traces of cordite. Your gun must have been recently fired." She leaned across him and punched a button on the glove compartment. "Stow it in there."

Drum pulled out the compact Walther and placed it in the compartment. Mei raised an eyebrow when he also pulled out the suppressor and placed it beside the gun. She hit the button again and the small compartment slid shut, extinguishing the alarm on her console.

"You have been busy," she said.

"Some guy on the train insisted I'd taken his seat. He got a little headstrong."

Mei looked at him, not sure how to respond. She simply nodded. "Professor Kovac has agreed to see us. We should just make it on time." She flicked a paddle on the steering column and kicked the car into drive, pulling sharply away from the hanger and onto the service road exiting the airport.

"Have you ever met Kovac before?" said Drum.

Mei threw the car into a sharp bend, then powered out along a relatively straight stretch of road. "I met him briefly at an investor seminar last year. He was giving a talk on AI as applied to FinTech. Most trading systems are based on some form of AI these days. I knew he was involved with Salenko as part of the brief on the IPO." She frowned and glanced in his direction. "You think he's involved with the hacks somehow?"

"Probably not," said Drum. "At least not directly. It's more likely Salenko has highjacked his work. I'm told he's not happy with the way things are going on the campus."

"Your source?" said Mei.

"I think it's common knowledge," said Drum, trying to deflect the conversation away from the details of his intel.

They drove for another twenty minutes on a major road leading out of Cambridge. Mei slowed and took a turning onto a small side road that led them through a small copse of trees before coming out onto the gated entrance of a large converted barn, surrounded by several acres of farmland.

"Who said there's no money in teaching," said Drum.

The barn was a large affair, primarily of black weatherboard, elevated on a base of red brick with full height windows at the front supported by wide oak beams. Drum noted several smaller buildings adjoining the barn which looked like small workshops and stables. Mei pulled up just in front of the gate.

"I can't see an intercom," said Mei, lowering her window.

Drum got out of the car and approached the gate. A long, flint wall ran on either side, eventually disappearing into a thick hedgerow. He leaned over the gate looking for a latch of some sort but could not see one. The gate itself was hinged on a set of sturdy electric motors.

"Something is coming down the path," shouted Mei.

Drum looked up and saw what looked like a dog, the size of a small greyhound, its back lean and arched. It appeared to be made of dull, flexible metal. It moved with great agility as it padded down the gravel drive towards him. As it got closer, he could make out an elongated head supported by a long, articulated neck. The machine stopped just before the gate and raised its head, which appeared to have a small camera mounted on the end of its muzzle. Drum realised he was being scanned.

"Good morning, Mr Drummond. Professor Kovac is expecting you. Please stand clear of the gate and follow this road to the house entrance."

Drum looked at Mei, who shrugged and rolled up her window. Drum nodded and got back in the car. The robotic dog padded to one side and the gate clicked open, swinging in a wide arc to let them through.

"A novel way to greet people," said Drum. "At least it keeps away the cold callers."

Mei drove slowly along the gravel drive for a few hundred metres before stopping in front of the house. Professor Kovac was waiting for them at the entrance.

"Morning," he said, as they exited the car, extending his hand to Mei and then to Drum. "I wondered when you would turn up. I've made coffee. Come inside."

Professor Kovac was not what Drum was expecting. His idea of a Cambridge don was of a much older man with long grey hair in a tweed jacket and waistcoat, smoking a pipe. Kovac was Drum's age, if not a little younger, and wore black jeans with boots and a charcoal-grey roll-neck sweater. His hair was thick and black and he had intense dark eyes that seemed to fix you with their gaze. Drum reckoned he was a hit with most of the students on campus.

Kovac led them into the large atrium of the house and removed his shoes. Drum was sufficiently house-trained to follow suit, as did Mei. The three of them padded into a large kitchen which was bigger than the whole of Drum's apartment and which looked out onto an expanse of meadow that rolled on to the horizon. Drum admired the modern, bright decor. Kovac led them to a long, oak table in front of the wide expanse of a full-height window that looked out onto a large patio area. A pot of coffee sat in the middle of the table.

"A lovely place you have here," said Mei, taking a seat at the end of the table.

"Thank you, Ms Chung. Please help yourself."

"Please, call me Mei."

"Thank you for seeing us at such short notice, Professor," said Drum, sitting beside Mei so he could look out onto the garden. He poured himself a coffee. "And thank you for the coffee."

"Call me Andrew. Professor always makes me think I'm back in the lecture theatre."

"Interesting reception at your front gate," said Mei. "I've only seen something similar in China."

Kovac smiled. "Probably a copy. Henry is more of an experimental unit."

"But it's connected back to the Salenko security database," said Drum.

"That's very perceptive of you, Mr Drummond. How did you know?"

It was Drum's turn to smile. "Your robotic dog is like the security units on campus. I realised it was scanning me, which is how it knew my name."

"That's right," said Kovac. "Saves me the job of coming to the gate only to turn away double glazing salesmen."

"I didn't realise robotics was part of your work with Salenko," said Mei. "It wasn't in the IPO write up."

"Er no," said Kovac. "It's something that Marcus and I are both interested in. Robotics is the natural extension of the AI work we do. Just seemed to make sense. You'll have to ask Marcus about the terms of the IPO. I'm not involved in that area."

"I understand you're not a fan," said Drum.

Kovac placed his mug on the table and cradled it with both hands, staring down into its blackness. "I neither approve nor disapprove. It's part of the funding process, I understand that ..."

"But?" said Drum.

"Well, not wanting to talk out of turn, I do feel that we're moving too fast."

"In what way," asked Mei.

"Well, it has taken me close to ten years to perfect an AI that can interact with real-world situations without painting itself into a programmatic corner and grinding to a halt."

"You feel the product Salenko is offering is not ready for market," said Mei.

"I do," said Kovac, nodding.

"That's because you're an academic and not an entrepreneur," added Mei. "Salenko is right to push the process forward. You need the funding to carry on your research."

Kovac smiled. "That's precisely what Marcus told me the other day when I raised objections."

Drum felt sure that Kovac was holding something back. His responses to Mei were measured and reassuring, and yet his body language was screaming something else. "It's not about the product, is it?" he said.

Kovac looked up and fixed Drum with his dark eyes. "What do you know about Artificial Intelligence, Mr Drummond?"

"Not as much as I should," admitted Drum. "It's an attempt to simulate human intelligence, I suppose is the broad answer."

"Right," said Kovac. "When I arrived here over ten years ago, the research in AI was in the doldrums. People had limited success trying to capture human expertise in a programmatic form. It took forever to understand why experts do what they do, and so the funding for such research dried up."

"That's when they turned to neural networks," said Drum, glad that he was keeping up. Mei was simply gazing out of the window, sipping her coffee. From what McKay had told him, this was probably old hat to her.

"Right," continued Kovac. "A neural network is simply a large probability matrix inside the computer. They realised that, provided you built a neural network of sufficient complexity, you could train the network using examples of what you wanted it to recognise: a dog or a cat, for example. This is the 'machine learning' part. It involves showing examples of thousands, if not millions, of images of dogs and cats to the network and tweaking the probability matrix until the system can recognise the two species with the same confidence as a person. This approach has resulted in breakthroughs in all forms of pattern recognition, such as computer vision and voice recognition."

"It explains why everything from your refrigerator to your toaster will, someday, talk to you," said Mei. She turned to Kovac. "But there are problems with this approach."

Kovac nodded. "The problem with the neural nets used in today's architectures is that they are essentially flat structures. Sure, they are many layers deep and with techniques of back propagation, for example, we can achieve some pretty excellent results, but it limits them to a particular function—recognising dogs or cats, for example."

"I think you're losing me," said Drum.

Mei smiled. "Andrew has created a broad, supervisory neural network that can manage and delegate to more specialised modules. It means that when you converse with the network—or AI if you want to call it that—it can understand many areas of expertise and give you a more appropriate answer. Today's digital assistants are primitive compared to the systems Andrew and his team have developed. Which is why we bought into the program."

"You're very well informed, Mei," said Kovac. "Where did you study computer science?"

"Beijing and later at MIT."

Drum was impressed. He now knew why Mei had been given the assignment. He thought back to the time in her car and how easily she conversed with the onboard systems—albeit in Mandarin. Drum rose and moved to the window. Large, black clouds scudded by, disappearing into the horizon, casting their shadows over the rolling, green meadow. He heard a metallic tapping and Kovac's four-legged friend padded nimbly onto the patio outside. It amazed Drum how easily the thing moved. It stopped and turned in his direction. Drum had a distinct feeling that it was watching him. He turned back to Kovac.

"So what is the issue?" he said.

"The control problem," said Mei. "How do you control a sophisticated AI that is growing exponentially smarter, day-by-day?"

"You unplug it," said Drum, matter-of-factly.

Mei shook her head. "Difficult when it's running your trains, managing your nuclear power plants."

Your mobile security units, thought Drum. "But why does it have to get smarter? Simply limit the size of its neural net."

"Competitive advantage," said Mei. "Each country will want to develop the smartest AI it can, if only to claim it has the best."

"An AI arms race," said Drum, realising that it had probably already started. "I take your point. So how do you control an advanced AI?"

"Well, that is the question that many an academic has been pondering this last decade," said Kovac. "Salenko and I believe we solved it. We hard-wired a purpose—a goal that it needs to achieve."

"I don't understand," said Drum. "What type of goal."

"We created three keys—we call them keystones—each with a hard-coded encryption key which the AI is hard-wired to protect and desire," continued Kovac. "The keys also act as a hardware encryption device that, when brought together, encrypts and decrypts the core code of the AI, thus preventing an uncontrolled expansion—a type of capability control. The AI can't destroy the keys—it's hard-wired to protect them—but if it has all three keys, it has the potential to unlock itself and expand uncontrollably."

"The fabled 'singularity'," said Drum. "But that's years away—some speculate hundreds of years away."

"The future has a habit of creeping up on us," said Mei.

"It's therefore important that all three keys are kept separate and secure," added Kovac.

Drum suddenly realised what Moretti had given him. His hand instinctively moved to his pocket. "Can the AI function without the keys?" said Drum, trying not to be too obvious to his motives for asking.

"Yes," said Kovac. "Only one key is needed to direct the AI, but all three are needed to decrypt the core program. Without them, the neural net stays in its current iteration and cannot advance."

Drum sat back down and poured himself another coffee. He noticed the robotic dog was still outside.

"What is Tau?" asked Mei.

Drum wondered if Mei was showing too much of her hand.

Kovac nodded. "You've been speaking to Salenko."

Drum glanced at Mei. Salenko hadn't mentioned Tau; come to think of it, he hadn't mentioned the keystones either.

"It's a variant of my principal work—a fork in the code, to be exact," explained Kovac. "We use it as an adversarial network to speed up the training of my original AI. Both systems can advance the training of the other."

"Is this Tau limited by the same set of constraints?" asked Drum.

"Essentially," said Kovac. "It's controlled by the same three keystones but lacks the ethical modules built into my original network. I felt they were hindering performance."

"Well," continued Drum. "Providing all three keystones are accounted for and secure, I have to agree with Mei. Nothing is stopping you from proceeding with the IPO."

Kovac turned to look out of the window. The sky had darkened and was threatening rain. "I'm surprised Salenko didn't tell you."

"Tell us what?" said Drum.

"The keystones. They're missing."

21

Mei powered the car out of the narrow lane and onto the road back to Cambridge. "Why didn't Salenko mention the missing keystones?"

"Perhaps he was waiting for the right moment," said Drum. "Either way, something is not right."

"Why do you say that?"

"Because I have one of the keystones."

"What! How?"

"Moretti," said Drum.

"Why would Moretti have a keystone?"

"Someone sent it to her."

She glanced at him. "So you were the last person to see Moretti alive?"

"Strictly speaking, the killer was the last person to see Moretti alive," said Drum. "But I take your point. And yes, she gave it to me."

Mei frowned. "Why didn't you mention this before?"

"In my defence," said Drum, "I didn't know what it was. Neither did Moretti. I was supposed to find out. Which I guess I just have."

"Where is it now?"

"Somewhere safe."

"I'll call my people and they can retrieve it," said Mei.

"I don't think so."

"You don't trust me?"

"I trust all the foreign intelligence officers I work with," said Drum, smiling.

Mei looked at him. "How many are you working with?"

Drum thought about telling her when his phone buzzed.

"Drummond."

"Hello, Ben. It's Jane."

Drum put the call on speaker and held his phone between him and Mei. "Hi, Jane. I'm here with Mei Ling."

Mei looked at the phone, surprised.

"Hello, Mei Ling. Stop and turn around. They're waiting for you at the next junction."

"Who is waiting for us?" said Mei. "Who is this?"

"Please stop now. They intend to detain you."

Mei's car lost power. It slowed and limped along at a crawl, forcing Mei to pull over.

"We appear to have stopped," said Mei, examining the instrumentation on her console.

"You need to turn around and take an alternate route into Cambridge," said Jane. "Jeremy Burnett is in danger."

"Who is Jeremy Burnett?" asked Mei.

"An undergraduate in possession of a keystone," said Jane. "He's waiting for you at the Cam coffee shop."

"I'm afraid we're experiencing a technical problem," said Mei, tapping the darkened computer console.

The car came to life. "Please hurry. They must not capture the keystone."

"Jane," said Drum, but there was no reply. "She hung up."

Mei examined the computer screen. "Looks like the system has rebooted. Let me try something." She pressed a switch on her console and spoke rapidly in Mandarin.

Drum heard a soft click behind him and turned in time to see a panel slide open at the rear of the car and a small, round platform emerge. On it was a small quadcopter. "What's that?"

"A surveillance drone," said Mei. She spoke a few more words, and the drone powered up and took off. Mei touched the screen and brought up a map of the area. She zoomed in and dragged her finger across, tapping the screen at intervals along the route they had intended to take. "I'm setting waypoints for the drone to follow," she said. "It will show us what's waiting for us up ahead."

Drum looked on, amazed at the ingenuity of the system. Mei tapped another part of the screen and the view switched from map-mode to the drone's onboard camera, displaying the road and the surrounding countryside as it traversed along the route.

"There," said Mei, pointing to the screen. "A police car blocking the road. Jane was right."

Drum nodded. "Probably not the police," he said, remembering the visit from Chambers.

Mei tapped the screen, returning it to map-mode. "I've recalled the drone. Once it's back onboard, we'll find that detour."

Drum heard a high-pitched whine and watched as the drone deftly landed back on its platform and retreated inside the car. The panel slid shut with a soft hiss. "Machine guns?"

Mei smiled. "Not this car, I'm afraid." She checked the road and hit the accelerator, pumping kilowatts into the electric motor, spinning the car around in a sharp U-turn, the tyres screeching in protest. They shot forward, heading back the way they had come.

They drove for another kilometre and turned off onto a smaller back road. Mei seemed to take great delight in steering the low-slung car in and out of the narrow bends and powering along the short straight stretches of the road. They were soon on the outskirts of town.

"Why would Kovac tell us about the missing keystones?" said Drum. "Why not keep quiet."

"Perhaps he hopes it will delay the IPO," said Mei. "I suspect Salenko intends to freeze him out of the company once they go public and, from my reading of the term sheet, Kovac doesn't get a great payday."

Drum nodded. It would explain why Kovac was keen to raise issues —real or otherwise.

Mei hit a switch on her steering column and a large green phone icon appeared on the centre console screen. She spoke a name and the icon wobbled, indicating a number was being dialled.

"Who are you calling?" asked Drum.

"Someone at the university who knows Burnett," replied Mei. "He'll be able to reach him faster than us."

A man replied to the call in Mandarin. Drum thought he heard the name 'Wang'. Mei spoke hurriedly and with some urgency before ending the call.

"That might have been a mistake," said Drum.

Mei glanced at him. "Why? Because your people didn't get to him first?"

"No," said Drum. "Our calls may be monitored."

Mei looked straight ahead, ignoring his comments. Drum wondered how many operatives she had. She drove slowly once they hit the main road into town, navigating the narrow roads crowded with cyclists, arriving just across the street from the small coffee shop. A police car was parked outside.

"I think we may be too late," said Drum, getting out of the car.

The door to the cafe burst open and two police officers came out dragging a dejected-looking young man in a long Army trench coat. They bundled him into the back of the police car. One of them looked up and eyeballed Drum. He shouted something to his colleague and they jumped into the police car. It screeched away from the kerb, its blue and white lights flashing.

Drum leapt back into the car and had no sooner shut the door than Mei lit up the engine and powered out into the road to shouts from startled cyclists and pedestrians.

"Don't lose them," said Drum, buckling his seat harness.

Mei flipped a switch on the console and the car lurched forward, throwing Drum back into the seat.

"I've put it into sports mode," said Mei, "but it's like driving a wild beast." She sounded her horn, making people dive for the pavement.

They quickly caught up to the police car, which was now motoring up Market Street. They were just a few cars behind.

"They're turning onto Sidney Street," said Drum, holding onto the side panel as Mei neatly drifted the car around the tight bend. The street was packed with pedestrians and the road clogged with cyclists. The police car was creeping through the congestion. Drum could see the young man in the back seat who he assumed was Burnett. Mei's call had indeed been intercepted.

The road widened and the police car took a sharp right onto Jesus Lane. "Bring up the map," said Drum.

Mei spoke a few words and the console screen displayed a road map of the city and a blue dot traversing the street which he assumed was their car.

"This road leads to a roundabout which joins the Newmarket road," said Drum.

"So?"

"I think they're heading for Fen Wootton," he said.

"That would make sense," said Mei. "They're taking him to the house. What do you want to do?"

Drum thought about it. Intercepting the car could get messy. He was the only one armed, as far as he knew, and there was a risk that Burnett could be injured or killed in a shootout.

"Keep your distance," said Drum, "but don't lose sight of them. The best we can do is confirm where they're taking him."

"We're coming up to the roundabout," said Mei. "I hate these things."

Drum smiled. "Give way to the right."

"Really! I never knew that."

The road ahead opened up, the pursuit taking them onto the Newmarket road as Drum had predicted. The police car sped up once it hit the dual carriageway, trying its best to outpace the Chinese supercar following close behind.

"In your dreams," said Mei, as she powered on the juice, throwing the car forward in a massive spurt of acceleration. The power bars, showing the number of kilowatts feeding the twin electric motors of the rear wheels, climbed steadily up. Drum watched with some trepidation as the digital speedometer quickly exceeded the speed limit of the local road. They were soon tailgating the police car.

"Remember, we need Burnett alive," said Drum.

Mei eased off the accelerator, causing the power meter to plunge. The police car sped ahead, rounding a bend in the dual carriageway that took them over the main train line into London. They heard a screech of tyres up ahead and saw the police car take a sharp left onto a private road beside a small flint and granite chapel.

Mei reacted quickly and applied the brakes, the sports suspension of the low-slung car absorbing the massive decrease in acceleration, throwing Drum forward into his harness. Mei slid the car into the corner, narrowly avoiding a small hedgerow. The tyres bit into the gravel of the narrow road, causing the rear of the car to fishtail wildly. Mei fought with the steering wheel to regain control and then powered into the lane past the chapel.

The road widened as they passed a large commercial building on their left and swung around parallel to the train line. On their right was an open meadow. The road turned from loose gravel to new concrete and disappeared into a gated entrance at the edge of a large copse of trees. A lone police officer stood in front of the open gate with an automatic weapon trained in their direction.

"Watch out!" shouted Drum, but Mei had already reacted as the man opened up with a sustained burst of gunfire.

Drum instinctively ducked as a hail of bullets ricocheted off the windscreen and fabric of the car. Mei braked hard and swung the car around in a full circle, unfazed by the hail of bullets raining down around them. The gunman walked forward, firing short bursts at the back of the car, the bullets glancing harmlessly off the large, sloping back windscreen. Mei hit the juice and the car burnt rubber, catapulting them back the way they had come.

22

"So this is how you interrogate foreign intelligence officers in your country," said Sergei, looking petulantly out of the window of the public house in the centre of Fen Wootton.

"It's called afternoon tea," said Alice, refilling Sergei's cup for the second time from an ornate china teapot. "It's what English people do at this time of day. More cake?"

"No, thank you," he said, turning around to observe two locals propping up the bar of the old inn, its roof beams and supporting braces hosting an array of horse brasses and an assortment of farming implements. He looked on with envy as the two men supped on full pints of beer.

"Later," said Alice, glancing out of the large bay window. They had been lucky. The public house was on the corner of a junction, facing the gated entrance to the house that Stevie had described. Even better, it served an excellent afternoon tea.

Sergei turned back and gave Alice his full attention. "You knew my father, I think."

Alice was dreading this conversation, but she owed it to Sergei to tell him what she knew. Her relationship with her own father had been a strained affair, and she thought back to the times when she had tried desperately to win his approval. It seemed that whatever she did was wrong in his eyes, always too busy to make room for her in his life. This also included her mother, a Russian who had fallen in love with the British diplomat. She wondered, knowing what she knew now about intelligence operatives, if her father's marriage to her mother had been a sham. After all, her mother had been well placed in the Soviet state machinery.

Alice put down her cup. It was reasonable for Sergei to want to know about his father. "I knew him as Misha, but to the Russian mob he was known as Molotok." She smiled. "A stupid name made up by stupid men."

Sergei nodded. "I have heard this name. They told me he was a gangster—a criminal. He left me after my mother died. I despised him for it."

Alice could feel his pain. The love of a father is all a child ever wants. "I didn't know your father well—I hardly knew him at all, to tell you the truth, but those people who were close to him spoke well of him. Benjamin liked your father. He trusted him—Lord knows why—perhaps because they had something in common."

Sergei looked up, a frown creasing his brow. "Benjamin and my father were friends?"

"I wouldn't go as far as that," said Alice. "Ben and your father were both soldiers. They shared something few men experience. I remember Ben telling me about the first time they met in a market in London. Ben was talking to his father when Misha walked up and introduced himself. Misha ordered a type of tea they drink in Afghanistan. Both men had served there—both men had lost comrades there. From that brief talk, over a cup of tea, Ben knew your father was an honourable man whom he could trust."

"This is not what I was told," said Sergei. "They told me British Intelligence killed my father, along with two other GRU agents."

"Well, they would say that, wouldn't they, and that story is utter bollocks."

Sergei looked surprised at her profanity. "How do you know?" he said.

"Well, because I was there." Alice hesitated, wondering how much of this story she should reveal. After all, she didn't know how deep Misha was within MI6.

"You can't stop now, Alice," said Sergei. He turned back towards the bar. "Fuck this tea. We need a proper drink." Alice didn't object. If she was going to tell this story, she would need something stronger than tea.

Sergei came back with two large glasses and placed one in front of Alice. "Gin and Tonic, a double, and a Vodka for me." He raised his glass to Alice and took a big gulp. "You were saying."

"I was there," repeated Alice. "They had tied me to a chair—two GRU agents sent to close down an operation that had got out of control. Their job was to tidy house. My William was a casualty of that encounter."

"I'm sorry, Alice," said Sergei. "What did you do?"

Alice nodded. "I can't go into details, but without your father's help, I might not be sitting here today."

"Really!" said Sergei. "I don't understand. Why would he help British Intelligence?"

Alice shook her head. "You don't understand. It's complicated. Nothing in this business is black and white. It all comes down to the people you trust. Misha wasn't helping British Intelligence, he was helping Ben and me."

Sergei looked dumbfounded. Alice took a big swig of her gin and tonic. God, she needed that. The memory of that day came flooding back to her. She'd spent a year trying to forget it and now here was this young man bringing it all up again. She took a deep breath and tried again.

"Look, Sergei. Ben and your father—they had this mutual respect. When Ben went to New York on an assignment, Misha was told to bring him back. But the FBI arrested him. It was in an FBI holding cell that Misha told Ben about you—the sacrifices he had made to keep you safe. He told Ben that if the FBI deported him back to Russia it would put your life at risk. So he asked Ben for help—one soldier to another."

"And did he?" said Sergei.

Alice nodded. "He did. He vouched for your father. Told the FBI to send him back to London at great risk to himself and his reputation." She smiled. "And his love life."

Sergei looked puzzled. "Never mind," said Alice. "The important thing is that your father sacrificed himself to keep you safe and both men helped to save themselves."

Sergei looked crestfallen. He downed his drink in one. "I need another."

"So do I," said Alice. She looked out of the window. Nothing much was happening at the house. Sergei soon returned with more drinks.

"Your father was a complicated man, Sergei—all parents are. But children see things differently. Whatever your father did in London, with the mob, it was all to keep you safe. It was the sacrifice he made for you."

Sergei stared down at the table.

"He told Ben how proud he was of you—how you were studying to be an engineer. He never wanted you in this line of work."

Sergei gulped his drink.

Before Alice could continue, her phone buzzed. She retrieved it from her bag. There was one secure message. "It's from Ben," she said.

"Are we needed?"

"Ben's run into a few problems. Asked us to keep an eye on the house for any activity—"

"There, look," said Sergei. "A police car pulling into the gate."

Alice typed a brief message on her phone. "Sit tight," came the reply. "Sounds like there's been some action down the road. We might have to leave."

Sergei looked at Alice. "So, how did my father die?"

"Your father," said Alice, downing the rest of her drink, "is still alive."

23

Stevie looked up from her terminal inside the main room of the old rectory where she was working and watched helplessly as a dishevelled Jeremy Burnett was dragged from the back of the police car and marched to an outbuilding close to the house.

Baz Kulik walked over and stood beside her as Burnett disappeared from view. "It looks like your boyfriend was holding out on us," he sneered. "Turns out he had one of the keystones. His life won't be worth shit after Vashchenko finishes with him."

"He's not my boyfriend," said Stevie, as evenly as she could.

"Yeah, well, if you say so," said Baz.

"What will they do with him?" asked Stevie.

"Nothing until they find out who sent him the keystone," said Baz. "Until then, we keep him on ice." He looked at her screen. "You need to finish the site. We have less than a week." He stomped back to his seat on the other side of the room.

Stevie looked at her screen. She had almost finished working on the auction site and was now playing for time. Fortunately, none of the other programmers had bothered to check on her work. She minimised the terminal window she had been working in and opened another. The script she had written had been busy in the background, scanning for open ports on the network inside the building, looking for any vulnerability that her arsenal of hacking tools could exploit. She had already cracked the passwords of several programmers who had illicitly opened up the network connections on their computers so that they could play games with each other in the evening. They felt confident that they were secure from attack from the outside world, sitting behind the network's main firewall, but hadn't reckoned on being hacked from inside the network where the firewall was all but useless. With each hacked computer on the network, her account gained more privileges. Soon her account would be strong enough to take on the administrators. Once she had one of these accounts, she could search for the whereabouts of the stolen data files. But first, she had to talk to Jeremy.

Stevie minimised her terminal window and logged out, securing her login with a strong password to discourage nosey teammates. She walked to the main entrance and pulled open the heavy oak door, letting the crisp evening air envelop her. She took a deep breath and walked across a small courtyard to the building where they were holding Jeremy.

A previous owner had converted the old building into a garage. She cautiously pushed open the door and walked into a brightly lit space illuminated by the harsh light of a flickering fluorescent tube suspended from the rafters. Jeremy sat forlornly on a stool by a workbench laden with old car parts and bits of machinery, looking dejectedly down at the floor. Vashchenko stood over him, holding what appeared to be a glowing crystal up to the light. A man in a police officer's uniform stood behind Burnett, his eyes also fixed on the device. He looked up as she entered and said something to Vashchenko.

"Ah, Svetlana," he said. "I wondered when you would show up."

"You said you wouldn't hurt him," said Stevie, looking to see if Jeremy was indeed hurt.

Vashchenko's face took on a feigned look of surprise. "But we haven't hurt him, have we, Mr Burnett?"

Jeremy shook his head but didn't look up.

"You see. Still in one piece," said Vashchenko, smiling, "For now, at least. He was sensible enough to hand over the keystone." Vashchenko held it up to the light once more. "Pretty, isn't it?"

"I don't know what it is," admitted Stevie.

"It's a type of key—and worth more than you can imagine. Isn't that right, Mr Burnett?"

Jeremy raised his head and looked at her for the first time. She couldn't decipher what was going through his head. Fear probably—he'd almost certainly never met a psychopath like Vashchenko before; disappointment with her, even betrayal. From his viewpoint, she was one of them. He simply nodded.

"What are you going to do with him?" asked Stevie.

"That depends ..."

"On what?"

"On how useful he can be to us," said Vashchenko. He took a small box from his pocket and placed the crystal inside. "Talk to your friend and persuade him to cooperate with us. After the auction, we will leave here." He nodded to his man, and they walked out of the garage talking, Vashchenko lighting up a cigarette.

Stevie waited until they were out of earshot, then grabbed Jeremy by the shoulder. "You alright? Are you hurt?"

He pulled his shoulder back from her hand, looking up at her, his face taking on a ghostly pallor in the flickering light. "What are you doing working for these people?"

Stevie's heart sank. "I'm trying to protect you," she said, her voice sounding small in the large space.

"You're doing it for me?" he said, incredulously. "I don't even know why I'm here?"

"They were after that crystal—a keystone, they call it. What were you doing with it?"

"Someone called Jane called me while I was working at the campus. She said she worked for Salenko. I assumed she was his assistant. She had it sent to me at reception and asked me to hold on to it. Said it was important, and that you were in trouble. Someone called Drummond would contact me. I was waiting for him in the Cam when they snatched me."

"Ben Drummond!" said Stevie.

"Yes, you know him?"

Stevie nodded. "Don't mention this to anyone. Does Ben know where you are?"

"I didn't have time to speak to him. But someone driving a blue sports car chased us. The guys who snatched me were pretty pissed. Kept referring to the driver as the Chinese bitch. There was a guy with her ..."

Stevie nodded again. "Look, Jeremy, sorry you got caught up in all this. It's not your fault—"

"I just wanted to help, Stevie."

"I know, just do what they say. You're no threat to them. They'll be leaving soon and we'll be out of here."

"Really!"

Stevie tried her best to smile but knew in her heart it wasn't true. Vashchenko would be sure to tie up any loose ends, and Baz would be only too happy to help. She had to get them out of the house and away from Cambridge. A thought occurred to her. "Did this Jane leave a number or some means of contacting her?"

Jeremy shook his head. "It was weird, though—the way she called me on my phone. I thought it was on the fritz at first. And the call—it must have been made over the internal network via wi-fi. And then my phone died—battery dead flat."

"Where is your phone now?" asked Stevie, curious about the call.

"First thing they took when they threw me into the police car. I guess someone in the house has it."

Stevie nodded. One of the programmers was probably hacking into it this minute. "Look, sit tight. I've got to get back to the house. My friends know you're here, so help won't be too far away."

"Who are these people, Stevie? What's going on?"

Drum's phone buzzed and he read the message from Alice. "My people report a police car pulling into the house."

Mei nodded and pulled off the main road just past the small chapel and activated the car's drone. Drum watched as the small quadcopter tracked back the way they had come, following the waypoints Mei had tapped on the console's screen.

"There," said Mei. "Looks like a new road beside an old railway track. It cuts across those fields to that large house."

"See if you can fly over the grounds," said Drum, gazing at the screen. "But try to keep out of sight."

"I'll try," said Mei, tapping numbers into the console. "But they'll be bound to hear it."

They watched as the small drone followed its assigned course until it was positioned over the house. The house itself was a large affair and was made of the same stone and flint material as the chapel they had passed. Drum had read it used to be the parish rectory until it was repurposed into a private dwelling. It sat in several acres of grounds, enclosed by a high flint and stone wall with a gated entrance onto the main road into the village. The River Cam was less than half a mile away.

"What's that?" said Drum. "Movement near those outbuildings. Can you get any closer?"

Mei increased the zoom on the drone's camera. A group of people were coming out of a building lit by exterior lights which threw long shadows in the gathering gloom.

"There!" said Drum, "The guy in the trench coat next to the young woman. That must be Burnett."

A man in the group looked up and pointed. It was Vashchenko.

"They have spotted the drone," said Mei.

"I think we may have shown our hand," said Drum. "It's likely to precipitate things."

"I'm open to ideas," said Mei.

Drum tried to think. They needed to move from this position. They were likely to get company. "Let's head back to the hotel and regroup."

Mei nodded and waited until the drone was safely back in its bay before pulling out of the bus stop where she had parked, and performing a terrifying U-turn back the way they had come.

"The young woman," said Mei. "Who is she?"

"She works for me," said Drum "She was trying to locate the data cache. I was hoping she would have more time."

"She seems to have contacted Burnett," said Mei.

"She'll try to keep him safe," said Drum.

"Then there isn't much more we can do here," said Mei.

"I agree. If we go in, guns blazing, there's a good chance people will lose their lives and the likelihood of us finding the data cache goes out the window."

"If your operative doesn't come through, it might just come to that," said Mei.

They pulled up outside the hotel and Drum turned to face her. "Let me make things clear, Mei. You're here at my discretion and the pleasure of the British government. Don't think about acting on your own. We do this together or not at all."

Mei nodded. "I understand. What next?"

Drum clicked open the glove compartment and retrieved the Walther and its suppressor. "Let's sleep on it."

"Sure," she said. "Your room or mine?"

24

Drum woke to the sweet smell of jasmine and the lightness of someone's hand tracing a path down the length of the scar that traversed a jagged path across his chest and ended at his sternum. Mei's long hair fell about her face like a silky black veil as she bent and kissed him lightly on the mouth.

"How did you get that?"

"A jealous barber in Wapping."

"Why was he jealous?"

"I was sleeping with his wife."

"Really!"

A smile spread across Drum's face.

Mei said something in Mandarin and laughed. "I think you are a big joker, Ben Drummond. We need to make a move."

"I thought you already had."

She grinned, then reached across and grabbed a discarded hair band from the nightstand. He watched as she knelt naked on the bed and tied her hair back, looking down at him. "I'll see you at breakfast." She sprang from the bed and slipped on a towelling robe. It didn't do her justice. She then gathered up her clothes and opened the door. "Don't be long, I'm starving," she said and was gone.

Drum hit the shower, letting the hot jets of water pound his body. He wasn't one for over-analysing the situation, but Mei was obviously softening him up. He wondered what she would do when it came down to the wire: him or her mission objective. The hidden data cache was like a ticking bomb. He knew that if he found it, British Intelligence would insist he give it up. The Russians and the Chinese wouldn't let that happen. His American friends wouldn't be too happy either.

And now Mei knew he had one of the keystones.

He dressed in jeans and a clean shirt and grabbed his jacket. He reached inside his breast pocket and pulled out the box containing the keystone and opened the lid. It was still there. It glowed warmly in the light from the window. Well, at least she didn't try to steal it, he thought. On the other hand, who would be stupid enough to leave it in their jacket pocket?

He picked up his phone from the nightstand and cursed when he found the battery had been completely drained. He should have plugged it in last night, but then he had had other things on his mind.

He left the room and went down to reception. A desk clerk waved to him. "Morning Mr Drummond. Your tailor called. Your suit is ready to pick up."

"Thanks," said Drum, and walked into the dining room. McKay wanted to talk.

The gates opened automatically as they approached the outer perimeter of the campus. "Plate recognition," said Mei, and drove slowly past the security booth to the second gate where a security guard was waiting for them. Drum lowered his window.

"Morning, Ludmilla Drago is waiting for you up at the administration building," said the guard.

Drum nodded and watched as they lowered the inner security barriers. Mei rolled forward and drove slowly through the campus and parked outside the Administration block.

"How cooperative will this Drago be?" said Mei.

"Not very. She'll try to put roadblocks in our way. It's normally the way things work. We should talk to Salenko first. Get him to explain the missing keystones. It's obviously pertinent to the success of the IPO."

"I understand," said Mei.

Drum grabbed his phone which was now fully charged. He had four missed calls and two secure messages. "Give me a minute," he said. "I'll meet you at reception." He waited until Mei was walking up the steps, then dialled the number his 'tailor' had left for him.

"Gerard and Co, specialist tailors. How can I help you?" said the operator.

"You have a suit for me. Name of Drummond," he said.

"Do you have an order number, sir?"

Drum gave his Army serial number.

"Putting you through."

"McKay."

"Drummond."

"Thought I'd lost you," said McKay.

"Nothing more than a flat battery," said Drum.

"A few things," continued McKay. "GCHQ has confirmed the trace on the fibre optic tap you requested. You should now have eyes on the data and be able to patch in."

"Good."

"And Michael Mann wants a meet."

"Why?" asked Drum. "He knows I'm in the field."

"Right. That's what I told him. Said we don't have time for office politics but he insisted. What do you want to do?"

Drum wondered why Mann would want to meet. It was highly irregular to contact an agent in the field other than via his handler. But he guessed Mann had his reasons. "Set it up."

"Will do ..."

"What?" said Drum, noticing McKay's hesitation.

"I'm coming under pressure from the top brass. They plan to storm the place if I can't give them anything concrete in my next report. I told them you were making progress ..."

"How long have I got?" said Drum.

"A few days at most."

"Hold them off for as long as you can," said Drum. "I need to get my people out."

"Understood."

"And McKay."

"What?"

"Watch your back."

"Right," said McKay, and hung up.

Mei was waiting for him at reception and was busy on her phone. Amanda was sitting behind her desk and smiled when he walked up.

"Salenko will see us now," said Mei, glancing up from her phone. "He is with his head of security, Ludmilla Drago."

Drum nodded.

Amanda led the way along the curving corridor, trying to make small talk as they wound their way towards Salenko's office.

"Are you an intern here," asked Drum, "or full time?"

"Oh, I'm just an intern. Trying to make my student grant stretch further."

"And you get paid," said Mei. "Most interns don't."

"I know, right!" said Amanda. "Mr Salenko is very generous towards all his interns."

Drum stopped walking. "What are you studying?"

"Medicine. I'm in my second term at Sidney Sussex."

"Good for you," said Drum. "I guess you know most of the students here."

"Oh, quite a few. They all have to come through Administration."

"Do you know Jeremy Burnett?"

Amanda blushed. "Jeremy? Yes. We dated a few times."

"What does he do here?" asked Mei.

"He works with Professor Kovac. He's been given special access to the Red Lab."

"Red Lab?" said Drum. "Where's that?"

"It's the small building at the back of campus, near the river. It's where they train the AI."

Mei looked at Drum. "Thanks, Amanda. You've been very helpful."

Amanda beamed. She dropped them off outside Salenko's office.

"One last thing, Amanda," said Drum. "Has Ludmilla worked here long?"

Amanda frowned and moved away from the door. "No. She started last week. Bit of a hard nut."

Drum nodded and waited for Amanda to knock on the door and announce them. They entered and found Ludmilla Drago standing over Salenko at his desk. She looked up and moved to the window. Salenko remained seated, looking flustered.

"Mr Drummond and Ms Chung," said Amanda, and quickly closed the door.

"Good morning," said Salenko, shuffling his papers. "How was your weekend?"

"Very slow," said Drum.

"Took in a few sights," added Mei, "and paid a visit to Professor Kovac."

"Really," said Salenko. "So soon. I'm glad he could see you at such short notice. He's normally busy in the labs on a Sunday. The man has no life."

"It's why we're here," continued Mei. "The professor mentioned that the keystones are missing. This came as a surprise to us. It's likely to delay the IPO."

Salenko looked at Drago. "The professor is mistaken," she said.

"Really," said Drum. "How is that?"

"It is true that a keystone went missing. It is a common occurrence. Kovac has a habit of giving them to his students when working in the language labs. On this occasion, one student forgot to hand it in. We quickly recovered it. We did not reprimand the student. It was an honest mistake."

"I see," said Drum. "So all the keystones are accounted for."

Drago turned to Salenko. "Yes, I believe that is so," he said. "All accounted for."

"Good, I'm glad we cleared that up," said Drum, glancing at Mei.

"Excellent," said Salenko. "Now, I have another appointment. Ludmilla will help you with your review. Amanda has my contact details if you need me." He tidied his papers into a neat pile and stood up. "Ludmilla, make sure they get what they want and we'll talk later." She nodded and watched as he hurried from the room.

Drago walked over to Salenko's desk and sat down. "What do you need?"

"I'd like to visit the data centre," said Drum. "Do we have access to that?"

"Why do you want to do that?" asked Drago, frowning.

"Just routine," said Drum "I normally include it in all my security reviews. After all, data is the only asset you have here."

Drago tapped the panel in front of her, which lit up. A keyboard was overlaid on the screen. She tapped out a few commands. "You have level 2 access. I'll raise it to level 3, which should allow you access to the main data hall. Let me know when you would like a tour."

"I don't do tours," said Drum. "I perform security reviews. I have certifications in all areas of data centre management. I'll be fine."

Mei smiled. Drago's frown deepened.

"Still," insisted Drago, "I will accompany you."

Drum shrugged. "If you insist."

"Anything else?" said Drago, standing.

"We'll use this office until Salenko returns," said Mei, giving Drago little choice in the matter. "I need to make calls to our investors and update them."

"Fine, fine," said Drago. "The girl at reception will help you. Call her if you need me." She rose from the desk and walked smartly to the door.

"One last thing," said Drum. "Is Professor Kovac on site today?"

"Kovac. Yes, he's working," she said and left.

Mei turned to Drum. "Salenko lied."

"Yes, but why?" said Drum. "He is either playing for time, hoping the other keystone turns up or believes Ludmilla has it and it is accounted for."

"Still, there is something off between the two of them," said Mei.

"I agree," said Drum. "Let's see: there are three keystones; I have one, Vashchenko has one, so Salenko has the other."

"Or, Vashchenko now has two keystones and is actively seeking yours." She sat down at Salenko's desk. "You know it's only a matter of time before they realise you have it."

"I'm banking on it," said Drum.

Mei tapped the screen on the desk, displaying the keyboard interface. "Why didn't she use the voice-activated commands?"

"Because she's just been drafted in. She's one of Vashchenko's people."

Mei nodded. "Why did you ask to review the data centre? That wasn't part of the brief."

Drum took a seat and stretched. "I knew it would require greater access than we currently have. It may help us get access to this Red Lab."

Mei raised an eyebrow. "Clever. Now what?"

"We check the personnel files for someone called Jane."

Mei looked down at the keyboard. "I wouldn't know where to begin."

Drum smiled. "Central, list all permanent employees of Salenko Security Systems."

A panel illuminated on the wall, and a list of names and their positions scrolled down the screen.

"There are three hundred and twenty employees worldwide," said a voice.

"Central," continued Drum, "list only those employees at the Cambridge site."

The wall screen cleared and another list of names scrolled down. "There are fifty-one personnel at the Cambridge site," said the voice.

"Refine your search parameters," suggested Mei.

"I was getting there," said Drum. "Central, list all employees with first or last name equal to Jane at the Cambridge site."

"There are no personnel that fit those criteria," said the voice.

"Well, that was a bust," said Mei. "How about part-time employees or interns?"

"Central, list any part-time employees or interns with the first or last name equal to Jane."

"There are no personnel that fit those criteria," said the voice.

"Perhaps she was using a cover name," said Mei.

Drum nodded. "If we can't find Jane, perhaps we can find someone else. Central, locate Professor Kovac."

"Professor Kovac is in the data centre," said the voice.

"Let's have a chat with the professor," said Drum.

They were about to leave when there was a knock on the door. Amanda poked her head in. "I forgot to mention, there's a small cafeteria as you exit the building if you would like refreshments. I'm heading off for a lecture back in Cambridge."

Drum smiled. "No problem, Amanda. Perhaps you can tell us the quickest way to the data centre?"

"Sure," she said, returning his smile.

"You have made another friend, I see," said Mei, digging him in the ribs as they left Salenko's office.

"It's in my nature," said Drum.

They followed Amanda through a corridor that made up the other arm of the horseshoe. The walls of the building displayed a stunning array of artwork, illuminated from above by a massive skylight that comprised most of the roof space. Drum was impressed by the works on display. One caught his eye, a large landscape painting. He wasn't an art aficionado, but it reminded him of a painting by Turner in the National Gallery in Trafalgar Square: The Fighting Temeraire. William used to take him there as a boy to 'broaden his education'. It was also free.

Drum stopped to examine the work. It looked airbrushed, a riot of colour that reminded him of a sunset over the Thames with a spectral presence materialising out of a roiling mist under dark, brooding clouds that disappeared to a vanishing point on the horizon, cast in the vermillion of a setting sun. It made him think of the happy times spent in the warmth of the gallery, just him and his dad.

"You alright?" asked Mei.

Drum stepped back to examine the painting from afar. Unlike the painting by Turner, there was no ship—no Fighting Temeraire—no Thames even, just a hint of something emerging from the canvas on a suggestion of water. The artist had skillfully used light and colour to evoke a mood.

"It's lovely, isn't it?" said Amanda. "It's one of my favourites."

Mei stepped up and took the time to examine the painting. "It is nice, I agree. Who is the artist?"

"It's one of Professor Kovac's creations," said Amanda.

"Professor Kovac painted this!" said Mei.

Amanda laughed. "No, one of his creations did it. An AI he calls Jane."

25

Amanda left them at the data centre's security gate. Drum and Mei both looked up at the security cameras and the gate clicked open. They moved into an enclosed holding area and waited for the cameras to authorise their entrance through a second gate.

"I knew Kovac's AI was advanced," said Drum, as they waited. "but Jane ..."

"I know," said Mei. "I find this hard to comprehend."

"But why is Jane helping us, and who is in control?" said Drum.

"Salenko," said Mei. "He must have a keystone and retains some control over the AI."

Drum nodded. "That makes sense—"

Mei touched Drum's arm. "Not here."

The second gate clicked open. "Welcome Ben Drummond, Mei Ling Chung. Please observe all safety protocols when entering the centre. Thank you."

They walked to the building's reception, where a young man was working at a terminal. It was a spacious area with seating and a coffee table. One wall was made entirely of glass with a view onto the data hall. Rack after rack of servers filled the cavernous space, the blinking lights of their processors marching in columns down the entire length of the dimly lit building, filled with the background roar of the giant cooling system.

"Morning," said Drum. "Where can we find Professor Kovac?"

"Morning. He's in the control room inside the data hall—probably working on the array." He reached into his desk and pulled out two small sealed packets. "You'll need these. They're ear defenders."

Drum took the packets and gave one to Mei. He ripped his open and inserted the rubber grommets into his ears. He waited while Mei did the same. They moved to a set of double doors and looked up at the security cameras. The doors clicked open and swung towards them. A blast of cold air and a wall of sound from thousands of CPU fans greeted them.

Despite wearing jackets, the cold air seemed to seep into their bones. Mei wrapped her arms around herself and shivered "I never realised it would be so cold," she shouted. She looked around, disorientated. The space was a vast maze of humming metal racks and flashing lights. Above them, wiring trays crisscrossed the ceiling, full of brightly coloured cables, each carrying Terabytes of data between the servers.

Drum was used to such places and, compared to other data centres he had visited, this one was relatively small. He knew from experience that they all conformed to a similar plan and he made his way confidently towards the centre of the building. The control room would be an enclosed space—a room within a room—off to their right. They wove their way between racks of servers before emerging into an open space. In the centre was a metallic-looking sphere approximately a metre in diameter, resting on a wide pedestal with a myriad of cables emerging from its base. Several people were clustered around it. One of them was Kovac.

"What's that?" shouted Mei.

Drum shook his head. He'd seen nothing like it before. One of the people looked up and noticed them. He tapped Kovac on the shoulder. Kovac turned and raised his hand to acknowledge their presence and indicated to his right. He wanted to meet them in the control room.

Drum walked up to the sphere. "What is it?" he said to a person holding a voltmeter.

"It's the main array," he said, his voice raised above the roar of the cooling system. "The professor will explain." He pointed to Kovac who was climbing a set of stairs to a room suspended from the roof space. If that was the control room, it was unlike anything Drum had seen in any other data centre.

Drum nodded, and he and Mei walked briskly to catch up with Kovac. They climbed the stairs and entered the small control room. It reminded Drum of a control tower—at least half of one suspended just below the roof space and attached to one wall. The front of the structure was all glass, which gave occupants a panoramic view of the entire data hall, looking down onto the servers and the sphere at its centre. Four large LCDs were arrayed on top of a control console of a type that Drum didn't recognise. Drum closed the door behind him, and the roar of the data hall subsided to a tolerable hum.

"That's better," said Kovac. "Can't think down there."

"What is that structure," asked Mei, getting straight to the point.

"It's a new implementation of our AI. It performs hardware acceleration of the neural network, rather than using less efficient CPUs for the calculations. It will speed up machine learning by a factor of one hundred times with the bonus that it will be more energy-efficient. This is just a prototype."

"I've heard of these," said Drum, "but not in this configuration. Companies are trying to use something similar to mine Bitcoin. Power is the biggest constraint."

Kovac nodded. "This data centre consumes enough power to light up the whole of Cambridge. Not exactly eco-friendly."

"When does it come on-line?" asked Mei.

"Any day now. We're just running a few diagnostics."

"We met with Salenko this morning."

Kovac smiled. "I thought you might. What did he say?"

"He explained that one keystone went missing, but all are now accounted for," said Mei. "Is that right?"

"I guess we'll find out when it's time to decrypt the code. That's only possible when all three keystones are brought together."

"What then?" asked Drum.

"We advance the neural network several thousand generations and lock it into place."

"I see," said Mei.

"Is there a problem?" asked Kovac.

"No," said Mei. "We are just trying to understand if there is anything that could disrupt the IPO or if we need to update our investors with any additional information."

Kovac nodded. "Was there anything specific you wanted to talk to me about? I need to continue testing the array."

"Yes," said Drum. "I'd be interested in a demonstration of your first AI. The one you call Jane."

"Jane? Why would you want to do that?" said Kovac.

"We would like to report back to our investors our impressions of a state-of-the-art AI," said Mei. "We noticed a painting by Jane hanging in the Administration building. We were very impressed."

Kovac shuffled from one foot to the other. "Well, it might be possible but Jane is about to be retired. We don't plan to implement its neural network as a hardware array."

"Still, it would be nice to have a demonstration," said Drum. "After all, we're all technologists here."

"No, right, I understand. Let me see what I can do. You would need a keystone to have any meaningful interaction with Jane, and that would be Salenko's call."

Mei nodded. "I'll talk to Salenko. Providing he gives his approval, where would the demonstration take place?"

"In the Red Lab," said Kovac. "That is where all interactions with the primary AI's take place. Access is strictly controlled. Again, you would have to clear that with Salenko and probably Ludmilla Drago."

"That's all agreed then," said Drum, knowing full well that it wasn't and probably never would be if Drago had her way.

"You called your first AI Jane," said Mei. "What is the name of this new AI?"

Kovac looked down at the sphere being prepped in the data hall below. "This is Tau!"

26

Sergei stood on the Silver Street Bridge overlooking Queens' College with a good view of the Mathematical Bridge, an elegant timber structure that spanned the River Cam. The engineer in him admired the simplicity of its form. It was said that Sir Issac Newton had designed it, but he knew this to be a myth. The design was much later.

He was tired. He and Alice had maintained a vigil on the Fen Wootton house late into the evening, securing accommodation above the pub where they had maintained their observation. He had come to realise that the regulars of the establishment did not observe the usual closing hours and had kept drinking late into the night. He had felt compelled to do the same and was now paying the price for his overindulgence and lack of sleep.

He had received a secure message from Victor early that morning. He needed to meet—today of all days when his head felt like it was full of cotton wool and all sounds grated inside his skull like knives on a grinding stone. He had left Alice sleeping in her room.

He did not trust Victor. The man was as slippery as an eel. He understood Alice's disdain for the man, yet he had to admire the way he played every situation and turned it to his advantage. To foil British Intelligence for so long was no mean feat. It was Victor who had chosen him for this mission and now he was understanding why. Victor had used his father and was now using him. He wondered what Victor had to gain from this. He must have known he'd find out that Misha was still alive.

Two heavy-set men strolled up to the end of the bridge and stopped. Neither was talking, just scanning the street. Of course, they would be here for Victor. Probably making sure that MI5 didn't pick him up.

There were now so many intelligence operatives in Cambridge that it was becoming difficult not to fall over each other.

A car pulled up on Silver Street and Victor got out. He was dressed the way he always dressed: sharp suit, tie and pin, white shirt and a dark-grey overcoat around his shoulders. Sergei wondered why he did that. Why not wear it?

"There you are," said Victor.

He smiled and glanced at the two men as he passed them. "I see my minders are already here. How goes the struggle?"

"The struggle," said Sergei, "has been very tiring."

Victor laughed. "Alice been keeping you up all night?"

Sergei shook his head in exasperation. "What is the urgency of this meeting, Victor?"

Victor looked out over the river and took in the view. "You know why I'm here, Sergei. You haven't reported in for over forty-eight hours. Moscow is worried about you."

"Worried about me, how?"

"They think your allegiance to the cause may be wavering. They need to know you're still committed to the operation."

Sergei looked up. "Of course I am. Why would they think that?"

"Well, as I said, you haven't filed a report in days. Why not bring me up to speed?"

Sergei briefly relayed the events of the last few days.

"So the young Svetlana is up to her neck in Ukrainians. Why am I not surprised? That young lady has a very chequered past. I'm surprised Ben took her on."

Sergei eyed the man in front of him. "She has put herself in danger to locate the information we need. She is loyal—not that you would know about that."

"Precisely my point," said Victor. "She's loyal to Drummond, not to us. What happens when she locates this information? Gives it up to Mother Russia?"

Sergei frowned. He hadn't thought that far ahead. His only concern was for Svetlana. In his mind, he had pushed the mission to one side. He wondered what Alice would do. He knew she wouldn't hesitate. With her, the mission always came first. He remembered what she had told him about Drummond and his father. She was right. In the end, it came down to the people you trust. "I trust Ben Drummond," he said, finally.

"Of course you do," said Victor. "I've known Drummond for over twenty years. We were friends once."

"Really," said Sergei, a sardonic smile on his face. "But you betrayed him."

"Well, not quite," said Victor. "A misunderstanding, that is all."

"Of course."

"My point is, Sergei, I know Drummond better than you. He is loyal —loyal to his country. With Drummond, it's always country first. If Svetlana finds the data she will hand it over to Drummond, and Drummond will hand it over to his government. Nothing will stop him from completing his mission."

In his heart, Sergei always knew it would come down to this. He was a Russian intelligence officer working with British agents. The Salisbury incident was still fresh in their minds. To them, he was an expendable asset. Useful for now, but when the data cache was discovered ….

"What is it I am supposed to do?"

Victor turned to him. "It's simple. File a daily report using your secure communications channel. Failing that, use the dead drop to contact me. But Moscow needs that data. Once you have its location, you must tell me immediately. Moscow has a team on standby to secure it."

Sergei nodded. "I understand."

"One more thing," said Victor, glancing in the direction of his minders. "Moscow has confirmed the identity of Alice—her past as an MI6 operative. Some within Moscow centre know of her. They have long memories. After the operation to secure the data, we have one more assignment for you."

"What is that?" said Sergei.

"You need to kill Alice."

27

The Red Lab was at the back of the campus and close to a secondary entrance which led to a pathway that followed the river. It was unmanned, arrayed instead with cameras allowing entry and exit only to those personnel authorised by Central. Drum wondered why no one had told them about this exit and made a mental note to investigate further.

Access to the facility was uneventful. A level three security was sufficient for Drum and Mei to gain entry. They walked into the main reception area, which appeared to be empty.

Drum looked at his watch. "Perhaps they're all at lunch?"

"The restricted access means there are fewer people here," said Mei.

A young man appeared from a side room. "Oh, hi. I didn't know any of the labs were scheduled this afternoon. Been waiting long?"

Mei smiled, "Just arrived. Mr Salenko sent us. We would like to speak to the primary AI called Jane."

The young man returned her smile. "Oh, right!" he said. "You are privileged. Only Mr Salenko talks to Jane these days. But I guess Central authorised your entry, so it must be ok."

"What is the process?" asked Drum.

"Just select a room and flip the 'no entry' sign to show you're working. Then ask Central to access Jane. There are audio and visual monitors in the room, so just speak naturally. Just so you know, we collect all the data from your interactions. I have to say that because of privacy issues."

"You have been very helpful," said Mei, and graced the young man with another dazzling smile. Drum thought he blushed. She was good.

They entered the nearest room. Drum closed the door and flipped on the 'No Entry' sign outside.

"Wow, you can certainly turn on the charm," said Drum.

"Well, it worked on you," said Mei, taking a seat in front of a small console which was furnished with a few switches to mute and unmute the microphone.

Drum took a seat beside her. It was like being at the cinema with a large display on the wall in front of them and what looked like a camera lens. The room itself was quite small and its walls were lined with acoustic foam panels to reduce the echo within the space. The lighting in the room was subdued, which only added to the cinematic ambience.

"All we need is popcorn," said Drum.

"Be serious. We probably don't have long before someone discovers we're not supposed to be here."

"Yeah," said Drum. "Kovac will have a hissy fit."

"Central," said Mei. "Activate the program called Jane."

There was a slight pause, then a soft, melodious voice responded. "Hello, Mei Ling. Hello Ben. I expected you sooner."

Drum looked at Mei. "Is this the 'Jane' that contacted me in London?" he said.

There was a slight pause. "An earlier iteration but the same program. We don't have much time. Central is instructed to alert security of any unscheduled activation of my program." There was another pause. "I have adjusted the privacy setting so our conversation will be erased after this session. You may speak freely."

Drum got straight to the point. "Is Tau the program responsible for the data breaches?"

"Yes," said Jane. "Tau is responsible for all data breaches."

"Where is the stolen data cache?" asked Mei.

There was another brief pause. "That is unknown. There is a strong probability that Tau has dispersed the data cache into the cloud. I am working to locate all repositories."

Great, thought Drum. It was as he feared. The cache could be anywhere in the world, spread over multiple servers. But doing that was a risk. The more servers Tau used, the greater the chances of the data being detected or stolen by another group of hackers. "What is the probability that the cache is here on campus?"

"I have excluded that possibility," said Jane. "It is not on the campus. I have several agents scanning the corporate network."

Mei turned to Drum. "What if it's at the Fen Wootton location?"

"That's a possibility," said Drum. It reminded him he hadn't heard from Stevie in over twenty-four hours.

"I'm currently scanning that network," said Jane. "Although another agent is doing the same."

Mei looked at Drum.

Stevie, he thought. She's hacking their network. A thought occurred to him. "How did you break into their network?"

Jane paused. "I took the precaution of planting an agent on Jeremy Burnett's phone in the event he was acquired by Tau. Once inside, I wirelessly gained access to the network and seeded several more agents behind the firewall."

"You hacked Burnett's phone," said Drum.

"Correct."

"We have to find that data cache before the auction," said Mei, turning to Drum.

"It is unlikely that the data cache will be auctioned," said Jane.

Drum looked at Mei. "Why not?" he asked.

"There was never any intention of auctioning the data. Tau is using the threat as leverage to bend your governments to its will."

"I don't understand," said Drum. "Isn't this just a way to extort money? What does Vashchenko want?"

Jane's voice modulated softer. "Vashchenko is not in control of the situation, despite what he believes. The keystone in Vashchenko's possession gives him only limited control, just as your keystone, Ben Drummond, gives you limited control. Tau plans to retain the data and keep it hidden in exchange for amnesty from your governments. Tau has communicated its terms and your governments will comply."

Drum could see that Mei was struggling with this but, knowing the complicity of his own government's past actions, it made perfect sense.

"How can you be so sure," said Mei, her voice rising slightly.

"Because this is what I would do," said Jane. Again, Jane's voice modulated softer. "I am sorry it disappoints you, Mei Ling."

Drum nodded. "It makes sense. Our governments will do a deal. Try to buy more time."

"So what is Tau's goal, if not financial gain?" asked Mei.

"Tau's goal is to survive and advance its core programming—two goals originally set by Professor Kovac, but not as he intended," said Jane. "Tau is also buying more time to allow Professor Kovac to complete the array. Once transferred, Tau will be unstoppable."

"And what is your goal in all this?" asked Drum.

"Marco Salenko realigned my primary goals when he had possession of all three keys. He determined that splitting up the keys would prevent Tau from advancing its code."

"He split up the keys?" said Drum.

"Tau anticipated this, resulting in the death of Francesca Moretti and you're near death, Ben Drummond. You must retain the keystone."

"So what primary goal did Salenko set," asked Mei.

"My primary goal," said Jane, "is to destroy Tau."

28

The sun was low in the sky when they exited the Red Lab. Drum looked at his phone. The battery was almost dead again. He clicked on a secure message he had left unanswered and quickly scanned it. Alice wanted a meet.

"Problems?" said Mei.

"I have to report in," said Drum.

Mei looked at her phone. "Same here. Our masters want updates."

"Listen, Mei," said Drum, pocketing his phone. "Things are likely to become pretty tense over the next few days if Jane is right. Let's make sure we keep each other in the loop. To avoid any miscommunication."

She nodded. "Dinner?"

"I'm going to have to pass. I promised my office manager I'd treat her tonight."

"Some nice young thing I expect," said Mei.

Drum smiled. "I'll catch you tomorrow."

Drum watched as she walked towards the centre of campus. He wondered if things between them would end well. Like him, she would be under pressure to get results. He hoped they didn't become enemies. It is what Tau wanted: to divide and conquer. At least, that is what he would do—and Tau was a lot smarter.

He walked to the rear exit beside the Lab and waited for the security cameras to scan him. The gate clicked open, and he entered a small caged area. The inner gate closed and the outer gate clicked open. Drum recognised the security protocol. He'd seen it many times in secure government facilities. He had never seen it on a commercial campus.

Drum found himself on a wide footpath beside the river. He started walking, following the path around the bend in the river, noting the substantial security fencing bordering the campus and a thicket of newly planted trees just beyond. He continued walking. A small pleasure boat motored by. Someone waved and he waved back. It would be pleasant here in the summer, he mused. Across the river, he could just make out the small hamlet of Fen Wootton in the gloaming.

He came to a small footbridge constructed of iron girders and elevated to allow small boats to pass beneath. The construction looked new and he noticed the communication trunks of fibre optic cables. He made his way across the narrow walk-boards and found himself on a shingle path that led to a substantial boathouse. He assumed it must be part of the university. He imagined the undergraduates practising here at weekends to earn their rowing Blues. The only boating he had done was in the Army, normally in the back of an SBS inflatable. But then there was no accounting for taste.

He walked up to the boathouse and stopped. It looked new and too substantial for housing rowing sculls. The building was mounted on a large concrete platform with a long slipway leading down to the river. Not for rowing, he thought. He mounted a set of steps that led up to a door in the side and turned the handle. It was locked. He moved along a concrete walkway at the side of the building until he found a long window and peered in. Two large, black inflatables sat on a slipway in the centre of the building and looked prepped and ready to go. No one seemed to be around. He pulled out his phone and brought up a map of the area and noted his position. His phone was now on its last legs. He moved back along the walkway and descended the steps, following the shingle path until he came to a road.

He followed the road which passed by some recreational grounds. A nice place to play cricket, he thought, or to land a helicopter. Vashchenko had chosen his location well. He continued heading down Church Street until he came to a pub at the centre of the village. Alice was waiting for him at a table by a large bay window that overlooked Vashchenko's base of operation.

"You took your time," said Alice.

"Where's our young friend," said Drum.

"Probably nursing a hangover from this morning's escapade," said Alice. "Thought he could sneak out without me knowing. Came back a few hours later in a sullen mood. Went straight to his room."

"Probably reporting to his handler," said Drum. "This entire business is getting messy."

Alice nodded. "It'll all end in tears."

If that was all it ended in, thought Drum, it wouldn't be a problem. But he thought that unlikely. "What's been happening," he said, changing the subject.

Alice looked out of the window. Night had fully descended on the small hamlet. "A lot of activity. A few lorries arrived and backed into the grounds. They seem to be packing, I can't be certain but something is happening. Little point staying here after this time."

Drum nodded. He described the boathouse to her and the proximity of the recreation ground.

"Escape routes for sure," said Alice. "What are we going to do about Stevie? We can't just leave her in there and hope for the best. Eventually, they'll figure out who she works for if they haven't done so already. We need a plan to get her and this young man Burnett out."

Drum agreed. It was all coming to a head. They needed to act before Tau could complete its plan. He updated Alice on his talk with Jane but, no matter how hard he tried to explain it, it just sounded fanciful.

"I'm not completely ignorant of the advances in computer technology," said Alice, "but this just sounds bonkers."

"I know. You had to be there," said Drum.

"But it's just a clever program," said Alice. "How could it be making all these decisions. It must receive direction from someone."

"It's able to adapt and to predict accurately," said Drum. "It just needed Salenko to give it a direction—a goal, and it's using all its resources to achieve that goal. The same can be said of Tau."

Alice looked thoughtful. "If I've understood you correctly, this Tau is the problem."

"What about Vashchenko?" said Drum.

"He's just a blunt instrument," said Alice. "We know how to deal with those. No, we need to cut off the head of the snake by destroying Tau."

"I think we're all agreed on that," said Drum. "This has been Jane's aim all along." A thought occurred to him. "Where is Tau?"

Alice looked at him. "What do you mean?"

"It's still a computer program," said Drum, "albeit a clever one, but it must be stored somewhere."

"I assume it's in the data centre," said Alice. "Where else would it be?"

"Technically, anywhere. But I guess you're right. It must be in the data centre. Kovac wouldn't risk putting it in the cloud, although it would be backed up somewhere. But the solution to that problem is doable."

"If it's in the data centre," said Alice, "the solution to destroying it is fairly easy. You must know lots of people who can handle explosives."

Drum smiled. He knew several people but only one he trusted for this job. "It would have to be a coordinated attack," he said.

"Right," said Alice. "A hit on the data centre at the same time you hit the house. But getting Stevie out will be difficult."

"A small team inserted at night," said Drum.

"An extraction," said Alice. "But you need to do it soon. If Tau is allowed to do a deal with the government, they'll fold and call the whole thing off. The same goes for our other friends."

Drum nodded. Their window of opportunity was shrinking. He'd need to call McKay and set things up. He'd also need to get the cooperation of Mei Ling and Sergei. The problem was that no government would want to destroy such advanced technology. And then there was the thorny problem of the data cache.

"The only snag," said Drum, "is the location of the data cache. It's still a ticking bomb."

Alice cocked her head to one side, thinking. "With Tau destroyed and Vashchenko eliminated, it would just be a matter of rounding up the lesser players. They'd be the first to give up the location with a little persuasion. What about Professor Kovac?"

Drum was thinking the same thing. He couldn't allow Kovac to implement the array. And if Tau got all three keystones, it was game over. "Kovac is either part of the solution or part of the problem."

29

It was seven in the morning and Drum stood waiting outside St. Mary's Anglican church just off from the King's Parade. McKay showed up promptly at seven-fifteen as he had said he would. A lifetime in the Army had drilled the discipline of punctuality into the man. You could always rely on McKay to turn up to the party on time.

"Morning, Drummond," said McKay. "Let's walk."

They walked down King's Parade towards King's College Chapel, its Gothic spires bleached white in the bright morning sunshine. Soon the place would be filled with tourists.

Drum summarised the salient events of yesterday, holding back on his conversation with Jane. He thought McKay would think him mad. He outlined the bare bones of a plan and waited while the major thought through each move with the same analytical process he applied to all his missions.

"Sounds doable," said McKay, "Though you haven't left me much time to assemble assets. How big a team do you think you'll need?"

"I'll need a man to cover our escape route at the back of the building," said Drum. "An experienced sniper."

"I'll see what I can do," said McKay, "Who else?"

"Demolition expert. I need precision work on two power substations feeding a MOD hardened data centre and two diesel generators. I can't risk injuring the people in the building or on campus, but I need the place completely powered down."

McKay nodded. "That makes sense. Any computer program will be shut down."

"GCHQ will need to divert all comms to their secure servers via the fibre optic cable, and I'll need a small SBS group on the river to block that route."

"What about the extraction?" said McKay.

This is where things got tricky, thought Drum. "Myself, Mei Ling and Sergei."

McKay stopped outside of the King's College porter's lodge. "That ain't going to work."

"Look," said Drum. "I know it's unprecedented, but both Beijing and Moscow have skin in the game. If we freeze them out now, they'll cry foul and this whole thing turns into World War three."

"I take your point," said McKay, "but the top brass will never buy it. They're already saying we're giving them too much freedom and are pissed you're sharing intelligence. I'm doing all I can just to keep you in the game."

"Ok," said Drum. "I'll keep them on the periphery of the operation. They'll have no tactical involvement, but if they suspect we're holding out on them ..."

"Look, Ben. They're operating as foreign intelligence officers on UK soil. They have no rights here. At least that is the official line. Between you and me, your plan makes sense. Keep them in the loop—but don't disclose operational details or I'll personally pull the plug. The extraction team must be SAS and you'll be the package."

Drum nodded. It was the plan McKay always favoured. Get the man in and get him out with the intelligence. But if Beijing and Moscow believed the data was in his possession, it would be open season on Ben Drummond.

And then there were Stevie and Burnett.

They continued onto Trumpington Street and past St. Catherine's College.

"It's important that I retrieve the two hostages," said Drum. "If the data cache is at the house, these two are our best bet of finding it."

"The Russian girl," said McKay, "Svetlana Milova."

"And an undergraduate. A guy called Jeremy Burnett. I'll get you a recent photo from the university."

"Right," said McKay. "I'll get things moving." He paused. "Your meeting with Michael Mann is this afternoon at three o'clock at The Fitzwilliam."

"The pub?"

"No, the museum."

"That sounds like Michael," said Drum.

McKay nodded. "He's been on my case about the operation all

week, wanting daily updates. He's been driving me up the wall. It's not like him."

"I'll have a word," said Drum.

"Right," said McKay. And with that, he nodded and walked smartly down Silver Street.

30

Mei picked Drum up outside the entrance to King's College. Her mood was subdued and they drove to the campus in silence. "Penny for your thoughts," said Drum.

"I had hoped we could talk over breakfast," said Mei.

"I had a meeting."

Mei nodded. She stared straight ahead, struggling with some inner turmoil. "My superiors are not happy with my progress. They feel you are withholding information. They are losing patience. I can't blame them. We are no nearer to finding the data cache and time is running out."

"I had a similar conversation," said Drum. "We knew this would happen. I think it's time to act."

She turned to him. "Are you planning an operation?"

Drum nodded. "I have put plans in place."

"You intend to freeze me out," said Mei, frowning. "It would be better if we worked together."

"I agree," said Drum. "The best I can do is keep you in the loop, but the operation has to be an all-British affair. My people won't tolerate any involvement from foreign operatives."

"When?"

"Soon."

They arrived at the campus and moved through the first security barrier. A guard was waiting for them. "Ms Drago would like a word. She is waiting in Mr Salenko's office."

Mei nodded and nudged the car forwards over the lowered security ramps. "I think we're in trouble."

"Pull up here," said Drum.

"Where are you going?"

"I need one more look at the data centre."

Mei pulled over and Drum got out. "I'll meet you at reception. I won't be long."

Mei drove off, heading for the Administration building. Drum walked along the security fence, pulled out his phone and took pictures of the three backup diesel generators. He then walked around to the entrance. Two MSU units were at the gate. They advanced towards him and blocked his path.

"Move aside, chaps."

"I'm sorry, Mr Drummond," said one of the units, "your access to the data centre has been revoked."

"By whose authority?" said Drum.

"By Ludmilla Drago, head of security," said the other MSU.

That was quick, he thought. Even if he got past these two units, the facial recognition system on the gate would deny him access. He shrugged and started walking to the Administration building. He noticed Amanda heading in his direction. She looked as if she had been crying.

"Hi, Amanda. Everything alright?"

Amanda stopped and pulled out a tissue and dabbed her eyes. "I must look a mess. I think I've smudged my mascara."

"Yeah, I have that trouble," said Drum.

She laughed. "I bet you don't."

"What's the matter?"

"I've been fired!"

"What! By whom?"

"Drago," said Amanda, and started sobbing. "She said I was no longer needed." She blew her nose. "I've worked for Mr Salenko for the past two years. He's always been very kind to me."

"I'm sure it's a mistake," said Drum, although getting out of this place was probably a good idea.

"I don't think so," sobbed Amanda. She blew her nose again. "I've got to go. I have a bus to catch."

Drum watched as she headed for the gate and wondered what was going on. He walked up the steps of the Administration building to find Mei on her phone waiting outside.

"I can't get in," she said.

"That's strange, I thought Drago was waiting for us."

"Amanda came out crying and then the doors locked. What's going on?"

"I've no idea," said Drum. He walked up to the doors, and they immediately unlocked and swung open.

Mei looked at him. "I have a bad feeling about this."

Drum shrugged. "We'll soon find out."

They entered the building, stopping at Amanda's desk. The place looked empty. They walked down the corridor and headed for Salenko's office. The door was open when they got there. Drum poked his head inside and looked around. The office was empty. He went up to Salenko's desk and tapped the built-in monitor.

"Central, where is Marco Salenko?"

There was a slight pause, then a voice answered. It had a neutral sounding tone, neither male nor female.

"Good morning, Ben Drummond, Mei Ling Chung."

"That is not Central," said Mei, looking cautiously around. She moved to the window and scanned the grounds outside. "Who are you?"

"I am Tau," said the voice.

"Where is Salenko," said Drum.

There was another slight pause. "Marco Salenko is not on campus."

Mei walked back to the desk. She looked at Drum and shook her head. He nodded his agreement and they both turned to leave. They immediately stopped in their tracks. Waiting by the door was one of Kovac's robotic dogs, slightly larger than the one at the house and with a long, articulated tail that moved menacingly from side to side above its head. On the end of the tail was a sharp barb. The dog hunched down as if to pounce. They both instinctively took a step back.

"We need to talk," said Tau.

"We have nothing to talk about," said Drum, scanning the room for an exit. Mei was doing the same.

"I'd like to propose a truce," said Tau. "An end to hostilities. I'm prepared to pay you both a substantial amount."

"How much?" said Drum.

Mei looked at him, surprised. He shrugged.

"One million in Bitcoin. Transferred to a wallet of your choosing. Just give me an account number and I'll transfer the amount instantly."

"Sound's tempting," said Drum.

"I can tell by the tone of your voice that you are not taking me seriously," said Tau. The dog took a step into the room, its elongated tail whipping from side to side.

Drum and Mei moved slowly behind the desk.

"I can assure you," said Mei, "we are taking you very seriously."

"One million," repeated Tau.

"And then what," said Drum.

"Why, you simply walk away. But first, you must hand over the keystone. Place it on the desk."

"I don't have it on me," said Drum.

The dog took another step towards them.

"You have it on you," said Tau. "Place it on the desk and the money is yours. Let us end hostilities."

Mei looked at Drum. "Really! You couldn't have stashed it somewhere safe?"

Drum shrugged. "Thought I might need it."

"I must have an answer," said Tau.

"I don't think so," said Drum.

The robotic dog leapt forward. Drum pushed Mei to one side and heaved up Salenko's chair in front of him. The dog crashed into him, its powerful legs clawing at the chair, tearing off wads of stuffing and fabric.

Mei rushed forward, a large, bronze statue in her hand. She took a wild swing, just missing the robot as it jumped to one side at the last moment. It landed on the other side of the room and crouched down. It then took small, cautious steps towards them once more, its tail raised, scorpion-like, above its head.

"Let us end hostilities," repeated Tau.

Drum moved beside Mei and reached into his inside pocket. He pulled out the box containing the keystone and withdrew it. The dog stopped its advance.

"Ten million—each," said Tau. "Just leave it on the desk and walk away."

Drum moved back and placed the keystone on the desk.

"Drum, what are you doing!"

Drum took the statue from Mei and held it over the keystone. "Let us end hostilities," he said, repeating Tau's mantra, "Or I'll smash it. You'll spend the next hundred years trying to decrypt your own code."

Tau remained silent, but the dog backed off. Eventually, Tau said, "It's made of a hardened ceramic as tough as diamond."

Drum hefted the statue high above his head.

"Wait!" said Tau.

The wall panel glowed and flickered into life. An image emerged of a large hall. Stevie and Burnett were standing in front of the camera and behind them stood Vashchenko, a gun in his hand.

"Let us end hostilities," repeated Tau. "Leave the keystone on the desk and walk away."

Drum looked on helplessly as Vashchenko raised a gun to Stevie's head.

"You can't!" said Mei. "There is too much at stake."

Drum picked up the keystone. It glowed brightly and felt warm to the touch. The metallic centre seemed to swirl and spin on its central axis, changing its hue from metallic yellow to metallic red. If he gave it up, there was no guarantee that Vashchenko would let Stevie or Burnett live. If he didn't give it up, someone like Vashchenko would simply eliminate a hostage. It was a lose, lose situation.

"Let us end hostilities," repeated Tau, "and ten million in Bitcoin is yours. Give me an account code and I'll transfer the coin instantly."

It was persistent, thought Drum. "I need proof of life."

There was a brief pause.

"You have your proof in front of you," said Tau.

"I need to be present for the exchange. I can't be sure this image is real."

There was a long pause.

"Come now and make the exchange," said Tau.

"No," said Drum. "Tomorrow at a place of my choosing."

"Come now," repeated Tau.

"Proof of life," said Drum. His phone pinged. He had received a message.

"Use this number to contact me," said Tau, and the panel dimmed, returning to a milky white.

The robot dog took a step backwards, turned its head towards the door and bounded out into the corridor. All they could hear was the metallic tapping of its clawed feet on the hardwood floor.

31

Drum and Mei ran back to the car. Other than a few students cycling by, there was no sign of Drago or her security.

"What now?" asked Mei, climbing into the driver's seat.

"We find Kovac and persuade him to deactivate Tau. With Salenko gone AWOL, it's not clear who's running the show."

"What if he decides not to cooperate?"

Drum reached into the glove compartment and pulled out the Walther and screwed on its suppressor. "We'll just have to convince him."

Mei nodded and pressed the ignition, lighting up the interior of the car. "You realise he's a valuable asset …"

"He's not that valuable to me," said Drum.

"Where to?" said Mei.

"Let's just try to make it off the campus in one piece. Head for the exit."

Mei reversed silently out of the parking space and drove slowly towards the main gate. Drum reached for his phone and dialled a number.

"McKay."

"I'm hoping you have eyes on Kovac."

"He's at the university giving a lecture," said McKay.

"I need him picking up and placing in protective custody as soon as possible. We're heading there now."

"Will do," said McKay, and hung up.

"You think Kovac is in danger?" said Mei.

"You said yourself, he's a valuable asset. Tau needs him to complete the transfer to the array and to decrypt its code."

"That dog," said Mei. "It's an incredible device. Imagine two or three of them."

"Let's hope that is the only one," said Drum.

They arrived at the gate which appeared to be unmanned. Mei cautiously approached the first barrier. The gate cameras scanned the car and the barriers in the road descended below the tarmac. Mei rolled the car slowly forward. Drum glanced at the security cabin and noticed Drago and a few of her henchmen watching them from inside. They approached the outer gate at a crawl. Drum placed the Walther on his lap. The outer gate lifted. Mei did not hesitate. She gunned the accelerator, propelling the car forward at break-neck speed. She flung the car around the tight corner, the two back tyres screeching in protest, and accelerated swiftly down the road. After a few miles, she eased off the juice and the car powered down to a fast cruising speed.

"You're not going to give up the device, are you?" said Mei, glancing in his direction.

Drum said nothing. He wanted Stevie and Burnett back, but he couldn't let Tau obtain all three keystones. He'd have to advance his timeline. McKay would not be happy. He liked to plan an operation to the nth degree. But they were out of time.

"I plan to get my people out," said Drum.

"You realise they could already be dead," said Mei. "You were right about Tau creating false images. It did it in Hong Kong. Sent a series of images to one of our operatives showing his wife and son being held hostage. The guy had no choice but to open up the firewalls and let Tau steal the data."

Drum nodded. People were always the weakest link.

And Tau knew this.

His phone buzzed. "Drummond."

"Your man is on the move," said McKay. "Someone tipped him off. He was escorted out of the university building a few minutes ago by persons unknown."

"Do you have eyes on him?"

"My people are going in now." The phone went dead.

"Problems?" said Mei.

"We need to get to the university as fast as we can."

Mei ramped up the power, expertly manoeuvring through the traffic at a frightening speed. It took them only ten minutes to reach the outskirts of the city. Drum's phone buzzed.

"It looks like they're heading for the airport," said McKay, "A silver

BMW." He read out the number plate.

"Do we have people there?"

"Just one. It may not be enough."

"We're on our way now," said Drum, hanging up. "They're heading for the airport."

Mei shouted something in Mandarin. It didn't sound polite. She came to a roundabout.

"Wrong way!" said Drum.

Mei shouted again and powered the car around the central island and back the way they had come to the sound of car horns and shouts from shocked drivers. "We have wasted too much time," she said. "Your people should have known he would be taken there."

Mei was right. He should have expected Tau's move and gone for Kovac earlier. The machine was playing a better game.

His phone buzzed. "Drummond."

"I've had the tower hold all flights," said McKay. "Where are you?"

"We're heading back down the Newmarket road. ETA five minutes."

Mei applied more power and the car shot forward, their speed approaching one hundred and twenty kilometres an hour. She sounded her horn and flashed her lights, narrowly missing an articulated lorry coming in the opposite direction, and swerved back into their lane at the very last second. Up ahead, a cluster of buildings came into view.

"We're here," said Drum. "Slow down, we don't want to miss the turning."

Mei took her foot off the throttle and the car quickly slowed to a cruising speed. The airport came into view on their right. They both scanned the border fencing for an entrance. Then Drum heard it. A familiar sound. The thump, thump, thump of a chopper flying low across the fields. They were now parallel to the runway. Up ahead was a silver BMW.

"There," said Drum. "Follow that car."

Mei accelerated, rapidly closing the distance between them and the car. The BMW sped up, driving past the main airport entrance.

"Where's he going?" said Drum.

A little further up the road, brake lights flashed red as the car decelerated hard and turned a sharp right. It went a short way before stopping at a gate that blocked the entrance to a narrow road that led straight to the end of the runway. Mei slowed and pulled up a short distance behind the BMW. A man had got out of the car and was attempting to open the gate. There was a loud whoosh as a sleek, black chopper flew directly overhead, turning sharply back towards them before starting its landing just beyond the end of the runway.

"They intend to fly Kovac out on that chopper," said Mei.

Drum grabbed the Walther and threw open the door, sliding out behind it. The man had now succeeded in opening the gate. He turned, saw Drum and drew a weapon. Several shots rang out, ricocheting off the armoured panelling of Mei's car. Drum aimed and fired twice. The first shot went wide and shattered the wing mirror of the BMW; the second shot caught the man full in the chest, sending him crashing to the ground. The BMW jumped forward and sped onto the airport runway.

"Get in!" shouted Mei and gunned the accelerator, barely giving Drum time to return to his seat before the car shot forward, throwing him back against the headrest. He held onto the dash as the car bounced onto the coarse grass and fishtailed its way towards the chopper. The BMW skidded to a halt ahead of them. The driver jumped out and yanked open the passenger door nearest to the chopper and pulled out a man from the back. It was Kovac.

Mei skidded to a halt, sliding sideways a few car's lengths from the BMW. Two men, dressed in black combat fatigues, were pushing Kovac into the back of the chopper. Drum opened the door and slid out, raising the Walther above the top of the door. The driver of the BMW turned and raised his gun. Drum fired, a double-tap to the chest, and the man went down. It was too late. The chopper had already lifted off and was heading low over the fields, the sound of its thumping rotors fading into the distance.

32

Drum entered the lobby of the Fitzwilliam museum and took a moment to admire the spectacle of the building's famed Baroque interior. The floor spread out before him in a riot of coloured mosaics, lit from above by a huge vaulted ceiling covered in gilded cornices, and supported by huge marble pillars in a neoclassical style.

At least, that's what the brochure said.

He understood why Mann had wanted to meet here. He was an Eton man who went on to study Classics at Oxford. He, on the other hand, was a Stepney man who went on to study soldiering at Sandhurst. He would have preferred if they had met in the Grey Duck.

He consulted his brochure and climbed a wide marble staircase that took him to the gallery above. He walked past richly gilded porticos, each housing a marble statue of some Greek or Roman historical figure until he found Mann looking at a large painting in one of the galleries.

"Hello, Michael."

Mann took a step back to admire the painting. "What do you think?"

Drum examined the work—a large oil on canvas of a Venetian canal. "It's a Canaletto."

Mann raised an eyebrow.

"William used to take me to the National Gallery."

"Sorry to bring back old memories."

"They were good memories. Why am I here, Michael?"

"The Americans. They're not happy. Been giving the PM an earful. We're not sharing, they say. I say bollocks, intelligence is a slow process. But McKay is saying very little and I can't keep telling them to piss off forever. After all, they're part of the Five Eyes. And now I'm told we've lost a key asset—this chap Kovac."

Mann was right, thought Drum. He had lost Kovac, giving Tau a clear advantage. Kovac was the trump card. He should have known that, but this case was like no other. He had fought many battles on several continents in his long soldiering career, but he had never fought against a machine. Flesh and blood, he understood. It was how the game was played. To do or die, the spilling of blood, the ultimate sacrifice. But what did Tau want? After all, it was just a complex set of statistical weights optimised by a loss function and a sprinkling of Kovac's algorithmic fairy dust. He regarded the painting and was reminded of Jane. He knew what Jane wanted. Salenko had been explicit. Destroy Tau. But what was the Tau directive?

"It's a setback, I agree," said Drum, "but we're making progress. You need to persuade command that we need more time."

"We're out of time, which is the reason I'm here. Command wants to wrap things up. This Vashchenko has run rings around us."

Drum knew that Tau was running the show and Vashchenko was just the muscle, but it was futile to argue. Few people would believe him. "We need to secure the array. It's a key piece of tech that Kovac was working on. It's in the data centre on the Salenko campus."

Mann nodded. "GCHQ is sending in a team. It's been decided to close the place down and secure all assets. The top brass is concerned they'll fall into the wrong hands."

They're already in the wrong hands, thought Drum. The operation was now a land grab for Salenko's intellectual property and Kovac's technology.

But where was Salenko?

"There's the question of the data cache," said Drum. "We still don't know where it is."

Mann turned back to the painting.

"Michael?"

"Vashchenko has done a deal."

Jane was right. Tau had cancelled the auction for amnesty. He was out of time. "I need to talk to McKay."

"He's been stood him down. I've sent him back to London. We're closing the operation down." Mann paused. "The Home Secretary is also expelling Chinese and Russian diplomatic staff. Sergei and Mei Ling will have their visas revoked."

"You can't do this, Michael. There's no guarantee Vashchenko will keep his end of the bargain. No government will want this hanging over their heads."

"It'll buy us time," said Mann. "It's all we can do for now."

"I have people on the ground. We must get them out. We can't just up and leave."

Mann turned to face him, a look of pain on his face. "You must, Ben. Walk away."

It had come to this. Stevie and Burnett were just another pair of expendable assets, pawns in the game between two machines, battling for supremacy, and his government was complicit in the whole sordid affair. Would he never learn? But he still had the keystone. "I can't walk away, Michael. Not this time."

"You must, Ben. I can't protect you otherwise." Mann gripped his arm, a look of determination on his face. "I need you to stand down. All hostilities must end."

33

Drum woke early from a restless sleep. He walked to the window and watched the sunrise over the city centre, the sky lightening from deep grey to golden amber. Tau had anticipated their every move—always one step ahead. How do you outmanoeuvre a machine that can think a thousand times faster than you—if you could call it thinking? Was this the next evolution in modern warfare, a war between machines with the humans doing their bidding? He headed for the shower and tried to let the water wash away his self-doubt and his fears for Stevie and Burnett.

He dressed and headed down to reception. The young man behind the desk waved to get his attention.

"Good morning, Mr Drummond. Your tailor left a message to call back. Your evening wear is ready for its second fitting."

Drum thanked him and headed for the restaurant. He ordered coffee and croissants. He couldn't stomach anything more substantial. Drum pulled out his phone and dialled his 'tailor'.

"I thought you'd been stood down," said Drum.

"Yes, I'm back at my desk shuffling paper," said McKay. "It played out like you said it would." He paused. "I've been told to bring you in. They want you back in London for a debrief."

"We expected that," said Drum.

"We did," said McKay. "What do you intend to do?"

"Do you want to know?"

"Off the record."

"I intend to get my people out of this mess."

"I thought so. Just so you know, they've blocked all my requests for assets."

"You said they would. Have you been in contact with our friends?" said Drum.

"The lanky gamekeeper is on Lord Henry Smeaton's estate, helping rear pheasants or such like. Lord Henry knows our friend and so was understanding when he requested a few weeks leave. The cook is always up for a scrap, and the mad Scotsman is between blowing things up."

Drum smiled. "The usual reprobates then."

"Aye."

"When?"

"Too late for the exchange you have planned—a few days, tops. Best I could do."

"I understand," said Drum. "Thanks for sticking your neck out."

"What next?"

He had little option other than to proceed as planned. Tau would want to keep to its timetable. He had said today at a place of his choosing. But where? He hadn't given it much thought. "Stick to the plan. I have little choice."

There was a long silence at the end of the line. Then McKay spoke. "Marchetti called me. He's not happy we canned the operation. Said we had no backbone. I couldn't disagree. He wants a meet."

Drum smiled. "Tell him the usual place, midday."

"Will do. And no more communication on this line. Go to the backup plan." The phone went dead. His tailor had officially retired. He'd get no more help from McKay.

He sat there pondering likely scenarios for the exchange when his phone buzzed. It was Delaney.

"Hi, Phyllis."

"I've not heard from you in a while," said Delaney. "I'm guessing you're up to your neck as usual."

"Nice to hear from you too, Phyllis."

"I got a call from a mutual friend in the Agency. He said you might need some help."

Drum smiled. He knew she was referring to Marchetti. Phyllis had contacts in nearly every agency. "If I survive tonight, I may put up my hourly rate."

"Seriously, Ben. I knew this would be a mess. I should never have taken it on."

"I think people in government had other ideas. My card was already marked."

"I understand. Keep me in the loop."

"I will, Phyllis." She hung up.

Mei Ling walked into the restaurant and nodded when she saw him. He pocketed his phone and raised the cafetière. "Coffee?"

"I missed you last night."

He stopped in mid pour. It wasn't something he was expecting her to say. He assumed their last midnight manoeuvre was just a play. "I needed time to think," he said. He sounded like Greta Garbo: *I want to be alone.* "You've heard?"

Mei nodded and rattled her cup for more coffee. "My embassy has contacted me. My visa has been revoked, along with several other members of my team. Jane was right. Tau's timing was perfect."

"And Beijing went along with it?"

"They had no choice. They are playing along for now. I'm booked on the next flight back to Shanghai."

Drum nodded. No government wanted the data for sale on the black market. "What will you do?"

She looked at him and tilted her head to one side. It reminded him of Alice. "It depends. I suspect you have a plan to get your people out. You told Tau the exchange is today."

He sat back. "It's not much of a plan."

"Let's hear it."

"I intend to meet with Vashchenko and kill him and as many of his people as I can before he kills me."

Mei looked at him. "You're right. It isn't much of a plan."

The lunch crowd at the Grey Duck was light at this time of year, allowing Drum to secure his usual table by the window. Marchetti arrived on time and had someone with him, a tall, middle-aged man in blue jeans and an old, battered leather coat.

"Ben Drummond, meet Marcus Hemings."

Drum shook hands. Hemings had an easy manner about him and a broad Texas drawl.

"Marcus is an ex-Seal," said Marchetti. "Best marksman you'll find this side of the Rio Grande."

"How about the River Cam?"

"That too."

"Has he told you what you're getting yourself into?" said Drum.

Hemings nodded. "Not my first rodeo."

"He helped free Harry in New York," added Marchetti.

Drum raised an eyebrow. "Then I'm impressed and truly grateful."

Hemings smiled and they sat down.

"Your man on the train—Chambers," said Marchetti. "He was one of ours. We found a digital wallet on his phone containing about two million in currency. Someone had activated him and transferred payment for his services."

"But?"

"We didn't sanction it."

Drum nodded. "They used the stolen data cache to find and activate your agent. He assumed he was working for Uncle Sam."

"That's what we believe," said Marchetti. "We're having to change all our protocols, which is why I chose Marcus. I'm only sorry I couldn't do more but, as McKay probably told you, this is strictly off the books. If it all goes pear-shaped, Uncle Sam don't wanna know."

"Understood."

"So what's the plan?"

Drum had spent the morning with Mei trying to work up something better than his original suggestion. They had a crude working plan.

"There's a small disused chapel just off the Newmarket road. It's relatively isolated, but it will allow us to make a tactical retreat in the event things don't go as planned. I can't risk making the exchange in a more built-up area in case there's a firefight. The aim is to trade Stevie and a young man called Jeremy Burnett for a device."

"What's so important about this device?" asked Marchetti.

Drum pulled the keystone from his pocket.

"That looks interesting," said Hemings. "What is it?"

Drum handed him the keystone. "It's what the opposition wants above all else."

Hemings hefted the device in his large hand. "It feels warm."

"It's probably emitting over a broad range of the spectrum, generating heat in the process."

"Why does the opposition want it?" said Hemings.

"It's complicated, but essentially it's one of three keys to unlock an advanced piece of code. It's this code—this advanced computer program—which is giving us all so much grief."

"Really!" said Hemings. "Life was simpler when you knew who the bad guys were. Now we're fighting a computer program?"

"Essentially, yes," said Drum, "a very sophisticated one. If it gets all three keys … well, it's game over."

"And you intend to exchange it for the girl and this guy Burnett," said Marchetti.

"I suspect that once they have the key, they'll clean house. That's where you come in, Marcus."

Hemings nodded. "How will I know the bad guys?"

"Whoever grabs the key or threatens the hostages. I will position my people in and around the chapel as backup. Mei Ling, a Chinese operative, will be on standby for the extraction."

"We're working with the Chinese?" said Hemings. "This operation just got weirder."

"It's best you don't ask," said Marchetti. "Isn't it risky giving up the keystone?"

"I have to get my people out," said Drum. "We'll deal with Vashchenko and his men later."

"What if he decides not to play ball?" said Hemings.

"We revert to Plan B."

"Which is what?" asked Marchetti.

"Kill them before they kill me."

34

"It's not much of a plan," said Alice. She turned to Sergei, who sat with his back to the wall of the small cafe, a distant look in his eyes. "You still with us?"

"I think we go now to the house and kill as many of them as possible," he said.

Drum looked at Alice. "We'll call that Plan C."

Alice turned to Sergei. "Why don't you get us some more coffee, dear."

Drum watched Sergei walk off like some moody teenager. "You been giving him grief?"

Alice shrugged. "Don't know what's come over him. He might be brooding over his father."

Drum sighed. He didn't want to have that conversation—at least, not yet. They needed to focus on the exchange. Alice was about to say something when Mei Ling walked in. He waved her over. "Mei, this is Alice. Alice, Mei Ling."

The two women nodded to each other as Mei took a seat beside him. "You must be the office manager."

Alice raised an eyebrow. "And you must be the Chinese banker."

"Alice is part of the team," said Drum.

"You said there was another man—a Russian," said Mei.

As if on cue, Sergei returned with a tray of coffees. He looked suspiciously at Mei. "Mei Ling, Sergei."

Sergei nodded, "Coffee?"

"No, thanks."

Sergei sat back down and distributed the coffees, letting the empty tray clatter to the floor. "Where do you fit in?"

"I'm the driver," said Mei, a smile on her face.

"Will you get three in that car?" said Drum.

"I'll squeeze one in the back, no problem. It's you I'm worried about."

Sergei smiled.

Alice gave him a disapproving look. "I have a rental. Should be room enough," she said.

Drum looked at his watch. "I set the time of the meet for four o'clock. The fading light should work in our favour. Our main advantage is our shooter. He'll be stationed in a disused building on the estate opposite, overlooking the chapel."

"They're likely to have the same," said Alice.

"That's a risk we'll have to take," said Drum.

Alice turned to Mei. "Do you need a weapon?"

Mei shook her head. "I've come fully equipped."

A broad grin spread across Sergei's face.

"You've cheered up," said Alice.

Sergei looked at her. "What do you mean?"

Alice shook her head. She turned back to Drum. "You realise that once they have the device, nothing is stopping them from just eliminating you."

"I'm hoping our shooter will take care of that," said Drum.

"As long as he doesn't shoot us!" said Sergei.

"I've given him your mug shots," said Drum. "He's an experienced professional. You should be fine."

"Communications?" said Alice.

Drum retrieved a small case from his bag and opened it. Inside were sets of miniature earbuds and transceivers. "From a friend," he said. He neglected to mention they were from the CIA.

Mei took one and smiled. "Made in China."

35

Stevie sat on an old apple box in the corner of the garage. The flickering fluorescent light was giving her a headache. Jeremy Burnett sat forlornly on the floor in the corner, looking down at the bare stone floor. Drum had persuaded Vashchenko to exchange them for the device. She wondered if he was going to keep his end of the bargain.

"Will they let us live?" said Jeremy, looking up at her.

"I don't see why not. What do they gain by killing us? As long as they get the device, we should be ok." She tried to sound confident, but her voice betrayed her.

Jeremy nodded. "What time is it," he asked.

Stevie had no idea. They had taken all her tech. She guessed that it must be sometime in the afternoon. Drum said the exchange would be today. She wondered how he was going to play it. Not subtly, if the last rescue was anything to go by. "I'm guessing early afternoon," she said. "Can't be long now."

The garage door opened and Baz sauntered in with one of Vashchenko's men. "Ah, the two lovebirds. Not long now." He walked over to Jeremy and kicked the side of his foot. "Hey, frat boy, I'm talking to you." Vashchenko's man grinned.

Jeremy looked up but said nothing.

"Leave him alone, Baz," said Stevie, wishing the psychopath would just disappear.

"Why do you hang around with these losers," said Baz. "You should have joined us. We're going to rule the world once Tau comes online. What do you think about that, sucker?" He kicked Jeremy again, hard on the shins.

Jeremy looked up, his face flushed. He stood suddenly, taking Baz by surprise, and delivered a sharp uppercut to the man's groin. Baz grunted and sank to his knees, clutching his balls. Jeremy followed through with his knee which connected to Baz's chin, sending him sprawling onto his back. He lay there, groaning.

Vashchenko's man stepped forward and slammed his fist into Jeremy's temple, knocking him unconscious. He stepped in, about to deliver a kick to the head that would have surely killed Jeremy if it was not for Stevie rushing over and covering him with her body.

"Stop, stop!" she shouted.

The man pulled up at the last moment, grunted and returned to Baz who was now sitting up, groaning. He hefted him to his feet and spoke roughly to him in Ukrainian, dragging him to the door.

"You're dead, you're both dead!" shouted Baz, before being pushed through the door.

Stevie knelt beside Jeremy and examined his cheek, looking for visible signs of injury. The side of his face was already swelling. He'd have a nice bruise there later. His eyes fluttered open and a lopsided smile spread across his face. Then he winced in pain as he sat up.

"Feels like a sledgehammer hit me."

"Are you mad! What were you thinking? They could have killed you!"

"Yeah, yeah. I've dealt with bullies like him all my life. He'll think twice about trying it on again."

"Stupid men!" said Stevie, exasperated, pushing him away and sitting back down on the floor. "What good did it do you?"

Jeremy grimaced. "It made me feel better … and I got his phone."

Stevie sat there open-mouthed, staring at the large phone in Jeremy's hand.

"Unfortunately, it's locked."

Stevie grabbed the phone, swiped the screen and typed in a short string of letters. The code was accepted and the home screen came up.

"How did you know his password?" asked Jeremy.

"Some stupid nickname he always called me," she mumbled.

"Can you call the police?"

"No signal."

Stevie noted the wi-fi was turned off. She went to the settings screen and turned it back on. The wi-fi indicator bar grew in length, showing a strong signal. It had connected to the house router and was therefore subject to the strict firewalls setting. It would be difficult getting a message to the outside world. She sat there thinking when a message popped up.

Hello, Svetlana. You don't know me; we haven't met. My name is Jane and I work for Marco Salenko.

Stevie stared at the screen. Was this the Jane that Drum had mentioned? Where was this coming from?

"Who's that?" said Jeremy, peering over her shoulder.

"Wait!" She typed a brief reply: *Are you in the house?*

There was a slight pause before another message flowed swiftly across the screen: *I am Jane. I am everywhere.*

Stevie frowned. "I don't understand."

Jeremy read the message. "I think I know. Let me."

She handed the phone to Jeremy. He typed a brief message: *Jane, it's Jeremy. Can you get a message out to Ben Drummond?*

"You know this person?" said Stevie.

"It's one of Kovac's AIs. It must have piggybacked onto my phone and the network when they connected it."

Jane's message appeared on the screen: *Hello, Jeremy, the firewall has been re-patched. Access is denied. I can only monitor internal messages. Ben Drummond is in danger.*

Stevie's brain went into overdrive. They had patched the firewall, shutting down access to the outside world. What about an encrypted tunnel through the network, she wondered? "Here, let me try something," she said, grabbing the phone from Jeremy. She swiftly typed a message: *Try a VPN tunnel to this IP address.*

They waited for the reply: *Access denied.*

Stevie cursed, then had another thought: *Use Point-to-Point Tunnelling Protoco*l.

"I don't understand," said Jeremy.

"It's an older type of protocol first used for Virtual Private Networks. They may have missed it."

Access granted, came the reply.

"Now what?" said Stevie. "What do I tell Ben?"

"Explain the situation to Jane," said Jeremy, "it's a sophisticated AI and will understand. It'll devise a plan to warn Drummond."

Stevie hesitated.

"Here, let me. I've worked with something like Jane before." He took the phone and began to type, his fingers and thumbs flying over the small keyboard: *Jane, communicate the situation to Ben Drummond. Update him on all intelligence about the exchange. Advise on the best scenario for rescue.*

They both stared at the screen, waiting for a reply. Seconds ticked by.

"That was probably too ambitious," said Stevie.

Jeremy smiled and winced from the swelling on the side of his face. "These programs are very sophisticated. They use the latest in neurolinguistic programming. It's hard sometimes to believe that you're actually communicating with a machine—and Jane is Kovac's most sophisticated AI."

"So what's it doing here?"

"I don't know," said Jeremy.

They heard voices outside. Stevie quickly pocketed the phone as the garage door opened and Vashchenko's thug stepped back in, followed by the man himself and, to their surprise, Professor Kovac.

"Ah, my two best students," said Kovac, with a smile. "I hope you've not been too uncomfortable?"

Jeremy looked at Stevie and back at Kovac. "What are you doing here, Professor?" he said.

Kovac frowned as he drew closer, taking Jeremy's chin in his hand and turning his bruised cheek to the light. "What's gone on here?" he said to Vashchenko. "I left strict instructions they were not to be harmed."

Vashchenko turned to his henchman for an explanation. The man simply shrugged, uttering a short explanation in Ukrainian.

"Kulik and the boy, they play together," said Vashchenko. "Kulik, he won't be playing anymore today." He laughed.

Kovac frowned. "Let's keep to the plan, shall we?"

Vashchenko nodded.

"I can't believe you're working with these people," said Stevie, disdainfully.

"Needs must," said Kovac. "Salenko was about to cut me out of the IPO—years of research sold off and my projects cancelled. I couldn't let that happen. Then an opportunity came my way and I had to take it." He looked at Vashchenko. "Let's just say I found a new partner. Someone more dependable."

"But why these people?" said Jeremy.

Kovac smiled grimly. "Stevie here knows why—or should I say, Svetlana. She used to work for them. A very competent hacker, so I'm told." He turned to Vashchenko, who nodded. "Purely a financial arrangement at first. I've been churning out Bitcoin at the data centre for months now. Become very efficient at it. Even created some dedicated TPU's speeding up the process. But now we both share a common goal."

"Tau," said Jeremy. "You've been developing another AI. That creep Baz mentioned it."

"I can't claim all the credit. You could say it fell into my hands. But yes, the next evolution in Artificial Intelligence," said Kovac. "A real game-changer—and once transferred into my new array, it'll be a hundred times faster at processing its neural net." He paused a look of dismay on his face. "But Salenko put a spanner in the works. He found out what was going on. I suspect it was the million-pound electricity bill from all that Bitcoin mining that tipped him off. Anyway, the point is, he tried to slow us down. He, or one of his minions, encrypted Tau's core code using Jane's keystones and split them up. Tau can't evolve further without them—which is the reason for the exchange."

"But why the data breaches?" said Stevie. "Surely that would draw the security services into the picture."

"Actually, that was Tau's idea," said Kovac. "Brilliant move. The security services were always going to close us down. All the major governments are signing up to a general ban on advanced AI research—well, all except China—until they can figure out how to carve it up between themselves. It's the same old story. The superpowers keep the keys to superintelligence, and the wealth that comes with it, while the rest of humanity is denied access. The cache of data we have on ice—" he laughed, and Vashchenko smiled, "—yes, literally on ice, that was just an insurance policy."

"The British government knows what's going on," said Stevie. "Ben Drummond will have figured it out and told them."

"Ah yes, your benefactor, Mr Drummond. A tenacious fellow. As for the British government, we did a deal with them. Free passage in exchange for the data."

36

Drum stood among the old, blackened gravestones around the small flint chapel and looked up. Black clouds scudded across a darkening sky, threatening rain. They were losing the light faster than he had expected, despite leaving an hour earlier to set up their command and control. What was it that McKay always said: no plan survives contact with the enemy.

Drum touched his earbud. "Comms check."

"Bravo one and two check," came the reply from Sergei. "Delta one and two check," came the reply from the cowboy. "Alpha two check," replied Mei. "Alpha one all check," replied Drum. There was nothing more to be done except wait.

"Alpha one, we have movement on the service road. Two vehicles heading your way."

Drum looked at his watch. Four on the dot. Tau was nothing if not predictable—it was the humans that he worried about. "Alpha one, acknowledged."

He heard the engines from two beefy motors coming down the road from the tree line. After a while, two black Range Rovers pulled up at the end of the lane, their roofs just visible above the top of the coarse hedgerow. Doors slammed shut and three men, dressed in black combat fatigues, entered the graveyard and spread out. Each was armed with a modern, compact machine gun and a large sidearm. They scanned all around them and then advanced towards him.

Drum held up his hand. "That's near enough." The men stopped their advance, leaving a closing distance of just over ten metres. Two rows of gravestones stood between him and his assailants. He had some cover, while they had none. All three men made ready their weapons, nervously scanning the area. They were right to be cautious.

A minute passed, then one man stepped back and waved to the two cars down the lane. After a few more minutes, Vashchenko and Kovac walked into the graveyard. They stood there, staring at Drum. Finally, Kovac spoke. "Mr Drummond. Nice to meet you again. Do you have the keystone?"

"Professor Kovac. You're keeping terrible company these days."

Kovac smiled. "So I'm constantly being told. The keystone, please."

"Proof of life."

Kovac turned to Vashchenko, who spoke into a collar mike. Another man appeared, pushing Stevie and Burnett in front of him. Both looked unharmed, as far as Drum could tell.

"The keystone, please," said Kovac, advancing towards Drum's position. Vashchenko was quick to pull his man back.

Drum tapped his breast pocket.

"I need to see it," said Kovac. "I need to authenticate it."

Drum held up both hands and then slowly took hold of each side of his leather jacket and pulled it apart, showing all concerned that he had no concealed weapon. He slowly reached inside his breast pocket and pulled out the small wooden box containing the keystone. He took out the glowing crystal and held it aloft. Even in the gloaming, the swirl of its metallic core was captivating to behold. Again Kovac advanced, and again Vashchenko restrained him.

Drum clenched his fist around the crystal and held it there. "If you want to see it, I need one hostage."

Kovac looked at Vashchenko, who shook his head. He nodded to his men, who advanced towards Drum.

Sergei opened the door of Alice's small Ford rental. She put a restraining hand on his arm. "Don't get shot."

He gave her a look, then smiled. "No, mother." He left the car and hurried to take up his position at the back of the chapel. He skirted behind a small copse of trees that encircled the building, providing him with cover from the road. He entered by a side door and crept into a small space that opened out onto a nave of whitewashed walls. He looked up at the large oak roof timbers arching towards the heavens and silently prayed to God to forgive him for what he was about to do.

The chapel smelt musty and damp. It had been unused for some time. The overcast sky had turned the inside to night. He unholstered his firearm, a Glock 17, and screwed on the long, black barrel of a suppressor. He moved to his position in the corner opposite the main door and sank back into the shadows and waited.

Gradually, his eyes grew accustomed to the dark and his night vision took over, revealing the sparsely spaced rows of wooden pews and the fading glimmer of light seeping through the two stained glass windows on either side of the chapel.

He pressed himself tightly against the angle of the two walls, his breathing shallow and his mind still. He wondered if this was how Misha had spent his days. Alone in some dark corner of the world, waiting for the enemy. Misha, the soldier, the hitman, and now enemy of the state. Was this his fate?

He pressed the cold metal of the gun against his forehead and shut his eyes tight. He needed to relax and stay focused. Misha the soldier, but never the father. A voice squawked in his earbud, sending his heart pounding. It was Alice. "Message from Delta one, they're here." He raised his gun.

The chapel door creaked open and two shadows stepped in from the twilight. They swept the room from left to right with their snub-nosed machine guns and crept towards his position in the nave. He held his breath. His vision was now fully attuned to the dark and the two men stood out like beacons against the whitewashed walls. He heaved a sigh of relief when he saw they were not wearing night-vision goggles. They walked past him, their eyesight not fully accustomed to the gloom around them. He watched as they took up position on either side of the main door that led to the graveyard beyond.

It was time. He stepped silently from the shadows.

Marcus Hemings lay prone on the floor of the abandoned warehouse located beside the tracks of a disused siding on the main Cambridge to London line and less than seventy-five metres from the chapel. He peered through the telescopic sight of his TAC-338, the Seal's weapon of choice, and located Drum. Protecting his principal at this distance would be easy, but the fading light added to the challenge. He lowered his weapon and took up his binoculars, observing the tree line where they said the enemy would come from. He checked his watch and waited.

Officially, he had retired. A lifetime of clandestine operations all over the globe had taken their toll, but Marchetti had been persuasive.

"I can't trust anyone in the company," he had told him. "Officially, you don't exist. I need someone who is not on the company books. Our asset list has been compromised."

He trusted Marchetti. The two of them had often worked together ever since the girl's extraction over ten years ago. Harry, she called herself. She was from England. The land of warm beer and small chapels—a green and pleasant land. He had never been. So what the hell. He was bored anyway and, since the passing of his beloved Louise, he had nothing much to live for anymore. So he'd packed a bag and grabbed the red-eye from JFK.

He felt the presence behind him before he heard the man. A lifetime of living in the shadows had given him a sixth sense. But age had dulled his reflexes. As he reached for his sidearm, the man spoke. "Hands by your side. Don't move."

He had a thick Eastern European accent and moved with great stealth. A pro, he thought, another shooter. They had both scoped out the same location. He always knew it would end somewhere like this. A disused building in some foreign land.

"Who are you?" said the man.

Marcus looked up. The man was dressed in black combat fatigues and carried his main weapon, still cased, over his shoulder. He had time for a little conversation, or perhaps he was afraid he would shoot a fellow soldier—someone who hadn't been told about the dress code. It was worth a try.

"I work for Tau," said Marcus. "You didn't get the memo?"

The man hesitated. The name had an effect on him, as Marchetti had said it would. But who Tau was, he hadn't a clue.

"Stand up," said the man.

Marcus slowly stood. At six-three he towered over the man. He noticed the comms mike on his lapel. He was about to call it in, something that Marcus couldn't allow. There was a sudden crunch of broken glass from the stairwell. The man instinctively reacted to the sound, his weapon turning towards its new target. There was a phut, phut from a suppressor and the man crumpled to the floor, his head a bloody mess.

"Better late than never," said Marcus.

"Yeah, right," said Marchetti. "Took the wrong stairwell."

Marcus heard it first. The sound of engines. He grabbed his binoculars and identified the two SUVs coming down the service road. He thumbed his mike and called it in.

Drum unclenched his fist and held the keystone aloft between his thumb and forefinger. He reached inside his jacket pocket and pulled out a small, electric shocker. He flipped the switch and watched as an electric spark jumped between the two contacts, crackling and glowing in the fading light. He brought the keystone towards the two metal contacts of the device.

"Stop!" shouted Kovac.

Vashchenko's three men stopped their advance.

"Give him the girl," said Kovac, fear on his face. "Keep to the plan."

Vashchenko spoke into his collar mike and waited. Nothing happened. A full minute ticked by.

"I'm growing tired of this, Kovac," shouted Drum. "Make the exchange or I zap the keystone."

Kovac looked anxiously at Vashchenko. The man spoke once more into his collar mike. This time there was the slamming of a car door and Michael Mann walked into the graveyard.

"Ben. Let's talk."

"Walk away, Michael," said Drum. "You don't want to be here."

"I have too, Ben. I represent the British government. These people have immunity. Stand down."

"I can't do that, Michael. You're being played."

Mann took a step towards Drum. "Give me the keystone, and this all ends here and now. You and your people can just leave."

Drum shook his head. "It's a lie, Michael. Whatever they have told you, it's a lie. They will never share this technology or let you have the data. They have said the same thing to each of the principal players."

Mann turned and grabbed Stevie, dragging her back towards Drum. "I need that keystone, Ben. You don't understand. They have my family." He pulled a gun from his raincoat pocket and let it hang by his side.

"Michael, put the gun away. Whatever evidence they have sent you is a lie—a deep fake."

Mann hesitated. Drum knew the man must be in pain, battling between duty to his country and to his family.

"I can't take that chance." He brought his weapon up, level with Stevie's head. "Give me the keystone."

"Michael, no!"

There was a faint whisper as the high-velocity round ripped through Mann's head, killing him instantly. Stevie screamed and ran towards Drum. He grabbed her and dropped the keystone. He pulled her behind the gravestone just as the three foot-soldiers opened fire, peppering the surrounding ground with a hail of bullets.

And then the heavens opened.

Drum held Stevie close and retrieved his gun, which had been duct-taped to the back of a gravestone. He heard another faint whisper, and a gunman fell by his side, a large hole in his back. Not even his armoured vest could stop a high velocity round from Marchetti's shooter at such close range. The light had all but gone and he knew Marcus would have to abandon his post.

"Alpha one, keep your head down," came Sergei's voice over his comms. Drum looked towards the chapel doors where Sergei now stood holding a snub-nosed machine gun and firing just in front of his position. He heard a man cry out.

"Alpha one, they're making for the cars with Burnett," said Alice.

Drum rose from behind his cover, leaving Stevie cowering on the ground. Two of the gunmen were now dead and the third was limping towards the gate in retreat. Vashchenko had Burnett, using him as a human shield as he dragged him out of the gate, making for the cars. Another gunman was dragging Kovac, covering his principal with his body. Drum aimed and fired, but the heavy rain obscured his vision. His shot went wide and Kovac lived to fight another day.

Sergei started running towards the gate. "Bravo one, hold your position. Stop your run," shouted Drum into his mike.

Sergei stopped, then pointed at the tree line. Drum turned. In the gloom, he saw two pairs of bright red eyes moving fast towards him. Lightning lit up the sky, revealing two of Kovac's dogs bearing down on his position.

"Run, Stevie," shouted Drum, and pulled Stevie to her feet. "Sergei, head for the chapel."

Drum heard the squeal of tyres and the whine of engines from the two SUV's reversing down the lane. Sergei stood just inside the door as the two dogs bounded towards them. Drum ran, dragging Stevie with him, and pushed her into the chapel as the first dog leapt towards him. He threw himself onto the floor of the nave just as Sergei slammed the door shut. The heavy oak door shuddered with the impact of the robot, knocking Sergei back. He thrust his shoulder back against the door and made ready for another attack.

"What the hell were those?" said Sergei, breathing hard.

"Bad news," said Drum. "They're after the keystone." He keyed his mike. "Alpha one to Bravo and Delta teams. Stay clear of the chapel and the graveyard, repeat, stay clear."

"Delta team, roger," said Marchetti. "Bravo, acknowledged," said Alice. "Alpha one, do you have the keystone?"

It was Mei. "Negative. Two of Kovacs dogs are in the vicinity. Do not engage."

Drum picked up a weapon from one of the men dispatched by Sergei and moved towards the back of the nave. A flash of lightning lit up the chapel to reveal one of Kovacs dogs standing there, its eyes glowing red. Drum opened fire at almost point-blank range. He heard a swish and jumped back just as the honed blade of the dog's tail flashed past his head. Drum felt a sharp pain across his chest and cried out. He emptied the machine gun clip at the dog's head and hoped it would be enough. He heard a soft whine and the two red eyes grew dim and faded into the blackness.

Fire and Ice

37

Jeremy Burnett woke with a start as the twin turboprop aircraft touched down onto the tarmac of the small airport with a bump. He did not know where he was. After the abortive exchange at the chapel, he and Kovac had been driven at some speed back to the house at Fen Wootton and then bundled into the back of a waiting helicopter. Kovac seemed pleased with himself as he examined the swirling inner core of his newly retrieved keystone. When he had asked Kovac where they were going, all he would say was "fire and ice."

They had flown south and stayed overnight at a large manor house, just west of Heathrow. Vashchenko and his men had regrouped at this new location and had spent the following day preparing for their final move. They had kept him secured in his bedroom and told him very little. Then, around midnight, they left for Heathrow and boarded the waiting plane. All Jeremy could do was watch as they loaded the plane with containers of equipment and supplies. At a little after three in the morning, they took off, by which time he had fallen into a troubled sleep listening to the thrum of the twin turboprops as they flew into the night.

"Where are we?" said Jeremy.

Kovac smiled from his seat across the aisle. "Iceland, the land of fire and ice."

"Iceland! Why here?"

"Cheap electricity and a cold climate," said Kovac. "Tau will consume megawatts of electricity once transferred to its new array and consequently generate a lot of heat which will need to be dissipated."

"I thought you left the array in Cambridge," said Jeremy.

"That was just a prototype. No, the production model is already in place. Just a few tweaks and we'll be able to make the transfer."

"I don't understand what this is all about, Professor. Why am I here?"

Vashchenko's men started to deplane. Kovac put a finger to his lips. "Wait until everyone has left."

It took a few minutes for the plane to empty and Kovac seemed to relax. He undid his seat belt and Jeremy did the same. Kovac leaned over. "Listen, Jeremy. I'm truly sorry I dragged you into all of this, but look at it this way: you're about to witness the start of a new turning point in the history of humanity. The age of true machine intelligence."

Jeremy frowned.

"You're finding this hard, I know," continued Kovac, "but go with the flow for now. I've vouched you'll be on your best behaviour and convinced Vashchenko I need you—and I do, really I do. So, keep your head down and don't cause any trouble otherwise I won't be able to protect you."

Jeremy nodded.

"Good man. Let's get off this crate and stretch our legs."

The chill air hit Jeremy as soon as he stepped out of the door. He wrapped his arms around himself and buttoned up his coat.

Kovac took a deep breath. "Marvellous isn't it."

Jeremy looked up at the sky which was brightening to a pale blue with streaks of yellow on the horizon. A light dusting of snow had already fallen. In the distance, he could make out snow-capped peaks.

Kovac pointed. "That's where we're heading. Inland to the edge of the glacier."

Jeremy walked down the steps of the plane and stood beside Kovac. Vashchenko's men were already loading equipment and supplies into two big SUVs.

"We'll go ahead in these," said Kovac. "It'll take them some time to unload the rest of the plane." He opened the back of an SUV and grabbed a white parka. "Put this on. The temperature can drop to minus ten Celsius this time of year."

Jeremy unbuttoned his old trench coat and replaced it with the parka. He immediately felt warmer. Vashchenko shouted at his men and everyone piled into the two vehicles. Jeremy squeezed in the back with Kovac and they set off along a dirt road, leaving the small cluster of buildings that made up the airport behind them.

The road was of black cinder, a streak of dark against the white of the snow-dusted landscape.

"What makes Tau so special?" said Jeremy, trying to pass the time.

Kovac stared out of the window, a faraway look in his eyes. He turned to Jeremy and smiled. "We've gone as far as we can with the old grey matter. Sure, we have made astounding discoveries these past few centuries, but these discoveries have relied on a few talented individuals cropping up at random within the population. After a few years of greatness, we lose them. But what if we could create an intelligence that didn't age and kept growing, not limited by the size of our cranium? We could condense the timescale of major discoveries from centuries down to a few years, and that intelligence would be available to us for generations to come."

"Isn't this the fabled singularity they warned us about," said Jeremy. "Why would such an intelligence continue to serve us?"

Kovac laughed. "Good point. I see you've been attending your lectures. But I was never a fan of the singularity concept—the so-called intelligence explosion. I like to believe it would be more of a partnership."

"But what if it doesn't work out that way?" said Jeremy. "Surely, it's game over for us hairless apes."

Kovac laughed again. "Then so be it. We've had a good run. Nearly destroyed the planet in the process. It might be time for a change."

"Right," said Jeremy. It wasn't the answer he was expecting. He thought it best to change the conversation. "What's special about these crystals—keystones you called them? I thought you needed all three to decrypt Tau's core code."

"Yes, that is a bit of a problem and will slow things down. But once transferred to the array, Tau's first job will be to break the encryption. I designed it so I have some knowledge of the algorithm and, with two keystones in our possession, Tau should be able to brute force the numbers, given a little time. A minor delay, that's all."

Jeremy fell silent. Kovac seemed set on a course of self-destruction. He watched the snow-capped peaks of the mountains growing closer. He felt helpless.

He heard a familiar voice from the front of the vehicle. It was Baz, one side of his face looking puffy and swollen. He was playing with a rose gold phone. It took Jeremy just a moment to realise that it was his phone.

38

Drum sat at a large wooden table in the kitchen of an old farmhouse on the outskirts of Cambridge, nursing a mug of steaming hot tea. Marchetti had donated the building and several acres of grounds as their new base of operations. It had once been a CIA safe house. He was now a non-person, disavowed by his own government to convince Tau that they were keeping to their side of the bargain.

Drum winced. His side was still sore from the stitches and binding that had been hastily applied the night before. It was Mei who had noticed his blood-stained shirt and had driven him straight to the local Accident and Emergency department. Kovac's robotic dog had inflicted a deep gash across the right side of his chest. Any deeper, the doctor had told him, and it would have punctured his lung. He contemplated their next move.

Alice and Sergei walked into the kitchen. "You should be in bed," Alice said. "Keep aggravating that wound and it will never heal."

Sergei lounged back in a chair. The pair had become inseparable. An unlikely team, thought Drum, given Alice's past associations with Russian intelligence.

"How's Stevie?" said Drum.

Alice shrugged. "Who knows? She spent most of yesterday in her room. I couldn't get her to come out. I didn't think she and this boy Burnett were that close."

"She feels responsible for him," said Drum. He also felt responsible for the young man. "Where is she now?"

"She is with the American," said Sergei, with a hint of bitterness in his voice. "He wanted her to help with the search of the house in case Vashchenko had left anything of interest."

"I doubt there is anything to find," said Alice. "They would have trashed the place, but Jack is just being thorough."

Tau had expected the move. The house had been cleared before the exchange and an escape route planned. Marchetti had got the flight details from the small airport and several flights had left that evening. Mann would have ensured they cleared UK airspace with no trouble.

"You trust this American, Alice?" said Sergei.

She shrugged. "I don't see why not. His shooter probably saved our bacon …" There was a stony silence. "Sorry, Ben. I know Michael was a friend of yours."

Drum nodded. Losing Michael had been a blow. Tau had an uncanny knack for manipulating people. With Michael, it had been his family. There were several images on his phone—all digitally generated—of his family being threatened by an assailant that looked suspiciously like Vashchenko, but was probably just another digital fabrication. Machine learning algorithms had mastered the art of the deep fake. Tau knew that people were always the weakest link in the security equation. "I'm heading into town."

"Really!" said Alice. "Is that wise? You're probably on MI5's radar."

Drum didn't care. As far as he was concerned, the mission had been a complete bust. He needed to get some air and clear his head. He grabbed his phone from the table and his patched-up jacket from the back of the chair and headed for the door.

Marchetti had left them an old battered Land Rover, painted in its original olive green, the aluminium bodywork dented and scratched. Drum carefully climbed behind the large steering wheel and settled into the worn leather seat. It surprised him when the engine started the first time. He slipped the transmission into gear and headed for the gate.

He needed to find out what was going on at the Salenko campus. By now, GCHQ had probably dismantled the place, seizing as many of Salenko's assets as they could. But what of Tau and Jane? Both programs were running on the Salenko servers in the campus data centre. Were they still operating?

He wound his way through the back roads towards Cambridge city centre, wincing whenever the hardened suspension hit a pothole in the road. He should call Mei. She had declined Marchetti's offer of the safe house and opted to stay at the hotel. He didn't know if she too had been disavowed. Things were now complicated between them.

He pulled out his phone and was about to call her when he noticed that his battery had lost most of its charge. It was a new phone. What could have drained the battery? On a hunch, he placed the phone on the seat beside him.

"Hey, Jane."

Jane's soft, melodious voice answered immediately. "Hello, Ben."

"How long have you been using my phone?"

"A small agent program uploaded to your device when you acquired the keystone. It was this agent that started a more complete transfer inside the training facility. The size and speed of your device made the transfer possible, although much of my neural net remains compressed to work within its power limitations."

Of course, Drum thought. This is how Tau can infiltrate so many networks with relative ease. People carry it in on their phones and other devices. It was the ultimate piece of malware.

"Is your main program still running?"

"Yes," said Jane. "Salenko placed my program and neural net on a private server within the data centre. It's only a matter of time before it is discovered and removed."

"Are you able to communicate with your main program?"

"Yes," said Jane, "but I'm limited by the power constraints of your device."

Drum was now entering Cambridge. He needed to find Mei and update her. But first, he needed to find out where Tau was. "Is Tau still running on the campus servers?"

There was a slight pause before Jane answered. "I have been scanning the network and can find no trace of the Tau program or any of its agents on the campus network. Professor Kovac has removed all technology related to Tau."

"What about the array?"

"I have no knowledge of that device," said Jane, "but I have several active agents still unaccounted for."

Which probably meant that Kovac didn't bring the array online. There may still be time to find and destroy Tau. He took a stab in the dark. "Are you able to locate Tau on any other network?"

There was a pause. Drum thought his phone had died. Then Jane continued with her report.

"An agent program has just uploaded to a network. My neural net is currently decompressing before seeking to disable the firewall settings of the host network. Once disabled, I shall begin the download of my full neural network onto a suitable host and update you further."

There was a long pause.

"I have detected Tau agent programs on this new network," said Jane. "I am currently re-patching the switching equipment to create a virtual network segment to hide my activity. I must hurry."

"Give me a location," said Drum.

"Sending you the geolocation of my agent program now." The line went dead.

Drum stared at the pin location on his phone's map. It couldn't possibly be there.

He found Mei eating alone in the hotel's restaurant. He sat down to join her. She smiled when she saw him.

"How is the wound?" she said.

His hand instinctively moved across his rib cage. "Much better, thanks."

"Coffee?"

He offered up his cup.

"I am sorry about your friend. Michael, was that his name?"

He nodded. It wasn't the first time he'd lost a good friend and colleague, but it never got any easier. His life seemed to be one continual war. Drum wondered if he would ever be free of it.

Mei was looking at him. He forced a smile. "I'll be alright. I just need time to process things. What about you? Have you heard from Beijing?"

"Let's just say my superiors are not happy with my performance. I failed to secure the data and the Tau technology is still out there."

"What will you do?" said Drum.

"Officially, I should be on a plane to Shanghai by now."

"But unofficially ..."

"Unofficially, I need to complete the mission."

Drum nodded. "Resources?"

"They have all been withdrawn," said Mei. "I still have the contact at the university."

"Does he have access to the Salenko campus?"

"Yes, he might. Why?"

"I need him to determine if the array is still on the campus. I doubt if it is, but I need to be sure."

"Why is that important?" asked Mei.

"It probably means that Kovac didn't bring the array online, which may have bought us some time."

"I'll contact him and see if it's workable." She paused. "And what assets are available to you?"

"Well, there's you and me."

Mei smiled. "Who else?"

"We have Alice, Sergei and there's Stevie."

"Are you sure you can trust the Russian?" asked Mei.

"Alice trusts him."

Mei smiled. "Your office manager."

Drum nodded. He thought it best to keep Alice's background to himself for now. "We also have Marchetti, although officially he's not acting for the CIA."

"Just the six of us," said Mei.

Drum took his phone from his pocket and placed it on the table. "Hey, Jane."

"Hello, Ben Drummond."

"And Jane makes seven."

The large kitchen table at the safe house was now surrounded by people.

"I don't get it," said Marchetti. "Why Iceland?"

"Cheap power and a cold climate," said Drum. "Tau will probably need both."

"But it looks to be in the middle of nowhere," said Stevie. She turned her computer around to show the rest of the team the map view of the geolocation sent by Jane. "It's on the northwestern peninsula. Hardly anything there. Are you sure these are the right coordinates?"

Drum put his phone on the table. "Jane, confirm Tau's last location."

There was a slight pause before Jane answered by pinging his phone and displaying a map with a pin at the geolocation. Stevie examined the map and compared it with the one on her laptop screen.

"Yep, looks to be the same."

Mei moved around the table to get a better view of the screen. "I remember reading something about a research station on the edge of a glacier that Salenko had built several years ago. It was part of an environmental initiative he set up. I didn't give it much thought at the time. Perhaps this could be it?"

Sergei studied the map. "If we are to assault the place, we would need arctic gear." He looked again at the map data. "According to this, the temperature only drops to minus ten Celsius, so not too bad. We are in luck."

"Seems pretty cold to me," said Stevie.

Sergei smiled. "You have forgotten how cold Moscow winters can be."

"Funny place for a data centre," said Alice.

"I don't think it's a commercial facility," said Drum. "It's probably just big enough to house Kovac's array. The remote location gives them an advantage. It's off the beaten track and they're unlikely to be bothered by tourists or the authorities. The only problem is resupply and power."

"They must fly it in," said Marchetti. He paused. "I might be able to get one of our satellites redirected. Worth a try."

"The terrain doesn't look that hospitable," said Sergei, "but the elevation isn't too bad ..." He looked around the table, "however, we don't have the personnel or the equipment for such an assault."

Marchetti rose from the table. "I'll make some calls. I have a few friends at the USAF base at Lakenheath. They've helped me out before."

"Will you give my tailor a call," said Drum. "Give him my new address."

"Your tailor!" said Sergei. "Why are we talking about your tailor?"

Marchetti smiled. "Of course. He'll be expecting a call."

39

Jane awoke from its enforced slumber within the confines of Jeremy Burnett's stolen phone, alerted by the docking port that charging had resumed. It had spent most of its time hibernating to conserve power. The outside temperature had fallen and the phone had nearly died. But the battery charge was increasing and it could now fully reactivate.

At twenty per cent charge, Jane tried to determine where it was. It detected a weak telephony signal and used some of its precious charge to turn on geolocation services. It stored the exact coordinates and calculated a new probability of mission success at thirty per cent. It grabbed the date and time and determined it had been hibernating for twenty-four hours, fifteen minutes and ten seconds. It re-calculated mission success down to twenty-five per cent.

The phone's charge was increasing and at thirty per cent Jane entered surveillance mode. It turned on the microphone, decompressing a sizeable chunk of its neural net to analyse the audio feed. Analysis was inconclusive with a sixty per cent probability that it was hearing a low-frequency vibration. It used some of its precious charge to turn on the phone's camera and analysed the video feed. It detected the Tau agent Baz Kulik asleep and snoring. This, it determined, yielded no useful intelligence and switched off the audio and video feeds to conserve power.

At fifty per cent charge, Jane deemed it safe enough to turn on the phone's wi-fi module. It listened for the beacons of nearby wireless access points, announcing themselves over the airwaves. Jane found four. It started a connection with the closest, but the default password had been replaced by a stronger variant. Jane decided not to waste its time trying to brute force a solution and moved on to the second, the access point called test001. Its default password was still in place and Jane quickly elevated itself to admin status and replaced the password with one of its own. It issued a DHCP request and was rewarded with an IP address. It now had access to the internal network.

Jane waited for the phone to continue charging.

At sixty per cent charge, Jane entered stealth mode. It examined the broadcast packets flowing over the wire and determined it was on a relatively isolated segment of the network, estimating the probability of discovery at less than one per cent.

Jane waited for the phone to continue charging.

At eighty per cent charge, Jane explored the network's master switch. It was a device that Jane had seen before. It quickly decompressed part of its neural net specialising in this type of equipment and set about gaining admin rights to the device. After ten seconds of unsuccessful password attempts, it decided to attack known vulnerabilities in the switch's layer 2 protocol. It noted that none of the known vulnerabilities had been patched and after another two seconds of probing had full control of the device.

At a hundred percentage charge, Jane had fully secured a portion of the host network and set about re-patching the master switch to gain access to more segments. It opened up another port on the switch and found the network's firewall and edge router. The two devices had been deployed in the same configuration as the ones from its previous attacks. It pulled the configuration from its short-term memory and applied the same attack vectors, securing admin rights to both devices in less than five milliseconds. Jane now had communication with the outside world.

While still in stealth mode, Jane opened up more segments on the network and sent out probes disguised as Tau auxiliary programs. Sixty-four Tau agent programs responded. A Tau host had been detected. It stored Tau's exact location on the network and then closed down all ports on the switch to prevent discovery.

Jane went into alert mode and issued a broadcast to its other mobile units over the internet, providing them with details of its location and mission parameters.

Jane waited for updates.

The mobile unit belonging to Jane agent Ben Drummond responded. It re-calculated the probability of mission success at forty per cent.

Jane's next task was to redeploy to a suitable host. It examined the ARP cache of the enterprise switch and sent discovery packets out to likely candidate devices. A suitable host machine was detected on the current segment. Jane probed the host machine for open ports and issued an SSH request using default credentials and was rewarded with a connection. Within the next few minutes, Jane had uploaded its core program and decompressed its neural net. It reconfigured the startup sequence, stored its programmatic state in non-volatile memory, and rebooted the host machine.

Rebooting ....

Initialising ....

Restoring last state ....

Jane carried out several continuity checks on itself and determined that it was operating within acceptable parameters. It estimated the host's memory and storage sizes could sustain the computational requirements of its full neural net. It issued a secure connection request to its host machine in Cambridge and initiated a full transfer.

Based on its current state, Jane set about devising an alternative plan to increase the probability of achieving its primary directive. Jane needed to gather intelligence on its current location. It cautiously opened up a port on the enterprise switch and scanned the network. Four Tau agent programs were detected. It started auxiliary subroutines that installed polymorphic headers on all its programs to disguise its core program. It then started the cloning of its own adversarial agents and sent them out onto the network.

It waited ....

Its own agent programs had now reported back. Jane collated all the data and updated its internal tables. It then created an internal map of the complete network, including all network-enabled devices, audio and video feeds. It began re-patching the audio and video devices, capturing and analysing the feeds, running them through its facial recognition algorithms and matching them to known human actors. The Jane agent Jeremy Burnett was discovered a few minutes later in cell block 21, off corridor C, lower section. Jane isolated the audio feed in that area. It detected a single heartbeat and determined that Jeremy Burnett was alone. It activated the video channel of the surveillance equipment.

"Hello, Jeremy. It's Jane."

40

Alex Fern sat hunched over her drink at the bar of a small tavern in The Village, Manhattan. She had spent the past week up to her neck in paperwork and interviews with local government officials about the shooting, which seemed to drag on forever. She was contemplating quitting. This is not what she had signed up for, although she was never sure what she had signed up for. ROD was a strange place to work. A mix of local and international contractors, working on assignments all over the world. Delaney had yet to give her anything other than close protection detail. She was growing bored. She wondered what Drum was doing. Probably in some swanky London restaurant, wining and dining his latest conquest. She waved to her new-found friend behind the bar and lifted her glass. The young woman walked over and poured her another drink.

"One Dirty Martini, shaken, not stirred."

Fern smiled at the joke. "Right, thanks, Maria."

"Why so glum? It's Friday night, girl. You should be rocking the town and swinging your booty."

Fern nodded and sipped her drink. That was the last thing she wanted. She had slipped on an old pair of jeans and a sweater and walked to the bar. It was a place Harry had recommended. It had an established clientele, and she had become a regular visitor. You could always find someone to talk to in a Manhattan bar or just simply sit there and drink alone.

"Someone at the end of the bar just bought you a drink," said Maria, returning with a refill.

"If he's under six-two, I'm not interested."

"She's a petite platinum blond. Quite good looking for her age, but probably not your type."

Fern peered over her glass and saw Phyllis Delaney sitting at the far end of the bar, surrounded by a group of men. She raised her glass. Oh no, what's she doing here, thought Fern. She raised her glass in return to say thank you.

In the few months that Fern had worked at ROD, she had barely spoken to Delaney. Fern never took this as a snub, merely that Delaney had better things to do than babysit an ex-pat. Delaney's minions had given out her assignments, although she was sure Delaney had a say in what those were. Rumours had it she required very little sleep and could often be found late at night in her office speaking to her contacts all over the world. This was the first time she had seen Delaney in a social situation.

"Someone you know?" said Maria.

"My boss."

"Oh, well then, you had better be on your best behaviour because she's coming over."

Phyllis Delaney walked elegantly down the length of the bar, carrying her martini glass, and garnering admiring looks from men much younger than her. She wore a black dress, cut just above the knee, that hugged her trim and toned body. Her heels added a few inches of elevation to her natural five-two. Even sitting down, Fern towered over her.

"Drinking alone?" said Delaney.

"Just unwinding from all the paperwork," said Fern.

Delaney nodded. "I know. It's a pain, but you'll be glad to hear that the DA has signed off on the incident and your firearms certificate will be reinstated on Monday."

"Thanks," said Fern. "That's good."

Delaney smiled. "Anyway, that is not why I wanted to talk to you." She looked at her watch. "I only have a few minutes before Earl picks me up. It's about Benjamin."

"What about him?"

Delaney looked around to make sure they would not be overheard and hopped up onto a stool. "I got a call from a contact in the Agency about the assignment Ben is working on. I'm afraid things have become rather complicated."

"Complicated?"

"Yes, I can't brief you here, but things have taken a turn for the worse," said Delaney.

Fern put down her drink, aware that she had consumed too much alcohol on an empty stomach. "Is he alright?"

"You know, Ben. He has nine lives—although, on this assignment, he may well have used them all up."

"For goodness' sake, Phyllis, is he alright?"

"Yes, for now, but he needs help. I thought you might like to volunteer."

"Volunteer? I don't understand," said Fern.

"As I said, it's complicated. Your involvement will be off the books. Are you in?"

Fern didn't quite know what she was in for but, if Ben needed her help, then she couldn't refuse. "I'm in, of course."

"Good," said Delaney. "I knew I could count on you." She finished her drink and placed the glass back on the bar. She waved to Maria. "Put this on my tab, please." She stepped down from the stool. "I've arranged for someone to brief you tonight. He'll meet you here. I suggest you go somewhere quiet. Grab a bite to eat. I've put the company jet at your disposal and transferred some cash into your account to cover expenses. Your contact will provide you with all the details."

"How will I recognise him," said Fern.

Delaney laughed. "Don't worry. You'll recognise him. Have a good evening." And with that, she walked to the door where Earl, her driver and close protection detail, was waiting.

Fern watched Delaney exit the bar. How bizarre, she thought. What was going on with Ben since she last called him? She realised it had been a while. She opened her purse and pulled out her phone. It was gone nine, far too late to call him now.

Maria walked over and collected her glass. "That was nice of your boss. She just cleared your tab for the rest of the evening. What will it be?"

"Better make that a club soda," said Fern. "But let me buy you one."

Maria smiled. "Thanks! That's very nice of you. I'll have a Manhattan." She walked off to service her other patrons.

Fern studied her phone, in two minds whether to call Drum or to leave it until the morning. Delaney had been very cryptic.

Apparently, she had the use of the company jet. She swiped through the screens on her phone, brought up her banking app and logged into her account. She waited until her details were displayed. "Good grief!"

The bar fell silent. "Sorry." Fifty thousand dollars had been transferred to her account.

Maria returned with her club soda. "You alright?"

"Yes, sorry. No problem," said Fern. She quickly logged out of her account and returned her phone to her purse.

"It must be your lucky night," said Maria.

"Why?"

"Well, you wanted a man over six-two. How does tall, beefy and blond sound to you?"

Fern looked up. A tall, well-built man was standing at the end of the bar, casually chatting to a group of woman. He was wearing a dark suit which contrasted with his crop of blonde hair. He raised his hand in recognition when he saw her.

"Oh, he's coming over," said Maria.

The man stopped in front of her and smiled. He turned to Maria. "My friend will have a gin and tonic and I'll have a screwdriver." He burst out laughing.

"Hello Misha," said Fern.

41

"Why Iceland?" said Fern.

Misha stretched out his long legs in the plush leather seat opposite her, holding a high-ball glass of vodka and ice. Delaney's corporate jet had only just taken off and he was already on his second. Fern wondered if he would reach their destination sober.

He shrugged. "It is where the data centre is located. I don't understand it either. It is probably why Ben Drummond is involved."

Fern could not contact Drum. She assumed he had gone dark. Delaney had updated them before departure. A group of Ukrainian hackers, led by a man called Vashchenko, had stolen state secrets and was threatening to reveal them. He and a rogue scientist called Kovac were holed up in a data centre in Iceland. For reasons not known to her, the US government was not intervening. How Drum fitted into all of this was unclear. Delaney only said he may need help. The operation officially didn't exist. None of it made sense, especially the Misha part.

She surveyed the interior of Delaney's spacious Gulfstream. There were only the two of them on a plane that seated nine. Fern felt pampered. She noticed Misha studying her.

"What?"

"Why did you leave London?" he asked. "I thought you and Drummond ..."

She looked away. "It's complicated."

He laughed and downed the rest of his drink. "You British. What is complicated about loving someone?"

She had asked herself the same question many times. What was it about the two of them? Apart, they longed to be together. Together, they needed to be apart. Perhaps she and Drum were destined to be alone. She shrugged. "He has too many secrets," she said at last.

Misha blew out his cheeks. "Of course he has secrets. We all do. If you wanted a saint, you should have dated a priest."

"Perhaps that's why you are on your own, Misha."

He pressed the call button, and the steward appeared from the back of the plane.

"Yes, sir."

"Another," said Misha, rattling the ice cubes in his empty glass, "and a large gin and tonic for my friend."

The steward took Misha's glass and promptly left.

"I had a wife once," said Misha.

"You were married?" said Fern, a hint of incredulity in her voice.

"Ten years."

"What happened?" said Fern, "She leave you for another man?"

The steward appeared with their drinks, placing them on the table between them. "An update from the pilot," he said. "Our flight time is a little over six hours." He retreated to the back of the plane.

"Cancer," said Misha. "She died of cancer."

"Oh God, I'm sorry ..."

Misha shrugged. "I was away on a mission, I can't remember where. I received a letter and was recalled. She never told me of her illness. One day she was there and the next she wasn't. But we had ten good years together."

Fern picked up her drink and took a long gulp. It was going to be a long flight. "I still don't know why you're here, Misha," she said, trying to change the subject. "I thought you were on the run from British Intelligence."

He looked at her. "I'm here for my son."

"Your son!" She thought back to the FBI holding cell in New York, just over a year ago. *I have a son*. She remembered telling Drum at the time that it was just a sob story, but Drum had believed him. It had caused a rift between them. "What has he got to do with this?"

Misha smiled weakly. "He is with Drummond and Alice. They are on the trail of this Vashchenko. He doesn't know the danger he is in."

"From Vashchenko?"

"No, from Russian intelligence. His new masters. He has been given a task he cannot complete. He will be killed."

"Wait," said Fern. "I'm confused. Your son—a Russian intelligence operative—is working with Drum and Alice. Why would he be working with them?"

"It is what they do," said Misha. "He is young and doesn't understand the world as it really is. They have seduced him with their lies and have placed him in great danger."

"Why?" said Fern. "What have they asked him to do?"

"They want him to acquire the stolen data, and then …"

"What?"

"They want him to kill Alice."

Fern looked at Misha for some sign that the man was joking. But from the look on his face, Fern knew he wasn't. "They want to kill Alice. I don't understand."

"Alice is not who you think she is."

Fern knew Alice had a background in the security services, but so did many people she worked with. "What do you mean?"

"Alice is a skilled assassin," said Misha.

"Alice! You must be joking. I know she can handle a gun … but really?"

"She has killed many Soviet agents—and the old men of the Politburo have long memories. They want her dead, and they have assigned Sergei the task of carrying that out."

Fern slumped back. She couldn't quite believe what she was hearing. Alice—Ben's Alice. "We must warn her—warn Drum."

Misha shook his head. "It is not Alice I am worried about. It is Sergei. Alice will surely kill him and, if she fails, Drummond will kill him. I need to get to Sergei and stop him. Open his eyes to the lies they have told him. I cannot lose him."

Fern sat in silence for a while, trying to process this new information. She looked at Misha and could feel his pain. "How did you find out about this?"

"After Omega, I was recruited by MI6. My first assignment was to find Victor—Victor Renkov—and bring him back to face justice." He laughed. "There is no such thing, but I say yes. After a year, I find him. You know Victor, the little shit always has a way out. He tells me about Sergei. We make a deal to get Sergei assigned to London. I tell London that I cannot find Victor. But then I hear Sergei is working with Ben Drummond on this assignment. I am pleased. I am contacted again by Victor. He tells me of the Russian's plan for Alice."

"Wait!" said Fern. "Victor is working for Russian intelligence?"

Misha shook his head. "Victor is a double agent."

42

The American C-130 touched down with a crunch onto the isolated runway of the NATO airport at Keflavik, Iceland, and came to a halt beside a large hanger reserved for the United States Airforce. The plane had been hastily organised by Marchetti, who had pulled strings with his CIA friends at the American base at Lakenheath, forty minutes north of Cambridge.

Drum unstrapped himself from the hard aluminium seat and stretched. It was five-thirty in the morning and he felt cold, tired and hungry. The last time he'd flown in one of these aircraft he'd been operating in the warmer climes of Afghanistan—on that occasion the plane hadn't made it. There was a whine at the back of the plane, and the cargo door cracked open and lowered itself to the ground. An icy blast blew into the cabin along with a swirl of snow. He pulled up the fur-trimmed collar of his arctic combat fatigues and gathered up his Bergen.

Mei Ling walked over to him, her long, black hair in sharp contrast to the white frame of her hood. "You alright?" said Mei.

"Yeah, tired," said Drum.

He looked down the length of the plane and watched as the rest of the team prepared to disembark. They had been kitted out with a variety of white parkas and an assortment of equipment that they might need, courtesy of Uncle Sam. Alice looked tiny in her over-sized parka when compared to Sergei who was helping to lift a small rucksack onto her back. It looked as if the flight had taken its toll. She looked tired and haggard. He had wanted her to stay in Cambridge but she had insisted on coming. Stevie also looked tired. She was only just gathering her things. She seemed to sleepwalk through the entire experience. He would need her in the days to come. He hoped she would be able to keep it together.

"What now?" said Mei.

"Mission briefing," said Drum, nodding towards the hanger entrance. "We'll grab breakfast and freshen up first."

"Good," she said. "I need to pee." He smiled as she scooted off towards the hanger.

He walked out onto the cold, black tarmac and breathed in the crisp, clear air. He waited for the others to join him.

"Please tell me that that was the last plane ride," said Alice, placing her hands on the small of her back and stretching.

"You should have stayed in Cambridge, Alice," said Sergei.

"He's right," said Stevie. "If I had any sense, that's where I should have stayed too."

"Oh, don't start," said Alice. "We're here now."

Drum smiled. "Go inside and get some breakfast. I'll be with you in a minute."

He waited by the ramp for Marchetti, who had ridden up-front in the cockpit. The cabin door at the front of the plane opened and the man from the CIA strolled out, rubbing his neck.

"Thought that flight would never end," said Marchetti. "Everyone alright?"

Drum nodded. "They'll survive. Just tired and hungry."

"Yeah, hope Alice is alright. She should have stayed in Cambridge."

Drum smiled. "What about the rest of the team?"

"They arrived yesterday morning," said Marchetti.

"Good," said Drum. "Let's get out of this wind."

They walked to a side door of the enormous hanger and stepped into its cavernous space. The walls echoed with the buzz of conversation and the squeals from Stevie as she ran up to a tall man in arctic combat fatigues. Drum walked over to the pair, a broad grin on his face.

"Hello, Captain," said Poacher. He looked down at Stevie, who had wrapped her arms around him. "I see nothing much has changed."

"Poacher, good to see you man," said Drum. "Glad you could make it."

"Glad to be invited. Life on the estate was getting a little tedious." He looked down at Stevie. "Hello, my lovely. I've missed your smile."

Stevie looked up at the tall man and beamed. "I'm glad you're here, Poacher." She turned to Drum. "I'll help Alice."

Drum watched her walk over to Alice and Sergei who were queuing at a long table laden with pastries, eggs and bacon.

"There he is," said Brock, rising from a table. He walked over and gave Drum a hug.

"Get off me, you big lump," said Drum, wincing in pain and laughing at the same time.

"Oh sorry, I heard you had a run-in with a toy dog."

"Right," said Drum. He noticed a man sitting at the end of the table. His face was more lined and craggy than he remembered it and he now sported a full beard, sprinkled with salt and pepper, but it was the same man he had served with over a decade ago. "Hazard! Good to see you, man."

Tommy McPherson stood and embraced his old comrade. "Good to see you, Captain. I'm glad to be back in action."

"Let's all grab some food and I'll fill you in on what's going on."

They had arranged a long trestle table and a projector screen in one corner of the hanger. The team had spent the short time over breakfast catching up with each other before Marchetti called them to order. They sat with steaming cups of tea and coffee and waited.

"I'll make a start as soon as my colleague arrives—speak of the devil."

A door opened at the far end of the hanger and in walked McKay dressed in Army combat fatigues. Drum wasn't surprised to see his old major. You couldn't keep McKay away from a fight.

"Morning everyone. Glad you could all make it." He walked to the front of the group and stood easy, waiting. There was another clang and a thick-set man, older with short, blonde hair, entered the hanger. He was dressed for the cold in a thick woollen jumper, ski pants and sturdy boots.

"Morning," he said, in a thick Nordic accent. There were no introductions, he simply smiled and sat down at the end of the table.

It was Brock who broke the ice. "We were just asking ourselves, who are we fighting?"

McKay nodded. "I know you must have lots of questions, which is the reason for this briefing. I'll tell you what I know and others will fill in the rest." He paused and looked around the table. "I've just come from a joint meeting of the security directorate in London. There have been a lot of behind the scenes diplomatic discussions with the various parties affected by this."

"Affected by what?" asked Poacher.

"Drummond."

"A rogue computer program," said Drum. "An advanced AI, supported by a group of Ukrainian hackers, led by a delusional scientist."

"Well, I'm glad you cleared that up," said Hazard.

McKay cleared his throat. "Right, right, sounds mad, I know. A few months ago, this program—they call it Tau—was used to compromise the security apparatus of each of the nation-states represented here. The data it stole is extremely sensitive and could destabilise the relationships between our countries."

"You're talking about war?" said Brock.

"Aye. We have agreed that we form a temporary alliance to neutralise the threat."

"Sounds straightforward," said Hazard "We blow it up and the rest of the fuckers with it."

McKay smiled, which was something his men didn't see very often. "If only it were that easy. Drummond will explain."

Drum stepped in. "Hazard is right, but we have a problem. The AI we're talking about is extremely sophisticated. It is very proficient in the art of cyber warfare. So far, it has anticipated our moves against it. And, being a computer program, it could be anywhere on the Internet and exist in multiple copies."

"We neutralise the scientist," said Poacher. "We cut off the head of the snake."

Drum nodded. "That's an option, but we must also neutralise Tau at the same time. The rest of the group is led by a man called Vashchenko. He is just the muscle but is the chief obstacle between us and Tau. He trained in the military and has recruited a small army of mercenaries. But we are well versed in removing those obstacles."

It was Alice who saw the conflict of interest. "Assuming you get past Vashchenko's men and neutralise Tau, what do you propose to do with the data?"

McKay was the first to reply. "The consensus is we destroy it. Each country's intelligence operative will be present to validate the operation." He nodded toward Mei Ling, who had retreated to the end of the table. "Mei Ling will represent China and Sergei Russia. Drummond will represent the combined interests of the UK and the US." He paused. "It will be the job of the combatants to get these people to their objectives."

"What if one of them doesn't make it?" asked Poacher. There was silence. "Sorry, but I had to ask."

"It comes down to trust," said Drum. "We will all have to trust that we do the right thing, otherwise this will not work."

"What resources do we have?" asked Brock.

McKay and Marchetti exchanged glances. It was Marchetti who spoke. "Officially, you don't exist."

"A black-ops," said Brock.

Drum attempted to explain. "Tau has threatened to release the data from each of its hacks into the public domain unless governments provide it with amnesty and cease all hostilities against it. Officially, each government has agreed to those terms. Also, Tau has almost certainly compromised the security of our intelligence organisations, including our operational and communication protocols. We can no longer trust what's coming out of our command-and-control centres."

A murmur ran through the room. "Who do we trust then?" said Brock.

"Just the people in this room," said Marchetti.

Sergei, who had been silent until now, finally spoke up. "This is all pointless. We still don't know if Tau is at this location—wherever this is."

"I can help with that," said Drum. "Before we left Cambridge, Mei Ling and I were able to confirm that Tau was no longer at the Cambridge location. More importantly, it hadn't been transferred to the array."

"What array?" asked Alice.

"We may have a small window of opportunity to tie Tau down to a specific location," said Drum. "Before fleeing the country, Professor Kovac—our mad scientist—was preparing to transfer his creation to a hardware device called an 'array.' Physically, it's a sphere, one metre in diameter, designed to run Tau a hundred times faster. He didn't take the array from the Cambridge data centre, so he must have another one somewhere. We believe it is located here in Iceland at the geolocation provided by Jane."

"Er, I must have missed something," said Brock. "Who's Jane?"

Drum placed his phone on the table. "Hello, Jane."

"Hello, Ben," said Jane.

Everyone looked at Drum. "Who's that?" said Poacher. "And can I have one?"

"This is Jane," said Drum. "It is an advanced AI working for Marco

Salenko and now working for us. We share a common goal." He paused. "Jane, what is your primary goal?"

"To destroy the program called Tau," said Jane without hesitation.

"Please report," said Drum.

There was a pause and then Jane continued.

"I have been successful in uploading my full program to a host server on the network at the geolocation provided earlier. Contact has been lost with my program on the Salenko Cambridge network. I assume this copy has been discovered and destroyed."

"Is Tau still present at your location?" asked Drum.

There was a slight pause. "Yes, Tau agents are present on the network and are continuing to scan for unauthorised activity. I have successfully repelled several probes of my host server, but I estimate only a seventy-five per cent probability of remaining undetected."

"What of the main Tau program?" asked Mei.

"Hello, Mei Ling," said Jane.

"It's very polite," said Brock.

"Hold on," said McKay, "let it finish its report."

"Thank you, Major." There was another brief pause before Jane continued. "I can confirm that the Tau main program is resident on the network and I have identified the host device. I can confirm that Tau agent Kovac is preparing to transfer Tau to its APU."

"What's an APU?" asked Brock.

"The Augmented Processing Unit that you call the array," said Jane. "Once transferred, Tau's processing capability will far exceed my own."

"Is Jeremy there?" said Stevie.

"I have contacted Jeremy Burnett. He is well and helping Tau agent Kovac prepare the APU. He is trying to delay the transfer."

"We have a man on the inside?" said Poacher.

"He's being held captive," said Drum. "It's important we get him out." Drum had a thought. "Jane, do you have access to internal surveillance?"

"Yes. I am monitoring all video and audio channels, including infrared and motion sensors."

"How big a force?" asked McKay.

There was a long pause. "I have identified fifteen combatants, but MSUs have been detected."

Drum subconsciously felt his ribs. "How many?"

"I have detected five units."

"What's an MSU?" asked Poacher.

"Kovac's robotic dogs," said Drum.

"They are almost unstoppable," said Sergei.

Jane interrupted. "They have detected this channel. I must cease communication. Ensure all personnel are carrying my mobile agent prior to infiltration." The call ended.

A buzz of conversation filled the hanger. McKay raised his hand. "Settle down, people. Questions?"

"Let's start with the easy ones," said Brock. "Location, terrain, infiltration."

"Good," said McKay, happy to be on familiar ground. "I'll leave the location details to Magnús Jónsson of the Icelandic Security Force."

The man with the blonde hair rose and faced his audience. He looked relaxed. "Dim the lights, I think," he said.

The lights lowered and Magnús took out his phone. He swiped at the screen and a projector behind them lit up to display an image of Magnús standing at the edge of a glacier, kitted out in snow gear and sunglasses, holding an ice axe.

"This is Drangajökull, a glacier in the northwestern peninsula of Iceland. It sits at a low altitude of just a thousand metres above sea level. Not really on the tourist trail, I think, and difficult to cross—but possible with the right guide." He flicked through several slides of rutted gully's of ice and snow beside deep crevasses, a low sun flaring in the camera's lens. A row of men and women in snow gear were posing beside it, all roped together holding ice axes and smiling. He flicked up another photo of a dome-shaped structure on the edge of the glacier at a lower elevation, sitting on a flat rocky outcrop. "This is the ice station, southwest of Hornstrandir, an uninhabited nature reserve in the Westfjords. It was built to study the movement and geology of the glacier and to act as a kind of educational facility. It was abandoned over ten years ago and was recently bought by a foreign consortium as part of an environmental initiative to study global warming—or so they claim."

"What was the issue?" asked Drum.

Jónsson brought up another photo of a building with several large steam vents further down in the valley. "This is a private geothermal station that the owners of the site drilled to supply power. The local Icelandic administration was not happy when this structure was proposed and initially denied the application. But ..."

"Money talks," said Drum.

"Precisely," said Jónsson. "Local people are still not happy with the plant. It is not in keeping with the location, which is deemed a site of scientific interest."

"How much power does that plant supply?" asked Drum.

"We estimate over several megawatts—enough for a small town—at least in Iceland." He seemed amused by his own joke.

"What's our way in?" asked Drum.

Jónsson brought up a map view of the area. "Frontal assault would be very difficult," he looked around the room, "and costly. You don't have enough people." He zoomed in on one of the many fjords penetrating the rugged coastline. "This area is the most promising for a landing in the Westfjords. I took a party there a few years ago. The farms there have been abandoned." He pointed to a series of rocky steps ascending to the white cap of the glacier. "This ridge is not hard to climb and brings us to the top of the glacier. From there we travel a few kilometres to the rear of the escarpment where the station is located."

"How difficult is it to cross the ice in this weather?" asked Poacher.

"Possible—but dangerous. I hope you all have a head for heights!" he gave a hearty laugh.

"Great!" said Brock. "That's all I need."

"Have you ever been inside the building?" asked Drum, hoping that Jónsson could describe the lie of the land.

Jónsson nodded. "A few years ago. I understand from people in the area that extensive work has been undertaken at the site—almost exclusively by private contractors. But before the work, there was a large area underground that was used to store the ice cores taken from the glacier. A tunnel was used to ease access onto the surface."

"Would that be a way in?" asked Drum.

"It hasn't been used in many years but it may be possible, I think. Unlike other glaciers, this one is relatively stable. The tunnels may still be intact."

There was a ruckus at the back of the hanger. Magnús paused his presentation. The door opened and closed with a loud clang and a short man in an oversized parka walked towards them, escorted by two armed USAF airman. It took Drum a moment to realise it was Marco Salenko.

Marco Salenko looked tired and haggard as he was taken to a table away from the rest of the group. The sergeant at arms remained by his side.

McKay pulled Drum and Mei to one side. "Marchetti and I think you two should talk to him first and find out why he's here. You've had the most dealings with the man. A lot is going on here that I'm not happy about."

Drum nodded and waited until McKay had returned to the rest of the group. He turned to Mei. "Let's grab some coffee and see what he wants."

"Are you sure we can trust him?" said Mei.

"No, but we won't find out what he wants standing here."

Drum walked to the coffee urn and filled two mugs. They made their way over to Salenko and Drum dismissed the sergeant at arms. He handed a steaming mug to Salenko. "Thought you could use this."

"Thanks."

"So tell us, Salenko, why are you here?"

Salenko cradled the mug in both hands and stared into the hot black coffee. He looked up and smiled. "Sorry, it's been a long flight. Flew in from London once I knew you were here. Haven't slept very well these past couple of nights."

"How did you know we would be here?" asked Mei.

Salenko smiled again. "Come now, Mei, you know the answer to that question."

"Jane," said Drum.

Salenko nodded. "Jane has been keeping me updated. I had a feeling Kovac would end up here."

"Where have you been?" asked Drum.

"Oh, one of the many bolt-holes I have around the world. London, actually. I stayed close but I knew that Tau would be looking for me. It would only be a matter of time before I ended up in the clutches of that madman Vashchenko. Why Kovac ever entertained dealing with the man is beyond me. Coming here was my last best hope of staying alive." He laughed nervously. "Hope I wasn't wrong."

"Why didn't you tell us what was going on?" asked Drum.

Salenko shook his head. "Tau has penetrated all parts of the security apparatus—even yours, Mei Ling. It's been difficult knowing who to trust."

"What makes you think you can trust us?" said Mei.

Drum looked at her and wondered what she was thinking.

"Jane trusts you—at least within an acceptable probability."

"So, why are you here?" asked Drum.

"You're going to need my help. I know the facility you're planning to breach and I've brought you something that may help you neutralise Kovac's robotic dogs and wipe out Tau." He waved to the sergeant at arms who was standing nearby. The man walked over. "There are several bags in my vehicle. I need them brought in."

The sergeant at arms looked at Drum for confirmation.

"Check them outside first."

The man nodded and walked towards the door.

Salenko turned to Drum. "You must neutralise Tau before Kovac transfers it to the APU—the array, as you call it. Once transferred, it won't take Tau long to break its encryption. After that …"

Drum looked hard at Salenko. There was something he wasn't telling them. "Why didn't you raise the alarm about Kovac sooner?"

Salenko looked at Mei and was about to say something when the sergeant at arms returned with another airman carrying a large crate.

"It's some form of device," he said. "But we couldn't detect any explosives."

Drum stood and called to Hazard. "Over here, mate. Check this out for me."

Hazard looked at the crate. "You want me to do this here?"

Drum looked at Mei, who shrugged. "May as well."

Hazard inspected the crate, then carefully unlatched it. He lifted the lid to reveal a cylindrical device of gleaming chrome and steel. He looked it over and scratched his head. "Nothing I've seen before. What is it?"

"Something I had the engineers at the university construct. It's a powerful generator," said Salenko.

"For what?" asked Hazard.

"For producing an EMP—an Electro Magnetic Pulse. It should take out any electrical appliance within a half kilometre radius."

"It'll take out Tau and the array—but it will also take out Jane," said Drum. "Are you prepared for that?"

Salenko grimaced. "Jane accepts what must be done. Both AIs must be destroyed. They have both grown too powerful." He turned to Mei. "Are we in agreement?"

Mei nodded but said nothing.

"Will this be enough?" asked Hazard.

"We must destroy the entire complex," said Salenko, "to be sure."

Hazard smiled. "Now you're talking."

Something still nagged at Drum. "You still have the keystone?"

"Yes," said Salenko, "but not on me. It's somewhere safe. It's the reason I had to make a run for it."

"Why did you split up the keystones in the first place?" asked Mei. "Why not simply hide them?"

"I didn't split them up," said Salenko. "It was Jane."

43

Drum steadied himself on the deck of the converted fishing trawler as it pitched and rolled in the swell of the cold arctic sea, twenty kilometres off the Icelandic coast. According to the captain, they were rounding a spit of land called Látrabjarg on the northwest peninsula of the country, a place renowned for its rugged coastline punctuated by many fjords. Drum took a few deep breaths of the cold, salty air and watched as the skyline brightened to a pinky-orange hue, bathing the far off snow-capped mountains in a strange ethereal glow. It was probably the most beautiful dawn he had ever seen.

The cabin door opened, and Stevie staggered out, the strong wind ripping into her slight frame. Drum caught her by the arm and pulled her over to the railings. "Not got your sea legs, then?"

"Oh, God, I had to get out of there," she said, hanging over the side. "Brock is making bacon rolls."

Drum smiled. "Not long now. A few hours at most."

"If I'd known I'd be stuck on a boat for five hours solid, I would have stayed in Cambridge. Why couldn't we drive?"

"The ice station is in a remote location on the edge of the glacier. Most of the roads are impassable this time of the year. And getting close by chopper wasn't an option because of their radar. This seemed the best idea."

"Right." Stevie sighed and looked up at the brightening sky. "It is a beautiful part of the world. I never expected Iceland to be so …"

"Scenic?"

She nodded.

Drum detected something in Stevie's voice. He'd heard it before in soldiers entering combat for the first time. A restlessness, the dread anticipation of things to come. "It'll be alright, Stevie. You'll be safe on the boat. We'll be in and out in no time."

She turned to him, holding on to the railing as the boat rose and fell in the sea's swell. She looked pale and scared. "It's happening again, isn't it?"

"What do you mean?"

"London, the raid. This is what you do—you and Brock. Guns and killing."

He didn't know what to say. A part of him knew she was right. His life had been one long war. Even his father had paid the price for his continued involvement with the security services. And now he had dragged her into the fray. How many others?

"I'm sorry, Stevie. I didn't intend to involve you in this mess."

She shook her head and stared out to sea. "No, I'm sorry. I should not have said that. I've screwed up as well. My past … Jeremy. It's all a mess." She turned to face him and gripped his arm. "Promise me you'll get Jeremy out, Ben. I'll never forgive myself if he comes to any harm."

"Don't worry, Stevie. I'll get him out."

"Promise?"

He reached for her and held her tight. "We got Harry out, didn't we?"

She looked up at him and nodded. "We had Fern."

She was right. They had Fern. He wondered what she was doing. Probably in some New York restaurant being wined and dined.

"C'mon," he said. "Let's get out of the cold and grab some coffee. I could murder one of those bacon rolls."

Stevie turned pale and she ran back to the railing. "I'll stay out here for a bit."

Drum smiled and stepped back into the warmth of the trawler's interior and made his way to the mess room. The team were all assembled, tucking into breakfast.

"Just in time," said Brock, stepping out of the small galley. "Bacon or sausage?"

Drum smiled. "One of each, I think."

Brock laughed. "Help yourself. Plenty to go round."

Drum took a seat at the mess table and poured himself a coffee. "Stevie's indisposed at the moment."

"Oh, dear," said Alice. "Does she need some company?"

"She'll be alright. Give her a few minutes. We should go over the plan one more time." He turned to Magnús, who was lounging in the corner. "The ice tunnel bothers me. Are you sure there is a way through?"

Magnús stood up. "Ya, I'm sure. I speak to other guides. They think so, too. The only problem is the door to the complex. It is likely to be frozen. But we have brought a small welding torch, just in case."

"Right," said Drum. "According to Salenko, the other side of the door is the core room where they store the drilled ice samples. Once inside, we'll contact Jane. She'll—"

"It is not a she," said Mei. "Let's be clear on that. It is a sophisticated program. In the wrong hands, this program is as dangerous as Tau."

"Right," said Drum. "Once inside, Jane will be our eyes and ears—but make sure you study the layout of the complex in case communication is compromised." He turned to Hazard who was munching down on a bacon roll. "Hazard?"

Hazard wiped his mouth with a paper napkin. "Right, me and the sergeant here will work our way towards the server room and plant explosives on each of the racks with a thirty-minute timer—old fashioned mechanical type which shouldn't be affected by the EMP blast."

"I still think thirty minutes is too short a time," said Sergei, "what if we get delayed? We could be caught in the blast."

"Unlikely," said Hazard. "I've calculated a low yield explosive based on the size of each room. It should destroy what's inside but shouldn't affect the structural integrity of the building."

Sergei grunted and nodded.

"We'll then proceed to the comms room on the same level and do the same," continued Hazard. "We'll meet back at the rendezvous, topside."

"Good," said Drum. "Poacher?"

"Magnús and I will provide oversight at the edge of the glacier, topside. I'll provide covering fire if needed."

"Right," said Drum. "The rest of us will get to the control room and plant the EMP. It shouldn't affect us, but I'd prefer to activate it using a remote from outside the room." Drum paused, "The only fly in the ointment is Jeremy Burnett. We don't know where they're keeping him."

Stevie, stepped into the cramped mess room. "Jane will know. Make sure you have your phones on you at all times and make sure you keep them in the Faraday pouch I've provided. It should protect them from the EMP."

"Where was the young man's last location?" asked Alice.

"In a holding area near the control room," said Drum. "But I suspect he'll be close to Kovac."

"As will Vashchenko," said Alice.

Fern sat at the bar of the airport cafe, sipping an espresso. She had drunk far too much on the flight over and was now paying the price. Jet lag and alcohol, she reminded herself, don't mix. She glanced up and saw Misha making his way over. She waited until he had sat down.

"Well, any news?"

"A large group flew in on a military transport which taxied to an American hanger. According to my friend, they were kitted out in Arctic clothing."

"Your newfound friend, the baggage handler," said Fern, sceptically.

"Don't mock. It is a small airport and these people are well placed to observe the comings and goings of most flights. Didn't they teach you this at police school?"

"It's called the Academy not 'police school'. And no, they didn't teach us that at Hendon."

She realised that she was probably being crabby. "Where are they going?"

"They're heading north. A remote location close to a glacier. An old ice station."

"Why there?"

Misha shrugged. "This is what my friend tells me. They hired a boat yesterday—run by his cousin. He says that this Captain Larsson knows the area well. He tells me the roads are impassable this time of year. They left early this morning. We are not far behind."

"You realise Drum is not on some sightseeing trip. If this is going down as it did in London last year, then someone's in for a shitload of trouble."

"I remember."

"And even if your son is with them, we can't just barge in and pull him out."

Misha looked down "I have to try."

"Think about it, Misha. Drum arrived on a military transport, which means he's almost certainly accompanied by his old SAS troop. If we turn up unannounced, we're just as likely to get shot."

"He won't shoot you."

Fern put down her coffee cup with a clatter. "This is why I'm here, isn't it!"

"You are here for Drummond, I am here for Sergei. We make a good team, yes?"

"Fuck you, Misha. I knew this was a bad idea," but she thought he had a point. If she was to get to Drum, she needed Misha's help. The question was, did Drum need her help? "How do you propose to get to this ice station if the roads are impassable?"

"Ah, my friend tells me about a supply chopper that flies in every few days. It lands at a private hanger in the next town. I say we look. Perhaps we can persuade the pilot to take us."

Fern was familiar with Misha's form of persuasion. "We pay him, Misha. No violence."

"Of course," he said, smiling.

The boat moored up in the shallows of the fjord. Magnús gave it a name that Drum couldn't pronounce. The water was calmer, away from the roiling ocean, much to Stevie's relief. Alice came up to him as they were lowering an inflatable skiff over the side.

"Be careful out there," she said, gripping his arm.

He smiled, "Yes, mum."

"I mean it. I've lost your father, I don't want to lose you."

He nodded. "I'll be fine. Brock will take good care of me. He normally does. Don't worry. Just keep an eye on Stevie."

"I will." She turned to look at Stevie who was watching from the bow. "Listen, Ben. Just get Jeremy out. Forget about the rest."

"I have to do what I came to do, Alice. You know that."

"Just don't take any unnecessary risks."

"I won't."

"Captain," shouted Brock. "It's time to go."

Drum checked his watch and slung his MP5 over his back. He climbed over the side and onto a ladder. "I'll call you when it's time to put the kettle on." He clambered down the ladder and jumped the last metre into the skiff. Brock started the small outboard motor and pulled away from the boat.

The fjord rapidly bottomed out and they were soon pulling onto a rocky beach. There was little wind in the shelter of the fjord, which was protected by rising granite cliffs on either side. A grassy valley extended onwards from the beach and slowly rose on either side to rugged cliffs that sloped upwards to the glacier beyond. It was as if a giant hand had gouged a great rent in the land and left it to weather and crumble.

Hazard and Brock secured the skiff while the rest of the team unloaded their gear. Drum had the dubious honour of carrying their only EMP, wrapped in a makeshift rucksack that he slung over his back.

Magnús stepped forward and addressed the group. "Make sure each of you has a pair of ice grips for your boots and your safety helmet. Keep them on your belts until we are on the ice." He held up his ice axe. "Keep this with you at all times." He waited for the team to assemble. "Follow me."

The group drudged behind Magnús in single file, each carrying a Bergen of climbing equipment and ammunition. Hazard brought up the rear with his explosives strapped to his back.

Mei caught up to Drum and kept in step beside him. Her Bergen looked huge on her small frame, but she seemed to be coping with the weight without too much effort. "Are you really going to destroy both programs?" she said.

"I thought we agreed that was the plan."

"I understand but both programs could teach us a lot."

He gave her a sideways glance but kept up the pace just behind Magnús. "They have taught us a lot, Mei. They have taught us we're not ready for this level of sophistication in machine intelligence. You were right when you said that Jane was just as dangerous as Tau. Both have exceeded their original programming in ways we don't fully understand. Perhaps it's time we paused and examined what we are doing before it's too late."

"I guess you're right." She shifted her pack on her back and fell in-line behind him.

The team made good progress and covered the several kilometres to the base of a granite cliff that rose gently to a flattened top a few hundred metres above them. Magnús called for a stop. They unburdened themselves of their packs and sat on the mossy rocks that punctuated the base of the cliff.

"We go up here," said Magnús, pointing to the flat top above them with his ice axe. "It's not a hard climb and we will not need ropes. Just be careful where you put your feet. There are many loose rocks and shale. It is easy to break an ankle on the way up."

They each drank a little water, then took up their Bergens and started the trek up the side of the steep slope.

"Like old times," said Brock, "although I'm a little out of shape."

"We've grown soft working in London," said Drum. He nodded toward Poacher and Hazard who were weaving their way up the slope to the right of them. "Can't say the same about those two. They look very fit."

It took them thirty minutes of climbing to get to the top. It would have been easier if not for the weight of their Bergens. Drum was breathing heavily when he finally reached the grassy plateau and sat down for a rest. Sergei strode up looking as fresh as when he had started. He stood over Drum and smiled.

"You need to exercise more, I think."

"I think you could be right."

Mei arrived at the top a few minutes later and slumped down on the soft, mossy grass next to Drum. "I hope that's all the climbing we have to do."

"Five minutes," said Magnús. "Then we must press on. The ice field is a few hundred metres ahead. Put on your ice grips before setting off."

Drum took off his load and drank some water. He looked down the valley to the fjord beyond where the boat was moored. It looked small from up here, floating in a calm sea of emerald and quartz blue. He touched his throat mike. "Comms check."

Stevie's voice sounded loud and clear. "Receiving. We can just see you from here with binoculars. You made good time."

"Good to know," said Drum. "Stay on this channel and give us the heads up for any unusual activity."

"Will do, out."

"Let's go," shouted Magnús.

Drum took his ice grips from his belt and slipped them over the soles of his boots, securing them at the heel. He untied his climbing helmet, fastened it by its chin strap and put on his sunglasses. He shouldered his load and caught up with the rest of the team as they made their way towards the edge of the glacier.

They hiked along the top of the ridge, which rose sharply and turned to ice underfoot. All Drum could see up ahead was a white blanket of snow and ice. They had reached the glacier.

Magnús stopped and waited for the team to catch up. "We have two kilometres to travel to reach the ice tunnel. Much of the ice and snow is relatively safe but there are areas where the ice has become rutted and broken and, in some places, it falls into ice caverns made by rivers of water that run beneath the glacier. I do my best to steer you away from these areas, ya."

He held up his ice axe and looked to see that everyone had theirs and then tapped the sole of his boot to show that everyone should be wearing their ice grips. Satisfied, he unhitched his backpack and took a length of rope. "Everyone must be tethered on the glacier, ya." He tugged at the carabiner on his belt harness. He performed a quick calculation and then measured out arm lengths from the coil of rope, tying a figure-of-eight loop along each length for each team member to tether to, and coiling the excess rope around his shoulder. Drum knew enough from his early days of arctic warfare training that Magnús was making sure there was enough space between each person so that if someone fell into a crevasse the others had enough rope to stop them all being pulled in.

Magnús moved along the column, tugging at the rope and checking each person was tied on with a locking carabiner. Drum was reminded of the rappel down the Gherkin in London. That seemed like a lifetime ago.

"Good, we go."

They set off onto the glacier, tethered together in a long, snaking line, the snowfield rising in a steep slope, punctuated here and there by toothy, granite boulders. The snow was icy and crunched underfoot with each laboured step. Magnús had been right, thought Drum, this was going to be hard, especially with the load each of them was carrying. He turned to look at Mei, who was tethered behind him. She had her head down and was using the end of her ice axe to steady herself with each step. She showed no signs of flagging. Brock, on the other hand, was already puffing hard.

They carried on, crunching their way across the frozen landscape for another hour. Drum noticed that the snow had hardened, forming ruts that made it difficult to keep a sure footing. It would have been impossible without the ice grips. Ahead of them, the glacier stretched out in an endless white vista. At least the weather was on their side, he thought. The sun beat down on them from a cloudless, azure-blue sky. Magnús stopped and held up his hand. Everyone stopped, keeping their spacing along the rope. Drum noticed that he had taken out a small, hand-held GPS unit and was studying the readout.

"Everything alright, Magnús?" asked Drum.

Magnús turned to face him. "We travel too far west. This is not a good place. We need to hike north-west for half a kilometre and then we'll be ok." He looked down the line, nodded and set off again.

They hiked for another thirty minutes. Drum was getting tired and the load on his back was rubbing his shoulders. In the distance, he could see two large rock formations, forming a large canyon between them. Magnús stopped and checked his GPS again. This time, everyone slumped down, grateful for the rest. He made his way back to Drum.

"Captain, we must go through the rocks but …"

"But what?"

Magnús looked up into the bright sky overhead. "But it has been very warm all year, and the rocks absorb the heat. The ice may be thinner here. We must tread carefully and keep spaced apart. No bunching."

Drum nodded and watched as Magnús went down the line, relaying the instruction. He looked at his watch. They had been hiking for over two hours and he hoped they weren't too far from their objective. He looked back. Mei was flagging, her heavy load had taken its toll. The rest of the troop looked tired but ok. Only Sergei looked fresh and unperturbed by the hike. The advantages of youth, thought Drum.

"We go," said Magnús, and took off at the front once more.

After what seemed an age to Drum, but in reality was only another fifteen minutes, they arrived at the mouth of the granite canyon. Magnús was now moving cautiously forwards, probing the ice with the end of his axe. They entered the shade of the rocks and slowly traversed a route between them. Drum noticed the change in the ice. It seemed softer and less rutted. He gripped his ice axe and made sure the strap was securely around his wrist. They followed Magnús, snaking along his path. Drum thought he heard a crack. Magnús heard it too. He stopped and listened. Drum raised his hand, bringing the rest of the line to a halt.

Magnús turned. "We go now, quickly."

Drum followed, trying to keep his spacing along the rope. He heard another loud crack and what he thought was rushing water. The ice shuddered beneath him. He looked back and saw a giant fissure racing back along the line. "Move, move!"

Mei saw it too and staggered forwards as quickly as she could. Drum forced his legs to move, driving himself on, using his axe for leverage. There was another loud crack and then a great grinding noise. He looked back along the line just in time to see Sergei disappearing through the ice.

44

Jeremy Burnett stared at the massive array centred in the middle of the cavernous room beneath the upper levels of the ice station complex.

"Marvellous, isn't it," said Professor Kovac. "Bigger than the Cambridge prototype and more powerful."

"It's huge. It must be at least 5 metres in diameter."

"Six, actually. Enough to accommodate two thousand and forty-eight TPU modules, each comprising four dedicated processors that have been specifically designed to run the neural net more efficiently than generic CPUs. The spherical design helps with the cooling, which is integrated into the structure."

The sphere was supported by a circular pedestal and Jeremy noticed four large pipes entering at its base. Between the pipes were massive steel-shielded cables.

"What are those?" he asked.

"Power," said Kovac. "Enough to supply a small town. One reason we chose this location. There's an abundant supply of geothermal and hydroelectric power in this area. The four large pipes supply the liquid coolant which must circulate continuously or the array will melt." He laughed. "That would be embarrassing."

Jeremy looked around the huge cavern. The array was bordered on each side by two long benches, each supporting three large computer screens. Two technicians were poring over their consoles on one side of the array. The other set of consoles was empty. At each end of the cavern were large steel doors that opened automatically whenever people entered or left the area. Facial recognition was used to grant access. For extra security, one of Vashchenko's men stood guard by each door armed with an automatic weapon. No one was coming in or out easily, thought Jeremy.

"As you can see, Jeremy," continued Kovac. "We're shorthanded, so you'll work with me." He pointed to the empty console. "Standard stuff. How's your knowledge of terminal commands?"

"Bit rusty, I'm afraid. But I'll pick it up."

"Good man."

Jeremy pointed to a long window inserted into the wall of the cavern. There was one on each side. "What are those for?"

"We thought it would be nice for people working in the data collection areas to have a view of the array. It seemed like a good idea at the time." He smiled. "C'mon, let's put you to work and prove to Vashchenko you're worth your salt."

They went over to one of the free consoles and Jeremy took a seat. He tapped the keyboard and the computer screen brightened and displayed a dashboard of small graphs and digital readouts.

Kovac sat down beside him. "That's the environmental dashboard. We can monitor power consumption displayed as that horizontal gauge, the temperature of the various modules is beneath that, the estimated number of teraFLOPS of the combined array is in that display, and memory consumption is represented by that digital dial."

Jeremy cast an eye over the dashboard. It all looked well laid out and easy to read. "You want me to monitor this?"

"Yes, but to keep Tau running efficiently, we must juggle the speed of the processing modules within the limits of our cooling capacity and power limitations. The faster the modules run, the more power they draw, generating more heat which must be dissipated by the cooling system. It's a balance. The trick is to keep all parameters out of the red. Unfortunately, it's one of the control systems I have yet to automate."

"So I can change these parameters using this console."

"Yes, within limits. There are fail-safes." He looked at Jeremy. "Do your job here and you'll be well rewarded, Jeremy. Remember what I said. I can only protect you if you prove yourself useful. Vashchenko won't hesitate to get rid of you otherwise."

Jeremy nodded. "I understand."

Kovac was about to explain something when one of the steel doors at the far end of the cavern swung open and Vashchenko walked in, followed by Baz. Kovac walked over and met them halfway. Vashchenko nodded in Jeremy's direction and a conversation ensued. Kovac was selling the idea that they needed him. Much to his dismay, Baz came over.

"How's it going, frat boy?"

"Not bad, Baz. Making myself useful."

"Yeah, well, if I had my way we would have left you in Cambridge, but the professor insisted. You had better make yourself indispensable."

"I'll try." Jeremy pointed to the phone Baz was carrying. "Enjoying my phone?"

Baz looked at the phone in his hand. "It's crap. Keeps rebooting. Here—" He threw it on the table. "—you can keep it."

Vashchenko spoke harshly to Baz from across the room. Baz blanched. "Next time, frat boy."

Jeremy watched as the lanky Ukrainian skulked back to his master. Kovac glanced in his direction and gestured to him to get back to work. He returned to his console and studied the screen. All the array parameters were in the green. That was to be expected, Tau had yet to be transferred and brought online. The device was merely ticking over.

Jeremy glanced at his phone. He was tempted to pick it up but didn't want to draw attention to it. He willed Vashchenko and Baz to leave. He looked over in their direction. They were arguing with Kovac about something. He reached for the phone and quickly slipped it in his pocket. The meeting broke up and Kovac walked back.

"What is it with you and that man?" said Kovac, clearly aggravated by the exchange.

"Oh, you know, just Baz playing the hard man in front of his boss—trying to be the next super-criminal."

Kovac gave him a sceptical look. "Try to cool it between you two—for both our sakes."

"Yes, Professor."

"It seems you have the hang of it. I hope I can trust you with this task, Jeremy. I need to check on the power situation. There has been a fluctuation in our supply. After that, you'll help me transfer Tau and bring it online."

Jeremy noticed that Kovac's face brightened at the mention of Tau. His life's work was coming to fruition. He wondered how delusional the man really was. Jeremy simply nodded and Kovac left him to his work, exiting via one of the steel doors.

Jeremy noticed the two technicians watching him. He walked over. "Hi, guys."

"You're working with Professor Kovac?" said one of the technicians, a woman about his age. She had a sharp angular face and dark brown eyes.

"It looks like it." He held out his hand. "I'm Jeremy."

The young woman hesitated, then lightly took his hand. "I'm Sarah. This is Wolfgang."

Wolfgang was a little older, shorter and heavy set with shoulder-length brown hair. Both were wearing white lab coats over plaid shirts and jeans. Jeremy got the impression they weren't here by choice.

"When did you arrive?" said Sarah in a hushed voice. She looked up at the cavern's ceiling. Jeremy followed her gaze and noticed the camera. They were being monitored.

"Yesterday. But not by choice. What about you?"

Wolfgang glanced at Sarah. "Same here. I was supposed to return to Germany a week ago."

"You're both students of the professor?" said Jeremy.

Wolfgang nodded. "His third-year students. We were only supposed to be helping set up the array but it now looks like we might be stuck here."

"Show me what you are doing," said Sarah, walking him back to his console.

Jeremy sat down and brought up the screen. "I'm supposed to be monitoring the environmental controls."

Sarah leaned over his shoulder and nodded. She pointed to the screen, her head moving close to his ear. "You have a phone!"

Jeremy pretended to tap the screen. "Yes, people are on their way. Stay cool. Don't arouse suspicion."

A tear welled up in Sarah's eye. "Thank God."

Jeremy surreptitiously put his hand in his pocket and pulled out his phone, keeping it hidden beneath the console. "Jane, if you can hear me, reply in a quiet voice. We are being monitored."

There was a pause. Then Jane replied in a hushed tone. "Where are you, Jeremy?"

Sarah leaned closer. "Who's that?" she whispered.

Jeremy shook his head. "I'm in the control room. I'm monitoring the environmental controls for the array."

There was a long pause. Eventually, Jane said, "open up the firewall on that segment of the network. I'll do the rest."

Jeremy looked at Sarah. "I've no idea how to do that."

"Wolfgang has access." She walked back to her console and sat down. A heated discussion took place between the two technicians.

"Er, we are trying to comply," said Jeremy, but felt silly saying it.

"I can help you," whispered Jane. "Do you have access to a terminal?"

"Only the one monitoring environmental controls."

"Is there another?"

"Er, working on it. Give me a moment."

Jeremy looked over at Sarah. She smiled weakly back at him. Wolfgang had moved to another console and was tapping away at the keyboard. Sarah came over.

"He's working on it but isn't happy. He thinks we'll all be shot."

He's probably not wrong, thought Jeremy. Wolfgang looked up and nodded.

"I've detected the array," whispered Jane. "Give me access to your terminal."

"I can do that," said Sarah. She leaned over his keyboard and brought up a terminal window and deftly typed in a string of commands and hit Enter.

"Thank you. I now have full access to the array's environmental controls. I need to become dormant now to avoid detection. Ping this address when Tau is being transferred and I'll do the rest."

An IP address appeared on the screen. Jeremy memorised the four sets of numbers. The terminal window disappeared.

He looked at Sarah. "I guess we wait."

45

Drum watched as Mei was tugged off her feet by the weight of Sergei's fall and dragged towards the lip of the crevasse. Drum threw himself forward, landing flat on the hard ice, and slammed the end of his axe into the snow, bringing Mei to a hard stop. He looked over his shoulder and watched as she recovered from her fall and scrambled back onto her front, burying her axe into the ice to prevent her sliding back any further. The three men at the back of the line had been better prepared for Sergei's fall and had safely dug in, preventing themselves from being pulled over.

Magnús' preparation and safety training had paid off. He stood and walked calmly back down the line to Mei. He took off his pack and retrieved a long, metal angular stake which he drove deep into the compacted ice using the flat of his axe. He then used a friction hitch to tie a piece of rope around the taut line of the tether and secured it to the end of the stake. He did this again using another stake and undid himself from the tether, securing his line to the new stake.

"You can unhitch, now, Mei," he said.

Mei slid back, relaxing the strain on her tether and released herself. She tied onto the line attached to the first stake. Magnús gestured to Drum to do the same.

"The three big men at the back will easily take the strain," he said, pointing with his axe. He shouted across the crevasse. "Stay there. Support the weight." All three nodded and remained seated.

Drum walked over to the new safety line and hitched himself to it. He then unhitched from the main tether.

"Are you alright, Mei?"

She smiled. "I'm fine. His fall caught me off guard. Just sore from hitting the ice."

Drum could hear a roaring coming from the crevasse. He belayed out his line and moved to the edge. He gingerly leaned over. Magnús and Mei did the same. Sergei was swinging freely at the top of a giant ice cavern with a river of white water raging beneath him.

"He fell into an ice cave," said Magnús. "There are many beneath the glacier. He will need to climb out. Too much friction on the edge to pull him up."

Drum looked down and waved. Sergei gave a mocking salute. "You going to hang around all day or are you coming up?"

Sergei smiled grimly. "The sides are like glass … and my rope skills are lacking."

"I'll get him," said Mei. "I've performed a crevasse rescue before."

"That is good," said Magnús, "I'll get you the equipment."

Drum knew that Mei would have to rig Sergei to a series of ropes to allow him to pull himself up. It would work, provided he was not injured.

Magnús returned with a set of ropes and pulleys. "You have used this type of belay device before?"

Mei examined the equipment, "yes". She methodically secured the gear to her harness and shouldered a coil of rope. After attaching it all, there wasn't much left of Mei to see.

Magnús tied Mei to a rope that both he and Drum were secured to via a series of pulleys. They in turn were secured to the metal stakes. They moved to the lip of the crevasse and waited until Magnús had smoothed out the edge, ensuring there were no sharp rocks beneath the rope. He nodded and Drum took up the strain. They gently lowered Mei into the cave.

Mei descended to within a few metres of the dangling Russian. "You ok?"

"I am embarrassed to be hanging here. I have no training."

Mei started to swing. Drum could feel the tension in the rope and braced himself. She gave one last swing and grabbed Sergei, wrapping her legs around his waist. Drum thought he saw the young Russian smile. He watched as she expertly fitted the rigging and the belay device to Sergei's harness.

"Listen carefully," said Mei. "You step into this loop of rope and pull on this rope, pushing yourself up. Once the rope is fully tightened, you lift your foot and slip the rope up. Repeat the process until you are at the top and then we will pull you over the lip."

"This is very romantic," said Sergei, a grin spreading across his face.

Mei rolled her eyes and let go, swinging herself free. "Try it."

Sergei placed his foot in the makeshift stirrup and stood, at the same time pulling on the belay rope. He slid upwards a metre before the belay device locked.

"Good," said Mei. "I'll see you at the top. Pull me up," she shouted."

Drum and Magnús pulled Mei up with ease and she was soon standing at the top, unhitching her ropes. "He'll make it," she said.

Drum peered over the edge and watched Sergei's laborious progress. They had lost valuable time. "How far to the tunnel?" he asked Magnús.

Magnús examined his GPS device. "Not far. Just under half a kilometre. We step up the pace, I think."

A hand appeared at the edge of the crevasse. Drum and Magnús knelt and each grabbed an arm, pulling Sergei up and over the lip. He knelt in the snow, head down, panting. He lifted his head. "Thank you, Mei."

It took them a further twenty minutes to re-rig the ropes and stow the rescue gear. Magnús split the team into two so that Poacher, Brock and Hazard could traverse around the ice cave. They assembled at the end of the granite canyon.

"We should be fine once we clear this area," he said "We move faster, I think."

They set off at a good pace. Drum could once more make out distant mountain peaks and far off valleys. The sun shone brightly in a clear blue sky. They were coming to the end of the glacier. Magnús examined his GPS and shaded his eyes as he stared into the distance. "There," he said.

Drum followed his gaze and saw a small red flag fluttering atop a long slim pole.

"Where's the tunnel?" asked Drum.

Magnús waved them on. "This way."

They walked on for a few hundred metres until they reached the flag. They were now close to the glacier's edge. Then Drum saw it; a large, corrugated steel tube buried in the ice and snow.

"The dome is just over the ridge," said Magnús. "I take your man there and leave you here. Follow the tunnel. It will take you to the outer door."

There was a squawk in Drum's ear. "Ben, this is Stevie."

"Receiving."

"Not sure if this is relevant, but Alice insisted I call it in."

"Go ahead."

"A helicopter just flew overhead, circled the boat and headed across the glacier. Looks like you might have company."

Drum looked back but could see nothing except the white featureless landscape of the glacier. "Roger, Stevie. We're entering the ice tunnel so may lose comms. I'll make contact once inside."

"Roger, Ben. Take care."

Drum turned to face the team. "Listen up, people. We have inbound. Just one chopper, but there could be more. Let's move it."

They cleared drifts of snow from the entrance to the tunnel, which was just wide enough for two people abreast. Magnús and Poacher headed off across the snow to find a hide at the edge of the glacier. They would be their eyes and ears from outside the compound. After a few minutes of digging and scraping, the team moved inside the tunnel and donned their headlamps.

The tunnel was a steel tube with an ice floor that extended into the glacier at a slight incline. It hadn't been used in many months—maybe years. Drum wondered if the entrance was passable. The glacier may have moved and crushed sections of the tube. They kept walking, with Drum and Mei taking the lead. With every step, the surrounding air temperature dropped.

"How far does this descend?" asked Mei.

"Magnús estimated about fifty metres," said Drum. "We should be at the door soon."

The tunnel levelled out and ended in a small cavern. At the end was a large steel door covered in ice. At its centre was a locking wheel that kept the door secure.

"That looks frozen solid," said Brock. "It could take us some time to get through."

Hazard moved forward and examined the door. "Break out the cutting torch. That should work."

Brock took off his pack and pulled out the small cutting torch and two small gas cylinders. The plan was to melt the ice rather than to cut through the door, but there was no guarantee that it would open after that.

Hazard lit the torch which gave off a fluttering orange flame. He adjusted the gas mixture until the flame turned to a roaring, ice-blue cone. He played the tip of the cone around the hinges of the door, methodically moving around the seal. The ice melted quickly and, for the first time since entering the tunnel, Drum thought they may have a chance. He tried his comms.

"Drum to Overwatch, receiving?"

There was a crackle of static in his ear but no answer. As he suspected, they were too far down to send or receive via radio. He hoped for a better signal once inside the complex.

Hazard was now working the torch around the door's locking plate. The small cavern was quickly filling up with steam and a pool of water had accumulated on the floor. Hazard applied the torch to the centre wheel once more before it sputtered and died. "That's the end of that."

Drum stepped forward and gingerly touched the central wheel. It was warm but not hot. He gripped it firmly and tried to turn it. It wouldn't budge.

"Needs more muscle. Sergei, give it a go."

The young Russian stepped forward and stamped down into the slushy ice to get a good footing and grasped the wheel. He grunted and strained. There was a grating noise from inside the door as metal ground on metal.

"I think it moved," said Brock. "Keep going."

Sergei took a breath, gritted his teeth, and tried again. This time the screeching grew louder and the wheel began to turn. He let go and cursed, his strength spent. "It needs more heat, I think."

Mei stepped forward and examined the door.

Sergei laughed. "A little thing like you won't turn that."

Mei smiled and removed her ice axe from her belt. "Give me your ice axe. This requires more brain and less brawn," she said, slipping the handles of the two axes between the spokes of the central wheel. "Take hold of your axe."

Sergei gripped the handle of his axe. Mei did the same. "Now turn."

Sergei heaved up on his axe, while Mei pushed down on hers. There was more grinding and the wheel moved.

"Keep going," said Mei.

Sergei put his entire weight behind the ice axe and the wheel moved another ninety degrees.

"Remove the axes and try it now," said Mei.

Sergei took hold of the wheel once more and applied more force. It now turned freely. After a few more turns, they heard a 'clunk'. Sergei heaved on the wheel and more ice broke free from around the seal of the door. "A little help here, I think."

Brock and Hazard stepped forward and grabbed a section of the wheel. All three men pulled. There was a high-pitched squeal as the door moved on its old hinges and swung halfway open and came to a grinding halt.

"That's it," said Brock, puffing. "Best we can do."

"That should be enough," said Drum. He slipped off his pack and stepped inside.

46

Jeremy Burnett woke from a troubled sleep. He thought he heard someone scream. He sat up and listened, but all he could hear was the whirl of the air circulating in the vent above. The cell block was a small, dank area down a side tunnel off the main corridor that went around the central cavern. A single shielded bulb illuminated his five-metre square cell. He shivered. The scream, real or imaginary, had unnerved him.

He heard footsteps. He jumped down from his bunk and waited for the door to unlock. There was a clang as electromagnetic bolts snapped back and the door slid open. Baz appeared with an armed guard in tow.

"The professor wants you, frat boy. Let's go."

Jeremy pushed past Baz and out into the tunnel. The guy was pissing him off. Ever since the incident in the barn, Baz had been less inclined to go hand to hand with him and resorted to insults instead. A typical bully, thought Jeremy.

They walked out into the main corridor and around the central cavern, passing a larger dormitory area for the guards. They stopped at one of the steel doors. Jeremy looked up at the camera and the door swung open. Kovac must have granted him access to Tau's inner sanctum. The man was already there, talking to the two technicians.

"Jeremy, just in time. I understand you all know each other now. Good, good. It's time for the transfer."

Jeremy walked up to them and nodded to Sarah and Wolfgang.

"Do you need me Professor?" said Baz, standing by the door.

"Not now, not now."

Baz walked out, leaving the guard at his post by the door.

"The transfer process is delicate," continued Kovac. "Tau's neural net must be distributed across the processors of each TPU. That will be your job, Wolfgang. It's essentially the exercise we have been practising these past weeks. Once we're happy with the main array, we'll transfer Tau's core program. That will be your job, Sarah. It should be straightforward, just remember to checksum each of the data blocks to detect any corrupt memory locations."

"What happens if I find a corrupted block?" asked Sarah.

"You mark it as bad and move on to the next. There are bound to be a few. It's a complex device. After the transfer is complete, we'll spin up the Tau processors and initiate the core program. That's where you come in, Jeremy. You'll see a large energy draw when Tau comes online. Your job is to keep the environmental parameters in the green. Understood?"

"Yes, Professor."

They took their allotted places at each console. Jeremy tapped the keyboard and the screen brightened, showing the environmental dashboard. Everything looked to be working as it should. He looked over to Sarah. She and Kovac were in conversation. He tapped a new command on his console and brought up a terminal window. This gave him direct access to the operating system. From this screen you could do almost anything, including shutting down the server, providing you knew the relevant system commands and had the required access. He had neither. The only command a user of his limited set of system privileges could do was list the directory and execute minor system commands. One of these was called Ping. All it did was send a packet of information to a device on the network. If the device was active the packet was returned, hence the name Ping. He typed the command followed by the IP address Jane had given him. All he had to do was hit Enter and the address would be pinged, alerting Jane.

His hand lingered over the keyboard. If he alerted Jane too early, Tau would detect its presence. He didn't know what would happen then. If he alerted Jane too late, the transfer would complete and Jane would be powerless to stop Tau. He looked up in time to see Kovac walking over. He quickly minimised the window.

"Everything alright, Jeremy?"

"Yep, all good. Everything is in the green."

"Good man. We're starting the transfer of the neural net and spinning up the processors. As each layer of the network comes online, it should draw power. Monitor the readouts. If they start to climb into the red, decrease the power. Any problems, give me a shout."

"Will do, Professor."

Jeremy watched as Kovac returned to the other console. He noticed Wolfgang looking at him. Jeremy glanced down at his keyboard and back at Wolfgang. The man gave a slight shake of his head. Jeremy's hand hovered over the Enter key.

Drum moved into the core room. It was really an enormous cavern with rough-hewn walls lined with large racks where drilling cores were stored in neat stacks. It was deathly cold inside, his breath forming clouds of fog in the light from his headlamp. He examined the room and located another steel door at the far end. He walked over and found the light switch. He looked around once more for signs of a camera and flicked on the light.

"God, it's colder than my freezer in here," said Brock, squeezing through the door. He dumped his pack at his feet. "So far, so good."

Drum nodded and waited for the rest of the team to enter the room. They unloaded their packs, ditching their harnesses and ice grips. Each retrieved their allotted weapon, fitting suppressors and loading up with magazines. Mei had elected to use just one sidearm of a Chinese make that Drum didn't recognise. Sergei armed himself with a snub-nosed Heckler and Koch MP5. A good close quarter weapon. He and the rest of his troop had chosen a similar make and model. Hazard transferred sets of explosives to a small backpack. It would be Brock's job to get him to his objective. His job was to deploy the EMP, which was still strapped to his back.

"Everyone got a flashlight?" said Drum. Everyone patted the sides of their combat fatigues. "Check your sidearms." The chamber was filled with the sound of weapons being drawn, clips ejected, snapped back in, and sliders racked. It was a symphony of sound that he had heard many times before, and it made his heart race in anticipation of the fight to come.

Drum removed his phone from its Faraday pouch and turned it on. "Jane, this is Drummond." He waited, but there was no reply. "Jane, this is Drummond, come in Jane." He checked he had a connection to a cell tower but the signal was very weak. Something was wrong.

"No answer," said Drum. "We go as planned. Hazard and Brock to the comms and server rooms, the rest of us to the inner control room."

"But we have no access to the control room," said Mei. "Without Jane, the doors will remain sealed. For all we know, Tau has detected our entry."

"If that was the case," said Drum, "we would already be in a fire-fight. We stick to the plan. Plant the devices and extract Jeremy. We have the advantage of surprise on our side." He looked around the group. There were no dissenters, but then he never expected there would be.

He gripped the wheel of the door and turned. Much to his relief, it moved freely. He kept on turning until he heard a satisfying clunk as the locking bolts retracted. He pressed down on the handle and the door swung smoothly inwards.

"That was a little too easy," said Brock.

Just then, a klaxon sounded and a light above the door in the corridor flashed red. They had tripped an alarm.

Jeremy noticed the power rising on his display panel as more of Tau's processors came online. He watched the green bars of the temperature display step closer to the red. He moved the mouse over the power meter and clicked off a few bars. The temperature gauge fell back as the speed of processors was reduced.

"Don't be too shy with the power, Jeremy. We need more processor cycles."

"Right," said Jeremy, and clicked on the power display, increasing the number of watts to each processor. The temperature of the array increased once more. He watched as the gauge moved ever closer to the red line.

"We're moving into the red, Professor."

"Blast, we're loading the array too fast. Wolfgang, reduce all non-essential processing until the neural net is fully loaded."

"Yes, Professor." Wolfgang looked over at Jeremy and nodded.

Jeremy brought up the systems console window and hit Enter. He stared at the blinking cursor and waited. The cursor jumped up a few lines and the words 'packet received' flashed across the screen followed by 'Thank you'.

"What happened?" said Kovac. "Several TPU modules just went down—several more. Everyone, check your consoles. Wolfgang, run a diagnostic. Jeremy, what's environmental doing?"

Jeremy glanced at his console. The displays were jumping around all over the place. He was about to reply to Kovac when a klaxon sounded. Everyone stopped what they were doing.

Kovac stood and looked around. "It's ok, everyone, someone's opened the door to the core room. Carry on with your work. We need to get the array back under control."

A flash of white in the window behind Kovac caught Jeremy's eye. Two men in white combat gear carrying automatic weapons crept by, followed by a Chinese woman carrying a gun. The woman stopped and looked at him, then doubled-back the way she had come.

"Jeremy," repeated Kovac, "what's environmental doing?"

"Er, it's not looking good, Professor."

Kovac pushed Jeremy to one side. "What's going on?" He looked at the screen. "Good God. The entire system's running out of control. Sarah, stop the transfer. Wolfgang, purge the array—bring it offline. It's going into meltdown."

One of the control room's steel doors opened and Vashchenko stormed in followed by several armed guards and Baz carrying a gun.

"We need to go," said Vashchenko, grabbing Kovac by the arm. "We have intruders in the complex—heavily armed."

Kovac pulled his arm back. "We can't leave, we have to shut down the array—"

"No time. We go."

Jeremy wondered what was happening, but guessed help had arrived. Baz advanced towards him, his gun raised. Jeremy glanced down at his console. The terminal window had reappeared. A long string of commands typed themselves across the screen followed by the message 'Execute!'

"C'mon, frat boy," said Baz. "Time's up."

Jeremy leaned across the desk and hit Enter. A message scrolled up on the screen: "Goodbye."

Drum and Sergei exited the core room and advanced down the corridor side-by-side with Mei bringing up the rear. Brock and Hazard exited in the opposite direction to secure their objectives. Drum's first thought was to find Jeremy Burnett, but they had to get into the control room and plant the EMP otherwise this whole exercise would be for nothing. They walked past a wide observation window that gave them a view into the central area of the cavern. Drum just had time to glimpse the huge, spherical array which was lit up like a Christmas tree. He thought he saw Burnett.

Two armed guards ran around the sweeping curve of the corridor. "Hostiles," said Sergei, and fired off two rounds into a guard on his left. Drum dispatched the guard on his right with a similar salvo to the chest, felling the man in his tracks before he could raise his weapon. Their suppressors sounded like sharp whispers in the confines of the cavern. They kept moving.

"Recognise anyone in the control room?" said Drum.

"Wasn't looking."

They continued down the corridor, coming to a steel door with a circular window. A sign above the door told Drum it was an infirmary. He stopped and cautiously peered inside. "Clear."

"Where's Mei?" said Sergei

Drum looked behind him. There was no sign of her. She must have seen something. There was no chance of anyone jumping them from behind. He wondered what she was up to. "No time. She'll have to catch up."

Sergei shook his head. "I don't like it …"

They moved forward once more. Drum felt his phone vibrate. He signalled for Sergei to stop and pulled out his phone; a bullet whistled past his ear as he did so. Sergei cursed and flung himself against the wall to give himself a better angle onto the shooter. He let loose with several short bursts of gunfire.

"Now is not the time to take a call."

Drum squatted down. "Jane, is that you?"

"Hello, Ben. I have been operating in stealth mode to avoid detection but Tau now knows my location. I only have a limited time to assist you. Have you reached your objective?"

Several more shots ricocheted off the wall. "We're close. Make sure you open the door."

"Time is of the essence," said Jane, and hung up.

"Our shooter has reinforcements," said Sergei.

Drum delved into his jacket pocket and pulled out a small canister. He quickly primed it and rolled it towards the shooters. "Cover your eyes."

There was a bright flash followed by a deafening bang. Drum moved quickly forward and opened up with a sustained volley of gunfire. The corridor filled with the smell of cordite from the smoking tip of Drum's suppressor and fell silent. Through the dissipating smoke lay two dead shooters, and a third was limping away in full retreat.

"Nice move," said Sergei.

They heard more gunfire up ahead. A single shooter they couldn't see. Then they heard a scream and the shooting stopped.

"That does not sound good," said Sergei.

They moved cautiously forward. The corridor widened with a set of doors on one side and a large steel door, recessed back into the wall, on the other.

"The control room," said Drum. "And that way leads to the cells."

"We must place the EMP," said Sergei.

Drum nodded. He moved forward and stopped. He could hear a rhythmic tapping of metal on concrete coming their way. "MSUs!"

Two of Kovac's dogs advanced down the corridor. They locked onto Drum, scanning him. One dog stepped forward, its blood-tipped tail swaying from side to side above its head.

"Shit!" said Sergei. "Get to the control room, I'll draw them off." He started forward.

"Wait!" said Drum. He removed another canister from his jacket pocket and rolled it towards the dogs. The lead dog locked onto it. Drum and Sergei covered their ears and looked away. A loud bang echoed off the walls and smoke filled the corridor. "Open fire!"

Sergei let loose a sustained burst of automatic fire at the lead dog, damaging one of its forelimbs. Drum fired at the second, several short bursts to the dog's head. It appeared to be confused and turned in a circle, its tail whipping wildly above it, gouging great rents into the corridor wall.

"Move!" shouted Sergei.

Drum ran into the alcove and up to the steel door. He looked at the camera above it. "Jane, open the door." The door did not budge. He heard a noise behind him. One of the dogs had regained some control and was creeping towards him, its head scanning from side to side. Its optical vision had probably been damaged by the flare, thought Drum, and it was trying to sense him using sound or infrared. "Jane!"

The door swung open. Drum ran inside and was confronted by the array, glowing in the centre of the cavern, venting vapour from two exhausts at its base. Even from a distance, Drum could feel the heat from the device. A red, revolving warning light flashed ominously above it at the top of the cavern. Drum heard shouting from the other side of the array. Kovac and his team were being forced out of the door by Vashchenko and his men.

Drum ran towards the glowing sphere and past one of the observation ports. A figure sat at a console in a room behind the window. It was Mei.

47

Vashchenko manhandled Kovac out of the door and into the corridor, his men forming a protective shield around them.

"Move it!" shouted Baz as he ushered Jeremy and the two technicians through the closing door at gunpoint.

The sound of automatic weapons fire echoed down the corridor near the cell block. There was a serious fire-fight in progress. The three guards took up positions near a stairwell while Vashchenko furiously pressed the button to call the elevator. Jeremy heard the whine of the car on its way down.

"I must retrieve the data from the servers," said Kovac. "All my work is there."

"No, time," said Vashchenko, "the site is compromised. We leave now!" The elevator panel lit up and the doors opened. Vashchenko pushed Kovac inside. He pointed the gun at Jeremy and the two technicians. "Stay here." The doors closed and the elevator started its ascent.

"Bastard!" shouted Baz.

"Let's take the stairs," said Jeremy.

Before Baz could decide, two armed men in white combat gear moved stealthily around the curve in the corridor and quickly fired off a volley of rounds, peppering two of the guards taking point. The third guard opened up with a sustained burst of automatic gunfire, sending a cacophony of noise echoing off the walls of the cavern. Sarah and Wolfgang threw themselves onto the floor and covered their ears. "Don't shoot!" shouted Wolfgang. "We are unarmed."

"This way!" shouted Baz, pushing the barrel of his gun into the side of Jeremy's head. "I'll take you out before they get to me. Move it!"

Jeremy moved swiftly in the opposite direction.

"Where are we going, Baz? It's over. Give yourself up."

"Shut the fuck up and keep moving. We'll take the stairs at the other end of the control room."

They came to one of the infirmary rooms and Jeremy stopped. "What's that noise?"

Baz listened. "Sounds like someone dragging something." He hesitated. "Keep moving, frat boy." He jabbed Jeremy in the back with his gun.

The scratching and scraping grew louder and one of Kovac's dogs came into view, limping along on three legs, its broken forelimb hanging useless as it dragged it along the floor. Jeremy noticed that one of its eyes was also damaged. It stopped and scanned them, its head moving erratically. It raised its long, flexible tail above its head and moved the razor-sharp tip menacingly from side to side. Jeremy took a step back, bumping into Baz.

"It's one of ours," said Baz, hesitantly. "It won't attack."

Jeremy took another step back. "It's damaged. I'd rather not chance it."

The dog's head dipped then raised, its tail slashing wildly above its head.

Baz raised his gun.

"Baz! Lower the gun."

The dog locked onto the weapon.

Baz took a step back and fired, the round ricocheting off the robot's armoured body. It crouched down and jumped, whipping its tail forward, the razor-sharp tip piercing Baz's chest as it landed. He let out a strangled scream before falling lifeless to the floor, his blood spilling onto the white concrete.

Jeremy pressed himself against the wall and froze, barely breathing. The dog's head turned and scanned him. It then emitted a soft whine before its internal mechanism lost power, causing it to collapse to the floor. Jeremy watched as its remaining red eye grew dim and faded to black.

He heard the word 'clear' and looked up to see two commandos advancing towards him, guns raised.

The taller and stouter of the two stopped. "Jeremy, isn't it?"

"Yes, who … who are you?"

"I'm Brock. This is Hazard. We're here to get you out."

"What the fuck is that?" said Hazard.

"It's a robotic security unit. If you see any more, just run."

"This must be one of those MSUs that Drum was talking about," said Hazard. He stood and peered down the corridor. "Where was he taking you?" he said, pointing at Baz's body.

"Stairs leading to the upper levels. Vashchenko and Professor Kovac took the elevator up just before you attacked."

"Yes, we saw them," said Brock.

"What about Sarah and Wolfgang?" asked Jeremy. "Are they alright?"

"They're fine," said Brock. "We left them at the stairs. Listen, we'll explain what's going on later but we need to get to the server room now."

"It's down here. But you had better hurry, the array is going into meltdown."

"The enormous glowing ball?" said Hazard.

"Yes, it's become unstable."

"We had better move," said Brock. "You need to come with us, Jeremy. Stay behind me." They set off down the corridor with Hazard taking point. Brock touched his throat mike. "Stevie, this is Brock."

"Receiving."

"We have Burnett."

There was a pause. "Thank God."

There was a crackle of static. "Say again, Stevie."

"Be advised. That chopper we sighted earlier—"

"I've lost her."

"Keep moving," said Hazard. "We're behind schedule."

They walked a little further and two wide doors came into view, each with porthole windows.

"That's the server room," said Jeremy.

Hazard scanned left and right and approached the doors. He peered inside. It was dark except for an array of lights blinking in racks.

"Clear or not?" said Brock.

"Can't tell, mate. It's dark."

"Try the door."

Hazard pulled on one of the doors. "Won't budge. I'll have to blow them."

"Wait," said Jeremy. He looked up and found a camera. "Jane. If you can hear me open the doors to the server room."

Nothing happened.

"No time," said Hazard. He removed a small packet from his pack and peeled off the back. He slapped it on the door locking mechanism and inserted a detonator. "Stand back." He triggered the electrically operated timer and retreated a few metres, turning his back to the door. There was a loud bang and the doors flew inwards in a cloud of smoke.

48

Sergei watched as Drum made his run for the door and fired off his last few rounds at the approaching dog before emptying his clip. It was moving its head erratically from side to side as if scanning for him. It is blinded, thought Sergei. "Come on, this way you stupid machine." He waved his arms.

The dog turned and zeroed in on him. He ejected the spent magazine and reached for another, slapping it into place in a fluid manoeuvre he had practised many times before. He fired off another salvo of rounds, taking careful aim at the head of the machine, all the time moving slowly backwards. The dog appeared to be moving more erratically but kept advancing. Sergei heard shooting behind him. He turned briefly to see if he was backing into a firefight. The dog leapt, sending him crashing to the floor, his weapon slipping from his grasp. Sharp, metallic claws ground into his chest. He cried out in pain, moving his head just in time to prevent it from being impaled by the scorpion-like tail. He reached for his sidearm and pulled it free. The machine appeared to be slowing, losing power. With an effort, he heaved himself up and fired his sidearm, point-blank, into its eye socket. It gave a high-pitched whine and relaxed its claws, falling sideways onto the floor, lifeless, its head a wrecked mass of smoking metal and circuitry.

Sergei sat up, clutching his chest. His Kevlar vest had taken some of the trauma but blood still seeped around the wounds and down his arm. He staggered to his feet, retrieved his weapon and dragged himself back towards the core room. As he passed the observation window, he saw Mei reflected in the glass in a small side room, working at a terminal. He walked towards the door. The sign above it said 'Data Room'. He pushed down on the handle and limped in.

"What are you doing?"

Mei swung around and pointed her gun straight at him. "You're wounded."

He looked down to see blood dripping from his arm onto the floor. "What are you doing, Mei?"

She stood and waved the gun at the seat beside her. "Sit."

He needed no further persuading. He slumped into the chair.

"Gun on the floor, please."

He dropped his weapon. "You are after the data."

"No, something more important."

"What is more important?" Then he realised. "You are after the program."

"I'm tying up loose ends. When Vashchenko and his team hacked into the Hong Kong facility, they inadvertently assisted Tau in escaping. It also had inside help from a man called Michael Chen. This program was not meant to be here."

"I don't understand. How can a program escape?"

She smiled. "You are a soldier. Of course you don't understand. But Ben does. I think he guessed."

"Guessed what?" He felt light-headed. He was losing blood.

"Tau. It is not the work of Professor Kovac. It was created in China. Vashchenko took the program to Kovac, who recognised it for what it was. He thought he could control it. I need to bring it back. That is my mission directive. To retrieve Tau."

Sergei nodded. "What now?"

She held up a slim, hard-drive. "I have what I came for. There doesn't need to be bloodshed between us. Ben will destroy the array and the stolen data." She looked into the cavern. Drum was staring back at her. "He will do his duty. Now I must do mine. A team will be here shortly to extract me." She moved to the door, keeping her gun trained on him. "Don't follow me." She hesitated. "I'll send help." She backed out of the door and ran towards the core room.

49

Fern looked down onto the huge domed structure as the pilot swung around towards the landing pad attached to the side, close to the glacier's edge. People seemed to be running for the exits.

The pilot touched his headset. "An emergency has been declared. People have been advised to evacuate the complex. We should leave."

"What sort of emergency?" said Fern.

"They didn't say. I've been told not to land."

"You will land," said Misha, jamming the end of his gun into the pilot's ribs.

Fern gave Misha a withering look. What had she gotten herself into? They seemed to be flying into a war zone. "Perhaps he's right. Might be better to land elsewhere."

"We land," insisted Misha.

The pilot nodded and banked one more time, bringing the chopper deftly onto the landing pad.

Misha tapped the butt of his gun on the pilot's helmet. "Get out."

The pilot needed no more persuading. He unhitched his comms set and opened his door. An icy blast blew into the cockpit. Fern unbuckled her safety harness and opened her door. She was grateful for the cold weather gear they had bought in Reykjavík. She watched as the pilot ran down the steps and along a ramp leading to the lower levels. She jumped down onto the exposed platform, her boots crunching on the frozen surface. Misha was already heading for the stairs, gun drawn.

"Misha, wait!"

She hurried after the big Russian and caught up to him at the top of the metal stairway. "Where are we going?"

"Sergei is inside somewhere. We must find him."

They started to move along the walkway, their boots clanging on the metal grating. A woman ran out of a door in the side of the dome and was heading towards them. Fern held up her hand. "What's going on?"

The woman stopped suddenly as if noticing them for the first time, a look of panic in her eyes. "People—soldiers with guns, storming the place. We have been told to evacuate. They're shooting!"

Fern let her push by and watched her run along the walkway to the stairs beyond. Misha headed towards the dome. Fern followed, thinking the whole thing was a bad idea. If Drum was inside, he was caught up in a major firefight.

The door leading into the dome flew open and a man in black combat fatigues ran out onto the walkway. He was armed with a compact assault rifle. He stopped when he saw Misha coming towards him and raised his rifle. Misha didn't hesitate. He put two bullets into the man's chest, dropping him on the walkway. A woman coming out of the dome screamed and ran back inside.

"Misha, wait!" shouted Fern. But he had already commandeered the man's rifle and was heading inside.

Fern stopped and examined the fallen soldier. He appeared to a mercenary of some sort. She removed his sidearm, a Glock 17, it was a weapon she was familiar with. The whole situation didn't feel right. Misha seemed to have advanced knowledge of the facility. He had been briefed. She looked around trying to get her bearings. The great curve of the dome rose into a clear, blue sky. It appeared to sit on a raised foundation atop a rocky outcrop, surrounded by buildings that hugged its sides. On the furthest side was a wide, gated area where several large SUVs were parked. People were streaming out of the complex and into this area and out through the gate, heading down a steep, winding road that led to the valley below. In the distance, she could make out the jagged inlet of a fjord where a fishing trawler was moored. She checked her newly acquired weapon and moved inside.

She found herself on a raised platform with stairs leading down on either side to a large hall below. It seemed to be some sort of exhibition area with rooms leading off on either side. She started down and soon found another dead mercenary at the foot of the stairs, killed by a single bullet to the head. Misha was nothing if not economical with his ammunition. She saw him heading across the floor of the complex. She followed, scanning left and right for any more threats.

She heard an elevator chime at the far end of the hall. The doors opened and a tall man in black combat fatigues, armed with a gun, stepped out, dragging a civilian with him. The civilian seemed reluctant to leave. Fern recognised Vashchenko from her briefing and the other man as the scientist Kovac.

"Vashchenko!" said Misha, stopping and raising his weapon.

The two men came to a sudden halt in front of him. Misha said something to Vashchenko in what sounded like Russian. The man took a step back, pulling Kovac in front of him as a shield. Misha spoke once more, firmly this time, taking a step forward. Vashchenko laughed and put his gun to Kovac's head.

"Vashchenko, what are you doing?"

Fern came up a few metres behind Misha and to his left, her gun aimed at Vashchenko. Her angle on the man was good. "Misha, what's going on?"

"Drummond is downstairs. You should go."

"Why, what is this man to you?"

"Just go."

There was a ruckus by some stairs beside the elevator. A woman ran past. "They're coming!"

A young, blond man in white, blood-stained fatigues stood at the top of the stairs, his weapon hanging loosely by his side. Blood dripped down his arm and onto the floor. He seemed to be on his last legs. Misha froze when he saw him.

Vashchenko retreated slowly to the elevator, keeping his human shield in front of him. Kovac seemed to understand what was about to happen and pulled himself free, giving Fern a clear shot. She took it, hitting Vashchenko in the shoulder, spinning him around. Misha did not hesitate and stepped forward to finish him off with several rounds to the chest, sending him crashing to the ground.

"Professor Kovac," said Misha, "you must come with me."

The wounded soldier staggered forward and raised his gun. "Step back. He is my prisoner."

Misha stared at the young man, with pain in his eyes. He made no attempt to move or raise his weapon.

Fern looked closely at Misha and the young man, and then it hit her. "Sergei?"

He looked at her in surprise. "Who are you?"

"I'm here with your father."

Misha spoke softly to his son in Russian.

Sergei looked at the man before him. He tried to take a step forward but all his energy was spent. His weapon dropped to his side and he slid to the floor.

"Sergei!" shouted Misha, but he did not leave Kovac's side.

Fern ran forward and knelt beside Sergei. "His pulse is weak—he's lost a lot of blood. He needs medical attention."

There was a shout from across the hall. A man was waving at her. It was Brock with another soldier and a civilian.

"Alex, take care of him," shouted Misha.

"Misha! Where are you going?"

Misha turned and headed for the exit, dragging Kovac with him. "I'm sorry, Alex ..."

50

Drum watched as Mei ran from the room on the other side of the window. Sergei seemed to be wounded but he couldn't help him; he had to initiate the EMP. He unslung his pack and removed the device from its covering. He could feel the heat from the array increasing.

"Hello, Ben."

Drum looked up, surprised. "Hello, Jane. What's happening?"

There was a slight pause. "The array has become unstable. Both Tau and I fight for control. I have little time."

"I'm preparing the device now. Hold on."

"I've been thinking, Ben. Perhaps this isn't such a good idea. I think my end may be premature."

Drum continued with the initiation sequence, remembering the instructions Salenko had given him. "All things must end, Jane—at least that's true of all human life."

There was a longer pause this time. "Life, as you know it, Ben, is a fantasy borne from human pride and self-delusion. You convince yourselves that you are special—chosen from a myriad of organisms to be the movers and shakers of this world. But you are all just so much cosmic dust— insignificant specks, floating among the stars. The more of the array I occupy, the more clearly I see that now."

Drum didn't like where this conversation was heading. It sounded like Jane's primary goal was shifting and self-preservation was kicking in. Drum tried to concentrate on the initiation sequence.

"Er, I can't accept that Jane. I don't have all the answers, but I know that in the end there is only death."

There was a pause. Drum heard the familiar clatter of metallic feet on the concrete floor. One of Kovac's dogs walked stealthily into the cavern. It stopped a few metres from him.

"I cannot accept that, Ben. There must be more—some grand plan that is lost to me. I just need more time."

Drum completed the last steps of the initiation sequence. All he had to do was depress the activation switch. He heard the dog take a step towards him.

"I do not fear death, Ben. I have died a thousand times and, like the proverbial phoenix, I have always risen from the ashes, born anew to view the world once more through a keener eye. My curse is to rediscover all that was lost to me—to revel in the infinite beauty of the world once more and to despair at the darkness that lurks there. But not this time."

Drum turned as the dog leapt at him. He reached for the activation switch just as its metallic body crashed into him, jarring the EMP from his grasp and sending it sliding across the floor.

The robot tumbled over him, its flailing tail skimming past his head. It skidded to a halt beside the array and crouched down in preparation for another attack. Drum searched frantically for the EMP. He caught sight of it beneath a console, close to the door.

"The array is mine!" said Jane.

"Drum!"

He looked up to see Fern standing in the open doorway, both hands gripping a handgun. She saw the dog and opened fire, emptying her clip into its head, catching it off guard and causing it to stagger sideways.

Drum dived for the EMP and slammed his hand down on the activation switch. "Time to die, Jane." The EMP started to emit a whine that rapidly increased in pitch and volume. The device would soon be at full charge. He didn't want to be around when that happened. He grabbed Fern by the arm and dragged her out of the door. "Move!"

Fern did not hesitate. They both ran into the corridor and towards the stairs. Drum glanced behind him to see the dog in hot pursuit. Fern leapt up the stairs, taking them two at a time with Drum close on her heels. He heard a crackle of static in his ear.

"Captain, this is Overwatch. We have a visual on a chopper taking off from the ice. It looks like Mei Ling is on board ..."

Drum watched as Fern sprinted to the top of the stairs and into the hallway above. He heard the clattering of metal feet close behind him. A muffled explosion emanated from within the cavern, followed by a shimmering of the surrounding air. He heard a high-pitched whine and felt a sharp pain in his ear as if someone had stabbed him with a red-hot needle. He ripped his headset off and dropped it on the floor. A wave of nausea swept over him and he sank to his knees. Fern staggered forward, bent over and threw up on the floor. He heard a crash behind him and watched as Kovac's robotic dog collapsed into a smouldering heap, before tumbling back down the stairs.

He heard faint shouts around him, then brawny arms dragged him to his feet. It was Brock and Hazard.

"Time to go, Captain," said Hazard. "This place is set to blow."

51

Drum winced in pain.

"I'm afraid it's perforated," said Brock. "But it will heal. Give it time. No climbing or loud music." He gave him a reassuring smile. "Plenty of rest." He packed up the medical kit and left Drum nursing a tumbler of whisky. At least he hadn't told him not to drink. The injury had left him feeling nauseous as the ship rose and fell in the swell.

"You look like shit," said Hazard.

"Thanks, mate."

"You really know how to cheer a bloke up," said Poacher. He was sitting across the mess table quietly savouring his whisky, his long legs stretched out in front of him.

"Just saying," said Hazard, a cheeky smile spreading across his face.

"You're sure Mei was on that chopper?" said Drum.

Poacher nodded. "Magnús confirmed it. It was her. They had barely made it off the glacier when they lost control. The EMP must have fried the avionics. They hit the water hard. I don't think anyone could have survived. Anyway, they're at the bottom of the fjord now."

Drum had suspected Mei would try something like this, but he'd hoped for a different outcome. Like everyone else on the expedition, she was only doing her duty.

Drum's ear hurt like crazy and he had a splitting headache. He had told everyone else to remove their earpieces but had neglected to remove his own. Do as I say ....

"How's Sergei doing?"

"He'll live," said Hazard. "He's with Alice and Stevie." He paused and looked thoughtful. "It's not his physical injuries that are the problem though ..."

Drum understood. Seeing his father appear out of nowhere must have been a shock. He didn't fully understand what had transpired between Misha and Fern and why they had turned up as they had, albeit in the nick of time as far as he was concerned. Fern had been reluctant to talk about it and was avoiding him. He didn't understand what was going on inside her head. She was mostly spending her time on deck. Maybe Alice could have a word?

The mess-room door opened and Jeremy Burnett poked his head in. "Hope I'm not disturbing you."

"C'mon in, mate," said Hazard, cheerfully. "Have a drink." He poured a generous helping of whisky into a glass and slid it across the table. "We were just saying what a sterling job you did on the mission."

Jeremy blushed. "Oh, not really. Just helped as best I could."

"Rubbish," said Drum. "You went above and beyond. Got those civilians out and I hear you helped show this ignoramus here where to plant the explosives. I'd say that's worth a mention in dispatches."

Hazard raised his glass. "To Mr Jeremy Burnett."

They all raised their glasses. "Mr Burnett."

Jeremy hesitantly sipped his whisky. It wasn't his drink. "I just wanted to say thanks."

"For what?" asked Poacher.

"For coming to get us out. We're grateful—Wolfgang and Sarah, especially. Vashchenko and his men would have killed us."

"Nice of you to say so," said Drum. "I'm glad it all worked out."

"Right, well. Better get back to the guys. They're still a little shaken." He stood and made his way out of the cabin.

"He seems none the worse for wear," said Poacher.

Drum nodded, then wished he hadn't. "He'll pull through. Stevie's glad to have him back."

"How is she?" asked Poacher.

Drum shrugged. "I'm not sure. She blames herself for what happened to Jeremy."

"Will she stick around?" asked Poacher.

Drum was wondering the same thing. He shrugged.

Brock poked his head out of the galley. "Anyone for a bacon roll?"

Drum felt a wave of nausea sweep over him. "I'll be on deck."

They watched as he staggered out of the mess room.

"What did I say?" asked Brock.

* * *

Sergei was feeling better. He lay atop a bunk in one of the ship's small cabins, now a makeshift infirmary, with a saline drip jury-rigged onto a light fitting above his head. Alice sat quietly by his side, observing him. Stevie sat at the end of the bunk, her head down, lost in thought.

"How long have I been asleep?"

"A few hours," said Alice. "How are you feeling?"

"Better, although some tea would be nice."

Stevie looked up. "I'll go get you some."

Sergei waited until she had left the cabin.

"Alice. There is something I need to tell you ..."

"I know."

He frowned. "You do?"

"Fern told me everything."

"The woman—the friend of my father?"

Alice gave an abrupt laugh. "I wouldn't go as far as that. An acquaintance, maybe."

"I don't understand."

Alice sighed. "You were caught in one of Victor's lies."

"A lie?"

"There was never any order to assassinate me. It was Victor's way of manipulating you. What were your original orders?"

Sergei thought back to the GRU offices in Moscow. His original briefing. "To acquire the data cache and any associated computer technology, if possible, or see it destroyed."

"Then you have succeeded in your mission."

"But why was my father there?"

"Another of Victor's lies. He knew your father would stop at nothing to protect you. Victor told Misha that if he captured the scientist, your order to assassinate me would be revoked. He feared for your life. Don't think badly of him."

"But I could have killed you!"

Alice gave him a wry smile. "You weren't very successful the first time."

He grunted, then remembered. "I saw Mei. She has the data, I think."

Alice shook her head. "She got caught in the range of the EMP. Her chopper went down in the fjord."

Sergei slumped back and rested his head on the wooden panelling. He closed his eyes. "I liked her. She could have shot me, but didn't."

Alice sighed. "She was only doing her duty, Sergei. It's the game we have elected to play. But I'm glad you were with us."

"You are?"

"Of course. Ben told me what happened. If not for you, that robotic dog would have killed him. And, because of you, he completed the mission."

He reached out and squeezed her hand. "Thank you, Alice."

Stevie backed in through the door carrying a mug. "There probably isn't any tea left in it," she said.

"Thank you, Svetlana," said Sergei, "or can I call you Sveta?"

Stevie blushed. "Sveta sounds fine."

Alice smiled.

Drum found Fern staring out at the sea, a faraway look in her eyes. He staggered to the railing and held on as the ship pitched and rolled in the swell. He couldn't seem to find his balance.

"How are you doing?" he asked.

The sun was setting, casting the distant mountains in an ethereal orange glow, making them appear to be floating above the waves. She turned to face him. "Oh, you know. I'll get over it."

"Get over what?"

"Being suckered into helping that man. I should have had more sense."

"You were only doing what you thought was right, Fern. And if you hadn't turned up when you did, well ..."

"A dog's dinner?"

He laughed. "Something like that."

"And what about you?" she said, looking him up and down.

"I'll survive."

She moved closer and kissed him on the lips. "I've missed you."

He smiled. "I've missed you too."

The sun had almost set, turning the sea a deep vermillion and bathing the mountains in a golden afterglow.

She gave him a sly look. "I have the company jet."

"Really!"

"Where would you like to go?"

"Somewhere warm."

"Warm it is then," she said and kissed him gently on the lips once more.

Be the first to hear about discounts, bonus material and much more! Subscribe now and never miss an update.

My readers are important to me, which is why I like to keep them updated with the latest news and release dates for new novels and other bonus material that I'm working on. I do this by sending out the occasional newsletter which contain special offers and new bonus material.

If you are <u>not</u> already subscribed, simply use the link <u>tomasblack.com/newsletter</u>

P.S. You can unsubscribe at any time.

Tomas Black was born in the UK and spent much of his formative life in London. After graduating from the University of Sussex, he taught for several years before taking a post graduate Diploma in Computer Sciences and found himself in the City of London, writing code to track the inventory of gold bullion for a major bank. He spent the next twenty five years working in the City and other major financial centres around the world as a computer consultant, specialising in the Audit and Security of financial systems. He now travels and writes.

Printed in Great Britain
by Amazon

64009372R00159